The Bohemian Adventure

ജ്ഞ

F. T. Burke

Nightengale Press
A Nightengale Media LLC Company

THE BOHEMIAN ADVENTURE

For information about Nightengale Press
please visit our website at www.nightengalemedia.com.
Email: publisher@nightengalepress.com

Burke, F. T.,
THE BOHEMIAN ADVENTURE/ F. T. Burke
ISBN 13: 978-1-945257-23-0
Fiction

First Published by Nightengale Press in the USA

April 2017

10 9 8 7 6 5 4 3 2 1

Printed in the USA, Canada, European Union, United Kingdom,
Germany, Australia, Russia, Brazil, South Korea

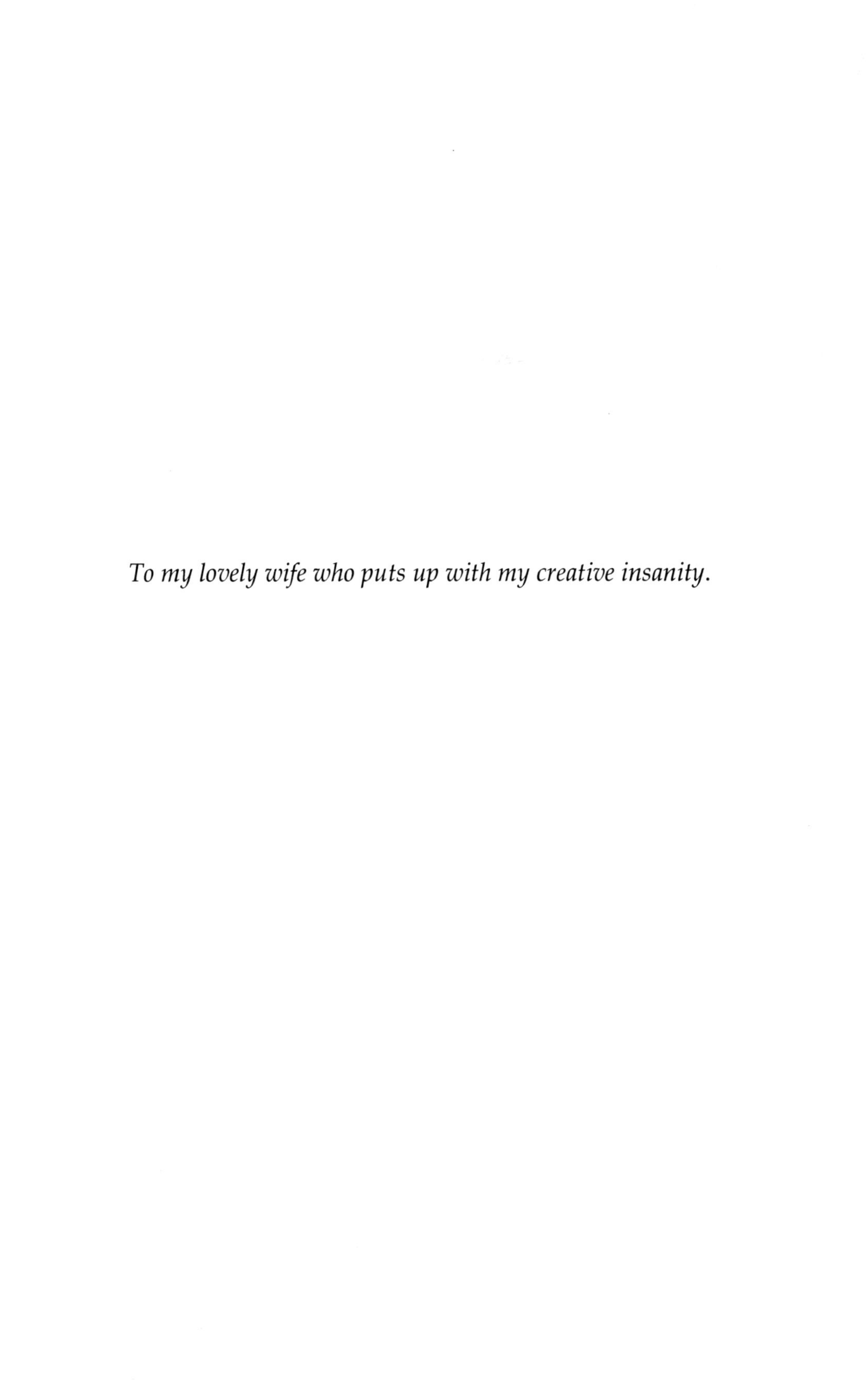

To my lovely wife who puts up with my creative insanity.

ACKNOWLEDGEMENTS

Many people inspired and influenced me during the writing of this book.

A special thank you goes out to: Lorie Lulick, Lisa Townsend, Gary Harris, Tim Brown, Don Mass, Steve Reifman, Danny Grinnell, Allen Glass, Valerie Connelly, Chet Budzynski, Reverie Beall, Kim Field, Bryan Watson, John and Kira Torbert, The Deadhead Community and The Rainbow Warriors of the Earth.

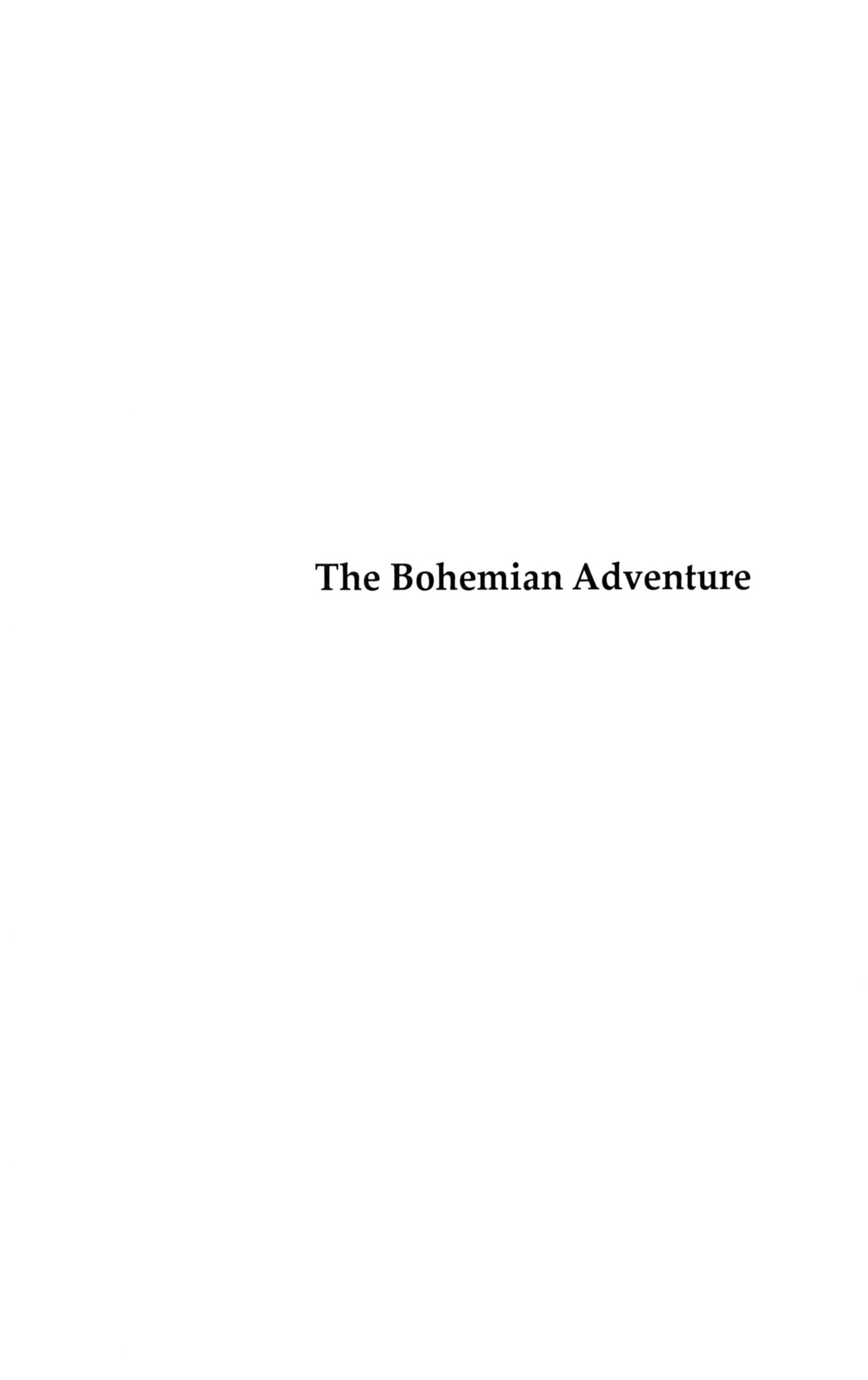

The Bohemian Adventure

PART I

A Bohemian

Bohemian: *Pertaining to or characteristic of persons with real or pretended artistic or intellectual aspirations who live and act with disregard for conventional rules of behavior. Living a wandering or vagabond life, as a gypsy.*

—Oxford Unabridged Dictionary

Enlighten me, O Muses,
tenants of Olympian Homes
For you are Goddesses, inside on
everything, know everything,
But we mortals hear only the news
and know nothing at all.

—Homer (9th Century B.C.)

ꕥ

Prologue

ꕥ

As I park my car in the garage after returning home from another day of work at the office—something isn't right. A taxi cab is parked at the curb in front of the house. I walk into my home to discover my wife, Julianne, waiting for me at the kitchen table with her hands clasped in front of her. Nearby I notice her luggage and then that her wedding ring is missing.

"What's going on?" I inquire.

"I'm leaving you, Ted. I had my lawyer draw up the divorce papers last week. All you need to do is sign," she says.

"Hold on here. I never saw this coming. We made a commitment to each other. You meet another man?"

"No!"

"You are my wife. I love you. I don't want a divorce. I know we've had some recent struggles. We can work things out," I say.

Julianne stands up and backs away from the table. I try to give her a hug and she pushes me away.

"I'm leaving you, Ted. The decision is made and it's final. I'm moving to Paris. I've fallen in love with Luca. We're moving in together! My plane leaves tonight."

"You mean to tell me you've been having a lesbian love affair and I never had a clue! You're playing a joke on me, right? Tell me it's not true. I'm being punked by my wife, right?

"It's true, Ted. I'm a lesbian. I just didn't know it till

recently. I'm sorry. It is what it is. I've been conflicted inside for awhile. Becoming friends with Luca has opened new doors for me."

"And closed the door to us," I say.

"I enjoyed our friendship, our relationship—but it's in the past now! The marriage is over. Time to move on," she says.

Julianne gathers her luggage and walks out the door. I watch her roll her luggage down the driveway. She hands her bags to the cab driver and he puts them in the trunk of the vehicle. Then she walks back up the driveway to the front porch where I'm standing, slumped over and shaking. Near tearing up, I gather myself and stand upright, throwing my shoulders back and clenching my fists as she approaches.

"Don't forget to sign the papers, Ted!" Then she turns around and walks out of my life. I watch the cab pull away until the tail lights disappear down the street.

ဢ

Chapter One

ဢ

The Campground Village of Chaos

My glow-in-the-dark watch stares at me. 3AM. A cacophony of sound pounds my ears. Banjos twang. Bongos and Tom-toms thump a beat. Tambourines jingle-jangle. Acoustic guitars sing a melody. Tribal chants and human claps tumble from another world. I unzip the window flap of my tent. I can't believe what I see.

Clusters of people mill about in all directions, like a band of gypsies on a caffeine high. A campground village is taking shape in Lake Minnawanna Park. Bonfires flame everywhere. Each campsite overflows with humanity. People clog all the roads. Engines rev. Car doors open and close. Headlights and brake lights flash. Music and voices fill the air.

I gaze out my tent window taking in all the changing scenes of organized chaos—fire-pits rage at each site as far as I can see. Tall shadows of bodies bob against the forested background. Chanting drums beat to a hypnotic Native American tribal dance. I slip into a trance taking it all in. I glance at my watch, 3:30AM laughs at me like a clown in a circus. Friendly, harmonious, total chaos explodes in the park through my waking dreams.

When I retired to bed for the evening and the last embers of my campfire fell into the pit—the night was quiet, serene and peaceful. I felt alone in semi-solitude. Only two other occupied campsites existed in the whole back half of the park. The light of their campfires glowed around the bend in the road. The quiet night breeze rustled the hickory and oak tree branches overhead in the quarter-moonlight. Nature holds the secret to my inward peace and serenity.

ᘓᘐ

Wide awake, I intend to get up to walk about and find out what's going on. Bright headlights illuminate my tent.

Neighbors.

I hurry to get dressed, fumbling around for a shirt and some shorts to put on. Unzipping the tent, a little six-by-six pup tent, I back out, right leg first, using both hands and my left knee for support. My right foot grazes, touches something. Startling, I fall forward into my sleeping bag in the tent.

Then I hear a voice.

"Excuse me. I'm sorry. Excuse me. We didn't think anyone was camping here tonight because you have no car. We're right next door and we'll have at least twenty people or more, five or six small tents. You don't mind if we go over your property line do you?"

I huddle inside my tent, peeking out the flap, as he continues.

"I'm going to park my VW right on the edge so we have room on the other side. I'm Jeff. What's your name? We're deadheads!"

ᘓᘐ

I exit the tent, stand up and face him to introduce myself. "I'm Ted. Ted Senario." We shake hands.

"It's great to meet you, Ted. Me and my brethren are

deadheads," he laughs, making air quotes as he continues, "We've come here following the Grateful Dead on tour."

I pause for the moment and look around at all the activity. It's not yet the dawning of sunrise. However, the whole park as far as I can see is bustling with peopled energy. Every campsite, fire ring, picnic table, vehicle and tent is buzzing with a symphony of sounds, motion, light, smoke.

Jeff speaks up. "I'm from Massachusetts, a suburb of Boston."

He wears a perpetual smile with his short red-top mop of hair on his medium-built frame. Jeff is thin and wiry. Muscled.

Five-foot-seven, a hundred thirty-five pounds?

He wears real thin braids with multi-colored material woven within, extending off one side of his head and down his back, where, at the end, several of these braids come together separately and are tied into a big colorful red, white, and blue ball. Jeff twirls the hair ball around and back and forth from each hand as he talks.

"I'm a college student on a summer vacation adventure. I sell devil sticks at the shows. Come on over to my site and I'll introduce you to some of the people I'm hanging with."

Jeff is all excited. Wound tight. Intense. Wired. He paces back and forth, hands in and out of his pants pockets, then back to twirling the braided ball in his hair.

I hesitate for a few seconds. "Sure man," I say with a wary sense of caution. "Lead the way."

During this brief introduction with Jeff, two flower-decaled VW mini-bus vans back in and park end to end in the campsite next to mine. They come to a stop less than two feet from my tent, serving as a wall, partitioning off my site from all the activities on the other side of the vehicles.

I follow Jeff around the other side of the VW's and here we are at a gathering. Happy mellow faces everywhere—tie-dyed shirts on just about everyone of the two dozen or so at Jeff's campsite. I meet John and Pete, Ann, Jane, another Jeff, another Pete, Judy, Carol, Lisa, Bob, Kent, Lois, Janelle, Ron, Betty, Trent, Joe, Lynn . . .

Everybody is from a different part of the country: Massachusetts, New York, California, Oregon, Colorado, Iowa, Alabama, Georgia, Maine, and Kentucky. I meet a couple from England, two guys from Spain, one guy from Germany, and a female—on student exchange—from Christ Church, New Zealand. Most of the people seem to be in their early twenty's, late teens—college students, I presume.

Pete is sitting on the edge of the picnic table by the campfire playing a banjo. He wears picks on each of his fingers and he moves them fast in a rhythm, a unison of perpetual motion, creating a blue-grass folksy sound. Jeff sat on the other side of the picnic table with a pair of bongos. He keeps the beat to Pete's banjo. Then Lynn joins in with a harmonica. Somebody offers me a beer. I stand by the campfire and watch them play.

John joins in with an acoustic guitar and they have a full band going now. The rest of the people start dancing, one-by-one, in a circle around the campfire. This is unlike any kind of dancing I've ever seen. It looks like the kind of thing you would imagine a three or four-year old doing.

Not full-fledged common-sense adults.

But common sense doesn't reign here—only the uncommon, unconventional sense of things. I watch in rapt attention with my right hand hugging my beer can. I take a sip. They move their arms and hands and fingers as if they are riding a wave.

The rhythmic frequency wave of the music creates a psychic connection?

I don't know. Very strange. Space cadets.

This spectacle I'm witnessing bewilders me. The dancers start hopping and skipping and twirling—like ballet or something—all the while still doing that wavy thing with their upper body. Each person is doing their own individual wavy twirl dance routine. Eyes often closed. Souls blissfully oblivious, lost in the freedom of the moment.

I stand transfixed, just observing the surroundings.

Soon it will be sunrise. The night delivers me into a day of a waking fantasy-like dream.

ཀའ

I walk away from the neighborly campfire scene of dancing and music to see some of the happenings at other campsites. As I saunter down a path that skirts along the back edge of the woods, I see more of the same type of activities—that strange dancing again, more musical instruments, big community circles around campfires. A commune of tents pitches up everywhere in any open space unoccupied by a vehicle, people or trees. The path I'm on leads to a park road, so I continue walking along, checking out the scenes.

Then I come across a campsite that is a little different. They have six medium-sized teepees in a semi-circle with a huge teepee in the center—a sort of community center teepee. Men and women are sitting in a circle with their legs crossed. Each guy has a drum. Some use sticks. Some use their hands. The girls shake gourds, castanets and tambourines. Everybody wears an American Indian leather outfit. Native frontier and wild looking. In the middle of this ring of Indians is the leader, the chief, I suppose. He's yipping and hollering to the beat of the drums and music. Pointing to the sky, he yelps some more, then picks up a handful of dirt from the ground and sprinkles it on his chest and arms.

"Yeeeoww! YeeYeeYipYip Yeeoww!"

Then everyone in unison yelps, hollers and chants. All the while the big Indian tail feathers of the Chief fly up and down and around as he skips and jumps around the campfire circle.

I startle from my watchful reverie. I notice groups of people leaving the huddles of their various campsites. People are congregating at a campsite across the road along the tree-lined forest edge. I decide to follow them and check out the situation. The Indians are completely oblivious. As I draw near the commotion, I hear rhythmic clapping and hollering and cheering. I squeeze my way through the tight crowd to see that, in the middle of the crowd, a couple is enjoying sex on a picnic table in plain view. A semi-circle of people gathers around them, cheering them on. I can't see the woman, other than her legs up in the air. The guy has long thick dreadlocks that covered up his whole back down to his ass. He's standing there at the end of the table with his pants down around his ankles. He must have pulled up the gypsy dress of his companion because she was still wearing it around her waist. They seem to be in their own far-out world—just humping and grinding along—unashamed in their carnal act.

A grey-headed, wild-haired, pissed-off elderly woman comes out of the crowd carrying a kayak paddle. She pulls back and starts whipping on the guys ass real hard—one—two—three—times! The humping stops. The cheering stops. Stunned silence lingers for a moment.

"Perverts! Disgusting!" She hollers at them, "You should be ashamed!"

The guy, holding his backside with one hand, pulls

his pants up with the other. He looks confused. The gypsy girl looks bewildered. She pulls her dress down, rolls off the table and casually strolls past everyone into the darkness of the woods.

As the crowd disperses and people head back to their various campsites, I decide to head back to my site as well. Walking around the loop in the road that heads in the direction I need to go, I become aware that I'm going against the main flow of traffic. I keep walking past group after group of tie-dyed deadheads. A group of guys, a group of females, some couples, gatherings of people all heading down the road that separates the front-end campground area with the back-end. This road is the midpoint of the park. I set up my tent weeks ago in the farthest corner of the back-end. In my wanderings I have looped around to the start of the back-half and am now heading in the direction of my campsite. There is a long quarter-mile stretch in the road that hugs the shores of Lake Minnawanna. It's the only place other than the public beach that has such an opening to the lake. Other than this entry point, the lake is surrounded by trees and hills and forest, up to the shoreline. I continue walking back toward my site, a bit hesitant and curious. Heading in the opposite direction, I notice Lynn and Pete along the road, the harmonica and banjo players from earlier. Lynn is carrying a folded blanket and Pete has his guitar strapped around his back.

"What's going on here? I'm afraid everyone's going to see Jesus, but me!" I joked to them.

"We're going to celebrate the sunrise!" they both blurted out. "C'mon Ted. Come with us. You've never seen a sunrise until you've celebrated one," says Lynn.

ꕥ

I join in with Pete and Lynn, and we saunter along the path.

"I've been following The Grateful Dead," Lynn says, "on the road, off and on, for two years. It's a great adventure. I meet new people, make close friends and enjoy the camaraderie, the harmony of the energy we create."

"This is unlike anything I've ever experienced before," I say.

"What do you mean? All us strange people?" Pete asks.

"Well…yeah…everything is so over-the-top! You deadheads all look as if you've been transplanted here from a 1960's time-capsule or something." Pete and Lynn chuckle. "What do you do when you're not following the band on tour?"

"We live in Rochester, New York. I'm eventually going to be a teacher when I grow up," Lynn jokes. "I have a Liberal Arts degree. I'm twenty-eight-years old and I love literature, history and music," Lynn boasts.

We continue our walk from the paved road to a dirt path along the shoreline. All the hair on one side of her head is braided. The other side is straight. She wears a long flowery multi-colored gypsy dress with bangles. Real loose fitting. Lynn tops that off with black combat boots. Plus she has big hairy bushes under her arm pits, I notice.

"I haven't shaved my legs in two years," she giggles as she pulls up her dress to show me.

I stop—aghast! Put my hand to my mouth to cover my stunned expression, but my wide open eyes are in shock. I've never seen such a sight on a woman before—way too much information. Lynn skips up ahead to rejoin with Pete and I hurry along after them.

Pete is quietly humming, content and happy with

himself, playing tunes in his head. He has an American flag bandana wrapped around his dark, curly, long black hair. Also with the requisite tie-dyed shirt, beads, jeans, moccasins, of the average deadhead. Pete shoulders his guitar upright and begins strumming. We draw near to the great gathering of people on the shores of Lake Minnawanna.

A hundred people or more all linger about this long narrow grassy strip between the road and the lake. By the faint glow on the horizon, I can see the sun will soon be coming up over the lake. We go over to a small alcove by the shore line and Lynn lays out her blanket. Pete drifts off into the crowd of people. We take a seat next to each other on the blanket and look out to the east. The pre-dawn darkness begins to dissipate. A slight milky fog hovers above the lake. The grass is wet with morning dew. Shimmers of pink, orange and yellow light brim along the surface of the horizon in the sky. The crickets and owls and frogs and noises of the night are giving way to the morning songs of the birds.

We both jump up from our sitting position to get a better view. We acknowledge the excitement and anticipation that fills the atmosphere of the moment, with stretched, anxious smiles, a wink and a slight nod. Everyone is still and quiet gazing out toward the peeking of the sun. The silence is deafening. Hushed moments of eagerness. I look out across the groups of people staring at the sky. A big blazing fireball slowly pierces the horizon as it rises and appears before us. A thunderous cheer goes up from the throng—a continuous crescendo of clapping, whistling, hooting, hollering—then a standing ovation for the radiant splendor! I've never experienced anything like this in my entire life. We all clap and carry on this way for a solid ten minutes. I feel the tingling hairs rising on the back of my neck. For the umpteenth time since awakening, I find myself transfixed. All I can do is absorb the moment and quietly observe. I watch several of the deadheads cavort and splash along the lake shore. I'm standing here with Lynn, but I'm in my own world, my mind is drifting…

Failure is like an anchor pulling me to the farthest depths of the ocean floor—bitter anger, self-pity, self-doubt. Pulling me under, pulling me down, sinking, sinking, going way way down. I miss Julianne…how is she? How has she been getting along? I lost my best friend. Oh, sweet Julianne. No place to share a home…no passionate dreams to care for as a team. My mind has been so unsettled…

Scenes from the last five years of my life go by: failure, heartbreak, divorce, misery, bankruptcy. The scenes and images flash before me. I'm staring out at the middle of Lake Minnawanna when the lake transforms into a big movie screen, filled with the images from my mind. I watch the toppling of the high aspirations and high ambitions I had for myself.

I'd done all the right things to a certain point in my life, and then I lost my way. Well enough is not good enough. Status quo is not good enough. I have to be more than I am and I know it deep down inside. I'm out on a limb—until the limb from the tree breaks and I fall into the abyss. I see the image of myself falling from the broken limb into Lake Minnawanna.

What am I looking for? How did I go so wrong? Three years wandering and refusing to fit in. The social net of society has hemmed me in. Here I am—free—and what do I want to be? see? do? experience? It all begins and ends within. Money worries, bills, creditors, loss of my love, loss of my home. I leave it all behind. I march forward into my great unknown…

Just then Lynn nudges me out of my reverie, bringing me back to the shoreline.

"Come on over here and let's sit on the blanket, Ted. What were you thinking about? I was watching you stare into space, and I could tell from the look on your face that you were far off and serious. Let's go over here and chat for a while." She points to her blanket and I follow her.

ꕥ

I sit on the shores of Lake Minnawanna with Lynn. The trees move in the slight breeze, as if they are just waking up.

"All my friends call me Cricket. You can call me Cricket," Lynn says.

She takes off her black combat boots and wiggles her toes in the water.

"Oohhh! It's cold!"

I skip a couple stones along the surface of the lake.

"I told you some stuff about my life and my background—what about you, Ted? What were you thinking a few minutes ago?"

I shrug my shoulders and skip another stone along the water.

"Come on—quid pro quo—What do you do? Where are you from? Did you go to college? How old are you? You married?" Cricket eagerly rattles off her questions. Then she falls silent, sits on the blanket, and then stares —waiting for me to speak.

Pete has wandered off, back to the campsites, along with the vast majority of the deadheads. Just a few groups of stragglers linger now. We edge closer to the shore to dip our feet in the water. I hesitate to speak for a moment, and continue to stare out across the lake. I'm not comfortable talking about myself with anyone.

Never have been.

I know I'm a loner at heart. Now I'm sitting here next to this complete stranger who wants to know everything, right down to 'Why?' my heart beats.

Cricket fires another flurry of questions at me. "What is your purpose in life? Are you a Dead fan? Do you have a wife and kids? Brothers? Sisters? Parents? Do you like to travel? Do you read?"

I throw my hands up in the air, making a 'T' sign for timeout.

"Your curiosity can be overwhelming Cricket! Please, one question at a time."

"I'm sorry! I'm just so excited about the start of a new day, meeting new and interesting people, enjoying my friends, and the energy of…being alive! Freedom! It's totally groovy man!"

She bursts up from her sitting position on the blanket and jumps in the air, looks up to the sky, throws her arms open wide, closes her eyes and smiles. Her energy is electric! Then she sits back down on the blanket beside me. Her facial expression morphs from her over exuberant state to a calm, peaceful, serene smile.

"I'm a witch!"

Startled, I draw away from her.

"What did you say?"

"I'm a witch," she repeats. "I'm a good witch though. I don't cast evil spells or nothing like that. I read tarot cards, study astrology and have an occasional séance now and then. I'm a student of Zen. You ever heard of Baba Ram Dass?"

I shrug and shake my head *no*.

"So, tell me about yourself, Ted. Wherever you want to begin, I'll be quiet and just listen," she says.

Once again I hesitate, looking out upon the lake. Then Cricket fumbles around in a pocket of her gypsy dress. She pulls out what looks like a shiny purple stone. She puts it to her mouth and blows air into it. She calls it her "Purple Whale." It's a unique looking pipe. She reaches back into her dress, another pocket—pulls out a plastic sandwich baggy all rolled up in a ball. She unwraps it.

"Are you okay with this?" Cricket pulls it back and clutches the material against her chest, giving me an imploring look.

"I'm cool, no problem."

I motion for her to continue with what she is doing. She crumbles some reefer into the blowhole of the purple whale. Then she reaches back into a pocket of her dress and pulls out a lighter and lights up. She inhales the smoke and passes the purple whale to me.

Feeling a little paranoid out in the open, I look all around. Nobody is paying any attention to us. It's just Cricket and me. I take a drag off the pipe and hold it in. The whale swam between us several times. Afterward, she puts the pipe, baggy and lighter back into a pocket of her dress. Cricket then stands up and tells me to stand up with her.

"Wanna do something different? Let's move all our fingers and toes at the same time."

So, like playing 'Simon Says,' I follow along. Here we are moving our fingers above our heads and wiggling our toes.

"I bet you haven't done that so freely since you were a child, Ted." She winks. "It's all a part of loosening up." Then Cricket sits back down in a folded leg position.

She touches the forefinger to the thumb of each hand. Her elbows rest on the inside of her knees. She tilts her head back so she faces the sky. She closes her eyes. I then proceed to follow all of her actions. We sit there, trance-like, meditating—several minutes of silence pass by.

I open my eyes and interrupt the moment. "I've never been good at this. I just can't seem to get to the essence of meditating. I've tried several times in my life and I just get frustrated with the process—"

"—the whole point is to relax and clear your mind of all thought. Detach from your thoughts. Pretend you are observing your thoughts and your thoughts are not part of you. It helps to concentrate and focus on just one thing—a word, a noise, a chant, an object, but best of all—your breath! Concentrate on this one thing at the exclusion of all else. Like that buoy out in the middle of the lake," Cricket says, "just concentrate on that and nothing else."

This great gathering is a fabulous social opportunity. Energy vibrations of unity. Senses aroused and heightened. All alert and tingles. A mingling meanderer I will be. The vast sea of people, countering the mainstream. I'm uplifting, drifting, arising. My eyes have seen the spectacular. Natural Nature! The magical mystery remains . . .

We go back to meditating for twenty minutes. Cricket seems like a master at the practice. The little gypsy girl, Buddha-like, soaring out of herself, I imagine as I peek through my half closed eye lids to view her countenance. Cricket sparkles and shines—the efflorescence of innate wisdom. A beacon of benevolent understanding, illuminate—or so I think as I glance at her now and then. Then Cricket opens her eyes and smiles real big and toothy as she jumps out of her sitting stance and leaps into the shallow water.

"What a great day! Life is wonderful! I'm so blessed! We are blessed!" Cricket beams from the shoreline. "Ted! Ted! Aren't you genuinely and sincerely thankful for this moment? this life? Don't you have so much passion for living? I can feel it now. It's flowing through me like a wave of peace. Don't you feel that passion for life, Ted?"

"Of course—sure!" I respond with enthusiasm. Her joy is magnetic. She exudes a sangfroid prescience—a powerful force of pure benevolent energy encircles my awareness in the now—the explosion of wonder! I feel like doing some creative writing, putting words together, seeking inner illumination . . .

"Ted, why don't you tell me about yourself?" Cricket the extrovert senses that she has finally broken through my introverted walls of protection. I am relaxed and feel comfortable and genuinely at peace.

"Well, I'm thirty-three-years-old and I've lived in Michigan my entire life. I earned a general business degree from Michigan State University in 1982. Then I worked in the automotive industry at General Motors for nine years. I worked in the engineering departments, but mostly with computer programmers at Electronic Data Systems, or EDS. It was a great learning experience, but I eventually fell into a rut with the daily routine. I got married to Julianne and we didn't last two years. Too young. Got divorced, failed in a business venture, lost a sizable investment in a bilking scheme from dishonest investment partners, then went bankrupt. I had it all at one time—money, cars, fat bank account, a new home, lots of friends, beautiful wife… and I lost it all."

Cricket looks at me with compassion in her eyes. "So, what do you do now?"

"I live in the woods—commune with nature. Write in my journal every day, read my favorite authors, write and read, write and read, take nature walks."

"You don't work?"

"This is my work for now. I'm living out in nature by myself in a tent for nine months straight. This is my fourth month so far. I'm going to be out in nature for five more months, coming out of the woods on Thanksgiving."

"Why?"

Cricket smiles at me with a quizzical expression on her face, an arched eyebrow squints.

"I had to make a drastic change, get to know myself at the root level—self and soul—know what I mean?" I say.

"You are a Bohemian! Yes, you are—a real bohemian!" Cricket blurts out with a delightful sparkle in her expression. She reaches back into the pocket of her dress for the purple whale. We pass the pipe back and forth several more times. "You need to learn the lessons from the failures and mistakes of your past, and apply those lessons-learned to the living present. Be here now! Ted, be here now!" Cricket exhorts me to get in touch with my presence. I don't really understand her now, but I hope to grow into this new awareness in my nature sojourn.

"I can't wait to read some of your writings, Ted. I participate in public poetry readings at coffeehouses, cafes and college campuses back home. What kind of stuff do you write about?"

"In my journal it can be just about anything—introspection, self-analysis, poetry, inspiration from nature, quotes from great authors, stuff like that," I say.

"Do you write stories or novels or screenplays?"

"No. I haven't ever attempted that kind of writing."

"What do you hope to achieve by taking such drastic measures?" Cricket inquires.

"I want to start over in my life with a new purpose and solid inner direction. I got so caught up in materialism, work-a-holism, get, get, get, go, go, go routine, that I lost myself in the process. I can't let my life be ruled by anxiety and stress or I won't be around much longer anyway," I explain. "Being in nature is like a cleansing of the soul for me."

We gather the blanket and each grab an end and shake it to get rid of the sand, dirt, grass and leaf mixture that stuck to the bottom from the wet morning dew. Then we fold the blanket in squares.

As I hand her the last folded half, I say, "Let's head back to the campsite."

Just then a group of hippies comes rushing over to us in an agitated panic.

"Cricket! Where have you been? Everyone is looking for you?" says one of the girls. Head nods of agreement come from the others in the group.

"What's the problem?" Crickets asks.

"Two groups of deadheads are arguing. We're all afraid it might turn into a fight. People have been scouting through the park looking for you, Cricket," says another girl in the group.

"Let's go!" Cricket says, getting up to leave.

She must have significant influence as a leader between these clans and tribes of people. I don't believe I have ever met anyone like this Cricket—er, Lynn. She has a magnetic presence, a mystical allure. Compassionate, discerning, warm-hearted, intelligent, curious, a great listener. What a special person!

After Cricket leaves with the group of deadheads, I sit at the edge of the shoreline of little Lake Minnawanna, staring into the soft wind-swept ripples in the water. Shiny diamond sparkles dance to and fro from the sunshine reflection on the surface of the lake. I ponder the things

I have said to Cricket, the things she said to me, all the events since awakening:

> *Why am I here? What have I become? Where am I going? I wonder often—and often don't know. This mysterious life is a riddle with no answers. Perhaps it's just me. Why do I have to search and seek so deep? Always on the edge, never satisfied and content with the view. Something hidden is lurking. I'm being summoned and I don't know how to answer. What is it, Ted? Do you know yourself—really know yourself? Wake Up, Ted!*

ꕥ

Chapter Two

The Counter-Culture

ꕥ

"The only people for me are the mad ones, the ones who are mad to live, mad to talk, mad to be saved, desirous of everything at the same time, the ones who never yawn or say a commonplace thing, but burn, burn, burn like fabulous yellow roman candles."

—Sal Paradise from On The Road by Jack Kerouac

Who Are the Dead?

I walk the path at the edge of the woods. Deadheads scurry about in every direction. An assortment of smiling faces mingle between groups, as they openly share their love for the Grateful Dead. I know the Grateful Dead is a band, but I have no idea what possesses these deadheads to do what they do with their cult-like following of the band on tour. It's truly a phenomenon to witness first-hand. I grew up on a good variety of music like Pink Floyd, Led Zeppelin, Ted Nugent, and Bob Seger. I have listened to Prince, the Gap Band, and other top-forty tunes. I even find myself appreciating some Beethoven and Mozart on a quiet evening at home. But somehow I have never come across 'the Dead.' I consider myself well versed in popular music culture, but suddenly I feel as if I have emerged from a cave.

Something very outrageous, phenomenal even, is stirred up within this devoted mass following of people. It seems like they are trying to recreate the 1960's—peace, music, flower power, summer of love! How could I have never known about this counter-culture existence? I've heard of the Grateful Dead through the years, mainly from the zany offbeat basketball player Bill Walton, when media would mention it. And I may have heard of a celebrity or politician who followed the band. But I never heard the music of The Grateful Dead.

Strange.

As I walk by a campsite I notice Pete, the banjo and guitar player, hanging out by an early 1960's creamy white classic BMW convertible—a beautiful beamer!

"Where's Cricket?" I holler at Pete to get his attention.

He shrugs his shoulders, "I have no idea of her whereabouts."

I walk over to within a few feet of Pete.

"I don't really know anything about the Grateful Dead and the deadheads. This whole thing going on here is so outrageous to me."

I shake my head in bewilderment and hunch my shoulders and upturned palms—clueless. Pete wears a big ear-to-ear grin. Then he snaps his fingers and points to the air. He puts his finger to the side of his head and says, "I got it!"

Next thing I know Pete is leading me to a campsite on the far side of the park. The whole way there he's talking a mile a minute.

"You're in for a treat! You are gonna hear from true historians, tapers, original sixties flower children. They can supply you with the real true essence of what we're all about."

He is animated and excitable, jumping around, circling me and walking real fast. I am in a half-trot jog just to keep up with him.

"I'm gonna introduce you to some people who are way out there, man!"

He is so enthusiastic that I begin to pick up on his vibe with anticipation. This should be fun!

We arrive at a campsite that has the classic VW minibus. This one is old and beat up. It has stickers pasted everywhere, coloring the metal surface of the vehicle. It's obvious that this thing is lived in year-round. A huge makeshift awning constructed of tarp and blankets and towels, serves as the entranceway into their home. It's dark and quiet inside. People are sleeping. The front window is covered from inside with cardboard and the curtains are pulled shut in the other windows. A couple of old army tents scatter around on the site. It's quiet, except for the loud snoring of a guy sitting at the picnic table with his head on the surface. I hang out by the fire ring, while Pete goes into the VW.

Pete comes back with a guy following behind him.

"Ted, this is Vincent or Vince—he goes by either name."

We shake hands. Tattoos spring out all over his tall and lean body. A long gray ponytail dangles down his shirtless back and stops at the waistband of his jean shorts. Patches and resewn seams cover his worn out Birkenstock leather sandals.

"Pete tells me you're a seeker! He says you want to learn about the Dead and the deadheads."

"He did? Right! Okay!"

Confused about the 'seeker' part, I catch on to where he is leading and nod in agreement. Vince looks to be in his late fifties. Deep furrows of crows feet surround his dark blue eyes that sparkle from his tan, weather-beaten face.

"Where's Jinx and Cricket? They need to be here," Vince says to Pete.

"I'll be back in a few. I'm going to hunt them down. I think I know where they'll be," Pete says.

Pete takes off on a jog and leaves me here with Vincent. We each take a seat on a folding chair and Vince starts in on my history lesson.

"The Haight-Ashbury district of San Francisco in the mid 60's is when it all started, man. I was there in 1966 and '67. If I could freeze time in life I would always want to be stuck in those days. I was a young rebel then."

He looks off in the air for several seconds, as if he is reliving the time period or searching the memory banks of his mind for a specific event.

"Buddha Bear and Pigpen were the founding members of the band. Pig was the blues man, the real thing. He drank himself to death before he got out of his twenty's. That was really sad when Pig passed."

Vince has a sour look on his face now. He takes out a cigarette and lights it up, takes a few drags, then continues his story.

"The Grateful Dead were founded in 1965 in California. I was living in the Santa Clara Valley during those days. Man, everything was in an upheaval then."

He clicks off his fingers one-by-one as if counting.

"Vietnam, student protests, sit-ins, riots, police harassment, hippie parties, flower children, social/political injustice and peace and love, man!"

Vince raises his voice near the end of his monologue, listing off the last couple statements. Then he throws out his hand to high-five me. His face is beaming! I return his gesture and he squeezes our hands together. His grip is tight. I can feel the intensity in his eyes as if I can peer into his soul and know his great experiences, or so I imagine. I am caught up in a wave of energy, ever since I woke up, and I know it well by now, so I just roll with it.

"I was ready to run away to Canada. I had no permanent address—went incognito."

Vince puts his sunglasses on, arching his eyebrows along the low slung glasses, like a sly sleuth.

"I never got drafted though—went to all the student protests around Berkeley and Stanford—met a lot of radical people. Most were well meaning, but as soon as it turned to violence and hatred—that was wrong!"

He pounds his fist in his hand to emphasize his meaning.

"Don't get me wrong—we had a lot of good times, every day was great, the summer of love, free love—I slept with so many women then."

He motions to the quiet VW and talks lower. "My old lady don't like hearing none of that shit, but she ain't out here."

He slows down to a whisper with a big grin on his face.

"I was getting it every night."

I leaned in tight as he continues. "Pussy everywhere and everyone so happy, acid trips and drugs and music. Everything was centered on music. Music made the world go round."

"So who's Buddha Bear?" I ask.

"Oh! That's what I call Jerry Garcia! He's so cool man, and so talented...plays guitar, draws, paints, composes songs, produces the albums. He's a genius! I always tell everybody—'Buddha Bear is full of glowing wisdom to impart subconsciously'—it's up to each person, how they connect with the raw energy, man!"

Pete wanders back with Cricket and two other people, a guy and a girl. I spot them approaching down the road and get up from my chair, pointing so Vince can see them too.

"Now it will really get interesting," he says. "You met Cricket?"

I nod 'yes.'

"I don't need to tell you then—but isn't she something? I always call her the 'Queen Bee.' Sometimes she doesn't mind, but if she's frustrated about something in one of the tribes or clans, she gets upset when I tease her with that name."

"I spent some time with her this morning at the sunrise. We talked for awhile. Her positive energy can be overwhelming. She's a force, that's for sure!" I say.

Laughing heartily, Vincent boasts, "Cricket is a genuine sparkplug! Yessirree!"

Cricket comes hopping and skipping along the road slightly ahead of the others. She waves her hand over her head.

"Hi Ted! Hi Vince!"

She comes running up to me and gives me a big hug. Then she hugs Vince. Pete soon arrives on Cricket's footsteps with the other couple. Cricket introduces me.

"Ted—this is Jinx and Mignon (pronounced min-yon). Ted is a writer, a thinker, and a seeker."

Just like that, she said it—I didn't know how to respond.

Mignon says, "Cool, that's groovy!"

Then Mignon walks over and hugs me, kisses my cheek and forehead, then takes a flower out of her hair, a daisy, and puts it in my hair.

In her late twenties, her long, dark, soft hair and delicately set nose frame her curvaceous, catlike eyes. Mignon is extraordinarily beautiful, exotic looking, like her name. She wears a gypsy dress similar to Cricket's, but she wears it tighter to her buxom body.

"Do you write poetry or lyrics, man?"

I look over to my right and Jinx is addressing me.

Another aging hippy historian of bygone years—he

wears coke bottle glasses with a scraggly beard and a body full of tattoos. His ensemble is complete with a biker's vest, jeans, boots, chains around his neck and a skull-and-crossbones-emblazoned headband scarf covering the crown of his head. We shake hands.

"All kinds of different stuff, it depends," I say. "I've been keeping a daily journal for many years now. Some days or nights I might feel the inspiration of a poet in me. But mostly, I just write what's on my mind or what the current events are of the given day. You know—What did I do? What happened? How do I feel? Then I write."

"Ted's here to learn and seek and grow," says a jubilant Cricket.

"We have the right mix of people here for that purpose," Pete replies.

We all find a seat around the fire pit. Jinx takes over and he's got some stories of his experiences for me to hear. There are six of us assembled together, but he just talks directly to me the whole time. With an intense glare he tells me about the history of Tapers at Dead Shows.

"I have a catalog of copies of every dead show ever done—many multiple copies of some of the greatest shows!"

Vince leaves the small gathering and goes to his VW for a couple of minutes. He comes back and hands a briefcase to Jinx.

"Thanks V—this is exactly what I need."

Jinx opens it up and hands me a magazine-type newspaper, *Relix*. I scan through it while he keeps on talking.

"Tapers are part of the inner sub-culture of deadhead tribes. I got my name from being a taper—Jinx. I screwed up sound systems and messed up quality tape reproductions in those early years. I was always experimenting—learning on the job, how the equipment works, what this control does versus this other control—stuff like that—anyways, the Dead crew started letting us dedicated tapers, plug into their sound system and mixing boards. It was cosmic man! A music revolution at hand! They empowered us listeners who truly hear…"

Jinx is in his own reverie now—his eyes are bugged-out and magnified through the thick glasses he wears. He is here with us, but at this moment he seems so far away within himself, living a vision or trying to catch the last glimpse before that very vision passes away. All five of us are quiet, captivated by the intensity of Jinx.

"I had to learn all the nuances and glitches to overcome to create the highest quality reproduction. I have the true raw purity of the greatness of the Dead—on live tape, show after show!"

Cricket chimes in, "An underground market of reproductions is passed down and copied by the most devoted of deadheads. They can learn who has the best quality tapes from show to show, year by year."

"Yeah—and Jinx's name is like 'Gold' in the inner circle now—people love to have copies of a Jinx reproduction," says Mignon with exuberance.

ஐ

"We are in a cosmic consciousness zone. I can feel it, sense it!" Cricket says, as she smiles real big and radiant. "I love everyone!"

Cricket and Mignon hug. The other guys look at them and smile with reverence. Cricket jumps up and starts cavorting, leaping, dancing around the campsite. Then Mignon follows her. They each have a bag of rose flower petals they pull out of a pocket in their dresses. They start sprinkling the rose petals around. Hopping and leaping like ballet dancers, they sprinkle rose petals on each of our heads. A couple petals fall into my hand. I hold them softly, the frailty and soft grace of the flower petal, the symbol of love in life. The girls continue cavorting about. The guys egg them on.

I ponder the true spiritual essence of being human—Love, Friendship, Thankfulness, Forgiveness, Moral Maturity, Happiness . . .

Pete nudges me out of my momentary daydream to pass the purple whale.

Cricket says, "We are all Searchers! Seekers! We spread the love, the energy, the message."

She is on her soapbox up at the pulpit as Cricket jumps on top of the picnic table bench.

"People become deadheads because they believe in freedom of consciousness, love of the earth, nature, thy fellow man. Society in the mainstream does not care about these most basic of things. What are we to do? Become slowly robotic and do what everyone else does—be like each other and live out our unimaginative days?"

"NO!" Cricket shouts.

"No! No!" shouts Mignon, Pete, Jinx and Vince.

Then they all sing in unison, "We are the deadheads and we are Grateful!"

I sit in my chair, all smiles and laughs, as I watch all five of them sing and dance and cavort about the campsite. I relish this moment—the brotherhood with complete strangers I am experiencing—solid rapport with people who make me feel like part of the family, a raw energy vibe of goodwill. Pete grabs his acoustic guitar and starts strumming away as everyone returns to their chair around the camp fire pit so we can continue with our talk.

Mignon says, "Educating yourself so you can work all your life and be tied to a job that is more important than your family and your life is backwards thinking.

People are so unhappy in this world. And the worst part is that most of them don't even know how unhappy they really are."

I interject, "The mass of men lead lives of quiet desperation—Thoreau."

"Yes! Exactly! You know what I mean!" responds Mignon. "I don't want to end up that way. Self-delusional conformity! Every day I see people who don't love themselves or appreciate life. It's like a wicked disease. I refuse to become afflicted with this malady. I love life! God is great! The earth is beautiful and magical."

"You go girl!" shouts Cricket, clapping her hands. "I taught her well—she is my protégée!"

Pete starts singing a song while strumming on his guitar. A couple of joints are passed around.

Mignon continues on, "I'm in my junior year of college credit eligibility. It's taken almost six years to get this far along—starting and stopping—I do correspondence school credits in Sociology and Psychology. My main thing is the society and environment of traveling with other deadheads across the country. This is my real life. There's such a sense of community. I have friends all over the country—people who really care about each other as a person."

Mignon clutches her hand against her upper chest to accentuate the passion of heart she feels.

"I'm part of the Greater Rainbow Family Tribe."

Then she walks over to Pete near the picnic table and watches him strum his guitar. Mignon closes her eyes and hums along with Pete. Cricket then takes over the discussion.

"Deadheads come from all factions of society: rich, poor, middle-class, high-society, the disaffected, disowned, trash heap of throwaways. I've met many people running from everything in their life, people so down from the pressures of living based on the expectations of mainstream society. Most people just need someone to care with compassion. To be real! To let them know they are valuable, to themselves, and the human race. I try to help the wonderful vibe of the Dead community by showing these types of people that another choice is available. It hurts me when I see people who do such deliberate self-damage."

Then Pete hollers over from the picnic table, "There's Cricket with her vision of saving all the lost children of the world!"

She hollers back, "We're all children you know, no matter how old we are, we are all just children learning everyday!" Cricket laughs at Pete's comment, realizing she's taking herself a bit too seriously. Then she goes over by Mignon and Pete to join them in a song.

ꕥ

Vince, at first so talkative then totally quiet, now takes over the discussion.

"There is a deep spirituality that I feel from all my years as a deadhead—each show is like a semi-religious experience that I share with 10,000 or more of my favorite brothers and sisters. I just radiate such love for people on those days—like it's a gift just to be a person—to be alive!"

"Halleluiah!" says Cricket. "Amen!"

Mignon and Cricket dance in a small circle with each other, more like ballet.

Vince has wound himself into a mystical reverie, recounting his passion for the ongoing movement within the deadhead community. His eyes sparkle and he wears a permanent grin, taking intermittent drags of his Marlboro.

"The Grateful Dead and The Stage show becomes

my Church. All my high-friends in the audience are the parishioners in fellowship. We make such high pure energy, all connected, so positive and real. It's cosmic, man."

"Halleluiah!" say Cricket and Mignon. "Amen!"

Cricket and Mignon break from their ring-around-the-rosie-pocketful-of-posey, gently holding hands.

"Life is a progressive journey from darkness to light, from ignorance to a knowledge of truth and wisdom, from spiritual infancy to soul supremacy!" Cricket proclaims, as she and Mignon raise their clutched arms over their heads.

"Halleluiah! Amen! Halleluiah! Amen!" says everyone in unison, even me! The energy of the moment rushes through me as I imagine I can see deeper and clearer for that moment. I see the bright radiant aura that glows, surrounding each individual—Jinx, Vince, Pete, Mignon, and Cricket, especially Cricket! A bluish-white ray of beaming light encircles her whole body, as a halo forms with a deeper intensity of light around Cricket's head.

I continue to take in the unfolding scenes. Jinx leans in between the girls, nodding their heads in agreement. Jinx glares at me.

"The music creates an aura, a general feeling, a total vibe, man! Like I said, it's cosmic, dude! You're going to the concert tonight aren't you, brother?" Jinx asks me.

I shrug.

"You must—you'll see for yourself!" says Jinx.

"What about the clothes and wardrobe most of you wear—tie-dyes, gypsy dresses, beads?"

I direct the question to the group, no one in particular.

"That's just leftover from the San Francisco hippy scene of the 1960's," Vince says. "Those hippies lived and looked exactly as we are today. It's all about freedom, man.

The hippies were just the carryover from the beatniks of the 1950's. You know Jack Kerouac, On The Road?"

"I read the book a long time ago in college," I say.

"That book is like a party-on bible," Jinx says. "I've spent many days reading my dog-eared paperback to fellow deadheads while traveling the roads from show to show. I like Kerouac, man. Dude, he knows what it's like to be me—to be like us!"

"Yeah, man!" agrees Vince.

They both have this far off look in their eyes—contemplating past adventures or slick golden pieces of Kerouac.

Then Cricket and Mignon rejoin us from their cosmic dancing reverie, to take a seat around the fire pit. Cricket wants to know if they told me about the Fan Club and the Art work yet? No one says anything so she starts in.

"The Fan Club has over 100,000 Deadhead members. They do a newsletter a couple times a year. Make special announcements about the band. Provide directions to shows and how to get Dead paraphernalia, artwork, patches, stickers, copies of tapes and such."

Cricket writes an East Coast and then a West Coast telephone number on a small crumpled piece of paper she pulls from a pocket of her dress. She hands me the paper. Then she continues on about the vast collections of Dead artwork.

"Jerry Garcia paints too! Deadheads across the country have been buying and trading in psychedelic inspired artwork from listening to the Dead. The Deadhead society has its own Picassos, Eschers, Dalis. I've seen some of the most far-out stuff."

Pete starts strumming a Simon and Garfunkel tune. Mignon skips in a circle around him. They start humming together. Cricket goes over and joins them. She pulls her harmonica from the "warehouse" pocket in her dress. Vince, Jinx and I sit around the campfire circle, watching them perform over by the picnic table. The one guy is still sleeping with his head on the other end of the table. He has never moved or been disturbed during all of our commotion.

I turn to Vince and Jinx and ask them to tell me more about tapers and the Sixties scene in San Francisco. I sit and listen as they talk about Janis Joplin, Jimi Hendrix, The Monterey Festival, Altamonte, The Hells Angels, The Rolling Stones, The Beatles, The Who, Grace Slick, Woodstock, the Acid Tests, Ken Kesey, Nick Cassidy, Timothy Leary, Alan Ginsberg…

ꕥ

After several hours of listening to Vince and Jinx fill my head with all their experiences and knowledge, I find my imagination swimming in a vast sea. Then I almost nod off. My eyes are open watching the two of them speak at me and to each other, but I do not hear them. I am tired, drifting off. Then I see an American Bald Eagle. I don't believe it is really there. But it is there in my mind's eye. I watch him fly up high, way above the trees, circling the campsite and the perimeter of the park. He just glides on the air current. I feel a connection with the eagle, like he is communicating with me.

I look at Vince and Jinx and they are still talking. Cricket, Mignon and Pete are still playing music and dancing over by the picnic table. I look up and there is the eagle. The backdrop of the bluish hue from the sky, mixed in with the milky white clouds, accentuates the majesty and glory of this bird of prey. The eagle continues to glide and circle and hover directly above. I close my eyes and I can still feel him there—see him hovering and gliding…

I have to find myself, know myself, get a hold of myself… I'm lost…Living in the woods and camping in the park allows me to write, read, think and probe deeper into understanding myself. But I can't live this way forever. Something's got to give and I don't have a clue what it is. I'm living in the woods like a hermit so I can wake up from this psychic slumber. AWARE, AWAKE, and ALIVE to the vital senses. But yet, I can't escape from this dream-state of living. Nature is my shelter.

Then the eagle disappears and I feel as if I've fallen from a higher plateau—a level of awareness I no longer sense. What did I lose? What did I see? I shake my head and blink my eyes, opening and stretching my mouth. I want to regain my wits and my senses.

Tuning back into the conversation with Vince and Jinx, they're talking about having tapes for over 3000 Grateful Dead Shows.

"I think Feb 13th in 1970 at The Filmore East in New York is the all-time greatest Dead Show. They never excelled at such a level," says Jinx. Smoking on his cigarette, he takes a drag and flicks the ashes. "The best after that…"

"The California gigs in the early years at Golden Gate Park, man! Those were special!" Vince interrupts with heightened excitement in his eyes to match his counterpart. "Nothing was like the everyday energy of the Bay Area in the late 60's man!"

He points his finger in Jinx's face repeatedly. "Not even Greenwich Village, man! Nothing compared to northern California then!"

Vince is now up in Jinx's face. They're standing chest to chest. "Just relax, man. Give me my space, dude."

They jostle around for a few seconds, pushing against each other until Jinx's glasses slip as he catches them just as they are about to fall.

"Sorry man!" says Vince, backing off.

"No! That's all right—I'm okay—but relax, man!" Jinx says to Vince. "Be cool, I'm with you, I know where your comin' from, dude. You just get all wound up and start coming at me, gettin' in my space—that's all, no big deal."

Jinx readjusts his glasses on his face after wiping them off against his pants. The both of them can talk forever about anything that has to do with The Dead. These two guys are truly oral historians of this counter-culture society. It has been an honor to learn about all these things from them.

I'm starting to feel the effects of lack of sleep. Yawning and yawning until I have to get up and move around to wake up from my malaise. Everyone else is full of energy, liveliness, intensity. This is just another day to them.

Quite frankly, my mind is blown over all this—an overload to the senses—mind-boggling sights, sounds and conversation. I feel invigorated as the noon hour approaches, but I can't keep up the energy with these people without my proper rest. I need to recharge. I decide to break free from here and go to my site to get something to eat and catch a nap.

"Excuse me guys—I have to head back. It was nice meeting both of you. Thanks for the great history lesson."

We shake hands and then the two of them go back to their conversation about all things Grateful Dead.

Cricket, Pete and Mignon are dancing and singing by the picnic table.

"Hey guys, I have to head out."

Pete stops strumming his guitar.

"You can't get away that easy," says Cricket. "You promised I could read some of your writings in your notebooks and journal."

"I know—you can, but I'm pretty tired right now. I'd

like to take a nap for a couple hours."

Cricket giggles and grabs my hand.

"Come with me for a minute. I have to show you something."

Mignon and Pete go back to singing and playing the guitar as I follow Cricket, hand-in-hand, over to one of the tents on the campsite. She folds back the tent flap window. I look inside. There must be at least fifteen people all huddled together on every piece of empty floor space in the tent. And they are all out cold. The dreadlocks and tie-dyes and beads and jeans all meld into one colorful heap of slumbering flesh. Looks like twice as many guys as girls in here. No movement, everyone dressed warmly, huddled, sleeping. Then Cricket takes me to another tent and we experience the same general thing—a sleeping mass of humanity. She giggles again with a big bright smile—shushing me with her finger over her lips as she flips the window flap of the tent.

We walk back over to the fire pit and the picnic table but everyone has gone. The sleeping guy at the picnic table is all that remains.

"I need to get going too!" I say.

"Can I walk with you to your campsite?"

I hesitate responding to her. I am tired and yawning more frequently now—just want to be alone, to get some sleep. But I feel compelled to continue visiting with Cricket.

I think of the vision of the circling eagle I saw earlier. Looking to the sky and above the tree lines—he wasn't anywhere to be seen.

"What are you looking for?" she asks.

"Oh, nothing! Yeah, let's walk to my campsite. It's way over on the other side of the park."

"Great!"

There she goes hopping, skipping and jumping ahead of me down the road. I follow behind her, moving along as fast as I can to keep up. All the while, I'm thinking of the eagle I had seen and look up toward the sky now and then. I feel like the eagle is trying to tell me something, to deliver a message—but I can't figure it out.

ꕥ

As we are heading down the park road together we pass a guy walking down the middle of the road straight at us. The guy wears over a hundred piercings in his face—lips, eyebrows, nose, ears, cheeks, forehead. He displays tattoos all over his body and he looks dangerous and menacing with a dark hatred in his eyes. We scatter to get out of the way, otherwise he would have plowed right into us.

Cricket snarls and hisses like a pissed-off cat. What an outrageous uncommon sound she produces.

"I know about him! Stay away! He's a bringer of bad karma," she warns me.

I look back at the shirtless, tattooed, pierce-laden heathen, as he stomps down the road in his black leather pants, biker boots with spurs, and chains dangling from places all over his body. Lost in his own mentally constructed world, he represents the opposite of everything I've seen so far.

"How is the criminal element amongst the deadhead society? A guy like that doesn't seem like he would be friendly to anyone," I say.

"You have to watch out for people like that," Cricket says, "and some others who will befriend you, then rob you blind when you aren't looking. Con-artists! Fortunately, very few people are like this. The word gets around about the thieves, criminals and distrustful ones. We share so much harmony, peace and love here, that when someone of this nature shows up, we can tune in and tune them out of our positive vibe."

We continue walking down the road toward my campsite, as I listen to Cricket explain her counter-culture society to me.

"All the true deadheads are like one big extended family—my brothers and sisters and children. A mother knows her children!"

Cricket points out a sticker on a bumper of a car. It says, "Mean People Suck." Then she points out the same message on a bumper of another car, then another.

Like a whirling dervish she twirls and swirls, hops, skips, jumps. I follow along as we walk the park road through the campgrounds.

"Those bumper stickers allude to people like that guy we just passed. I've seen him around many times and I've tried to talk to him to steer him down the right path, but he's just evil—out to do no good to whomever he can manipulate and take advantage of. All my friends are aware of him."

"Are there many people like that who follow the Grateful Dead?"

"There's a few here and there. They usually gravitate toward each other, when they're not alone, so we all know who they are and are aware of them. But enough about that," Cricket says, "they do not represent what we are all about—there is a positive energy flow, a harmonizing process, a creative flux—and each of the true heads work to perpetuate this ongoing feeling of bliss. Negative people with negative energy forces are not part of this process," she proclaims.

I drifted off into contemplation of the magnetic effect of my own experienced negativities:

The burden of depression slowly eats away the life force, bitter anger—melting me from the inside—burning, boiling, bursting, bubbling—anger and misery. Why do I choose to cause myself such struggle? Am I selling my one life short, adopting and conforming to the social norm? I can't live this way.

Cricket says, "The Deadheads are like one huge extended family—a gathering of relatives who mainly don't know each other. We each contribute our harmonic thoughts to the community gathering with total liberty to be free. We care about each other, but we don't interfere with anyone's trip. We don't condone violence, which means no negative energies. We love all things natural in nature. We bless the earth every day. Give thanks in humble prayers of gratitude for all living things. These virtues should be preserved and perpetuated by the human race. I'm glad for The Grateful Dead because they provide for the making of this community so we can experience it first-hand. This is not just about a concert or getting to a show. This is about a positive mindset of goodwill toward nature and your fellow man at all times."

"But what about people like that guy? He doesn't—"

Cricket interrupts me. "—fit! Doesn't fit! Is that what you were going to say?"

I shrug my shoulders and nod my head as we continue our walk.

"Let me tell you why he *does* fit. It's about freedom, Ted! Everyone has the right to choose the way they want to be. If we had rules that said you couldn't be mean, nasty, hateful, negative—then we would be telling people how to think and choose—that wouldn't be freedom!"

"So most deadheads choose the happy, flower power, positive vibe, mindset that I've mostly experienced then?"

"Yes! Yes!" Cricket jumps with joy, assuming that I'm 'getting it,' I suppose.

"We do get a lot of bad, misguided publicity, though. The media makes us all sound like a bunch of acid-soaked freaks. Yeah, people do that and some more than others, and some even all the time, but that's their trip they choose, man. When you have freedoms, some of us lose balance with our choices. That's why the community supports itself and each other. If you're on a bad trip you can come out of it. You can grow. I tell you I know for a fact that the average deadhead is happier in this community than the average person living out in the "real world" is with their fellow man. Humankind in society is generally an unhappy conflict-oriented community. We are the exact opposite of that. But we are so few in number, compared to the overall scheme of things, that we really have to work and participate to keep this energy flow going and growing."

We keep on walking along the park road as I listen to Cricket. She is fully animated as she punctuates her points with loud bursts of expression—huge eyeballs at me whenever she wants to make sure I get the point. Then Cricket jumps, hops and twirls for a few seconds then comes running back at me and starts right back where she last left off.

I feel like she is the PR Director of the deadhead community, ushering in a new way of experiencing spiritual awareness.

Cricket continues on as we circle around the bend in the road and head for my campsite. I haven't been back since I first met Jeff at 3am, and now it's mid-afternoon.

She starts railing about the media and all the negative images they inundate us with on a daily basis.

"Everyone always points out problems and bad things but no one ever offers solutions. Not government, big business, corporations, the armed services. They rarely solve anything. Just as long as the cash is flowing through the economic system and the big dogs are getting paid—everything is just fine!"

Cricket pounds her right fist into her left palm. This petite gypsy woman looks as if she is about to explode in frustration—her face is flush with redness and she is perspiring on her forehead and upper lip.

We're soon coming up to my campsite.

"Cricket! Cricket, you need to relax about all this. Take it easy girl. Here's my campsite, number ninety-nine. Go have a seat at the table and I'll get some charcoal ready to make some coffee or tea. Which do you prefer?"

"Tea, please. Thank You! Sorry Ted, I just get so upset at the way things are sometimes. For example, we have a healthcare system in America that is overburdened and yet other countries offer free healthcare to all their citizens. Our educational system of teaching and learning is not preparing these young kids properly. We already get taxed too much! Tax increases don't solve any problems!"

Cricket is full of exasperation, as if she is taking the weight of the world upon those tiny shoulders. Releasing her negative energy with a deep sigh, Cricket slumps forward as she takes a seat at the picnic table. I fumble around with the cookware and the grille.

"I'm all unwired and off balance, now."

She waves her hand in front of her face, fanning the air about her head. "This isn't me, usually. I focus my passions on the positive goodwill things of this life, but I can't ignore these other issues."

"Are you a political activist or have you ever thought of running for office?" I ask.

"No and No! The American political process aggravates me. Politicians stump for votes, say anything they feel sounds good—lie to the general public over and over—never intending to keep any promises they make. Heaven forbid, if I ever ran for office, though, I'd get involved first-hand and do things that solve problems, offer solutions, follow through on every promise. I would be inspired to unveil the truth of what I see, and expose the lies of others."

"You sound like you have some experience with the process."

"I had relatives and friends in politics. I see how people change."

Cricket is shaking her head slowly, disgusted and exasperated with the continuance of this topic of conversation.

"All right, onto something better, before I misplace my energy. Save me from this discussion, Ted. Show me some of your works."

"Okay!"

I go over to my tent to gather some reading material. Looking back out at the picnic table from the tent, Cricket is quiet and reflective now. She stares up at the sky, shielding her eyes with her right hand, squinting.

I pull a big-handled crate-like box out of my tent and carry it to the table.

"Here are some of my writings, journal entries, notebooks, index cards, loose papers, and poems. I usually fill up a three-hundred page notebook every two to three months. I've been writing for many years so I have a lot of journal notebooks. I saw you looking up at the sky, did you see an eagle or something?"

"No. I was just de-energizing myself of the negative chi I had," Cricket says.

"What do you mean by that?" I ask.

"We block our energies from flowing through our body correctly when we choose to concentrate on negativities, stress, tension. Then our bodily system is blocked. Meditation works well for me. But just now I have to flush my mind of the thoughts we've been talking about, the negative stuff. I have this thing I do to rid myself of negative energy. You're probably going to think I'm a fool, if you don't already!"

Cricket pauses for a few seconds, smiling at me.

"I've got an open mind—I try not to prejudge!" I stammer.

"Well let me tell you then, Ted. I imagine the sky as a vacuum of energy—positive and negative atoms all co-mingling throughout space. I visualize this vacuum sucking out all the residue of negative energy from my body and filling me up with positive healing light as it passes through. Swooosh!"

She must have read my disbelieving facial expression.

"See! I told you, you would think I was crazy!"

"No-no—whatever works! It obviously works for you," I say.

I open the lid from the box, sifting through my inventory, looking in my notebooks until I find a selection that seems to fit the moment. It has to do with my feelings on the New England Transcendentalists of the 1800's, mainly, Emerson, Thoreau, Whitman and Margaret Fuller.

"Here's some stuff that I think you will find interesting."

I give the notebook to Cricket to read, opened to the page I want her to start at. She grabs a folding chair, with her tea and the notebook, goes to the edge of the woods overlooking Lake Minnawanna. Cricket sits there and reads for a couple of hours. Not a word from her the entire time—just read in silence.

ЖОЖ

I am still tired, but for a moment I feel renewed energy. I sit at the picnic table with pen in hand and commence to capture the day's events in my journal notebook. Every now and then I look up at Cricket and wonder what part she is reading now.

I go back to writing in my journal. I ponder this counter-culture movement sustained by these deadheads. It still befuddles me that I wasn't aware of this minority faction in America and around the globe. I'm discovering that I'm essentially a disconnected and disaffected person—a literal dropout of society. I didn't like the direction of my life and I didn't know how to stop it, so I ran away from society to learn about myself to make a better go of it. Life is too precious to squander. There must be more. Then I wake up one day and stumble upon a mass gathering of the disaffected who want positive changes, too.

Maybe I'm a counter-culture type. This thought resonates with me as I continue to write in my journal.

Cricket is reading from my notebooks about the counter-culture of the mid-1800's. There is a common chord that runs right through the great movements of the past to present day—the worth of the individual! Enlightening oneself!

I consistently achieved the good grades, made the good money and rose up the corporate ladder. I've been happy and in love and enjoyed plenty of friends. Sweet happy memories. Yet, it seems like another's life, and I really wasn't ever present. Why can't I restart my career with a good paying job and just go forward from there? Because I'm still unhappy and I'd feel further constrained and alienated. Something within me wants out and I can't find it. Ted – Who Are You?

Just then Cricket comes over to the table where I'm sitting and gives me this big long hug. I hug her back but she keeps hugging. So I hug some more. She keeps hugging. She has her ear to my chest like she is listening to my heart as she hugs me. I start to feel uncomfortable.

What's happening here?

Cricket then pulls away and goes around to the other side of the picnic table so she faces me. Her eyes pierce mine.

"Thank you for blessing me with your words! Your art! Your gift!" she exclaims.

"Thank you! I'm glad you like it!" I say.

"You have a mission and a purpose, Ted! Your work must be read, heard and known."

I nod my head agreeing with her.

Cricket grabs my hands from across the table.

"But first," she says, "you must continue to explore the mystery, the essence of truly knowing yourself. True knowledge of self-awareness can only be gained through personal experience."

"I'm on this journey now!" I say to her.

Cricket nods in agreement. We squeeze each other's hands and continue our intimate stare down. I can feel the intensity radiating from her big brown eyes.

"All writers need experiences and adventure to stimulate the creative mechanism from within. I've got a great idea for you. We're going to heighten the process of artistic inspiration today. You are going to experience a 'Miracle' today."

"I feel like the whole day has already been a miracle from meeting all the heads and experiencing the vibe!" I explain to her.

"This is only the start—there is more to come!"

Cricket then breaks free from our trance and proceeds

to hop, skip and twirl down the road. I sit at my campsite staring at her as she disappears into the forest trail.

> *Idealistic notions and concern for the growth of society, individual by individual, is truly altruistic. Then reality sets in—I, too, am more of an idealist than a realist! This state of mind and decision-making has scrambled my foundations, unbalanced my character growth. Why should I care? Who am I to believe what cannot be? Mankind is still in infancy, humanity is just a mere baby. Growth and evolution is highly sporadic. Why do we, as the human species, sell ourselves so short? But yet, the enlightened individual can soar and fly!*

ഇര

Chapter Three

A Lifestyle of Bohemia

ഇര

Bohemia

1) *A district inhabited by people whose behavior is characterized by a disregard for conventional rules.*

2) *The social circles where such behavior is prevalent.*

The vision of Cricket twirling and swirling and skipping down the road entrances me as she reappears from the forest grove, heading back to my site.

"I almost forgot—I was wondering if you wouldn't mind if I copied down one of your poems and you sign it?"

"Sure, no problem! Which one?" I ask.

"I like the one titled, 'Sweet Passionate Earth' the best."

I reach into my box of writings and leaf through the notebook Cricket read. I find the poem and then give her a blank notepad to copy it. She sits down at the table and transcribes. When she is done it looks like artwork because she has transposed the poem into a calligraphy style of writing.

"That looks really neat. How did you learn to write like that?" I ask.

"I've been doing it most of my life, till it's like second nature to me now. My mom and sister taught me when I was a girl."

She slides the notepad over to me so I can sign my name. After I write 'Ted Senario' at the end of the poem, Cricket then takes back the notepad and writes 'The Bohemian' under my name. She proudly tears the sheet from the pad and re-reads her copy of the poem.

"This is great! Thank you!"

She gives me another big hug then off she bolts again, skipping, twirling and whistling, eventually disappearing on the path to the woods.

I decide it is finally time to take a nap. I need to put my box of journal notebooks in the tent and clean up the picnic table a bit.

Then Jeff comes around the VW-partitioned-wall and he's all wired up just like he was when I first met him early in the AM.

"Yo, man, I could tell you guys were having a real interesting visit and I didn't want to disturb you or anything. I fell asleep," Jeff says, "and then woke up an hour later and you two were in the same position, hardly moving—just reading. I spaced out staring at you guys, dude. Neither of you moved except for turning a page and I thought you became statues—I saw you as a statue! Then when you guys started talking and moving around finally—I started freaking out, man—until I realized I was daydreaming or hallucinating."

I joke back to him, "You've got to watch out what kind of drugs you're taking there, dude!"

Jeff snickers, "It's all about having a good time, man!"

He wanders around my campsite, pacing back and forth as we're talking.

"Would you like to see how I run my business so I can afford going from show-to-show across the country?"

"Maybe later—I'm pretty beat right now!"

I gather books, papers and notebooks on the table and put them in my box and take it to the tent. Jeff continues his pacing.

"It'll only take a few minutes," he says to me, as I re-emerge from the tent. "It's a wonderful operation, man. You'll be impressed! Come on, just a few minutes . . ."

"Oh, all right," I say, "sure, lead the way."

Jeff jumps in the air with excitement as I follow him over to his VW mini-bus. The vehicle is two-toned—white and sunburst yellow. He opens the backend of his vehicle and pulls out what—at first—looks to me like a built-in sewing table. He pulls it out on a hinge-type pulley apparatus, unfolds four legs underneath and positions the legs on the ground. Then he unhinges the device and pulls the equipment upright from within the table so that it fits on the table top.

"My Dad helped me custom-design this thing to fit in the back of the van like this," he tells me, his chest puffing with pride. "When I'm all done using it, it folds in nice and neat to where nothing is in the way."

"What is it?"

"It's a drill and a saw bench. This is what I use to make my devil sticks!"

"What the hell are devil sticks?" I ask.

"I'll show you!"

He makes some more fiddling adjustments, installs a drill piece, then turns the equipment on. Nothing happens. He starts to worry now—re-inspecting everything. Jeff goes around to the front of the van then comes back, then runs around to the front again. I'm standing there watching him scurry back and forth trying to figure out his problem. He tries to start his vehicle but it won't turn over—dead battery! Jeff comes running around to me near the rear of the vehicle.

I shake my head 'no' to him.

Jeff is working himself into a frenzy, throwing the ball in his braided hair, back and forth from hand-to-hand as he paces around the van thinking about what to do.

It is quiet at his campsite, just Jeff and me are milling about. He had mentioned to me earlier that each of the tents on his site are filled with people sleeping. It doesn't matter to Jeff now. He is loud and boisterous, scurrying back and forth, working on his machine. He wakes up the people in the other identical VW, by hopping in and pulling it around to face the hood of his car so he can use jumper cables. I can't see anybody but I can hear angry voices hollering at him while he is doing all this.

Jeff gets the cables out, connects all four poles—then to start his vehicle—nothing but persistent clicking noises! He readjusts the cables and then goes to the other van and sits in the driver's seat for ten minutes, revving up the engine. Jeff then jumps into his VW minibus and, at last, starts it up.

A loud noise explodes near me. Startled, I jump away several feet. His equipment motor is on and running. The contraption is vibrating and whirring real loud and one of the legs falls loose. I step back a few more steps. Jeff comes running around from the front of the vehicle and hits the power switch to save the day. He is sweating profusely.

"Dude! Dude! Yo—I just avoided a disaster!" he proclaims.

He reattaches the loose leg and gently strokes the metal surface of the equipment.

"If I'd broken this machine I would be done touring—immediately—with the dead! Whew!"

Jeff swipes his hand and arm across his forehead, staring off in the distance, trance-like.

After several minutes I woke Jeff out of his dream-like thoughts.

"Hey!" Snapping my fingers to get his attention, "Show me your stuff . . ."

"Hmm! Oh—right!"

Jeff proceeds to unhook the jumper cables, close the hoods, and re-park the other van. I stand off to the side by the fire pit and watch him do this. I can hear angry grunts of protestation coming from the van. Now Jeff's back at his machine. He reaches into the rear of the vehicle along the floor board and pulls out several long two-by-two blocks of wood, perhaps six feet in length. He readjusts the drill bit and replaces it with a saw bit. Jeff flicks on the switch, puts on goggles, then grabs one of the long sticks and promptly cuts it into four pieces. Then he shuts off the machine, grabs the wood pieces and then hands me two of them.

"They'll be 'Devil Sticks!' I can sell them for $20-$30 at the shows! I can barter and trade with them to get other things like food, concert tickets, weed!" he boasts.

"What do you mean—it's just pieces of wood?" I say.

"This is just the raw materials. I've got to finish making them. I can earn up to $500 each round before I have to stock up on material again," says Jeff.

"How much money do you have to put out to make $500 worth of product?"

"Just fifty dollars, man! That's what's so cool about this little business! I hunt down the nearest hardware store from town to town and re-supply." Jeff adds, "I can create a whole batch with a half-day's work for two people. The money usually lasts a week before I have to do it all over again!"

"Why don't you make some devil sticks so I can see what you're talking about. That won't take too long will it, because I don't have all day?"

"No, no, no. You just take a seat and watch and I'll be done in no time."

Jeff points over to a nearby lawn chair for me to sit and observe. I take a seat and watch him fumble around with his materials and equipment.

"I go to about half the Dead shows," Jeff says, "the other half the time I hang out at the parking lot venues selling my devil sticks and mingling with the people in the deadhead community. So I have a small business earning revenue in order to move on to the next venue, and I just repeat the process from show to show."

Being successful in business making money, I thought to myself, as Jeff went on and on about his exploits. I zone him out for a brief moment as I wonder about my own plight, drifting uneasily:

> *Why is success defined by money? Did my lost wealth form a false character? or my true character? Losing the nest-egg, the savings, the home and property, losing all our investments. How did I let it come to this? Did my lost wealth form an unbalanced ego? I want more, I am more, I can be more, and do more with this life I live. I'm determined to persist…*

"So what do you think about my setup, Ted?"

"What about your parents and school?" I ask, snapping back to the present moment.

"I'm going into my third year, so I should be a junior, but I barely have enough credits to qualify as a sophomore. There's too much distraction and too much fun on campus. Plus I have bad study habits."

Jeff continues fiddling with his equipment, installing a drill piece.

"I'm going to be more disciplined this fall semester, especially after going on my first all-summer deadhead adventure. My parents have been very cool about everything. They helped me find and buy this VW, and my Dad helped me install this equipment."

"Where did you say you're from?"

"My parents live in upstate New York between Buffalo and Syracuse, but I go to school at Boston College. I brought my buddy from school, John, on this trip, but things haven't been working out to well between us lately."

"What's the problem?"

"We don't get along anymore. Before we left on this trip we made an agreement to work together on the devil sticks. It's a two-man operation requiring four to five hours of work to produce a crop of devil sticks to give us enough money to carry on for a whole week. John refuses to help now, so it's all on me. All he does is complain that he wants to go home. We never party together or have fun with each other anymore."

I ask Jeff to make a set of Devil Sticks and show me how they work. He grabs the stick pieces and trims them down into an hourglass type of look. He then sands down the rough edges, making sure the stick is completely smooth. Jeff then goes into the back of his van and pulls out a big box that he brings over to the picnic table. It's full of red, white and blue leather lace. He wraps an intricate weaving pattern around the stick. The outer lace is glossy and shiny. Jeff ties off the end and cuts the lace. He twirls the stick in the air like a baton. Then he sits back down and starts to wrap another stick.

"I presented my parents a written, typed up business plan with spreadsheets and everything. The budget had weekly line items for gas, oil, food, car maintenance, hardware supplies. I had it all thought out and budgeted for the entire summer. I educated my parents about all the positive energy generated within the community of the deadheads. Mom was worried because I have never done anything like this before, but Dad was all for it. I found the VW mini-bus during spring break and Dad helped me rebuild the motor and customized the back of the van so I can run an entrepreneurial venture. It's been the greatest prolonged thrill of my entire life!"

"How did you hear about the Grateful Dead, deadheads, and doing something like this?"

"I have several friends in college who have done it. They were so excited and said it was the greatest adventure thing they had done in their lives. I listened to some live tapes and went to my first concert and was hooked immediately. I love the community sense of being a Deadhead."

All the while he's talking to me he's still working on his devil sticks. He talks about the venues and the things people sell at the shows.

"Everyone who wants to follow the Dead has to have a way to make money. Some deal drugs, but I didn't want to do that—too much of a risk. Besides, I'm prone to being paranoid anyway, especially when I party and get too high. If I was dealing I'd always be on the verge of freaking and wouldn't be having so much carefree fun."

Jeff jumps up and starts twirling the devil sticks in both hands.

"So that's why I came up with a business plan and presented it to my parents."

Then he throws smaller sticks up in the air and starts juggling the mini-sticks—with the larger sticks in each hand. He's doing flips and twirls, behind his back, over his head, constant motion. He looks likes some type of circus act. I sit and watch the movement, the circling, the continuous flow of the devil sticks. He's got a good thing going, looks like a magician—up, down, over, back, circling to and fro—constant motion. It actually becomes mesmerizing watching him. All of a sudden, Jeff stops, catches all the sticks in one hand and then sets the devil sticks on the table.

I pick the sticks up and try a go at it—and everything falls to the ground. Try again—same thing. I put the sticks down.

"All I have to do is stand by at a parking lot venue and do the devil sticks demonstration and people crowd around and watch. I keep doing it while my buddy collects the money and passes out the sticks. We made over a grand one day just doing devil sticks demonstrations all day and people buying. Usually, it's not nearly that much, but I was really stocked up that time and we wanted to see if we could actually clear a thousand in a day and we did!"

"You going to the show tonight? Everyone will be leaving in a few hours. You can ride with me," Jeff says.

I yawn. I shrug my shoulders—I'm undecided.

"I don't have a ticket and I can't afford to get one," I say.

"You need a miracle! In order to get a miracle," Jeff says, "you have to be where miracles happen! Ted, you must come with us tonight!" he pleads.

"I'm going to my tent right now to take a nap. I have to get some sleep. Come and wake me when it's time to get ready to leave and I'll see how I feel then—okay?"

Jeff nods in understanding, "You just wait, you're going to have a 'Miracle' tonight!"

When I get back to the tent my mind is whirring with high octane thought. I feel so inspired. I've got so much going on in my head—thought after thought—I've got to capture it and get it on paper. I lay out on my sleeping bag and write in my journal nonstop for forty-five minutes. Free flowing words, thoughts, ideas. My hand and pen can't move fast enough. Finally, exhausted, I drift off to sleep.

I dream I'm in a deep thick forest. I'm on a path, alone, just walking along the trail. Birds and animals come out and I know them by name, they are my friends—a raccoon, a squirrel, a blue jay, a cardinal, chipmunks, deer, a moose, elk, a black bear. We are headed toward a distant bright light on the horizon. The trees, wildflowers, ferns and dense forest growth are all alive and vibrant with thought and feeling. Peace of mind, in the universal force of nature. We all co-exist together harmoniously, walking down the trail.

I hear a voice outside my tent, "Ted, Ted. It's time to go. Wake up! Ted!"

It is Jeff. He's all wired and ready to go. I look at my watch—barely slept over an hour. Jeff unzips the bottom of my tent and sticks his hand in. He has a small pipe—a skull with a lightning bolt in the middle of the forehead—the Grateful Dead trademark insignia. He puts it down with a lighter next to it and tells me to—"feel free to take as many hits as you need, I have more where that came from. We have to get ready to start partying the rest of the day and night," he assures me.

"No thanks, man, I'm really not up to it."

I roll around in my sleeping bag, stretching and yawning.

"I need my rest!" I holler out to him.

"Dude, it's all set up. Tonight you are going to experience a miracle. All you need to do is point to the sky and close your eyes and concentrate real hard."

Rustling around in the tent, I ask, "What do you mean by that?"

I unzip the tent and crawl out, looking at him bewildered.

"I don't know what you mean by a miracle? What do you mean—it's all set up?"

Jeff wears a self-assured grin on his face. He proclaims that I will, "remember this day for the rest of your life, because you're going to your first Grateful Dead concert show!"

He says I will be "transformed."

He's actually starting to sound like a fanatic lunatic to me. I'm not so sure I want to follow through with this. Maybe I will just bow out. Jeff can sense that I'm still hesitant about the whole affair.

"You just have to go, Ted. You can't miss this!" he pleads. "I promise to stop being so hyper if that freaks you out, man. You can use the back corner of my van to sit and spread out, right over the top of my equipment, which is folded back in, covered with padded board and then a seat cushion over top of that. Come on, Ted!"

"Oh, all right," I say, at last. "Let's get this show on the road!"

Jeff jumps for joy, his sales pitch complete. I gather a few things and jump into the back of his van, resting my legs up on the cushion covering his contraption. I brought my book bag with me and set it right below my feet. Four more people then pile in, plus Jeff driving. I meet Candice, Julie, Mitch and John. Looking out the back window I see activity and packing at all the campsites. It's like you would imagine it if a fire bell went off. The roads in the park are becoming gridlocked. People are scurrying about and rushing around in all directions.

The passenger door opens and a female gypsy hippy with tons of beads around her neck and rainbow patches all over her dress, jumps in. We now have seven people. The two girls back here are the only ones that seem to know each other. They keep whispering back and forth and giggling. They look to me to be eighteen or nineteen years old. They wear the requisite tie-dyed shirts and jeans. The two guys in the back with us are staring empty into space. John is the buddy of Jeff, the driver. Now I see why they don't get along. The two of them are so opposite in nature. Jeff is energetic, enthusiastic, talkative, friendly. John is lackadaisical, fearful, unhappy, worried. He doesn't want to talk or make eye contact. Mitch, sitting next to him, is a space cadet, all drugged out. He can't complete a sentence or focus his eyes. He's just there. It takes a while to get out of the park and down the road.

The driver is laughing and having a grand old time with his front seat passenger. Jeff hollers back to everyone,"Ted is a writer!"

"How do you know that?" I shout back.

Jeff responds, "Cricket told me!"

Oblivious, the girls keep giggling and whispering to each other. The two guys pay no attention to any particular thing. Jeff then blasts the radio with Grateful Dead music. It is unlike anything I have ever heard.

Jeff turns the volume down and hollers—"This is Dark Star. This is Dark Star. Captain Trips, Man!"

Then he blasts the music again as we are driving down the highway heading to the show.

We arrive at the Palace arena parking lot in Auburn Hills, Michigan. I've been to this venue countless times for sporting events and concerts. It's usually the same type of scene—barbecue, have a few beers, tailgate, and then go in. Sometimes I just park and go in to the event. But what I see now is beyond anything I can ever imagine in my most wildest far-out dreams.

A literal parking lot metropolis has formed—a vast open sea of peopled activity. The entire parking lot in every direction I look is like one huge continuous flea market—a rock festival!

So this is how Jeff sells his devil sticks.

The parking lot eventually morphs from a vision of a vast flea market into an all-encompassing circus side show. Never in all my days can I imagine anything happening like this. I'm literally stunned. My mouth is gaped open, jaw-dropped as I stare in wonder at all the activities. I look out upon an ocean of vehicles and bobbing heads walking, a constant motion everywhere. It's like the parking lot is a huge heart beat and all the people and cars' movements are the energy of the blood flow. Pulsing. Pulsing.

Jeff hoots and hollers and shouts out the driver-side window. We are inching along, looking for a parking spot. The side door opens and Candice, Julie and Mitch jump out. They quickly disappear amongst the throng. Jeff is still hooting, hollering and repeatedly honking the horn. The female in the front seat is on an endless laughing trip. John, in the back just stares ahead with a doomed look on his face. Jeff finally finds a spot to park the VW bus. It's time to get out and look around.

"I'm going to take a walk and I'll be back in about forty-five minutes," I say to Jeff.

He gets his devil sticks out and starts doing a juggling demonstration. People gather and form a semi-circle around him. I use this as my cue to take off and explore.

I feel like I am in a zoo of people. The parking lot is a psychedelic festival. It seems like every deadhead has something to sell—beads, shirts, pipes, food, stickers, tie-dyes, hats, watches, jewelry, more food and more food.

I walk down one aisle then start all over in the next aisle. An endless procession of people, spreads out in all directions. I get in line and follow the flow—people, people everywhere! I can start to tell the difference between a deadhead and those who come from home to check out the scene.

A clean-cut family, husband and wife, with a couple of

nine and ten year-old children walk by. The parents' wear a look of awe and wonder and perplexity. The children, in contrast, are just beaming from ear to ear.

Various pieces of rock music blare from different directions—Led Zeppelin, ZZ Top, CCR, The Doors, The Who, The Beatles, The Grateful Dead…

I see row upon row of tie-dyes, long hippie hair, dreadlocks, baggy gypsy dresses, beads, a sudden whiff of cannabis smoke. The cops on horses look helpless in the unfolding scene. This is a true rock festival experience.

I squeeze and push my way through the tight crowd, taking it all in, as I pass from one remarkable scene after another.

I decide to make my way back to the VW van. I have been gone a lot longer than I said I would be. Maybe they already left. I try to hurry through the crowd to get back. As I come upon the vehicle, Jeff is still doing his devil sticks juggling. He has about ten to twelve people gathered around him. The side door and the back door of the van are open. No one is in the vehicle. Jeff spots me in his crowd, stops juggling, catching all the sticks in one hand.

He hollers out, "I thought you already had a Miracle."

"I was just walking around checking out the scene. It's a crazy atmosphere around here—I've never seen anything like it," I say.

"I've got to take you somewhere and show you something," Jeff says.

He shuts the door, rolls up the windows and locks the vehicle. The crowd from his juggling demo disperses. Jeff and I are alone now. We walk through the masses of people and activities, with him in front and me following. As we get closer to the entrance of the arena I see groups of deadheads pointing to the sky. They walk around in little mini circles, many with their eyes closed, humming and praying, chanting—all the while with their index finger pointing toward the sky. Some of them seem to be in a deep trance. I stop walking just to watch them. But I have to hurry or I will get too far behind and lose Jeff. We stop by a line that is the entrance to the arena. Jeff is jumping up and down like a Jack Russel Terrier.

"All those people you saw pointing to the sky are waiting for a miracle."

He paces back and forth at the end of the line we're in, hollering to me above the noise.

"The crowd gathers around all the entrance gates as it gets closer to show time. It's been a long Deadhead custom tradition to grant 'Miracles.' Many people see their first show this way. Come on—point to the sky! Have faith, Ted!"

How did I lose such faith in people. I use to have faith, sometimes blind faith, in relationships, mostly in people. Faith and hope kept me going for a long time. I've been so disconnected. Greed, envy, deceit. These character traits are nothing but trouble. But the norm in society is to be ruled by them. Anger, worry, jealousy and hate. The fate of an individual turns on these traits as well. Egotism, lust and intolerance—common human afflictions. So many people are controlled by these negative traits. I don't want to have these commonalities with my fellow-man. I am turning my back on these troubling defects of erroneous character building. Nothing is to be gained and everything is to be lost. Fear will not be my patron. I have the will to refuse—grand choices to make!

"Have Faith, Ted. Pray for a Miracle!" says Jeff.

I refuse to cooperate. Shake my head "no!"

He pleads with me to do this—"Come on, Ted!"

I start to walk away. Jeff leans over to me and grabs

my right hand and lifts it above my head.

He tells me, "Open your hand," and he puts something in it. I bring my hand down and look—it's a ticket to the show!

"I can't accept that!" I say, handing the ticket back to him. "Here, take this back!"

Jeff throws his hands up in the air and shakes his head 'no,' walking away from me.

"I can't take your ticket. I don't feel right about it," I complain.

"It would be a great honor to me to grant you a 'Miracle' to your first Grateful Dead show."

Then Jeff says, "Please be a gentle, kind receiver of this miracle."

I'm speechless—what can I say? I nod in agreement. I will go to the show.

"Yes! Yes!"

Jeff jumps in the air pumping his fist like his favorite team just scored. As soon as I get in line Jeff takes off, hollering back to me with cupped hands to his mouth, "I'll meet you at my VW after the show!"

Then he disappears into the crowd. So here I am standing in line to go to my first Grateful Dead show. I look over to my side at the people pointing at the sky. Some of them are praying and concentrating real hard. A girl in a gypsy dress leaves from the front of the line and walks over to three people—a guy and two girls. The three of them are walking in a circle, eyes closed, begging and praying to receive a miracle, pleading to the sky. The girls are openly crying, the guy is whimpering. The gypsy woman walks around the three of them, watching them—walking around them, back and forth, back and forth—then she touches one of the girls. They hug, jump up and down, scream, cry, kiss—a "Miracle" has been granted!

Once I get into the arena I just let myself be absorbed by the people, the music, the light show and the energy flow of the scene. I try to watch the stage but all the deadheads are more interesting. I keep twisting and turning to see who is doing what, and what I might be missing. My neck is in continual motion, looking around all night long.

I don't "get" the music. It is totally unfamiliar to me. I can't recognize one song—still having a great time though.

After the concert I find Jeff in the flea market rock festival parking lot. Jeff has three hippy girls hanging with him now. His buddy, John, is asleep in the van. We all pile in to head back to the campgrounds. Janice, Betty and Shirley are loud and boisterous. The music is blaring and Jeff is hooting and hollering. One of the girls sits up front with Jeff.

The two girls in the back make out with each other, holding hands and rubbing each other's body. They are totally oblivious of me as if I am not here.

John is still sleeping. We inch our way out of the parking lot. It takes close to an hour before we are freed from the gridlock chaos to exit the lot for the road back to camp.

I watch the dark silhouette of the women squirming and fondling each other, as we head down the road. What an evening!

We finally get to the campground around 2:00 am.

As we're driving down the park road toward my campsite I notice a big bonfire and a bunch of people at my site. When we get there and I rush out of the van, I discover Cricket and her merry band of friends.

"We've been waiting for almost an hour for you, Ted!"

Cricket gives me a hug and then asks, "Did you see the show?"

"I did and it was a great time!" I say.

"Yeah, I granted him a miracle!" says Jeff, running over to us, "and he almost refused it. But I got him to go!"

Jeff and Cricket high-five each other over the accomplishment of getting me into the show.

"We planned this together," says Cricket, "when you took a nap earlier. I had the extra ticket so I gave it to Jeff. It was his job to talk you into going and then get you to take the miracle. I told you a miracle would happen, didn't I?"

"So, both of you schemed together to grant me this miracle, huh? Well, thank you very much!" I say. "I'm appreciative and grateful for your generosity. Thanks, to both of you, for making such a great experience of all this since your arrival, and treating me like extended family."

The three of us stand there in a group hug for a good minute.

Then I pull away to ask Cricket, "Who are all these people at my campsite?"

"I met up with some new friends, they have tents, but it's too crowded everywhere—would you mind if they camped in your lot for just one day?"

"Sure—no problem!"

"It's only two small tents and five or six people. Most of the rest of these people already have a place to sleep."

Cricket skips over to the other side of the fire ring to tell her friends the good news. She calls me over and introduces me to them. Then we go over to the picnic table and she introduces me to the gathering there. The only person I recognize is Pete, strumming his guitar, leaning up against a tree.

Cricket hollers aloud, "Ted is a writer and a poet, a bohemian philosopher!"

She jumps on the table top and announces, "I'm going to read one of Ted's poems." Cricket pulls out a sheet of paper that happens to be the poem she copied and I signed earlier in the day.

She reads the poem with great expressiveness and passion—more like she performs it.

Sweet Passionate Earth

Sweet passionate earth
swirling in the mass void
Expressing yourself as Mother Nature,
an endless womb of reproduction,
give and take, ebb & flow.
Sweet lady earth, you bedazzle me
Your hills and mountains,
Fields and streams,
oceans, rivers and lakes,
A vast mass of creation to see!
Resting in the sky with a bed of stars,
Yourself a star and sun,
with one moonbeam too!
The revolving system of the Universe,
...day-night, month-end, year-gone.
Sweet passionate earth keeps rolling on!

Everyone claps and gives her a resounding applause when she is done. Cricket motions for me to stand on the picnic table beside her so we can bow together. I join her, standing on the picnic table, looking out at our small crowd of listeners and revelers. Several of the deadheads come over and offer to shake my hand. What the heck, this is so utterly unexpected—especially after such a long day.

It's past 3am, once again. I've had twenty-four solid hours of the deadheads in my life. Now this!

The group starts chanting "More! More! More!" Then they form a makeshift tribal dance around the campfire. "More! More! More!" As I continue to watch them carry on, standing atop the picnic table with Cricket,

I am compelled to pull a notebook from my book bag and start reading aloud.

I jump on top of a big boulder off to the side of the fire ring. Pete moves in closer strumming on his guitar. I read my poetry, inspirational thoughts, quotes from great thinkers, prose and poetry intermixed…

The people gather around the fire and listen to me. We go on until the new sunrise peaks upon Lake Minnawanna.

ꕥ

Chapter Four

The Road Show Invitations

ꕥ

"Lately it occurs to me, what a long strange trip it's been."

—Grateful Dead *Truckin'*
(The Band's unofficial Motto)

Last Day for The Deadheads

I slept in my tent the rest of the morning and all afternoon into the early evening. I was totally out, didn't dream anything. Just slept and recharged.

As I wake up I notice half the park has cleared out. There are still a lot of deadheads all over the place, but it isn't busting way past capacity like before, and I notice several empty campsites dotted through the park.

The deadheads are on the move to the next arena or stadium. The traveling parties roll down the rockin' roads to the next gatherings in the hoopla extravaganza.

Next door at Jeff's site only one minibus van remains. The other vehicle has vanished along with everyone else. Now only one quiet tent stands on the neighboring campsite. I don't know where anyone is. It feels like I'm alone.

Empty bottles and garbage are strewn around my campground. With a shrug of my shoulders I pick up around my campsite, pitching the burnable trash into the ashes of the fire pit, and collecting the bottles and cans in a big trash bag.

I hear quick footsteps approaching. Jeff is walking up the road heading to my camp site, with a fat balloon in each hand. Skipping and red faced, blushing with exasperation, Jeff blurts out some kind of high-pitch-cartoon-character voice. I laugh at his unnatural sounds. He giggles in a munchkin voice. I laugh again. As his voice blends back to normal sounding, Jeff holds out a balloon to me and says, "Nitrous Oxide, bro!"

I grasp the balloon nozzle and suck some air out of it, clamping my fingers on the nozzle again before passing it to Jeff. Holding my breath I continue to suck in deeper . . . hold it . . . hold it. I suck in one more breath. Hold it.

Suddenly a rush passes through me like a freight train. I hear the train whistle and the engine rev full blast, deep in my inner ears. My lips move but I don't know what I'm saying. Nor can I hear. Momentarily deaf and mute.

That damn train fills my head with the rattle of the tracks. The after effects. I sway on my feet as my equilibrium wavers.

Jeff takes a gulp of a breath from the balloon, grabs my arm to steady himself, as he starts talking in that cartoon voice again. I can hear now.

We laugh together like two silly hyenas!

Jeff gives me a balloon and tells me to keep it. Well, what am I going to do with this?

We decide to sit at the picnic table with our nitrous-filled balloons. We still can't stop laughing. Everything is hilarious!

We finally manage to stop and catch a breath and calm down a bit. Take another slow suck on the balloon. Clamp down on the nozzle—can't lose any nitrous—hold your breath as long as you can. Blow it all out. Ride the rush. Laugh like an insane clown posse. Repeat!

Every great balloon story must come to an end, and so it goes with this one. My belly is so sore from laughing that it seriously hurts if I laugh now. My neck muscles are strained. My eyes are leaking like a waterfall. My nose is running like a river. I've used up a good supply of Kleenex. I've laughed myself silly, from inside out.

"This is the laughing gas dentists use. Someone has a tank full of it down the road," says Jeff.

Oh—so that explains it!

All of a sudden I'd had enough—can't take it anymore! Back to being serious-minded.

"I can't continue on like this, Jeff. I need to mellow and settle my body down."

Then we both think that is the funniest thing and start laughing all over again. I have to get away on my own to break up this cycle of uncontrollable energy. My body aches everywhere. I can't take it anymore. I hand the balloon back to Jeff and head out to the woods by myself.

I take a short path leading from my campsite down to the swampy northern edge of the lake. I need to get away on my own to compose myself. Now I'm alone, but I keep erupting into short laughing hysterics by myself in the woods.

Just then Cricket, Mignon and Pete come by the campsite. I can hear their voices through the trees, weeds and bushes, as they talk and laugh at Jeff. He is bordering on the incoherent. He's entertaining to laugh at, but hard to talk with right now.

I recompose myself in the small cove. I have to climb two steep two-foot stairways on the path I took that led me here to this place of solitude.

I can hear them calling out to me now—got to get back and say goodbye to everyone.

Yes, it really will be goodbye!

I ascend the earth-trodden trail, through the woods, up the short path, and there they all are, milling about the campsite.

We hug each other in greetings. Cricket, Mignon, then Pete.

"We have been making the rounds and saying goodbye to people all day," says Cricket. "We plan on spending the night and then packing up and leaving first thing in the morning when it's still dark."

"We have to go to Ohio, Indiana, Chicago, and then over to Buffalo," says Mignon.

"I have most of our packing done," says a serious-minded Pete. "I'd like to leave under moonlight in the early morning hours. Time for some sleep."

"I've been doing that all day!" I reply.

"I have to go into town," says Jeff, "and find a hardware store and restock up on supplies for devil sticks."

We all watch him gather his disheveled self, with a balloon in each hand, stumbling to his van then disappearing from our view.

"Man, he is buzzed half nuts!" says Mignon. "Somebody found some Nitrous, it seems!"

"Yeah!" I blurt out laughing. "I was on my way to acting that way just a few minutes before you arrived. I had to stop—"

"Laughing is fun!" says Cricket. "Laughing is great for the soul. Stress relief. Peace of mind. Tension release!" Cricket jumps in the air as if doing a cheer, "Laugh and relief! Laugh and release! Laugh and peace!"

She smiles and laughs, giggling with delight, doing her cheer in front of me. Pete is disinterested, looking off into the trees of the surrounding forest and yawning now and again. Mignon just wants to dance and sing by herself.

She pirouettes around my campsite, humming tunes to herself. Everybody seems to have a different motivation.

"Laugh and relief! Laugh and release! Laugh and peace!"

Cricket is doing a personal cheer just for me it seems.

"Laugh and relief! Laugh and release! Laugh and peace!"

Nodding in agreement with a big smile on my face, I say, "I know what you mean. Cleanse your mind—refresh your soul—"

"Cosmically connect!" Cricket changes her cheer. "Eternal mind—spirit mind—universal mind!" She turns her new cheer into a rhythmic chant. "Eternal mind—spirit mind—universal mind! Eternal mind—spirit mind—universal mind—cosmic connect!"

"Have you ever read Emerson?" I ask.

I attempt to interrupt Cricket to say something but she's wound up in her trance-like chant—'Eternal mind—spirit mind—universal mind!'

Cupping my hands to my mouth, "Have you ever read Ralph Waldo?"

"Huh?" Cricket re-connects with me—focuses in on my question as she loses the blank stare. "Yes, of course! I was just reading about the Transcendentalists from your notebooks earlier."

"Actually I'm referring to a specific thing Emerson wrote and said to the effect of—'There is an ocean of universal mind and our individual minds are like inlet gates to this ocean of universal mind'—or something to that effect. You heard that before?"

She is all serious-looking at me now. "I've read that before and I believe it to be true and I know it!" Cricket says with certainty. She comes over and leans into me half whispering, "I want to read some more of your journals!"

"Well, that's what I was thinking when you did that chant. I was wondering if Emerson inspired you? Or Buddha? Or perhaps the ancient eastern mystics?"

Cricket walks over to the picnic table to look inside my book bag. I go over and pull out a notebook and hand it to her.

"I'm 'inspired' as you put it, by a lot of things—people, art, music, great authors! I'm attracted to unique people who shine in their own special way," says Cricket. "Everybody has special value, even if they don't see it or know it. Ted, every person is like a diamond—a diamond waiting to be discovered—waiting to be polished, and once discovered within . . ." She climbs on to the picnic table top and shouts to the sky. ". . . polished into a full radiance of sparkling shafts of light. Bright light! Crystalline light!"

I laugh out loud, still amazed at her genuine exuberance.

"Very Transcendentalist! Emersonian! Thoreauvian!" I reply.

Then Cricket rushes over to me with a look of sheer intensity and focus. I lose my smile, peering into her determined hazel eyes, such seriousness of expression she emanates.

"You know, Ted, it's going to be getting dark soon and I want to read some more of your stuff, so if you don't mind, I'm going to find a spot by myself to read."

"Okay—no problem!" I mutter.

Cricket grabs a lawn chair and locates a distant cove overlooking the lake. I can see her from the far corner of my campsite, as she sits there and reads from my journal notebook.

I proceed to gather some wood and stack it for the big campfire later tonight. Mignon has wandered off and Pete is still strumming his guitar at the picnic table.

Then Jeff comes back over minus his balloons.

"You all right now?" I snicker to him.

"Yeah! I'm okay! Man was that fun! I've been doing that all day. Here let me help you gather some kindling."

ᘓᘐ

After Jeff and I finish with the fire pit, we join Pete at the picnic table and watch him strum away on his guitar. Pete is oblivious of us with his eyes closed, softly humming. We sit across from each other at the opposite end of the table from Pete.

"You know—keeping cash flow flowing from show to show can be a real big problem sometimes," says Jeff. "I barely have enough money left to fill my tank and get supplies."

"That's right, you said earlier that you need to run to a hardware store in town."

"It's too late now. I'm not up to it. I'll just have to do that when I leave tomorrow. What a grind. You really have to pay attention and budget your money. I have a party fund and a business fund and I can't ever mix them. I screwed up once," says Jeff, "and lost everything. I was flat broke and the van was on empty!"

"How did you manage to get out of that bind?" I ask.

"I called home and my parents came through and wired me some money—saved my ass!"

"Where'd that happen?"

"Over by Tennessee and Kentucky. My parents were really upset at the time. My mom worked herself up all sick worrying about me. Dad settled her down and wired me the money. Yup! I always got to be thinking about keeping cash flow flowing…"

Jeff stares off into the distant trees, pondering his predicament. Pete continues strumming on his guitar and humming a tune. Cricket is still reading off in the shady cove. Mignon hasn't returned. I decide to go light the campfire and get some charcoal ready in the grill. Jeff is in a trance, daydreaming while I'm doing all of this.

"How do you guys do it?" Jeff snaps out of his fog directing his question to Pete.

"How do you pay for all the things you need from show to show . . . food, gas, party supplies?"

"Huh?" Pete stops playing his guitar. "You talking to me?"

"Yeah! How do you guys pull it off?"

"Pull what off?" says Pete. "Oh! Oh! The economics of being a traveling deadhead—you mean?"

"Exactly! How do you do it?"

"Simple! We each saved up our money," says Pete. He strums his guitar again. "We don't worry about it!"

This is not what Jeff wanted to hear. He is looking for a sympathetic ear on the subject of "Economic Road Show Fiscal Viability." No one else at this particular gathering has concern about that.

After witnessing the festival-type flea market in the parking lot last night, I can understand how all the deadheads have to keep the cash flow flowing so they can get from show to show. It's quite the organization of a non-organization—the whole planning process that goes into point A to point B to point C. They spearhead and launch this fantastic community spirit. Everyone lends a helping hand. Somehow, some way, they get from show to show. Everyone has a unique story to tell.

I really like Jeff's operation. If he can buy the raw material then construct his product which then sells, all told, a Ten-to-One payback—that's a good business model. Somehow, I don't think most of these deadheads put that much thought into the process like Jeff does.

Pete gets up and starts to wander off, then turns

back around and hollers to Jeff and me, "I'm going to my campsite and to find Mignon. I'll be back. Tell Cricket!"

"Okay!" we both say in unison.

I look down to the far cove where Cricket is. She's still reading. She turns her head and looks up and our eyes meet. Cricket hops out of the chair smiling real big as she skips over to Jeff and me at the picnic table.

"What happened to Mignon and Pete?"

Jeff begs off suddenly, telling Cricket and me, "I got to go!"

"They'll be back soon," I reply. "Are you done reading now? It's going to be dark soon."

Handing my notebook journal back to me, "Yes," she says. "I feel energized and inspired! I like some of the tangents you go off on in your writing—searching for purpose, meaning, soul—learning from mistakes, failures, heartbreak—learning to be thankful and forgiving! I think and do these things—and you have the ability to write these things—to express deep feelings and well-constructed thoughts. You have a rare gift, Ted!"

Cricket is so emotionally overcome that her eyes well up with moisture and a happy tear flows down her left cheek, leaving a dewy trail. She comes over to me and we hug real tight with her face nestled against my chest. We stood this way in silence for what seemed five solid minutes.

It's been so long since I felt this kind of peace and contentment, purpose and belonging. The resistance has lessened the hold of my struggle within. Tension has eased. I'm temporarily basking in self-acceptance. Where have I been? Why do I continue to travel the road of struggle so often?

Cricket says she was sad most of the day because she said goodbye to so many people. She said that Mignon, Pete, and she are driving together in Pete's car. Pete has a little enclosed trailer that he's hitched to the back of the car. He stores his musical equipment, their clothes, and other stuff, in there.

"After we packed we made the rounds," Cricket says. "I've been so emotional all day. Some people are leaving the tour and I won't see them again for awhile—so that's been the toughest goodbyes."

Just then she spots Mignon and Pete walking towards the campsite from up the road. "There they are!" She waves her hands like windmills to them as she jumps up and down, and shouting to me, "Here come two purveyors of living light!"

Pete arrives with his banjo. He hands his instrument to Mignon as I motion to him to help me move the picnic table closer to the campfire. All situated now, Pete sits on the corner of the picnic table with his feet propped on the bench and is strumming along. The rest of us take a seat around the campfire.

Day will soon be giving way to night. The sun disappears below the horizon as dusk settles in. The soft night air turns crisp, with the crackling sounds of the fire pit, mixing with the bullfrogs and crickets to form a swirling rhythmic nighttime cacophony.

"Hey, Mignon, what happened to Jinx?" I ask.

"He's just a good friend—already went on with another clan. I'll see him in Indiana or Chicago. He always likes to get to a new venue ahead of time so he can scope out his spot in the tapers section. All the tapers," Mignon says, "are like a sub-cult within a sub-cult. They have their own language and keywords and gestures for communicating. I don't understand any of the technical stuff they talk about. It's really fun to hang out with a group of tapers though, because they have their own special vibe they generate and it's fun to be a part of, groovy man!"

Cricket and Mignon lean in close to each other and whisper into each other's ear, back and forth. I'm curious, watching them, staring into the fire, and listening to Pete fiddle with his banjo.

I'm going to miss these people. Tomorrow when I wake up they will all be gone. I look around at each of them and think about how special the last two days have been. I stare into the campfire.

I'll always remember this moment in time.

Cricket and Mignon decide that our topic of conversation will be "Rainbow Families!"

"We want to talk about the network creed of the rainbow!" says Mignon. "Each of the colors of a rainbow has special meaning. A rainbow is a signpost!" she proclaims.

Cricket talks about all the people she has met over the years. "Some of my best friends and most authentic people I have known are part of the Rainbow Family. We have gatherings in National Forests, yearly, to pray for peace on the planet. They're into intentional community building, alternative lifestyles and non-violence. Many of the same virtues and freedoms the deadheads emulate."

Pete stops picking on his banjo to add, "Native American tribal traditions are copied and used as guidance by the Rainbow gatherers. The earth is the most crucial thing—Praying for the Planet!"

Then Pete goes back to picking the strings of his banjo.

"So, you guys are all part of the Rainbow Families?" I ask.

"A lot of us are, but not everyone. Some people are deadheads and some people aren't!" says Cricket. "The main thing is the planet, the earth, as Pete said—to pray for the health of Mother Earth."

Cricket reaches down and grabs a handful of sandy dirt and watches it crumble through her fingers.

"The colors of the rainbow signify points of energy and specific issues to focus upon. The color red," Mignon says, "is the root energy center of our body and it deals with balance and stability. The color orange deals with self-control, well-being, joy. The yellow color of the rainbow is in the energy center of the solar plexus." Mignon points just under her ribcage, "This is where the issues of self-esteem and empowerment come from."

"The color green in the rainbow is the energy center of the heart," says Cricket, with her hand over her chest. "This is where we find compassion, peace, generosity, forgiveness."

Cricket then points to her throat. "The energy center for the color blue is the throat. Creativity, willpower and sincerity are the issues related to this energy point."

Mignon then points to her eyebrows, with giggling energy, fidgeting on her seat. "My favorite color—indigo—corresponds to the energy center of the brow. This is where we get inspiration, intuition, imagination."

Then Cricket jumps up from her seat. "I got the last one! The color violet," she puts her hand on top of her head, "signifies the crown energy center of the body. Faith, gratitude and patience are the key issues here."

"I don't get it. What are you guys talking about?" I ask.

"The seven energy centers in your body that correspond to the seven colors of the rainbow!" Cricket blurts out. "Everything is one. We're all connected! It's about being balanced and optimizing your potential. Chakra alignment!"

I still don't understand but I can tell they sure do.

With confident smug looks on their faces, Cricket and Mignon start dancing around the fire with their arms encircled at the elbow, they go round and round, skipping and hopping.

Now Pete, strumming away on his banjo, starts singing a folk music tune. Mignon breaks away from her reverie with Cricket and goes over by Pete, harmonizing and humming in the background. Then Cricket joins in humming and then singing with Pete.

I sit here and watch and listen to them as I slowly drift off into staring at the campfire. I find my mind wandering far off. The campfire and the music are mesmerizing me into a trance-like mental state. Calm and steady, I stare into the fire.

I see a large bird flying in the sky-fire. The bald eagle from yesterday! He's flying in a circle, gliding round and round and round. I watch him as he glides, every once in awhile he will flap his wings. Then the eagle suddenly breaks up his routine and does a twisting movement—from a circle to a big twist, like two mini-circles within the big circle. He continues in this new pattern. I'm staring into the abyss of the camp fire, but I see the eagle flying this new sequence, with a twist. I focus closer on the pattern. The eagle is flying in a figure eight—flying a mobius strip! He's looking at me as if to say,"Ted, do you get it?"

I realize I have so many character defects to work on. Why am I the way I am? Have I made myself an enigma to my own self? The riddle must come unraveled. Who are you, Ted? What must become of you? What must I do? Worry is a waste of time. So is egotism, anger, envy, intolerance and greed. Why have these character defects become a part of me? What am I afraid of? What truths have I been hiding from? My patience sometimes wears thin. Procrastination, indecisive, self-deceit. My vanity of mind has been my partial undoing. The worst is to say you will do things and not keep your word. Business and money have given me troubles. It seems so easy to plan and hope and so hard to make the reality fit the vision. Where did I lose myself? How did I lose myself? The real Ted Senario is still waiting to find himself.

I snap out of my trance vision when the music and singing stop. Everyone is tired and worn out from the day's activities. Pete wants to get to sleep. He has to get up early and drive all day tomorrow. We shake hands and then he leaves. Jeff hasn't returned. He must have decided to go over to his VW bus and hit the sack. Mignon, Cricket and I are left sitting by the campfire.

"What an honor it has been to have met," says Cricket. "I'm still beaming from your poetry and journal writings I read from earlier this morning. It felt like Golden Code—a great exclamation point capper to the whole Michigan experience with the Dead."

"Thank you for the generous praise I don't deserve. You are way too kind. I have never done anything like this before. In fact, this whole experience has been sort of other-worldly to me."

Cricket hands me a letter. It's addressed to "Ted – Mr. Lake Minnawanna Sunrise." I open it up and it's an invitation to a wedding in Rochester, New York in a few weeks. Lynn (Cricket) and Pete are getting married.

"If it's meant to be, you will make it! I'm having a big show—a whopping four day nature party by a waterfall in the Finger Lakes region of upstate New York. You just get yourself to Rochester," says Cricket, "and we'll get you to the wedding."

"Yeah! We expect to see you!" says Mignon.

"I have enough space and room reserved to hold over a thousand people," says Cricket.

"I think there will be more people than that—maybe fifteen hundred," says Mignon.

I am speechless—I don't know what to say or how to say it. I stammer a few times trying to get it out. Nothing.

I open the invitation again and read the card—a folded piece of paper falls out—directions to the BIG SHOW nature party. I look it over while the two of them stare at me with bated breath. I fold everything up and put it back in the envelope and shrug my shoulders.

"Well…anyway…consider yourself invited as my honored guest," says Cricket. "Like I said—if it's meant to be, I'll see you. Want to know a secret?" Cricket motions for me to lean over so she can whisper something in my ear. I lean in. "I think you're going to make it to my wedding! I just know it!"

Then Cricket dances around the fire ring.

"Let's talk about something else now—we still have a lot of fire light and more wood to burn," says Mignon.

I offer to read a chapter of Walden. They both agree to this clapping their hands with big smiles on their faces. So, I walk over to my tent and get my copy of the book. I read the last chapter, the "Conclusion." We discuss the authors' deep meanings—debate what he meant at other times. I can barely get through a paragraph and we stop to have a discussion point. We each have our own favorite one-liner that we like the best over all others in the chapter—as we defend our reasons for picking the statement that is our favorite.

"The main commonality being—TRUTH—how the understanding resonates within us, individually, from reading and hearing spoken—Thoreau's seminal words from **Walden, or Life in the Woods,**" Mignon says to Cricket and me.

"We each have our moments of identification when the writer speaks cold hard truth to our mind and heart," says Cricket.

"It's all about knowing yourself to the utmost," says Mignon.

"The ancient philosophers knew," Cricket responds, "just like Thoreau knew, that truth is truth is always truth, regardless of the age or time. We each have to discover our own truth."

After we finish our discussion and reading of Thoreau, it is nearing midnight. All three of us keep yawning, sometimes all together. It is time to call it a day. I close the book and stick the wedding invitation inside Walden.

"Maybe I'll be able to make it some way. It's over three weeks from now—gives me something to think about. Thank you very much for the invite."

I hug the two women goodbye, and off they go to sleep at their own campsite.

ജര

Next morning, Jeff wakes me up. The park is really emptying out now. Vacant campsites blend into the forest. The deadhead vibe vanishes from the premises.

"I saw Cricket and Mignon earlier and they told me about the wedding invitation," says Jeff. "I can come back in ten days and pick you up. You can then ride with me to the Dead shows in Washington, D.C. Afterwards I can drive you to New York."

I don't know what to say about this proposition.

"I need to think about it."

"Think fast because I'm leaving in a few hours and I need to know."

Jeff's going to run up town to the hardware store to get some devil stick supplies. I hope I will have an answer by the time he gets back.

Cricket stops by for her final visit. She's beaming like the sun, bright and cheerful. I tell her about Jeff's invitation. She said she already knows. They talked about it earlier this morning when I was still sleeping. The two of them put their heads together and came up with this plan.

She says I can trust Jeff. "If he says he will come back in ten days and pick you up, he will!" she states with certainty.

"The whole point is that I have to agree right now to do this," I complain to Cricket. "That's a big decision to make."

"There is nothing to decide—just do it—go with the energy flow, Ted!" says Cricket. "You can have a true full-fledged Bohemian experience. You may never get another opportunity to do something like this for the rest of your life. You are a Seeker—remember? You have much to learn and know for your personal growth and evolution. This will be a great experience for your writing background."

I feel my resistance melting away. I can't deny the common sense of her pleading. How can I say no? I realize at this moment that I'm going to take a chance and do something like never before in all my days.

I began to think about my own failed marriage. How did I end up this way?I miss my girl, my friend, my lover. We were such friends at one time that it seemed then like it would last forever. We stared at the sky in the moonlight, wishing upon the stars—two young lovers. Oh Julianne, I miss you, I miss our friendship. Now I'm alone and lost and searching. I remember our laughs, our kisses, our great sex. It's all vanished but the faint memories still linger in my head. Yes, I will love you forever I said. Yes, I will love you forever, too, she said. Promises broken, promises not kept. I miss her, my former lover, my former best friend.

ജ്ഞ

Cricket says she has to leave now, just as Jeff pulls up in my campsite drive. I give her a big hug and a little peck on the cheek. We hold each other tight for a long minute and then I let her go. The little petite gypsy spark plug with hairy legs and an overzealous personality is now leaving me. I'm going to miss her company a lot. She waves to Jeff and off she goes.

Jeff jumps out of his VW full of energy. "You coming?"

"Yes, I am!"

He jumps up and down and grabs me in a big celebratory bear hug. We then sit down at the picnic table and discuss the reconnoitering plans.

"I'll be back in exactly ten days from today."

He walks over to the passenger side of his van, looks inside, then comes back with a calendar. We count the days off the calendar and Jeff circles a date.

"I'll leave the Indiana venue on the day of the last show so I can get ahead of the crowd. The Dead will be playing a three-to-four day set in Indiana before everyone begins to drive the Midwest, via state of Michigan way."

Jeff jumps up and down yipping and hollering.

"Wait till I tell Cricket! Yippee!"

Even though Jeff is so excited and I'm sure Cricket will be too—I'm a little apprehensive and low-key. Jeff hands me a card, the number to his parents' house, on the back of a hardware store business card. He wants me to call them on day number eight or nine and he will leave a confirmation message with them that he is on his way.

Jeff then went off to finish the rest of his packing and organization for the coming road trip. He has a full tank of gas, food, ice, and devil sticks supplies.

Jeff just needs to pack up his tent, clean up his site, and find John. John is nowhere within sight and the park is sparsely populated. Perhaps he went for a walk in the woods. Jeff asks if I'd seen him lately. I haven't.

A couple from Oregon and another couple from Kansas come by and say goodbye to me. I don't know who they are. They say they watched and listened to me reading on a rock.

"Oh, that night . . . I see! Yes, I remember now!"

I give each a hug or a handshake and wish them well and continued good times.

ஜ௸

I notice John, off in the distance, walking along the edge of the woods. He keeps glancing in my general direction as he walks further away. I decide to take a walk and catch up with him.

Jogging over to the trail in the woods as I draw closer, I shout, "Hey John." I wave. "Jeff is looking for you. It's time for you guys to go!"

It's obvious that John is upset—his eyes are all red and he looks panic-stricken. The only other time I have seen him was when we went to the Dead show, and he wasn't doing too good then either.

"What's the matter dude? You all right?"

John stares at the ground when he talks to me and he won't make eye contact.

"I'm dreading this road trip," he whines. "Jeff is always bossing me around! I feel trapped! I just want to go home!"

I continue shuffling along with him on the edge of the wooded trail.

"He treats me with disrespect. He's belligerent and aggressive!"

John is wearing jeans, tennis shoes, a woolen yellow pullover that says BC in the front. He keeps his brown hair combed over his face and forehead and eyeglasses.

I can see why this dynamic isn't working out—John's squeamish, introverted character coupled with super-hyper extroverted Jeff—the odd couple.

I decide to mollify things, intercede to smooth the situation out.

"Have you ever attempted to talk over these problems with Jeff?"

"Are you kidding! Plenty of times!" he says in exasperation. "It's useless. Hopeless!"

The poor guy is so dejected. He has the countenance of someone walking the plank or standing before a firing squad. Very depressed.

The two of us continue to walk the trails along the edge of the forest. I finally convince him to head back to the camp with me. The two of them have to have a heart-to-heart—to end the disharmony between them. When we get back to the site, Jeff is finishing up the final stages of packing. He smiles at me and sneers at John.

The three of us sit down at the picnic table to have a talk. I feel like I may have to be ready to referee a battle royal as they raise their voices in angry tones toward each other. Accusations fly back and forth. They attempt to out-volume each other with their angry shouts. They are not even listening to each other, just hollering and yelling.

I grab a nearby kettle pot and a stick, then jump on the picnic table, beating the pot as hard as I can till I drown out their noise. They both shut up—then I stop pounding. Quiet. We look at each other.

"Enough of that!" I shout at both of them.

I stare them down for a few seconds, both standing in opposition to each other at the picnic table. Then they start to holler and point in each other's face again.

"Enough!" I warn as I pound the kettle pot real hard again, jumping up and down on the table at the same time. Quiet again!

"Don't talk, and keep your hands and fingers to your sides. Just listen to me for a minute. The both of you are contributing to the combustible creation of negative energy—bad karma! You should be ashamed of yourselves. I thought you were on this road trip adventure to get away from the persistent negative energy in mainstream society. At least that's what everybody tells me. And here you guys are just contributing to the problem. Are you catching my drift?"

I peer down from the table at the two of them, with the kettle pot and stick still in my hands. Jeff looks up and snickers at me while John looks down at his feet. I set my makeshift instruments on the table and jump to the ground.

"What kind of modern day flower children deadheads do you two purport to be?"

I met stunned looks on both their faces. I must have got through somehow. The two of them are just looking at each other but not talking. It is as if they are deciding on a non-verbal plane to call a truce. I then speak about the great harmony and positivity the deadheads brought to this environment, hoping to push them into a final reconciliation.

"What happened to the Happiness? Goodwill toward fellow man? Appreciation of Nature and Love of Earth?"

They both, at the same time, get up from the picnic table, shake hands, and apologize to each other. Just like that. Situation resolved.

Jeff and John are soon thereafter ready to head down the road. I give each a big hug and handshake. Jeff says he will be back in ten days—with or without his friend.

We go off to the side of the van and he tells me that he's going to suggest a bus ticket home for John when they get to Chicago. He wants to know what I think about that. I tell Jeff that may be the way to go. I suggest he keep the peace and harmony till then. He promises to make that his goal. Another handshake, then Jeff hops in the sunburst yellow and white VW mini-bus van—driving down the park road and out of sight.

ꙮ

After they leave I go over to the fire pit to set some logs in place for a fire. It is time to get the grill going, make some coffee, and start cooking a breakfast. While I'm occupied with these activities a car is coming around the bend in the park road with the horn blowing and beeping in long stretches.

It is Pete, Mignon and Cricket! They haven't left yet! I thought they were long gone. They have the skinny travel trailer hitched to the back of the car. The top is down on the convertible. Both women sit in the back seat. Pete pulls right into my campsite and comes within a foot of where I am standing by the fire pit.

He has a shiny chromed, cream colored, BMW convertible. Pete has one of his guitars in the front passenger seat. The two girls jump out—all festive and full of energy.

"Hey, Ted! Hey, Ted!" hollers Cricket and Mignon.

"We get to say one last goodbye!" says Cricket with a make-believe pouty–lip face.

"I'm first!" says Mignon.

As I'm leaning down to light the wood in the fire ring, Pete backs his car away several feet. He gets out and grabs his guitar and starts strumming away.

I then proceed to share big long hugs back and forth between Mignon and Cricket. The three of us have a group hug. Then we call Pete over to join us. He puts his guitar back on the front seat of the car and comes over and squeezes in real tight. We all laugh with joy.

Cricket asks us to close our eyes and hold on tight and

be real quiet. She is going to say a prayer of thankfulness and friendship. Each of us close our eyes and continue our hug as she speaks.

"The Great Cosmos—The Universal Existence of Unknown Reality, Infinite Intelligence—Thank you for this gift of Life. Thank you for this moment in time. Thank you for genuine friends and friendship."

We all respond in unison,"Halleluiah! Amen!"

It is good to be around people, to share in great times and learn from experiences with others. I've really missed having close relationships with friends, or just palling around with caring buddies. I have been on the verge of becoming a permanent social hermit. It isn't that I don't like people. It's all me, only me, and how I fit in. The positive energy vibrations from hanging with the right mix of people allows me to look deeper within. Nature and people—people and nature—an equilibrium will arise. I am a seeker, learning, a seeker, growing, a seeker, evolving to uncharted depths…

Pete goes back to his guitar. Mignon trails behind him humming. Cricket and I grab a couple of folding chairs and set them up by the fire ring. She says she has something for me.

Cricket has some herbs in her hand. "This is sage. It has been used as an antioxidant for medicinal cleansing by all the great Native American Indian tribes."

She lights one end of the six-inch stalk of sage. Then she blows it out so it smokes. She directs me to stand up and step in the clear. Then she walks around me. Cricket says she is outlining my aura with the sage smoke. Then she brings it under my nose and around my head.

Cricket then proceeds to take the sage and put it on a plate. It's still smoking good! She unzips the entrance to my tent and sets the plate on the floor. Then she zips the tent back up. Cricket skips back to the fire ring where I'm standing. She has a big satisfied grin on her face.

"The Shamans use sage to cleanse their spirit surroundings. To detox their bodies so they can receive guidance from the Great Spirit," says Cricket. "Ted, you need to keep your presence, your aura, your environment—clear of negative energies. You must align your chakra energy. Have you ever done yoga?"

"No! I never have tried yoga."

"That's okay—I left a little beginner's yoga handbook in your tent with the sage. At least do the basic postures and breathing exercises—and keep on working on your meditation practice," she advises. "Then you will be able to receive proper guidance and inspiration when you write. We've got to go now, Ted! You take care of yourself and I hope to see you at my wedding. Jeff will be back to pick you up and bring you out east."

"I'm looking forward to the adventure! I'm already missing you guys and you haven't even left."

Pete and Mignon come over by the fire, singing in harmony, as he strums the guitar. They sing, "It's time to go my friends. It's time to go."

Mignon hums, then Pete does a quick solo, she hums again, then they repeat the chorus. "It's time to go my friends. It's time to go!"

The three of them get in the car and they are ready to leave. The women blow me a kiss. Pete waves. Their car disappears off in the distance of the park road.

The campground is vacant. All the energy from the people is gone. Only I remain. I feel sad at this moment.

There went my Bohemia.

Now it's back to me and nature—all alone.

Part II

A Bohemian Adventure

"You can have something that lasts throughout your life as adventures, the times you took chances. I think that's essential in anybody's life, and it's harder and harder to do in America. If we're providing some margin of that possibility, then that's great. That's a nice thing to do."

—Jerry Garcia
(from a Rolling Stone interview)

Transcendental:
1) transcendent, surpassing, or superior
2) being beyond ordinary or common experience, thought, or belief; supernatural
3) Philosophy—beyond the contingent and accidental in human experience, but not beyond all human knowledge

"I wanted to live deep
and suck out all the marrow of life..."
—Henry David Thoreau, Walden

"Know Thyself."

—Socrates

ഇര

Chapter Five

A Bohemian Adventure Story Unfolds

ഇര

"Men esteem truth remote, in the outskirts of the system, behind the farthest star . . . In eternity there is indeed something true and sublime. But all these times and places and occasions are now and here."

—Henry David Thoreau
from ***Walden,*** in the chapter
"Where I Lived, and What I Lived For"

I spend the rest of the day in solitude with nature after the deadheads leave Lake Minnawanna. I take my little skinny hardcover book of ***Nature*** by Emerson, and Thoreau's ***Walden,*** and I read throughout the entire day. Every now and then I stop to jot something down in my notebook. I keep myself busy like this till sundown and bedtime. I decide to number my journal entries, counting down till Jeff's arrival, to begin my bohemian adventure.

Day #9

I choose to spend the day on a long trek throughout the park. I have over five thousand wooded acres with paths to roam. I light Cricket's sage this morning and wave it around the outline of my body, like she did. Then I wave it around in the tent. I miss all of the people. I'm still amazed at all that happened—so fast and quick. Now it's just a memory that will fade further with each passing day. But right now it's all still so fresh. That first morning at the sunrise was outstanding, all the people cheering the sun by the shore. I can see the whole thing in multi-colored images unfolding in the memory of my mind... but now they're all gone and it's so quiet. Regular campers will be coming this weekend. I'll just keep to myself and live within my books and notebooks, enjoying the raw elements of the outdoors.

Day #8

I slept really well last night. I'm full of energy today. I'm going to walk the other half of the park. I'll hit all the trails I didn't take yesterday. I did Cricket's sage ritual again. I wonder where all the deadheads are congregated now? I imagine they have taken over some other State Parks or National Forest. If it's the day of a show the deadheads will have their row-upon-row, aisle-upon-aisle setup of "Rock Festival" flea-market activity. There is nothing like being in the midst of an experience in that scene. The whole vibe and energy flow is hyperkinetic. I've been to countless concerts and sporting events—and nothing is comparable.

Day #7

I'm going to spend today in a canoe out on the lake. An old college buddy of mine left it out here for me to use last week. Lake Minnawanna is a small inland lake. More like a big pond than a lake. It's comparable to Walden Pond in size, but not depth. Lake Minnawanna has served as my Walden, in this life. Early on it was just a place of recreation and fun times. Now it's become so much more. It is my refuge from the chaos I experience trying to fit my way into society. I know that it all boils down to my not knowing and understanding my "Self" well enough. I have to dig deeper and mine for my truth:

I have much to learn and a solid character growth to re-grow. So much I've learned. So much I didn't know. So much I still don't know. The wandering seeker! I don't know how I fit in to the overall scheme in society or if I ever will, but I'll keep searching!

Day #6

It's cloudy and overcast today. Looks like a good storm will be passing overhead. I light Cricket's sage again. It's now down to a three-to-four inch stub. I light the sage and it billows smoke on a plate in the tent. The billowing cloud rings are drawn to the outside air from the tent screen—out flies the smoke, like signals to the cosmos. Today is going to be my reading day. I'm going to enjoy Plato, Socrates and Goethe. The verbal logic, reasoning and questioning of Socrates astounds me at times. Once the platform is his and he starts questioning the people in his presence about values, concepts, wisdom, truth—Socrates is truly a Master. I imagine—whenever I read or hear told a Socratic anecdote—Plato in a corner of a room with a clay wax tablet, stylus in hand, capturing the words of his teacher philosopher, Socrates.

My reading of Goethe is with "Faust." I'm at the point where Mephistopheles entices Faust for the cost of one thing—his Soul. What a choice, eh? Unlimited fame, wealth, riches for anything you can buy. Reminds me of the deal that author Oscar Wilde made with his main character in "Dorian Gray." There is a mystical underlying theme, just under the surface, that applies to the human condition. We all struggle with the individuality of being human. Everyone should want the best for themselves—our Higher Self. But few are willing to pay the proper price, to earn whatever it is through diligent constructive personal efforts. The vast majority seek shortcuts to the finish line, cheat sheets, steal, lie—whatever it takes. Why is this? The mystery of the human condition…

Day #5

It's a nice day today. I'm going to go for a long hike. After spending almost the entire day in the tent and around the campsite reading yesterday, I'm ready to stretch, move and go. I only have four more days before Jeff will be back to take me on this bohemian adventure. I wonder if he will really show up? Hmm, I'll call his parents in a few days and find out.

Day #4

I'm going to go out and fish in the canoe today. I usually end up throwing everything I catch back into the water. I love the feeling of releasing a life to be free again. I watch and feel the fins and tail flap and twitch from my grip as the latest catch disappears into the depths of the dark blue-green water.

Day #3

I wonder what the deadheads are up to today? I see Cricket and Mignon swirling and twirling around, singing, dancing, and spreading rose petals around as Pete strums his guitar or banjo. Tomorrow I will call Jeff's parents. I'll also make my final packing preparations. I can't take everything with me, so I'll need to streamline and trim down my supplies. I'm going to read Walt Whitman throughout the day.

Day #2

I call Jeff's parents today. They each have a phone so I talk to Tom and Jan at the same time. Jeff is coming and will be here tomorrow afternoon. They ask about my writing and said Jeff told them about the night I was on the large boulder rock reading to a crowd. They are happy their son is meeting up and connecting with such interesting people. I told Tom he did a stand-up job fixing the back of the van with the drill and saw contraption. He is all proud and explains some of his problems when he first started. I have to cut the conversation short because I'm running out of quarters at the park concession stand phone booth. So Jeff will be here tomorrow for sure. I'm really going to go on this bohemian adventure!

Day #1

Last night I called up my old college dorm room buddy, Ervin. I had him come over to the campground to pick up a lot of my camping supplies, books, papers and things. He lets me store my personal property in an outdoor shed he has behind his barn. I've been keeping in touch with him every ten days to two weeks or so, this spring and summer—actually, ever since I decided to spend the year out in nature every day, back in early March. It's now past mid-June. I've been out, steady in nature, mostly in solitude for four months now. I plan on living this way right till Thanksgiving. That would give me nine solid months living under the bare sky, mostly. I had an epiphany one night in the middle of the dreary days of winter—and I knew in the morning that this was what I had to do. I was staying in a room at my Aunt's house. I told her in the morning. She looked at me like I'd gone over the brink and was now insane, or partially nuts anyway. Maybe I am. I've had enough attempts at trying to mold myself into mainstream society. Holding down a string of successive "wrong jobs" didn't help the matter either. I need the freedom to evolve and educate myself on my own terms. A nine-to-five, forty-hour week, does not allow for this. My aunt, my buddy Ervin, and my sister, bring me food and supplies and check up on me every so often. It has worked out well and now I'm ready to go on this bohemian adventure for a few weeks.

I am packed and ready in the morning. When noon rolls around and still no Jeff, I move my supplies to the far edge of the campsite by the outer woods. It's no longer my site so I can't be on it in case someone registers. So I'm hanging out on the edge of the park forest by my old campsite all afternoon. Then it turns into early evening and dinner hour—still no Jeff. I'm real worried now. It's been a long day, sitting and pacing, waiting around.

> *Have I misjudged people again? Do I have a misguided trust of people—all types of people? I failed in the past by trusting and believing in the wrong people, the wrong situations. I wasn't in touch with my intuition. All I wanted to do was feed the greed of materialism. Get over it, Ted! It is what it is—you failed, got duped! Get over it. Move on!*

ꕥ

Looking down the park road—for what must have been my several hundredth time, pacing back and forth, I spot the old familiar two-tone VW mini-bus. It's Jeff! He is laying on the horn as he drives down the park road. There he is leaning out the driver's window hollering and waving.

Jeff pulls up, jumps out, and we give each other a big bear hug. He picks me up off the ground an inch or two and swings in a circle, a couple revolutions. He's pumped with adrenaline. Someone gets out of the passenger side door—she's the new sidekick.

Jeff must have sent John home and traded him in for this cute little darling.

Jeff introduces me to Brandy. They met in Buffalo at a concert show last week and they've been together ever since. They seem to be quite smitten with each other—perhaps in love. Brandy wears a constant, beaming, pearly white smile. Her blonde hair is in braids, cropped to her head. She's wearing an Indian leather outfit with beads. Looks like a squaw.

I pack my gear in the van—tent, sleeping bag, book bag, backpack of clothes, twenty-pound dumbbell, mini-cooler of food and drink on ice, and a small grocery bag of dried food goods. We pack it all in. He has plenty of room. I have the whole backend of the van to stretch out and relax and enjoy the adventure down the road.

Before climbing in I walk down by the Lake Minnawanna shore for a last look. I will miss this place.

I carry my book bag on my back. In it I have half a dozen pens, three highlighters, four notebooks, two books—Walden by Thoreau and Nature by Emerson. And I have my walkman cassette player with ear phones. I only brought two tapes of music—Led Zeppelin *"Greatest Hits"* and Pink Floyd *"Dark Side of the Moon."*

I am ready to go. I bid farewell to the park, the woods, and the lake.

Faith in others is like faith in a seed. Give it attention, caring and compassion, and it will grow. My new-found friends are filling a need I denied. I can adapt in a world of nature, distant from any close friends or society. But that isn't truly me. I just needed to get away and readjust. I'm getting there. I haven't lost my faith in the human race. I'm ready for this adventure, this temporary detour—ready to connect with life and harmony and easy going people. A sense of belonging! Why have I been running? I built a wall around myself, thick enough to never let anyone in. I can dismantle this wall, brick by brick. I sense a harmonic convergence from within. Just begin, Ted, brick by brick. Open up your life to the new influx.

We head south towards Detroit, and keep on going to the Michigan/Ohio border. Soon after entering Ohio around Toledo, we drive east on the Ohio Turnpike toward Cleveland. I ask Jeff how many shows he has been to since I last saw him.

He says, "One in Ohio, one in Buffalo, New York, where I met Brandy…"

I see them both holding hands in the front seat while he's speaking and hollering back to me and driving down the road. Every once in awhile Brandy looks back and smiles at me with her big white teeth and sparkling blue eyes.

Jeff continues, "Two in Kentucky, two in Chicago, and three shows in Indiana. I skipped the last one so I could make time and stop to pick you up. That makes nine shows. I saw the Dead at five of those shows…twice on miracles!"

"How did you two meet?" I ask.

"I had to get rid of John first. We left Michigan a week and a half ago and then went to Hebron, Ohio at Buckeye Lake for a show."

I am sitting in the backend of the van and they are sitting up front, so we continue to holler back-and-forth in our conversation.

"There really is a place called Buckeye Lake?" I ask. "It must've been near Columbus, eh?"

"Oh yeah! Oh yeah! It was a great setup, man! Had a real good time, dude. Then we drove from Ohio to Buffalo. I dropped John off at the bus station there in Buffalo. I bought him a one-way ticket back home to Watertown, New York and gave him a twenty dollar bill for food."

"How did you two get along till then—any more big arguments or disagreements?"

"We got along just fine once we agreed on the plan driving to Ohio. He was cool. We shared some laughs and more good times. I'll see him back in college in the fall. We were both relieved when I dropped him off at the bus station, though. This wasn't meant for him," continues Jeff, "because he couldn't keep up with the pace and the constant movement and doing things. He's a quiet and shy guy for the most part—you know what I mean?"

Brandy listens in the passenger seat, as Jeff and I go back and forth with our conversation.

"Yeah, I know what you mean!" I holler back in agreement.

"Thanks for settling our arguments last week. It was really getting bad and we needed to talk things out!" He shouts. Then I hear him in the front seat describing the arguments he was having with his buddy John, and how I helped them call a truce and create positive harmony once again.

Brandy listens with interest—probably already heard the story several times.

Jeff hollers back to me again as we continue on the turnpike in Ohio. "We were only together for three more days after we left you in Michigan—just went to the one show in Ohio—then drove straight to Buffalo and dropped him off."

Then Brandy turns around in her seat to face me.

"We met at Rich Stadium in Orchard Park, New York. We met outside in the parking lot. He tried to teach me how to juggle his sticks."

"Can you do it?" I ask.

She giggles, "No—not really! I tried quite a few times, but I can't do it."

"She was selling clothes and Indian costumes and tie-dyes at one of the market stalls when I found her."

Jeff reaches over and squeezes Brandy's hand and she smiles back at him.

"We both got a 'Miracle' that night," says Brandy, "and went to the show together. We had a blast!"

"Yeah! We were constantly on the move the whole show," says Jeff. "Must've seen half the people in the stadium and then again in the parking lot. Yahoo, it was fun!"

Jeff bounces up and down in the driver seat recollecting the great time he had. Brandy and I have a few chuckles watching him react. She playfully punches Jeff in the arm and says he's crazy.

I settle into a comfortable spot in the backend of the vehicle and put my headphones on. Listening to Pink Floyd and Led Zeppelin, I switch the cassettes back and forth as we roll on down the highway.

I lay back in dreamy wonder—my journey to "Bohemia" and the counter culture is straight ahead. I see visions of a rock festival parking lot, flower children, and spaced out people roaming about, Cricket, Mignon and Pete…Vince and Jinx… and new people I'll meet.

ꙮ

It's getting late in the evening and Jeff has been driving all day and he doesn't want to drive past midnight. He decides to pull off at a rest stop. We're about twenty-five miles from the Cleveland city limits. I get out my small tent and quickly put it up on the grass. We're off in a far corner of the rest area. It's quiet in most of the vehicles and trucks. When there is activity it's over by the rest room and vending machine area. We're parked as far away from the activity as can be, so we can get some sleep.

Jeff rolls up the top part of his mini-bus then pulls out a tucked-in bed. The two of them are all set for the night's rest and I'm snuggled into my sleeping bag in the tent. Time to catch some zzzz's. We will be doing road work all day tomorrow, too.

ꕥ

At three in the morning, I have multiple big lights shining in my tent. Near by, I hear dogs sniffing and barking and growling. I hear a voice. "This is the Police. Please come out."

I'm stunned and don't respond at first.

This time the voice comes again, it's louder with a tone of authority.

"This is the Police. Come out of your tent, now!"

I quickly unzip the zipper and climb out of my sleeping bag. Lights in my eyes everywhere—two cop cars with the red and blues whirling around, flashlights, flood lights, from the cop cars—I'm literally blinded by the light!

"What's the problem?" I ask, shielding my eyes from the bright glares and pulling my shirt tight against my body with the other hand.

There are three police and two of them keep pacing back and forth while the other cop continues to beam his steady flashlight on me and in my face. I am disoriented. I see these big silver and gray mounty-type-hats they wear—looking menacing and mean, glaring hard looks at me. The two pacing cops each have a dog collared on a harness—muzzled German Shepherds.

"This isn't a campground. It's illegal to pitch a tent at a rest stop. Let me see your driver's license."

The cop has his hand out waiting for me. I reach for my wallet out of the back of my pants pocket, find my license and hand it to him. He goes back to his police car to run a check on me.

One of the cops walking with a dog asks me, "Who are you with?"

I point at Jeff's VW in the parking lot.

His partner shines a flashlight in the window and starts beating on the door—"Who's ever in there—get up and come outside right now!"

It's all dark and quiet in the mini-bus.

Suddenly the vehicle starts rustling about and we can hear noises as Jeff and Brandy come out of the van. The police want to see their driver's licenses too. Jeff and Brandy, stunned like I was, and shielding their eyes from the prying beams of flashlight, fumble around to find their identification.

A cop is going through my tent with his dog. He pulls my sleeping bag out onto the ground. The dog sniffs all through it. Then he pulls the poles on the four corners to collapse the tent, and motions me over to take it apart and pick it up. So, I go and do as he commands. When finished, I take the rolled up tent and rolled up sleeping bag and put them in the van.

The three of us stand there like common criminals in a lineup as the police car lights whirl round and round. We had to stand and wait and wait some more as the police communicated with base to do a background search on us. The three of us look at each other now and then, keeping our eyes mostly facing the ground, like three naughty children, not saying anything.

The cop who took our licenses, comes back and hands our drivers licenses to each of us. "It's best if you guys be on your way… hit the road, now!"

"Yes, sir!" Jeff and I say at the same time.

We hurry up and jump in the van and get moving again. Here it is three-forty in the morning and we're back on the road. Nobody says anything. The moon is out full and bright. It seems to light the path on the freeway we drive. I look up at the stars in the sky from the back window. I locate the Big Dipper and the North Star.

As soon as we cross the Ohio border and see the 'Welcome to Pennsylvania' sign—after not speaking and staring at the road for so long—we all three clap and hoot in unison. "Yahoo! Yippee!"

Jeff pulls over at the Welcome Center rest stop. The sun is coming up and we are all tired, especially the driver. They sit in their seats up front and go to sleep. Jeff has a big cardboard window shield that he puts in to block out the daylight. I have the curtains closed on the windows in back. They fall asleep, almost immediately.

I slowly drift off into a dream or a vision. I visit with Cricket in a meadow. She has her right arm wrapped in leather, extending to a leather glove. She's training eagles, hawks, falcons and condors.

I watch as the giant bird folds in his wingspan and clutches to Cricket's arm. Cricket talks in bird language to the bird. She feeds him pieces of fish from a wicker basket beside her. Then the bird flies away as another big bird of prey flies in to land on Cricket's gloved hand.

In my dream or vision I crouch in the tall grasses of the meadow, unseen, observing the interplay between Cricket and the birds of prey. When suddenly—I start flapping—I have wings!

Now I am flying! This time the eagle is me.

I am the eagle…

ℵ

It's afternoon before any of us wake up. We decide to head to the nearest truck stop to take a shower and have some lunch. We're all moving slowly, keeping to ourselves. It's three in the afternoon before we get started back on the road.

We take Interstate 80 through the heart of Pennsylvania. Then we connect on I-81 heading south toward Baltimore, Maryland and Washington, DC.

I have been relaxing, kicking back, watching passing road traffic, and listening to Led Zeppelin and Pink Floyd on my headphones.

I see Jeff and Brandy talking and carrying on in conversation up front.

I'm in a great frame of mind—positive, optimistic, hopeful, adventurous.

I leaf through some pages of ***Walden***, rereading passages that I'd highlighted in previous readings—the 'golden nugget' stuff. I ponder on the metaphoric "Self & Soul" journey with nature that Thoreau undertook—his very own bohemian odyssey of his life. Then I muse upon Henry Miller roaming the streets of Paris in the 1930's on his bohemian adventures. Or what about John Reed and Greenwich Village in the early years of the 20th century. I consider Jack Kerouac and even Hemingway—all writers seeking personal experience for self-knowledge advancement—to create and give structure to the stories they breathe into public life. Each writer invented their life's bohemian roles. My mind roams this way on our day of travel—off on far-reaching tangents.

The music inspires me, the road inspires me! I write a couple poems and pen some entries in my journal. It's all about awareness! I keep thinking one idea over and over.

It's all about awareness! It's all about awareness!

I write in my journal, without consciously thinking. I'm in the zone, effortlessly gliding as a scribe along the papered lines with constantly moving pen. Flip the page and keep on going. I am just warming up, I consider. The inspirational insights come in droves. I'm prepared and ready as I capture the intuitive thought-streams when they arrive.

It is well past midnight when we pull into the rest stop at Frederick, Maryland, about twenty miles from D.C. There is nowhere to park. The whole place is filled with deadheads—they are everywhere. They have turned the rest stop into a virtual campground. Tents are up side-by-side in all directions. Vehicles are parked end-to-end, bumper-to-bumper.

Jeff gets out of the van to talk to a clan of heads. They give him permission to pull in real close. They move one of their vehicles to make it easier for him. I grab my tent and sleeping bag and go out amongst the vast crowd to find a small spot on the ground. My tent is up in five minutes and I'm in it—another day of road work done. Sweet dreams!

I wake up in the early morning. Jeff and Brandy are still sleeping in the van. I decide to head to the rest room and get a coffee from the vending machine. There's a lot of deadheads—tie-dyes, beads, gypsy dresses, long-haired hippies, milling about. I stop and talk to several groups on the way to the concourse. I meet people from Florida, Utah, Georgia, Idaho, Canada, Arizona, Oklahoma and Maine. Deadheads from all over the country, North America—perhaps the world over.

This whole community vibe is exhilarating. Camaraderie and kindness are common everywhere. All the people I talk to have happy faces. Every day is a road show experience when traveling in a deadhead community.

I've got my coffee now. I'm going to head back and pack up my tent and wake up Jeff and Brandy.

As I head back through the deadhead throng at the rest stop, I notice some people crying and visibly upset, guys and gals, both. I stop by one of the camps and ask what is the matter? The sorrow and extreme sadness is now permeating throughout the rest stop. The first couple of people I inquire from are too upset to talk.

Now a great crowd of people starts to form over at the north end of the rest stop. I see and hear the arrival of police cars and paramedics and more police cars. As I come upon the scene, a guy behind me asks if I know what is going on. I tell him I haven't found anything out yet.

The police are hollering in a megaphone for the crowd to get back.

"We have a serious injury and will need room!"

The cops wave people away and begin to form a human tunnel with the other police so the emergency workers have a pathway through with a stretcher. I can see panic, terror and grief on people's faces.

The couple in front of me turns around, motioning that we have to move, as the whole crowd starts backing away. In comes an ambulance.

"Do you know what happened?" I ask them.

"A guy got his head run over by a bus," says the weeping gypsy girl.

The boyfriend holds her tight as she wipes her tearful face on his chest.

He says, "The dude was sleeping under the back tire of the bus. When the driver disengaged the parking brake the wheel squished his head and busted open his skull. There was a big pool of blood and they think he's dead."

"Unbelievable!"

I don't know what else to say as we all squeeze together and crane our necks after the police had wedged a pathway through the crowd. Crying and wailing is going on everywhere in all directions now. I feel this deep pit in the depths of my stomach. Several deadheads are throwing up. People are hugging and crying on each others' shoulder.

I have to get back to the van and let Jeff and Brandy know about this.

I find out through the grapevine that his name is Hugh and he's from a small town in upstate Wisconsin. He's only nineteen years old.

When I arrive at the van Jeff and Brandy are just waking up. They are sitting in the front seat with both doors open. They share expressions of confusion and bewilderment as they survey the scene of unfolding chaos, sadness and tears.

Jeff spots me in the crowd and jumps out of the VW and comes running towards me, "What happened? What happened? What's going on?"

I stop walking and we stand there as I tell him what I have found out. Jeff asks me to go be with Brandy while he runs over to the scene.

There is now a helicopter overhead. They're lowering a gurney down to the accident area.

Brandy comes running from the vehicle.

"What happened and where is Jeff?"

I tell her the story. She grabs her face with her hands and busts out crying. I put my arm around her and hug her against my chest as we walk back to the VW. The two of us sit in the back of the van and watch the unfolding scene. Some people are walking around like catatonic zombies. Others continue to cry and wail.

Brandy is starting to worry because Jeff has been gone for over forty-five minutes.

The constant sound of the helicopter and the flashing lights from the cop cars, ambulance and paramedics never ceases. The moment is surreal, like it's a dream not really happening—but it is.

Brandy is pacing back and forth beside the VW, while I stare out at the unfolding scene. Just then Jeff emerges from the crowd and he is in total hysterics, crying intensely, his wiry body shuddering with each huge breath.

"Hugh was my friend! He's dead! He's dead!" Jeff wails. "Hugh was my friend! Now he's dead!"

Brandy and I go over to comfort and console him. He pushes us away! He's angry! He wants to throw something, punch something, kick something. Jeff finds a rest area trash can and kicks it repeatedly. Tears flow like a river down his face.

Now Brandy is in bad shape again as she observes Jeff's spastic response. She keeps repeating, "I knew him. I knew who he was. Hugh was a good kid."

She rocks back and forth in the front seat of the van, in a semi-catatonic mode, repeating, "I knew him, I knew who he was. Hugh was a good kid."

Jeff finally comes back to the van—he and Brandy tearfully embrace.

The helicopter is reeling up the gurney with Hugh. All the people in the crowd take pause from their crying and praying and fretting to watch the helicopter pull up the gurney.

It is a very solemn moment.

All I can hear is the constant "whooosh whoosh" of the rotor blades. Everything else is silenced.

I look out on a sea of sad faces.

Then the gurney is pulled in and the helicopter leaves the scene. I still have the "whooosh whoosh" sound going off in my ears like an echo.

Everyone meanders back to their vehicles, their small clans, their tents. I go to break down my tent. I pull out the two long poles that intersect to create a dome out of the tent. Then I roll up my sleeping bag and pack the tent tight. Many of the heads are off doing the same things—packing tents and sleeping gear, filling the vehicles up with stuff.

It is real quiet and somber everywhere I look. There are still a few people, here and there, crying and carrying on with grief-stricken emotions. However, the vast majority of deadheads are somber, quiet, and reflective.

> *Any moment of any day could be the day of our last breath. Precious life, precious breath, eternal death. Just a short time span to pack it all in. I've been so close to the edge twice—just hanging by a thread. I came back to live, to do something wild and great and beneficent. Doesn't everybody have a purpose? But how many seek? Are we all fools, throwing our created nature away? Losing a friend, a loved one, someone you may have just spoken to—gone—forever dead. Fragile precious life can end on any day…*

I carry my gear to the VW mini-bus. Jeff and Brandy continue to hold each other in a tight embrace, standing outside leaning up against the vehicle. Putting my gear in the van, I say, "We should be leaving soon, I suppose…."

"We can be at the show venue in an hour or so," says Jeff. He's all composed and back to his normal self for the moment now. "I'm going to find a place to park on dirt and grass so you can put up your tent. I can operate my venue right out of the back of the van. I'll set up my equipment so I can demonstrate how the product is made and juggle the sticks. Brandy—you can help collect money and wrap tassels and twine around the sticks."

The three of us hop in the van as Jeff continues on, "We can start selling right away because I have over a dozen sets ready to go. Plus I have all the supplies I need to make more."

We head down the road. Nobody mentions anything that just happened. Speechless silence prevails. We're each a universe unto ourselves with our thoughts. I'm sitting in the back thinking about life and death. It all can end so fast and so final. This is why the Great Masters, Buddha and Jesus, spoke of reverence for life and brotherhood with fellow man. It's why Socrates proclaimed, "Know Thyself." I ponder the "Self and Soul" of an individual human life:

> *Life. Death. What does it all mean? What purposes do we have with the "Self & Soul" we own? Is it about a proper daily balanced mindset? Family Love? Friendship? Self-control? Knowledge? Education? Love? Experience? I wonder about the infinite depths of life as I seek my own awareness and understanding! What is my purpose in this life? Where am I going? What have I learned from where I've been? Precious lifetime trapped in finite time. I can't waste it! I know that I don't know. . .*

ᘓᘐ

As we approach Washington, D.C., I look out onto the interconnecting maze of traffic patterns. It's easy to spot a deadhead vehicle. They all stick out amongst the traffic flow. Just about every deadhead vehicle has stickers and/or groovy paint jobs, day-glo bright colors, peace signs, etc.

The Grateful Dead trademark insignia of a skull with a lightning bolt in the forehead is standard-fare on just about every deadhead vehicle. Each VW mini-bus is a regular deadhead traveling mobile. They paint them up with rainbows, bright colors, graffiti, stickers everywhere.

I start counting all the deadhead mobiles in the traffic. Jeff is in the fast lane so we are whizzing by and passing them by the dozens. My count reaches a hundred in less than ten minutes. Okay—enough of that!

I look out the window and see signs for "Robert F. Kennedy Stadium." Jeff gets in the proper lane and follows the signs. I see another sign that says "Potomac River." This gets me to thinking about George Washington. I'd like to visit Mount Vernon one day. Then I see other signs for Pennsylvania Avenue, The White House and Capitol Hill.

Jeff hollers from up front and points to the horizon. We can see the Washington Monument from the freeway. Jeff calls it the 'Big Phallus' in the sky. I thought I didn't hear him right so I ask him to repeat what he said. He says it again. I heard right.

We follow the exit to "RFK Stadium parking." Jeff doesn't want to park close to the stadium. He finally settles on a parking spot that must be three-quarters of a mile from stadium parking. We park on grass in a field, by a river that borders the lot. All the riverside prime spots are taken. So, we set up our market stall venue directly across.

Is this the Potomac? A steep wooded decline keeps people off the riverside. Just then, through a clearing, I see a couple of deadheads have climbed down there and are walking along the rocks on the river's edge.

Jeff pulls out his "devil-stick-making" contraption and I start to set up my tent. Pausing, I look into the distance and see RFK stadium. I think of the NFL football's Washington Redskins. They've had some good teams and some great games played in this stadium.

Then my mind drifts back to Hugh. He was alive hours earlier. He was alive when we pulled into the Frederick, Maryland rest stop. Maybe he was alive when I first got up this morning. It's noon now, and he's dead. I wonder if the three of us will ever talk about it, as I unpack my gear and set up my tent.

ꕥ

Chapter Six

Washington D.C.

ꕥ

"For long you live and high you fly
And smiles you'll give and tears you'll cry
And all you touch and all you see
Is all your life will ever be"

—Pink Floyd
'Breathe' from ***Dark Side of the Moon***

The Deadhead Festival in the Parking Lot

The pace of activity and energy increase as the mid-afternoon sun shines bright in the rock festival parking lot. My tent is set up, and I have some notebooks and books strewn around on top of my sleeping bag. I take one notebook and two pens and leave on a long stroll. The merchants in the market stall venues resemble a bunch of worker ants scurrying about doing their jobs, setting up throughout the massive stadium parking complex.

It is a vast sea of swarming activity, bobbing heads, movement flowing in certain circles, energy vibrating from all directions. Jeff juggles and flips his devil sticks for the crowd as it gathers. Brandy passes out the set of sticks for the paying customers. Jeff fields questions from interested admirers, explaining how he makes his sticks and the tricks to the mechanics of his juggling act. He is a natural born salesman. Brandy soon has a fat wad of cash.

I look out on the venue, trying to decide which direction I want to go. Music and noise and echoing voices fill my ears. I walk all along the riverside corridor and then over to the next aisle.

I continue aisle to aisle through the parking lot, taking in every camp setup. Deadheads are selling glow-beads, stickers, tie-dye shirts, Grateful Dead shirts, chicken pitas, hot dogs, hamburgers, popcorn, soda, beer, tattoos, dope, grass, jewelry, watches, hair braids, peace signs, artwork, caricature face drawings, spray paint art, posters, and devil sticks.

From time to time I am captivated by a strange sight or an outlandish scene—like the old man with the "End of the World" sign. He says over and over, "Repent! Repent!" while walking in a circle, holding his sign overhead. He is gray and unshaven, wearing old tattered clothes like he has lived on the streets for quite a while. The old man holds his sign up high for all to see. "John 3:3" is written in faded marker.

"Repent! Repent!" I walk by and drop a couple quarters in his cup of change.

Next, I come to a gypsy psychic woman shaded by a purple tent. She sits at a round table surrounded by crystal balls, tarot cards, magic tricks.

"Hey, there, let me tell you your romantic future and all the riches you will make."

"No, thanks!" And I walk on.

I see a guy on stilts dressed like a tree, walking amongst the throng.

Then I see two well-dressed, clean-cut, teenage kids handing out small leaflets concerning the Mormon Church. Later on, I see and meet a couple who are handing out literature for Jehovah Witnesses.

After sauntering up and down the aisles for over an hour, I come across a group of five guys dressed in white robes jumping around in circles, the sun reflecting from their bald heads. "Hare Krishna! Hare Krishna! Hare

Krishna!" I continue on my way, winding through the crowd and gatherings, taking it all in.

The sights and happenings go on and on forever with no ending, it seems. Afterwards I come upon some menacing looking Hell's Angels biker-types. I nod 'hello' to a few of the guys and keep on walking past them. They have over a hundred bikes parked side by side stretching into a row of shining metal in the field parking lot.

I spot a priest walking alone. He wears an apprehensive look on his face, as if he is walking in to the depths of the pit of hell. I go over and talk with him.

"You look a little out of place here. Are you lost? Can I help you?"

He's very soft spoken. "My name is Father Carlos. Father Reysmadena Carlos." I lean in closer to hear him. "I'm looking for a poor lost soul."

He pulls out a three-by-five picture bookmarked in the small black leather-bound bible he carries.

"Her name is "Mercedes" and she's only fifteen years old." Father Carlos hands me the picture.

I look at the young girl and shrug my shoulders and shake my head 'no' as I hand the picture back. I say, pointing to the endless crowds of people fanning out in all directions, "I think you'll have a hard time finding her here amongst all this."

"I've been searching since early this morning. I've never before seen a gathering of people like this in my life," he says with a timid weakness in his voice. "Her mother is home with tremendous grief and I'm losing hope of finding her."

"Do you really believe she's here in all this chaos?"

"She has been threatening her family that she was going to run away when a music group came to town. The teenagers I talked to at my church confirmed that she would be out here. We've already turned in a missing person report to the police," says Father Carlos.

"The music group that attracts this mass following is the Grateful Dead. People band together in little groups and clans. She could be anywhere. I'll keep my eyes open. Good luck, Father."

An ivory rosary wraps around the hand and wrist holding Father Carlos' bible. I watch him stand there silently counting his beads and looking out at the Hells Angels bikers and the endless row upon row of heads constantly moving and mingling in the crowd.

His situation is hopeless and he is coming to this realization. With a shell-shocked look on his face he turns to me and says, "Will you please pray with me?"

"Excuse me?" I say.

"Will you pray with me? Are you Catholic?"

"I'm a Christian, but I'm not a Catholic," I respond. "I'll do a short prayer with you—sure—okay!"

He holds out his bible and I put my hand on it while he says a short prayer for the missing girl. Father Carlos conducts his prayer in Latin. It's no more than half a minute long. Then he crosses himself at his chest and kisses his rosary. He is anxious to continue his search. Father Carlos quickly thanks me and moves on until the crowd swallows him up.

I stand for a moment looking out on the sea of people as Father Carlos disappears, wondering if he will find that young girl along the way.

I decide it is time to make my way back to where we parked. I continue on the endless procession through the human zoo. The counter-culture deadhead scene is like a magnet that brings out the freaks and weirdoes in droves. The entire scene is akin to one vast stage where everyone is an actor, playing his part.

I saunter past groups and gatherings of people from everywhere and every walk of life. The excitement is infectious and encouraging as I absorb the life-energy vibe of all those swirling around me.

When I arrive back to home base I sit down on a blanket in front of my tent to have some lunch. Jeff and Brandy join me.

"We sold out our devil sticks!" says Jeff. "And we're all excited about that. Now we plan on getting tickets and going to the concert tonight!"

"You want to come with us?" asks Brandy.

"Yeah, man! Come on to the show with us," says Jeff. "It's on me!"

"I'm going to hang out in the parking lot," I reply. "Going to stay here by my tent, and maybe do some writing in my journal notebooks. I'm just going to soak this day in for a bit. You two go and have a good time."

"Are you sure?" asks Jeff. "I have enough money to get you a ticket, or you can hangout for a miracle. Are you sure you don't want to come with us?"

"I'm sure. Thanks anyway! You guys go and have a good time. I'll hold down the fort here," I say, pulling out my notebook and pens from the book bag.

Jeff and Brandy finish eating and then Jeff locks up the van and they take off. I won't see them again until well after midnight.

I sit down on the ground in front of my tent and begin to pen some words in my journal notebook. Every so often I look up to watch the people pass by. I find myself, every now and then, staring off into space at an unusual sight—a possible transvestite, punk rockers, big burly tattooed bikers, some sexy looking women, provocative sexy walkers, and wide-eyed, stoned, silly freaks, and cute little gypsy revelers. I continue on in this manner—writing and gazing at people—throughout the rest of the afternoon.

ଌଓ

Then I meet a strange looking biker-type. He wears long brown hair, a rust-colored shaggy beard, dark sunglasses, grim reaper tattoos down both arms, black leather Harley Davidson biker vest, shirtless, black jeans and big black army boots. The guy is six-foot and firmly muscle-bound. He wears a crystal black helmet with a spike right through the top of it. As he passes by my little venue spot, he notices me writing, and stops to ask me what I'm writing about.

"Anything interesting?"

"Huh?" Startled, I look up at him from the small folding chair I sit in, with my journal notebook resting on my lap as I write.

"Are you writing anything interesting?" he inquires. Motioning to my notebook with a nod of the head. And then he points at the page I am writing on.

I'm momentarily stunned with silence as I look at his intimidating countenance. The spike in his helmet holds my attention for a few brief seconds.

"I'm Baron Von Torchenstein!" He holds out his hand to shake hands with me.

I hesitate and then stand up to exchange greetings with him.

"I'm Ted. I'm writing in my journal right now. Just writing about life, my experiences, whatever catches my fancy at the moment. There's a lot of inspirational energy around here. I try to tune my mind into the vibration and then write whatever comes," I say.

"Sort of like creative writing? Creative thinking?" he says.

"Yeah! Yeah! What did you say your name was again?"

"Baron Von Torchenstein. You can just call me Torch

or Baron Von, if you want." He sits down on the ground next to me in front of the tent. "You mind if I read some of your stuff?"

I flip through several pages to where I copied down some great quotes from authors, scientists, and great thinkers, ancient Philosophs. I hand over my notebook. He sits there and reads, page after page.

Baron Von takes his spiked helmet off after he's been comfortable for twenty minutes, and lays the helmet on the ground beside him. His long rust-colored hair falls out of his helmet and descends half-way across his upper back.

He hardly moves or mumbles a word thereafter—just turns the page every so often, and continues reading from my journal notebook. A couple times I hear him mumble and I say "Huh?" in response. Torch only answers with a nod of agreement—"Sincerely profound!"—he'd mutter and continue on with reading from the journal notebook.

Baron Von Torchenstein spent a couple hours, the rest of the afternoon, reading.

"Do you have another notebook I can read?"

"Sure!"

I give him another notebook and take back the other journal. Baron Von Torchenstein settles back in and concentrates on more reading. We are in the midst of chaotic noise, excitement, and peopled activity—but we sit in silence reading, looking up every so often at the passing crowds, then back to reading.

I finally get Torch to take a break and talk with me.

"So where are you from, Baron Von Torchenstein? Myself, I came from Michigan when I met up with some deadheads at a state park and a guy agreed to come back and pick me up in ten days, and he did, and now I'm sitting here in D.C. talking to you!" I say.

"I'm from Michigan, too!" he says.

"All right, cool!" We shake hands again.

"Where at in Michigan? I grew up around Port Huron," I say.

"I'm from the U P originally, near Manistique. But I've been all over the entire state, back and forth across the bridge on my Harley," Baron Von says. "I just got out of jail. Hopped on my Harley and joined the caravans of deadheads in Indiana for a few shows. Then we came out here. I had to miss the Michigan shows because I was locked up."

"What were you in jail for?"

"Non-payment of child support to both my ex-wives—I'm way behind!" Torch says with dejection in his voice. "I've got a kid with each woman and it didn't work out. Every time I make anything they garnisheed my wages. Friend of the Court has me by the balls."

He grabs himself in the crotch as he shakes his head in disappointment.

"Anyway, I just got out and got on the road so I can get in on the last week of the tour!"

"You a big Dead fan?" I ask.

"Not really!" he says. "I'm here for the people and the gatherings. It's like playing in fantasy land—then it's back to the other reality of eking out sustenance and living."

"Sounds like you live on the fringes of society. I can relate!" I say. "But we come from quite different backgrounds, I'm sure. Where did you go to school? Do any college?" I ask.

"I was in the Marines from the age of seventeen to twenty-one. It was either that or jail, the truant officer told me. I played hockey all the time when I was growing up and I could've had a hockey scholarship at any school of my choice, but I blew that by getting in trouble with the law all the time," says Baron Von Torchenstein. "I had speeding tickets, parking tickets, racing tickets—and then they'd catch me with grass or open intoxicants—until I had a rap sheet a mile long before I was halfway through high school. I've never liked authority figures. I don't want anybody telling me what to do!"

"How did you survive the Marines for four years?"

"It wasn't easy! They made sure I wasn't so cocky and arrogant all the time anymore. Let me tell you, I spent many nights in the brig that first year. It was either, conform and go with the system or they were going to kick my ass every day until I had no energy left to fight and rebel."

"Did you go overseas?"

"Oh yeah!" he says. "The Philippines, Thailand, Korea, Hong Kong, Okinawa, Tokyo, Vietnam, the Samoan Islands. I remember we stopped in Sydney, Australia on our way to Guam when I first went over."

Torch stares off into space, reminiscing, perhaps thinking of distant comrades.

"I was in the service from May 1977 thru April 1981. I was in Lebanon and left there with my outfit just before the Marine barracks was blown up. I lost some friends that day. Yessirree, I've been all over the south China seas."

"So you've been out of the Marines over a decade now?"

"Yeah! Got out of the service and got married and had a baby boy right away. Then I got divorced and remarried again within a year, then two years later I had Brittney with my second wife. I work in Tool & Die shops as a QA Supervisor—always job hopping—can't stand it in one place too long," says Torch. "I lose my job every time they throw me in jail. Then I have to agree to get my wages garnisheed to start at another job. It's a bullshit system. I work for cash whenever I can, framing in houses on construction crews."

"What about that big long moniker of yours—Baron Von Torchenstein? Did you name yourself or did someone give you that name and it stuck?" I ask half-jokingly.

"Well, I've been called Torch since I was a kid in my early teens. Then I became Baron Von Torchenstein after the Marines. I survived two helicopter crashes and a near death experience from an accident on my Harley Davidson."

He stands up from his sitting position on the ground and pounds his chest like King Kong.

"I'm self-invented," he boasts. "Original and unique!"

"Well, it's good to see that you don't have a big ego or self-image and self-esteem problems," I joke.

He bends down and picks up his spiked helmet from the ground and fits it back on his head.

"I was a Baron in a previous life, during the medieval Dark Ages. I was also a leading Torch-bearer in another incarnation," says Baron Von Torchenstein, in total seriousness. He continues to pound his chest, intermittently, with his right fist to his heart area.

"I have a hard time believing anything about a previous life lived. What's the point?" I say. "People struggle in dealing with their own lives that they lead right now on earth."

Baron Von nods his head in agreement at first, then he shakes his head "no" and wags his index finger at me from side to side.

"I know through direct empirical instinct and personal intuitions. Most people don't know themselves this deep—I do!" he says, pointing his right thumb into his chest.

"My intuition brought me this understanding and

awareness through recurrent visions and dreams and meditations."

I look at him like I'm nobody's fool. At once, he is riled up over my disbelief.

Torch jumps up and in a loud threatening voice he yells at me. "I'm not making it up to have a story to tell!"

"Just relax, dude!" I say.

Now he looks like he is getting more visibly upset about this, like he may want to punch me.

"What does it matter if I believe you or not? It's your reality and you believe it. Cool!"

We meet each other eye to eye and endure a long uneasy silence between us. Then Baron Von takes off his spike helmet and sits back down on the blanket, spread on the ground. He is calm and relaxed of posture once again.

Finally, I speak to break the silence.

"I believe everyone should have freedom to believe as they please. I don't believe anyone's opinion or beliefs should be shoved down someone else's throat."

He nods in agreement.

"Sorry man, I'm wound up a little tight sometimes."

We shake hands and shrug it off.

"So, how long have you been Baron Von Torchenstein?"

"Since I got back from service," he says. "But I only discovered what I knew all along. I just had to re-remember… "

"Whatever that means?" I question him with a look of curiosity. "Re-remember, did you say?"

"That means I'm a real Baron now—and I've been a real Baron many times before! Yahoo!" he yelps and laughs at himself.

"You smoke?"

I nod and then he proceeds to pull out a joint from the inside pocket of his biker vest. We kick back and enjoy watching the crowds of people walk by. It is an endless procession of changing faces and bodies constantly moving along. Baron Von Torchenstein starts hooting and hollering at the pretty young girls that walk by.

We pass a long stream of time staring absent-mindedly into the milieu, fascinated by the constant pulsation of movement and activity of rock revelers of all ages.

All is one and one is all. Planet earth is vibrating with energy that charges every human soul and living thing. The great miracle is always present in every day creation. We are infinitely blessed and don't even acknowledge the blessings. The mystical rainbow beholds the energetic colors of manifestation. Earth people with lifetimes upon lifetimes, generation upon generation…

I receive a hint of inspiration at the moment so I proceed to write in my journal notebook.

Baron Von Torchenstein says he will be back in a few minutes. He is going to get his bike and park it next to the tent and hang out with me the rest of the day and night. Says he has a book on his bike that he's going to bring back and he wants to talk about it. Off he goes for over an hour. Meanwhile, I just sit in front of my tent and write in my notebook.

Baron Von Torchenstein returns with the most fantastic looking bike. There is a flaming skull on the gas tank, with very intricate details and multi-coloring blends.

He says, "I designed it and painted it myself."

The bike is a big Harley chopper, black, burgundy, and silver, shining luminescent in the sunlight. His arms are fully extended, holding onto the handles as he steers it to a spot between the VW mini-bus and my tent.

Once parked, Torch unzips a little black leather pouch he has behind the huge bar on the back of the bike. Baron

Von Torchenstein pulls out a little dog-eared paperback. It's Immanual Kant, Critique of Pure Reason.

He opens it up and finds his spot and then comes over by me, reading a passage out loud:

"*'Always act so that you can will the maxim or determining principle of your action to become universal law; act so that you can will that everybody shall follow the principle of your action.'* This, Kant called, the 'Categorical Imperative.' You ever heard of that?" he asks me.

"I'm familiar with Immanual Kant from my reading and studies of Thoreau and Emerson and Whitman. Yes, I've heard of the 'Categorical Imperative.' But, I'm not really too versed in all of Kant's philosophy. I find him to be a challenging read," I say.

Baron Von Torchenstein is a lover of all things Immanuel Kant. He just raves on and on about how he said this or he wrote that. He reads me several more passages from the I. Kant book.

Then we start talking about Copernicus, Newton, Galileo, the Catholic Church, Darwin, Einstein…

We just met, but it feels like we have known each other all our lives. Back and forth we go, talking about history, science, biography, intellectual movements, mathematics, inventions, physics, philosophy.

The sun will soon go down so we break from our conversation to get some refreshments, use the bathroom and check out the surrounding scene before nightfall. We can hear the concert in the far distance, mainly the cheering crowd in the stadium, percussion instruments, and a loud guitar riff now and then.

The parking lot rock festival is just as lively as it has been throughout the whole day.

Baron Von Torchenstein goes over to his bike and

pulls out a long tubular package that is strapped tight to the back of his long sissy bars. He comes over to me with this tube and pops off the cap on the one end. He has a couple of paintings in there.

"I did these in jail. I'm going to frame them and try to sell them so I can get some money in my pocket."

He pulls the paintings out of the tube. Baron Von Torchenstein unrolls the first painting.

"This is my 'Heaven & Hell' portrait," he says.

It's a picture of two androgynous angels. The brightness and light depicted in the far northwest corner of the portrait attracts one of them. The other angel has black wings and the black abyss in the far southeast corner of the portrait attracts his attention. Upon closer inspection, it's one angel—half-n-half—emerging from a flaming skull in the center of the painting.

Absolutely spell-binding! Reminds me of stuff I've seen by William Blake.

Baron Von Torchenstein is not just a normal painter. I discover him to be a bonafide ARTIST!

The next painting he pulls out of the tube is an up close facial portrait of a wizard holding a bright fiery crystal ball. Blood drips down the wizard's fingers. The wizard's eyes are in a trance—alive with the reflection of the light and fire. The wizard wears a long white beard and long, flowing white hair. The aura around his entire head is beaming bright indigo.

Baron Von Torchenstein asks me, "What do you think about this one?"

I am speechless! Words cannot convey the thoughts in my mind. I am enraptured, as if waiting for the wizard to speak.

Baron Von Torchenstein then goes back to his Harley and reaches into his saddle bag. He brings out a block of wood and hands it to me. Baron Von has been whittling and carving a fifteen-inch standing wizard.

"It's not done, yet," he says.

Torch has the robe, pointed hat, and facial features completed. The wizard has his right hand fully extended outward holding what looks to be a star or a shiny crystal ball.

"I just need to fix a few spots and varnish it," he says.

"You really have some awe-inspiring talent," I say. "How long did it take you to do this stuff?"

"It's just some jailhouse work and a hobby I do in my spare time."

"Well, aren't you modest and humble," I chuckle.

Then I hand the wooden wizard back to Baron Von Torchenstein.

"Can you watch my stuff for a few minutes?" he asks. "I need to frame these two pictures and I know a couple places I found around here, where I can get supplies and tools."

"You mean among these deadheads?" I ask.

"Yeah! I won't be long. I already arranged things earlier. I just hope the guy is still there. He said he would be, all night. If not, I got another guy I can check on. I'll zoom around on my bike and I'll be right back," he says.

"I'm not going anywhere. I'll be right here when you get back. Your stuff will be safe. Hurry back!" I say.

Misjudging people on appearance? Misjudging the choices in life? Missing out on opportune moments because of a closed mind? Wake up! Open up to the wide universals in Nature. Nature is! Nature was! Nature will be! What is the truth of your nature, Ted? Wake up, Ted! The ever present NOW is here! Connecting with the inner sanctum of my divine being! Closed off, clamped down? Open up! Wake up! Stop the struggle, Ted—and go with the natural flow!

ꕥ

Within an hour Baron Von Torchenstein returns. He's brought back an easel and a potato-sack. Inside the bag are various pieces of wood.

"I have everything I need to build my frames and put my art work on display," he says. "Maybe I can make a few bucks!"

"How did you manage to get this stuff?" I ask.

"I befriended a family earlier that had a big market stall of posters, paintings, and deadhead artwork. I showed my artwork to the guy who ran the place, and asked if he could sell my stuff for me, put it on display. Instead he offered to give me the wood to make my frames and use his tools," says Baron Von Torchenstein. "I told him I would get back with him after I found a place to park my bike and setup shop. We'll do it right here!"

He starts sawing and hammering and tacking his frames together.

No sooner does Baron Von Torchenstein get his wizard portrait framed than he already has two interested buyers.

Both guys are outfitted in loose ties, wearing sport coats, and it's obvious they have been drinking all day. They're Yuppy types, clean-cut, the Wall-Street-Stockbroker look. The first guy pulls out a crisp hundred dollar bill and tries to give the money to Baron Von. When he reaches for it the other guy pulls Torch's arm down. Then he pulls out two hundred dollar bills from his money clip.

Baron Von tells them both he has two paintings, but they both want to haggle over this one.

Soon the bidding is up to two-hundred-fifty dollars. I'm watching all this unfold with pure amazement. The final price settles at three-hundred-twenty-five dollars.

The other guy declines to top the offer!

The first guy counts out his money and puts it in Baron Von Torchenstein's hand. The new owner of the art work has a camera in his coat pocket and he wants a picture of himself with the artist and the artwork.

Baron Von excuses himself for a few seconds. He comes back from his bike with his spiked helmet on. I volunteer to take a couple of pictures. The guy then walks off with his prized painting.

Baron Von is elated. I congratulate him and we shake hands.

I ask, "Did you ever think you could get money like that for your stuff?"

"No! Not really!" he says. "I was hoping someone would see value in it and offer me a fifty or maybe a hundred at the most. Wow!"

Baron Von Torchenstein is just beaming ear-to-ear with the satisfied grin of a Cheshire cat.

We spend the rest of the evening in our little "market stall venue" in the parking lot. Torch buys us some food, beer and cigars to celebrate.

The Grateful Dead concert is ringing through the night air from RFK Stadium. We are far enough away to where we can't hear very well, but we hear it every now and then, especially when the crowd cheers.

I am getting inebriated and higher and higher. I need to keep things simple and fundamental now.

So what does Baron Von Torchenstein proceed to do? He talks of physics, science, and engineering. I am not understanding while in this present state of mind.

My head spins. I struggle to keep up with his talk.

He continues with his dissertation, anyway. Now he's into Newton and Einstein. He loves Copernicus.

"Everyone celebrates Valentine's Day on February

14th but I celebrate Copernicus' birthday. Humanity was stupid and dumb till then. Copernicus righted the ship, so to speak," he says.

I interject, "What do you think about the Catholic Church putting Galileo under house arrest near the end of his life because he said he could prove Copernicus was right?"

"I'm not a fan of the Catholic Church. That's why Copernicus didn't publish until his death. They would have accused him of being a heretic and burned him at the stake. All they do is deceive and take, deceive and take," he says. "The Dark Ages and medieval times were dark for so long a time because of Catholic lies, deception and thievery of the public at large. Jesus did not intend for this to be!"

We go on talking like this till the wee hours of the night.

Jeff and Brandy finally come back well after midnight. They are really burned-out of energy, especially Jeff. We try to talk to him, but he is in his own acid-reflex-universe and it is hard for him to join us. We hear him vomiting behind his van.

Brandy mostly looks just tired and whipped out. They've been going non-stop all day long. Jeff unlocks the van and passes out inside on the floor.

Baron Von Torchenstein makes a little fire between the tent and his bike. Brandy joins us by the fire. The three of us sit on a blanket on the ground, legs folded in. The summer night air has a soft chill.

I introduce Brandy to Baron Von Torchenstein. She acts like that is just the most normal name she has ever heard. We ask her about their day. She smiles big and talks about the concert and all the people and selling all their devil sticks and the things they saw and heard in the show. She perks right up as she gets into all of the details of their day-long-party-hearty atmosphere.

Then she stops abruptly in mid-sentence—Frozen!

She stares for a few seconds.

Then tears well up, her chin starts puckering, and she lets loose and begins bawling.

This knocks the buzz right out of Torch and me, all at once, as we watch and experience Brandy's sudden mood shift—from extreme happy thoughts and memories to extreme sad emotions.

All at once I realize that Brandy is thinking about what happened this morning at the rest stop in Frederick, Maryland. The tragic bus incident—the dead deadhead.

Thinking of the journey of Hugh's soul…

ഗ്ദ

Brandy eventually calms down. The three of us sit around our small fire and talk about what happened in the morning with Hugh.

"Why would somebody be using a bus tire for a pillow?" Baron Von Torchenstein wants to know.

"I met Hugh, and Jeff knew him well," Brandy says, sniffling. "The guy was mostly a loner and he hopped from ride to ride to get around to all the Grateful Dead shows. He was just having fun and enjoying himself every day."

"He was probably tired to the point of passing out after traveling and partying all day," I say.

"He maybe got lost, didn't have a blanket. It probably seemed warm under the bus," says Brandy, mournfully. "Sort of like a shield from the night air. He probably propped his head up on the tire so he could breathe right while he slept."

We all three stare into the fire as Brandy finishes surmising the story.

"Jeff had a real tough time when that happened," she says. "He was so angry and sad. I still can't believe it happened. I'm shocked!"

"It was a very surreal moment—something I will never forget!" I say. "Death and chaos and frantic gloomy faces everywhere! That's the most group sadness and grief I ever experienced."

"It's pretty amazing," says Baron Von Torchenstein, "a deadhead, dead, with a busted open head!" He snickers to himself.

On any normal occasion that would have been something to laugh about, if it weren't true. Torch wasn't there, so he can crack the quick quip joke.

Brandy continues to stare at the fire. I look at Baron Von with a warning look to watch what he says. He gets the message, with a crooked mischievous smile on his face.

This is followed by long moments of silence, staring into the fire, all three of us. Fatigue is quickly creeping in. The flames are getting low and barely a few inches high. We gather some more kindling sticks and twigs and Torch fans the flames.

Brandy asks about our day. Baron Von Torchenstein tells her how we met. Then we tell the story about selling his painting. We talk about all the different and weird people we had talked to and seen throughout the day. Brandy keeps yawning till finally she excuses herself to go to bed in the van. She's going to let Jeff sleep it off on the floor of the minibus. After she leaves we continue to visit for a short while.

Staring into the coals of our mini-campfire, we revisit the night's earlier topic once again. "Have you ever had a near-death experience? I did about six years ago on my bike. I was messed up real bad," says Torch. Then he points to a deep impression in his neck. "They had to do a tracheotomy to keep me alive. I flat-lined a couple times. They electro-shocked my heart back to beating."

"This happened from a bike accident?"

"The woman just stopped in the middle of the road for no reason, and I was going along thirty-five to forty miles per hour—then WHAM!—I flipped over my handle bars and over her car and landed on my head in the street. Deep lacerations! Needed brain surgery!"

"Damn, dude! That's a rough story. How long did it take you to recover from that?" I ask.

"I was done for a year, man! Couldn't do anything but recover. I lived with my Grandma and she nursed me back to health."

We both stare into the hot embers, yawning now and then, quiet and thoughtful. Then Torch asks me, "What about you? Did you ever die and come back to life?"

"Twice in my life I was involved in serious accidents where I should have died. When I was four years old I ran into the road after a beach ball and was run over by a woman going fifty-five to sixty miles per hour. I was in a coma. Wore a body cast. Five hundred stitches in my head. Then when I was in my sophomore year of college, on spring break, a buddy and I were out drinking and he ran through the stop sign at an intersection in town. Hit another car broadside! They had three guys, who were also drunk, out partying. Everyone died but me! The steering wheel went right through my buddy's chest and killed him instantly!"

"Shit, man! That's some tough stuff! We're brothers in spirit, man!"

Torch reaches over to me and holds out his hand. We stand up to shake hands, and pat each other on the back. Then we sit back down in our lawn chairs, fixated on the hot coals.

Billy! Billy, are you there? Are you alive? Can you breathe? Billy! Billy, are you dead? The car crash. The field, wandering. Red lights, blue lights flashing. Sirens. Screams and shouts. Am I dying? Drifting through a tunnel of light. Rising. Advancing speed. Rising. White light drawing me in. The hospital room emergency ward. Billy! Billy, are you there? Have you gone to heaven or gone to hell? I'm still here…

"Hey, man! Want to go visit the Memorials in D.C. tomorrow?" asks Baron Von. "We can leave at sunrise and visit all morning and then get back before things heat up in the early afternoon with the deadhead crowd. You can ride on the back of my chopper. It's a big seat. I got enough room. What do you say?"

"That sounds like a great plan! You ever done it before?" I ask.

"No, this will be my first time," he says. "We should hit the sack then. Sunrise is only a few hours away. I'm going to sleep right out here between my bike and the fire on the ground."

"All right, I'll see you in the morning!" I say.

There is still a lot of activity and movement going on throughout the parking lot but it is a lot calmer than it has been throughout the day. A drunk deadhead teenager comes by looking for his clan. I point him down the row and tell him to keep on walking. He continues on, like a zombie, following my orders. Thereafter, I crawl into my tent and fall asleep.

ꕥ

Next morning we get up real early at the break of dawn. All the deadheads are still sleeping, so it is very quiet. The entire parking lot resembles a huge, tightly-packed campground, surrounding RFK stadium. A few times we see a matted-haired deadhead with squinty eyes walk by, heading to the nearest porta-john. But it is mostly still and quiet amongst the sea of vehicles, tents and makeshift venues.

A stray dog, a Dalmatian, white with black spots, comes scurrying over to Baron Von Torchenstein and me with his tail between his legs. We pet him gently on the head and swoosh him to go. He won't leave so we both do a feint charge and stomp, and the poor dog takes off running down the parking lot row.

We make a small fire with kindling and brew some hot water with instant coffee.

"You know, I'm going to wake everyone up when I start up my bike. So when I do, you need to be on the bike and ready to go so we can get out of here fast," says Baron Von Torchenstein. "Here's an extra helmet."

He hands me a solid black helmet that he has attached to the back of his bike. Then Baron Von unscrews the spike from his helmet and puts it in his side saddle bag. We adjust the helmets on our heads and enjoy our coffee around the small fire.

"I'm glad you're not traveling with that spike on your head," I joke.

"Never do. I'd get in trouble with the law. I've done it a few times, but usually on back roads and by myself," he says.

I pack some things in my book bag—a water bottle, a few pens and a notebook journal. Baron Von Torchenstein ties it down tight to the back of the bike.

"You should read ***Zen and The Art of Motorcycle Maintenance,*** " he suggests. Reaching back into his side saddle bag, he pulls out a paperback copy of the book.

"I read this book all the time. This guy has a dual personality and he caused himself to go nuts with philosophical inquiry," Torch says.

He hands the dog-eared paperback book to me and I quickly fan through the stained and rumpled, marked-up pages. Then I hand the book back.

"I'll be sure to check that book out of the library when I get back home," I say.

I readjust the helmet on my head. We down our cups of coffee and kick out the small kindling fire.

"Are we about ready to go?" I ask.

"Sure, hop on the back," he says.

He kicks in the kickstand and holds the bike at the handle bars, steadying it as I hop on. He starts it up—Vroom, VVrroommm. I hold on tight to the back of the sissy bar behind my rear end. Baron Von Torchenstein shifts the bike into gear and we are off!

We soon discover that D.C. traffic is outrageous, even in the early morning hours. He cuts in and out of traffic, often passing in the fast lane on the freeway. Baron Von Torchenstein is very good at the operation of his bike. This is my first ride on a Harley. He guns the chopper down the road, switching gears and going full throttle. I hold on tight to the back of my seat, the wind rushing at my face makes my eyes water. I can feel the bike vibrating down my legs and up my back. I just watch all the scenes and traffic of early morning D.C. whiz by.

Whatever happened to all my friends? Friends from when I was a kid, friends from high school, friends from college, friends from my professional career? Displaced. Disconnected. To have a friend, I have to be a friend, and I can't be a friend if I'm not a friend to myself. But I can't run from myself—friend or no friend.

I have connected with a unique soul—science, literature, writing, philosophy. People who can converse and create amongst all these disciplines are quite rare. How did I become one of these types of people? The Great Thinkers and Great Writers have always held my sway. What is the universal essence of these common threads? Baron Von

Torchenstein has given me recharged inspirations—a soul brother, from a different mother.

We make it to our first stop—The Vietnam Veterans Memorial. We walk up and down the whole Wall. Baron Von stops at a couple of names he knows and feels the impression of their name on his finger tips.

We are silent with our heads bowed in honor of the fallen.

Then we move back down the Wall again, walking the length of the structure. A small dewdrop tear forms at the corner of the big, tough, biker, ex-marine's right eye, which he quickly wipes away.

Perhaps for some lost friends, and of reverence for those who have fallen, and those who have served, with the ultimate sacrifice of their lives.

We walk over to the Lincoln Memorial from The Vietnam Veterans Memorial Wall.

Awe-inspiring "Big Abe" sits in his chair. I stare up at the Lincoln statue for a half hour in utter silence—the greatest president in the history of the United States.

I muse on the Civil War era and what life was like for those living from 1860 to 1865.

The North versus the South. The Emancipation Proclamation. Robert E. Lee, U.S. Grant, Sherman, Gettysburg, Bull Run, Appomattox. Over 620,000 Americans died in the Civil War.

I spend another half hour just roaming around the Lincoln Statue reading inscriptions.

Baron Von is quietly sitting on the steps of the Lincoln Memorial looking out toward the Washington Monument and Capitol Hill.

Next, from here we get back on the bike and head for the Jefferson Memorial.

Baron Von says that Thomas Jefferson is one of his

"all-time greatest intellectual heroes."

Torch beams like a proud relative standing next to his world famous relation. He is more animated and full of excitement at this Memorial than at all the others combined. Usually he is quiet, somber, and respectful.

Not here.

We are the only vistors, so he starts hollering really loud up to the Jefferson statue—"Hey Thomas, tell me the story how you wrote the Declaration of Independence. Or how about the story behind the Louisiana Purchase?"

Baron Von Torchenstein beseeches the statue to talk. He wants to have a conversation with Jefferson. I shrug my shoulders and laugh at Torch, as I read all the inscriptions on the inner wall of the dome-like structure.

After we leave the Jefferson Memorial we cruise by the Washington Monument, Capitol Hill, and then the White House, down Pennsylvania Avenue.

It is now time to get back with the deadheads so we can continue our great day.

ꕥ

The rock festival market atmosphere blasts at full throttle when we pull in from our trip to D.C. on the chopper. Music! Noise! Activity and happenings!

Baron Von causes a lot of heads to turn when he goes anywhere on his bike. I watch it countless times, as people stop what they're doing and crane their necks to get a better look at his impressive Harley. The motorcycle enthusiast-types just drool with envy when looking over his machine. Baron Von Torchenstein assures me that he gets his share of wild women because of his bike.

I survey the looks of men and women alike as we coast down the aisles and rows at five-to-ten miles an hour. The flaming skull on the gas tank is like a beacon that draws everyone's eyes. I consider the women would have to be wild and daring to hang out with a character like this Baron guy.

Who else do you know who wears a spike on his helmet and names himself a Baron?

Baron Von Torchenstein pulls into our market stall camp spot. Jeff and Brandy are involved in manufacturing devil sticks. I introduce Jeff and Brandy to Baron Von Torchenstein, then as Torch, and finally as Baron Von. I let them know he prefers all three names.

"Cool name. I dig your look, man," says Jeff.

He walks over to the bike to check it out as Baron Von Torchenstein refits his spike to the top of his helmet and then puts it back on his head.

"Wow, this is awesome!" says Jeff.

"I designed and painted the flaming skull gas tank myself," says a proud Baron Von Torchenstein. "It is a time-consuming process that took a whole winter to complete in my spare time."

Jeff marvels at the bike and brushes his hand across the flaming skull. I leave Baron Von to mingle with Brandy and Jeff, while I go to my tent. I decide to take a nap. I can still feel the vibration of the motorcycle and hear the loud sound of the engine and smell the exhaust fumes of the freeway. Time to relax and recharge. I drift off to sleep.

I sleep most of the early afternoon away.

When I get up the three of them are hanging out, drinking beer, eating food, and talking. Jeff and Brandy have finished making a new batch of devil sticks. They don't know if they will go to the show, but they plan on walking around with some sticks, sell a few, then come back and get more to sell.

Baron Von Torchenstein frames his "Heaven & Hell" portrait. He has the artwork on display on the easel while preparing to varnish his wooden wizard sculpture.

"Have you ever worked on chiseling rock or marble?"

I ask.

"No," he says, "but I'd sure like to one day. Wouldn't that be a trip! I can imagine myself chiseling out a statue of myself standing next to my bike," says Baron Von Torchenstein, in total self-admiration.

He stands next to his bike posing for himself, while he looks up in the air above himself, concentrating on his artistic vision.

"What about that wooden wizard you whittled?" I ask. "It wouldn't be hard to imagine you putting that into stone marble."

Torch picks it up and fingers his miniature wooden creation, as he comes out of the momentary artistic vision. He mulls it over, studying the details, while sanding and smoothing fine points and rough edges of emphasis on his wizard.

I walk over to his newly framed portrait and study it for awhile. Jeff and Brandy come over and look at the painting with me.

"Isn't this great?" says Brandy. "Sort of scary though…"

Jeff, who is usually super-hyper and excitable about everything, is reserved and quiet in contemplation of the portrait. He stares at it and into it as if he is mystified.

Brandy pulls him away. "Come on, let's go, Jeff." She tugs at his arm. "Let's go find a miracle!"

And with that, he snaps out of his momentary reverie and the two of them rush into the throng.

"Did you see those two checking out your "Light & Dark" painting here?" I ask Baron Von.

"Yeah! I don't think they like it," he says with a boastful laugh and a shrug of his shoulders. "It's too deep for their young minds!"

Then he adds, "If I don't sell this painting before nightfall then I'm going to have to take it off the frame and role it back into the tube. I've got some money in my pocket but it would be nice to have some more."

"What are you looking for?" I ask. "I'll be your agent! We just need to find some people like those guys last night."

"What do you think—two-hundred, three-hundred dollars?" considers Baron Von Torchenstein as the two of us stand in front of his "Heaven & Hell" portrait in anticipation of the day's transaction.

"If I sell it, I'm going to find me some poon-tang tonight," Torch says with a devilish expression and a sparkling gleam in his eyes. "I'm just itching to get out and troll around. I think I might go to the last show. What are you going to do?"

"I'm just going to hang out here like yesterday and write, while checking out the ongoing festival atmosphere. We'll be heading to New York tomorrow morning. Then I'll need to catch a bus to upstate New York in Rochester," I say.

"I mean tonight?" he says. "You want to go see the Dead's last show?"

"No, not really! I saw them in Michigan. I'm low on funds," I reply. "This great gathering and loyal following of all the people out here, this rock festival atmosphere, is my Grateful Dead experience."

We hang out together the rest of the afternoon, into the early evening, before the last concert show begins. Baron Von Torchenstein finishes the varnish on his wizard sculpture and sets it in my tent to dry, and so it won't get knocked over.

We have a bite to eat and share a few beers and smoke. Baron hoots and hollers at many of the fine looking girls who walk by. The parking lot aisles are jam-packed with people moving in all directions, a constant flow of the throng.

We both notice a rich-looking, upper-class couple. He

is middle-aged and she is younger and quite-striking with her long blonde hair, short shorts, lipstick and nails. They are accompanied—slightly behind them—by another scantily dressed woman. The unattached friend is lagging back ten to fifteen feet. The two women share enough resemblance that they could be sisters.

The couple walk up to Baron Von Torchenstein's "Heaven & Hell" portrait and they are immediately transfixed—utterly fascinated!

"Is this for sale? I want this," says the guy to his girl.

The young blonde in pink hot pants, with pink wet lips and a low cleavage, a revealing chiffon blouse, nods her head in agreement.

I look over at Baron Von Torchenstein and he isn't even paying attention to these people. He is distracted by the cute friend. He keeps darting his eyes at her while the other two gawk with excitement at the painting. The young woman turns away and heads in the other direction—embarrassed—once she notices Baron Von Torchenstein's prowling stare.

I nudge him from his preoccupation.

"You can really make out here," I say. "This guy seems to be the person we are looking for. Come on over here."

I walk over to the side of the van and away from the couple staring at the portrait on the easel. Baron Von Torchenstein comes over to me but he still has his antennae out for the roaming friend who is still within eyesight.

"Hey, you want me to talk with this guy? I'll get the deal done for you!" I say.

"If you can get at least what I got yesterday, that would be cool," he says.

"All right!" I say, as we shake hands on the agreement. I leave Baron Von Torchenstein to continue his stare-down of his prey while I go over to the couple at the easel.

"Nice painting!" I say. "You want to own it?"

"How much?" asks the man.

"Make an offer! The artist will have to agree on the final price but he gave me authority to sell it," I say.

"He's the guy that painted this?" asks the girlfriend, as I point to Baron Von Torchenstein.

"Yes, he is!"

"I'll offer him a couple hundred dollars," says the man.

I shake my head 'no,' together with a wave of my finger.

"He sold a much smaller painting than this yesterday for about that much. I'm sure he wouldn't go for it," I say.

The guy and his girl step away for a brief second and whisper back and forth in each other's ear. Then they come back over to me in front of the portrait.

"I will offer him five crisp one hundred dollar bills to take it right now," says the man. "I want it for my girlfriend's apartment. It's a symbol for all the relationships I've had with women—Heaven and Hell," he laughs. His hot girlfriend playfully punches him in the arm.

"Just a minute, I need to consult with my friend," I say.

I look over to Jeff's minibus. Baron Von Torchenstein is gone. I bolt over to the other side of the vehicle and there he is talking with the woman he's been pursuing.

"Excuse me! Can we talk?" I interrupt.

"Sure, just a minute!"

Baron Von Torchenstein whispers something in her ear, then he comes over to me and we have a short discussion.

"The guy is ready to give you five-hundred bucks!" I say.

"No shit!"

"You giving me the okay?" I ask.

"Go for it!" he says.

Then he goes back to the side of the VW to visit with his new companion. I walk back over to the couple and tell them the good news!

"He says five-hundred-fifty and you've got a deal!"

The man reaches in his billfold and counts out the money and hands it to me.

"Thank you very much!"

The young girlfriend jumps up and down with excitement. "Can I get my picture with him? Can you ask him please?" she inquires.

I holler over to the vehicle for Baron. He comes around and I give him the money.

"Can you pose for a picture with your painting before they take it?" I ask.

Baron Von Torchenstein puts on his spiked helmet and stands beside his painting while the young woman snaps a few pictures with her camera. Then the two girls get in the picture with Baron Von by his motorcycle. I take a few pictures for them.

Meanwhile, the gentleman who paid me, is carrying around the painting with both hands clutching the frame, walking back and forth staring at the picture. Then he looks over at his women friends and tells them they have to go!

Baron Von Torchenstein starts packing his stuff. He's all of a sudden leaving immediately!

He comes back over and whispers to me, "The little blonde thing, the girlfriend/sister, she's staying with me on my bike. We're going for a ride, maybe to the concert, for sure to a hotel."

He's all excited and eager.

"You mean this is it—you're leaving?" I ask.

"Yeah, man! Got to go!" he says. "Here's some money for you for selling my painting."

He hands me a hundred dollar bill and a fifty dollar bill.

"Thanks! I really appreciate it! Money is tight for me too," I say. "This will get me going on the rest of my travels. Thanks again."

We give each other a big hug and a long handshake and wish each other well. "Look me up in Michigan at Lake Minnawanna," I say.

As he is getting on his bike, strapping his helmet back on after he took the spike out, his young, nubile, female friend adjusts her helmet as she sits on the back of the seat leaning against the sissy bar. She doesn't say much but she sure is good to look at.

"You ever been to Torch Lake?" asks Baron Von Torchenstein.

"I've heard of it, but I haven't been there."

"It's in northern Michigan, close to Traverse City. It's the deepest inland lake in Michigan, over 310 feet deep. Plus it's eighteen miles long," he says. "I'll be camping out there later this summer if you get a chance."

He buckles down his helmet, checks his passenger's helmet to make sure she has it on right, then he starts the engine and revs her up—Vroooom, Vrrrooommmmm—and there goes Baron Von Torchenstein.

It feels good to achieve, to be of service. I've missed these feelings of inner worth. The sale. The transaction. Magic money. Bad money. Good money. No money. Materialism. Works of art. The skillful selling of a product of creation. The high worth of the worthwhile effort.

ཀྵ

I am now alone, once again, in a sea of people. I can

hear the concert sound check from the stadium. Tonight is the end of the Grateful Dead East Coast Summer Tour—Masterpiece '93. The band is then going to take two months off before they start up in late August in Oregon and then northern California.

I learn of this earlier in the day when Jeff and Brandy are talking about it. This will be my last night with them, too. Then I will have to figure out a plan for getting to Rochester.

I've had my eyes on the lookout this entire trip for Cricket, but I haven't seen her. Several times I saw a similarly dressed resemblance to her, but upon closer inspection, it wasn't. All of Cricket's string of big parties start next week. She told me back at Lake Minnewanna, if I can get to her home within a few days after the last show, I would be around for a whole slew of parties they have planned.

It feels good to have cash in my pocket—I was nearly dead broke! Thank you, Mr. Baron Von Torchenstein. What an interesting character he is. I wonder if I will ever see him again.

When it gets late, near midnight, I go to my tent for the evening. Jeff and Brandy are still gone.

I am restless, so I get out ***Walden***.

It's too noisy, too much activity outside. I focus to close off the outer chaos to my mind.

I then flip through my notebook journal to a passage I had copied out of Baron Von Torchenstein's other book from his saddle bag by author Robert M. Pirsig, ***Zen and The Art of Motorcycle Maintenance:***

> *"I don't know of any other cyclist who takes books with him. They take a lot of space. A copy of Thoreau's* ***Walden*** *can be read a hundred times without exhaustion. I try always to pick a book far over his head and read it as*

a basis for questions and answers, rather than without interruption. I read a sequence or two, wait for him to come up with his usual barrage of questions, answer them, then read another sequence or two. Classics read well this way. They must be written this way. Sometimes we have spent a whole evening reading and talking and discovered we have only covered two or three pages. It's a form of reading done a century ago. Unless you've tried it, you can't imagine how pleasant it is to do it this way."

I transcend into the Philosophy of the Philosopher who lived along the shores of Walden Pond. Walden is a metaphor for Thoreau's exploration of the inner depths of his soul. My consciousness resonates with an equal yearning to understand my own soul. This bohemian adventure has me well on my way.

ꕥ

Chapter Seven

New York

ꕥ

Liberty of thought is the life of the soul.

—**Voltaire**

Land of Liberty

I wake up at early sunrise the next morning, having fallen asleep with ***Walden*** on my chest. I hear Jeff and Brandy getting back real late, keeping quiet and low-key. With this kind of lifestyle you sort of get in the habit of partying till you drop each day.

I was there a couple nights ago.

Now I feel all refreshed this morning. I feel in my pocket—Money! Excellent!

Now I have to break the tent down and start packing. I discover a lot of the people are already up at daybreak. Cops are walking down the rows and hollering for people to wake up. They want people to start packing and leaving. No one is moving too fast or actually leaving yet, but all the natives are stirring around.

The side door of the van opens and Jeff jumps out.

"You going to be ready to go soon, like in the next half hour?" Jeff asks, while stretching and yawning.

I am momentarily surprised at his sudden readiness to go, but I am already in the mood to get moving onto the next set of adventures.

"Sure! I'm breaking my tent down and gathering up

my stuff right now. Brandy up? Or are we going to take off and leave her sleeping?" I ask.

Just then I hear a voice from the van. "I'm up! I'll be ready to go whenever you guys are!" says Brandy.

Jeff looks at the watch on his wrist. "It's 6:20 right now. We're leaving at 7am! So if anyone has to go to the bathroom, pack, say goodbye to anyone or whatever—now's the time to do it. I'm heading several rows over to say goodbye to some friends but I'll be back before 7am. Later!"

Jeff combs his hands through his red hair, puts on a clean shirt and then takes off, jogging down the makeshift campground parking lot.

Brandy jumps out of the van. She wears a baseball cap slung low over her eyes. Jeff's coat envelopes her body as she creeps around the other side of the van to conceal herself and then hollers back over to me. "I'm heading to the bathroom! I'll be back!"

Then she scurries down the parking lot rows and cuts over to the pathway leading to the outdoor porta-johns.

I see all the people packing and moving about in their respective camp sites in the parking lot. I'm packed in the van and my two cohorts are still missing. I sit on the floor by the sliding side door and continue to muse and daydream about my adventure. I anticipate what the reunion with sparkplug Cricket will be like. I see visions or self-made visualizations in my mind of her hopping and skipping about as she converses on metaphysical wonderment and spiritual techniques, harmonious meditations, and deep discussions of great literary writers.

"Ready to go, Ted?" I hear someone holler. I look down the road and it is Jeff and Brandy, arm-in-arm.

He waves and hollers again—"Ready to go, Ted?"

"All packed up and ready!" I holler in return.

When they arrive at our venue parking spot, the three of us climb into the vehicle and take our respective positions. I put on my earphones to the walkman cassette player, listening to Pink Floyd then Led Zeppelin. Jeff pulls out of our parking space and heads for the nearest entrance to a highway. I stare out the side window at all the clans and groups and tribes of people we pass.

So long to the human zoo gathering!

We're back on the road now.

We just passed Baltimore, Maryland.

Now I'm seeing signs for Philadelphia and New Jersey.

We're heading to New York City. Jeff and Brandy want to see the Empire State Building and the Statue of Liberty. I'm coming along for the ride. This should be fun.

We soon pass a succession of signs for New York City, Manhattan, Long Island, Brooklyn Bridge, Lincoln Tunnel, George Washington Bridge, Times Square, Wall Street, Broadway. Jeff drives us out to the harbor where we can see the Statue of Liberty. I put a few quarters into the binocular-stand and proceed to look out at the statue.

From reading literature, pamphlets and placards, I find out: "This statue was a gift to the American people from France—completed in July 1884 by French Sculptor Frederic Auguste Bartyholdi. The statue was first exhibited in Paris, then dismantled and shipped to New York. It was formally dedicated on October 28, 1886 by U.S. President Grover Cleveland."

The formal name is "***Liberty Enlightening the World.***"

In 1903, the sonnet, "The New Colossus" by American Poet Emma Lazarus, was inscribed in bronze at the base of the statue. It reads:

Not like the brazen giant of Greek fame,
With conquering limbs astride from land to land;

Here at our sea-washed, sunset gates shall stand
A mighty woman with a torch, whose flame
Is the imprisoned lightning, and her name
Mother of exiles. From her beacon-hand
Glows world-wide welcome; her mild eyes command
The air-bridged harbor that twin cities frame.
"Keep, ancient lands, your storied pomp!" cries she
With silent lips, "Give me your tired, your poor,
Your huddled masses yearning to breathe free,
The wretched refuse of your teeming shore.
Send these, the homeless, tempest-tost, to me,
I lift my lamp beside the golden door!"

I look out through the binoculars and ponder what this statue symbolizes—'Freedom and Liberty!'

We are free, as individuals, to make the choices that determine our evolutionary destiny. We grow and develop or stagnate, based on our accumulative choices.

It's amazing to think that no other country in history ever offered such liberty and freedom to its populace, before the rise of America.

This freedom is precious to our growth as people, and to the attainment of deeper levels of understanding, as individual spirits in flesh.

Yes, this life is precious! I'm thankful and I am grateful our land was blessed with some amazing forefathers in those early birth years. From 1775 to 1865 the whole world of humanity changed because of what unfolded in the history of our young democratic republic. These were birthing years. It may take nine months for a human baby to form from an embryo seed—it took America ninety long years to permanently establish the Rights of Liberty and Freedom.

ᘓᘐ

Afterward, we head out to the ferries from Battery Park. We just have to see the old girl up close on Liberty Island. A short ferry ride later and we are on the island.

Jeff, Brandy and I decide to walk the outer three-hundred-fifty-four steps. It is quite demanding on all three of us as we near the top. The view of New York Harbor and New York City is spectacular. We have climbed from the pedestal to the crown of Lady Liberty.

I read placards, signage, engravings. "In 1984 the United Nations Educational Scientific and Cultural Organization designated the Statue of Liberty National Monument a World Heritage Site, and recognized it as a unique cultural site.

The statue depicts a woman escaping the chains of tyranny, which lie at her feet. She stands a stately 306 feet tall. In her right hand held aloft is the burning torch that represents Liberty. Her left hand holds a book tablet inscribed "July 4, 1776," but in Roman numerals. She is wearing flowing robes and the seven rays of her spiked crown symbolizes the seven seas and continents. The Statue of Liberty symbolizes ***Freedom*** throughout the planet."

What is harmony? What is personal security? What is inner freedom? Why do I feel so lost within myself? The struggle of the human condition—we all want security, inner freedom, harmony—but very few actually get all three. Money and wealth is not the answer. It only pretends to be the answer. It's something deeper—more soul driven—from the roots of one's being! That's it, I'm lost from the roots of my being—the soul that animates these bones and this flesh. I have a duty, a responsibility, an obligation to my spiritual nature to take ownership of this vast power within and use it wisely. 'Do it, Ted!'

I owe myself! I owe the nature of my nature as a living part of Nature!

After we get back from the ferry ride to Battery Park, we hop in the VW van and drive uptown in search of the Empire State Building. The tall edifice is located on 5th Avenue between 33rd and 34th streets.

Jeff gets us into a parking garage across the street from the majestic tower. We don't plan on climbing the stairs this time.

We take the elevator up to the observation deck. We stand in a long winding line, then stuff ourselves into the over-crowded elevator. My arms are pinned to my sides and my ears are popping as we ascend.

When we get to the observation deck, the expansive views are splendid. Awe-inspiring! Magnificent! We stay at the top of the Empire State Building for about an hour, walking all along the periphery.

Completed in 1931, the Empire State Building stands 1250 feet and has 102 stories of office space. I huddle in a corner by myself for several minutes and survey the horizon views.

I feel a vortex of energy emanating from this height. The endless people below, the surrounding buildings, streets, sidewalks and vehicles all combine to create a constant hum of vibration.

I "om" a sound from deep within my throat and visualize a universal energy from above, bursting through the crown of my head and down my spine—white sparkling hot golden flashes of light, searing through my body and down through the Empire State building, to the foundation. I feel grounded and connected, but yet boundless, free, unlimited, soaring!

"Ted, you ready to go?" says Jeff.

And just like that I lose my temporary state of

consciousness. I shake off the clouds of my imagination and step back into present reality.

"Yes, I'm ready to go! Where's Brandy?"

"She's over by the elevator standing in line waiting for us," he says.

I take one last grand look at New York City, a cosmopolitan capital to the world. I imagine the millions upon millions of individual life stories all taking place right now, below me. Stories of love and hate and anger and greed and goodwill and homelessness and power and friendship and life and death—the process of life carrying on the beat of humanity!

After we leave the Empire State Building, Jeff drives us through downtown to the Lincoln Tunnel. We cross the state line to New Jersey.

Jeff stops by the bus station and I purchase a ticket for Rochester, New York. The bus doesn't leave till late tomorrow night.

Back to the road, we exit at a nearby motel by the freeway in Secaucus, New Jersey. This is the final goodbye with Jeff and Brandy. Jeff pulls his minibus into the parking lot.

"Looks like this will be it for us, Ted," says Jeff. "You ready for the next part of your adventure?"

I gather my belongings into my backpack and open the side door to climb out. "Yes, I am! I really appreciate what you've done. I would never be able to do this type of thing without your involvement."

Jeff bolts out of his car seat and comes around to me and we embrace in a tight hug and then shake hands.

"Awe, isn't this cute," says Brandy, leaning out the passenger side window observing us. "You take care of yourself, Ted. It was nice meeting you," she says.

Jeff motions for her to get out of the van and come

over to us. The three of us have a group hug and then individual hugs and handshakes again.

"You can keep the dumbbells I brought with me, and the cooler. I won't be able to travel with those things anymore," I say to Jeff. "Now that I'm losing my chauffer, I've got to travel lighter."

Then Jeff secretly hands me something just before he gets back in the VW to leave—it's two hits of LSD.

"Thanks, but I'm not into this stuff," I say.

I attempt to give it back but he brushes me off.

"Keep it! You may decide to change your mind and try it one day," he says.

Jeff offered several times before but I always declined.

I put the LSD in my pocket. And then just like that they are gone and I am alone, looking out onto a sixteen-to-twenty lane freeway. My bohemian road trip is twisting off in a new direction of adventure, discovery, experience and wonder.

I check into the hotel and shower, get a quick bite to eat and fall asleep with the TV on.

ꙮ

The next day I take a cab to the bus station in mid-afternoon. My bus doesn't leave until near midnight. I sit around all day reading newspapers, magazines, a book, and eating from vending machines.

I drift in and out of daydreams at various times throughout my long day, pondering my experiences in the last couple of weeks. This bohemian adventure of mine is going further into uncharted territories, causing me to speculate and wonder what new experiences await me.

When the bus finally departs I fall fast asleep. When I wake up it is daylight and I am in Rochester, New York.

After I get my baggage and gear I call up Cricket from

a nearby phone booth. She answers the phone and I tell her I am at the bus station.

"Ted! You really came here! I'm so excited, I can't believe it!" she shrieks. "I'm getting ready to come down and pick you up right now!"

Click.

I replace the phone in the cradle, gather my backpack of stuff and go outside to wait for Cricket.

To have a friend you've got to be a friend. These people have such genuine sincerity. This is not how it works in the mainstream, the "real" world. Most people are out to use others, to disparage, to criticize, to judge, argue, disagree and hate. The basic instincts override the finer points. Why is this so? This community of gatherers sense this egregious error to the natural flow. Love, harmony, peace and compassion is a fireball of energy that flows like a current through this counter-culture, in spite of the currents of mainstream. People connecting with people—friends of friends of friends…

Ten minutes later and here she is once again. Cricket wears a big oversized gypsy flower dress. She is still full of a vibrant bounce, happy, joyful, enthusiastic—just pure kinetic energy! We hug and kiss like two long-lost great friends.

I load my stuff in her car, an early 80's dark brown Oldsmobile, a big boat vehicle. She drives a few minutes, makes several turns and then parks the car on a side street.

"Let's get out and take a walk, Ted."

We get out of the car. She locks it up and then we walk down the sidewalk together.

"How has your adventure been so far? Did Jeff come back and pick you up in Michigan and take you out to D.C.?"

"Yes, he did, just like he promised he would. I looked for you out in D.C., but that was an absolute madhouse of activity. I knew it would be tough to find you. Several times I thought someone was you, then as I got closer I realized that it wasn't you," I say.

"We only stayed for the first show and then we had to get back home. Did you enjoy the trip and the traveling?" asks Cricket.

"Yes! Jeff had a new sidekick, Brandy. He dropped off his buddy in Buffalo and met her and they seemed to be very attached to each other. I've been having a great time!"

"And now you're here with me!"

She jumps in the air and skips ahead and twirls in a pirouette as I catch up with her along the sidewalk.

"The next two weeks are going to be so fun, Ted! I have so many plans in the works. I promise you will never regret you made this trip!"

We walk down some more side streets and then we enter a back alley. "Where you taking us?" I ask.

"Come on, Ted, don't worry, this is a shortcut!" I continue to follow her down the long back alley way. We pass a couple poor beggars. Cricket walks up to them and places her hand on each of their heads—calls them by name and drops some change into their cup.

She does this same act three separate times with the bums she meets. I stand off to the side and watch her go about her business. The first couple of times she does this, I am quiet and follow along. Each of the winos are meek, docile and receptive to her.

When she rejoins me on the third instance of this behavior I ask her, "Why do you do this? Aren't you afraid of these people and this environment?"

"No, Ted! I have no fear! I have compassion for people who are stuck in this self-destructive way of life.

My heart goes out to them."

"Why do you put your hand on their head?"

"To pray for them and bless them with positive energy. I visualize my goodwill energy going through the crown of their head. Maybe one day, one individual at a time, they will take hold of their mind and make positive choices in life. I pray for this to happen to each one of them."

Then we come upon two winos, drunk and mean. They start swearing and hollering at us. One guy bluffs to charge, and Cricket goes right after him, hissing and screeching ungodly sounds.

He stops in his tracks. The two men turn around and run away from Cricket. She comes back huffing and puffing in her steel-toed black army boots.

"Most people are just innocent lost children. Life is a series of struggles. I try to assist those people and give them hope to find a better way," says Cricket.

"And then you have people like those two guys," I say.

"Oh, they're harmless—I know them. They just want to test me sometimes," she says.

"Yeah, but you could get mugged, raped, beat up, and abused, quite easily."

"I know how to handle myself around people, Ted! This is my home turf! I know that a vast number of people in the world are bloodsuckers and leeches with evil karma. They prey on the weaknesses and fears of others. I will always refuse to submit to these types of people. They only have power because our fears give them power."

We continue on through the alley way and back through a neighborhood. After a couple more blocks we arrive in a small-town commercial section of the city—multiple coffee houses, bookstores, cafés, and record shops.

"This is the 'Greenwich Village' of Rochester," she says, "artists, musicians, poets, writers, and deep thinkers, congregate around this section of the city."

We walk through a coffee house and she introduces me to several people. She tells everyone we meet that I'm a writer she met on her deadhead adventures.

Cricket whispers to me as we are leaving the coffee shop. "Most of these people have very interesting life stories. Very creative. They're all seekers—Bohemians."

Then she says in a louder voice as we're back on the sidewalk, "Bohemian, Ted! Bohemians just like you, like us!"

Then she skips and twirls up ahead. We visit a couple of bookstores, a record shop, and a couple more coffee houses. Cricket introduces me to dozens of people. She parades me around like I am a famous celebrity or something. She keeps telling people I am her honored guest. She overly exaggerates my writing skills. I feel embarrassed and humbled from her repeated praise of me to those we meet. I feel like I must say something great and profound to back up what she says. But I choose to just keep quiet mostly, and just follow her around. We spend a couple of hours at record shops and then a couple more at bookstores. Cricket knows everybody no matter where we go.

Have I always been introverted? I know I'm quiet and don't talk much, but I used to talk all the time and where did it get me? Am I a loner or do I just need long periods of being alone? Cricket is the polar opposite of me—but yet I feel a strong kinship and deep commonalities.

When I first met Cricket I could tell that she is totally unique from all the others in the deadhead following. That is saying a lot, because all these deadheads are unconventional and unique in their own ways. Cricket just stands out from all of them. Now, I'm here on her home turf and I see that her unique authentic self still applies.

ꟷ

Cricket and I walk back to her car. She says it's time to go home and get me unpacked and settled in. Off we go through the town and into the neighborhoods.

She pulls into the driveway of her home and I'm flabbergasted!

It's a huge structure—well over ten thousand square feet of room—a late 1800's built Victorian-type mansion. There are four floors and a basement, plus a huge enclosed wraparound deck patio porch. The back yard has a rock and water garden pond with tiny waterfalls and goldfish.

I follow her up to the fourth floor, where Cricket gives me one end of the attic room to store my stuff and a couch that pulls into a bed. She even has an empty chest of drawers for me to unpack my clothes and toiletries. She then takes me out to the far corner of her backyard and tells me I can pitch my tent there. These two spots will be my home base while I'm here.

I start setting up my tent right away. Cricket leaves me alone to go back in the house to prepare dinner.

After dinner Cricket wants to walk the neighborhood. We finish our little barbecue out back and she is ready to go. She wears a huge empty cloth bag slung over her shoulder. The bag is full of various rainbows, custom-made artwork.

"What is that for?" I ask.

"To carry things. Come on, let's go—you'll see!" she says.

Every house we saunter by has someone outside doing yard work or sitting on their porch relaxing. It is a warm, muggy summer evening. Cricket waves, smiles, and greets everyone as we walk the sidewalks of the neighborhood. In between all this repeated activity, she is giving me a running take on all the plans, events and things that will be happening in the next two weeks.

"There will be an endless stream of parties and celebrations, reunions! People are coming from all over the country," she says.

"When is your big wedding event?" I ask.

"That's not till the end of next week. We have a lot of other things lined up that lead into that. Everything is planned out and scheduled. The culmination will be my wedding to Peter beside a beautiful waterfall in the Finger Lakes region," she says.

Our first stop is at Pete's house—Cricket's traveling companion with Mignon when I first met them at Lake in Michigan. She walks up to the porch and knocks on the door until Pete appears.

We shake hands, and I congratulate him on his impending wedding. He looks at me quizzically.

"Do you know something I don't?"

"You and Cricket are getting married, right?"

I question the two of them with a look. I am met with a bursting laugh-out-loud response from Cricket and Pete. I am confused…

"This isn't the Pete I'm going to marry. We're just real good friends," Cricket says.

Pete shakes his head in agreement.

"You will meet Peter tonight when he gets home from work."

I scratch my head in disbelief. "All this time I've been thinking that the two of you were getting married, ever since you gave me the invitation in fact."

They both laugh heartily at my mistaken assumption.

"Pete doesn't want to get married. His life is his music," Cricket says.

"Besides, Cricket wouldn't have me anyway," Pete jokes.

"Come on in my house and visit for awhile." He opens the screen door and we follow him in.

When we first walk up to Pete's porch I notice a big striking gold, green and red plant. It looks like a seven-foot tall marijuana plant. I ask Pete about it. "Is that what I think it is?"

"His name is Herb!" says Pete, with a snickering grin. "He's a male pot plant!"

"Herbert!" says Cricket.

The two of them burst out laughing with their inside joke. Here we are in a neighborhood in front of a house and this guy has a tree stalk of a pot plant out front for everyone to see. I've heard of liberal places and states, but this doesn't measure up.

"Rochester isn't Amsterdam, so how come you can do this out in the open?" I ask Pete.

"I can grow it because it's a male plant. It has no THC properties. You can't get high from smoking it, in other words," Pete says. "I've had it for several years now. I dig it up and bring it in the house for the winter. It's my family pet."

We all laugh while we look out at Herbert through the bay window in his living room. The plant looks all shiny, vibrant and healthy. It seems to assume an air of conscience, standing proudly and erect. Pete has two long boards of wood with white cloth wrapped around the lower stalk to help support the weight.

"I got in a lot of trouble when I first decided to grow and replant Herb. I had to sign some papers at the courthouse and tell the cops and have chemical composition testing to prove Herbert here is devoid of

THC. Then they gave me my permit—reluctantly I might add. Everyone loves Herbert. He's the most popular thing in nature on my whole block."

"He's turned into a freak of nature!" I say. "I've never seen anything like it! He looks mystical."

Herbert's breadth of span is expansive, taking up the whole front bay window of Pete's brick ranch home. The multi-colored hues of green, golden yellow, and red, unfurl, taut as an umbrella, shimmy in the soft wind.

Pete leaves Cricket and me standing outside with Herbert, while he gets us each a soft drink. He comes back with his guitar strapped around his back. We follow him into the house and Cricket and I watch Pete strum and sing a Bob Dylan tune. Cricket passes around her purple whale.

Pete starts another tune and Cricket interrupts him.

"We've got to go! I just wanted to stop by and let you see that Ted is in town. Sorry to rush along."

I say goodbye to Pete and go back outside on the porch to look at Herbert. Cricket hangs out in the house for several minutes talking with Pete. When she comes out her big rainbow bag is stuffed with clothes. Pete has given her a bag of clothes and discards for charity.

We continue walking down the sidewalks and streets. Cricket greets and gestures hello to most of the people along the way. She keeps picking up clothes and garments from friends and neighbors as we proceed down the streets. Cricket barely weighs a hundred-ten pounds, and her overstuffed rainbow bag is as big as she is, it seems.

I finally take the rainbow bag off her and put it on my shoulders to carry. So here I am, with a big stuffed rainbow bag, walking the streets of Rochester, New York.

"What are we going to do with this stuff?" I ask.

"We have a special place to visit. We'll be there in a few more blocks," she says.

When we arrive at her destination point, I see a cement slab building in a field, full of weeds, and grass taller than us. There must be a dozen broken down vehicles strewn around the property. There are kid's playthings and toys in several areas of the unkempt yard. No one is around. Cricket directs me to a chair by the front door and she neatly takes out each piece of clothing and refolds it, and stacks the clothes in a neat pile on the chair. She empties out the whole rainbow bag.

Then she skips along with a big smile on her face and we're off down the driveway, down the street, across the road, heading home on foot.

It's dark now. Cricket's excited about all the parties coming up. She tells me once again how elated she is that I found a way to get here. We talk about the rest of the Grateful Dead Masterpiece '93 Tour. I tell her about meeting Baron Von Torchenstein in D.C. Then I tell her about Jeff and Brandy and the day we woke up in Frederick, Maryland—and poor dead Hugh.

"I heard other people talking about that at the end of the tour in D.C. I couldn't believe how a bus tire could roll over someone's head," she says. "I thought it was just a rumor!"

"It was for real and it happened that morning of the first show in D.C. It was very eerie at the rest stop, with the helicopter, all the cops and ambulances, and all the grieving people. Jeff took it real hard. He was a friend of Hugh's."

"The whole thing seems senseless to me," Cricket says.

We continue walking down the sidewalks and through the neighborhoods.

"Why was he there?" she asks.

"That's the big question that everybody wanted to know. Hugh only knows for sure and he isn't around to tell about it. Jeff, Brandy and I talked it over and we figured he partied all day and had nowhere to sleep when he was ready to crash so he crawled under the bus to keep warm and propped his head up against the tire as a pillow. When the bus driver started the bus in the morning and took it out of park, the wheel rolled back and pinned his head and his skull cracked open. It was a terrible sight."

"You know, Ted," she says, "life is so precious. Each one of us has been granted God's greatest gift just by being born. We have so much promise, hope and potential. It's frightening to see so much quality wasted. People do it all the time. I'm not just talking about Hugh, but life in general," says Cricket.

"I know where you're coming from," I say. "Life is an honor. More people need to see it that way."

ꕥ

When we get back to the house it is dark and late.

Peter is home. I meet him out back by the rock garden waterfall pond as he is feeding the fish and enjoying a beer.

Cricket immediately excuses herself for the rest of the evening, after introducing us, and leaves the two of us out back to visit.

"What do you do for a living to afford such a property as this?" I ask.

"I'm the Head Chef at a Spaghetti Warehouse Restaurant."

"No way!" I say in disbelief.

He laughs and shrugs his shoulders.

"You can really afford all this being a chef?"

"No, no, no—I'm only pulling your leg, joking around. I have a Masters degree in Engineering. I made a lot of money at a firm for five years after graduation. Lynn and I bought this place with cash. I just have taxes and maintenance upkeep. I quit my engineering job because I was burning out. I didn't like the long hours, corporate greed and office politics. The money was great but I had to get out for my own sanity."

"How long you been working as a Chef?"

"Not even two years. I basically manage the place. Plus I have flex hours and can take a vacation whenever I want. I can support us and keep this place going with that job."

"Don't you miss engineering work?" I ask.

"Sometimes, but not really," he says. "What I miss most is the money! I've thought about starting my own engineering firm one day. I still might. But for now this is just fine!"

Peter is thirty years old but he looks like a teenager. He wears curly brown bushy hair, rosy cheeks, hardly any stubble for whiskers, except on his chin and under his nose, a patch. With a six-foot two-inch athletic physique, Peter is youthful, laid back of personality, and a calm presence.

"How did you and Cricket meet?"

He laughs when I call her Cricket.

"That's Deadhead moniker," he says, "and I don't subscribe to any of that. She's Lynn to me."

"You mean you're not a deadhead?"

"Not really. I have my own music I like and the Grateful Dead don't do anything for me, if you know what I mean. Don't get me wrong—I think it's great with the loyal following they have, but it's not for me," Peter reiterates.

"What kind of stuff do you listen to?" I ask.

"Stevie Ray Vaughn, Jimi Hendrix, The Doors. I enjoy listening to some head-banging stuff now and then like AC/DC, Metallica, Pantera."

"So you and Cricket have multiple varied interests then."

"Yes—Lynn and I do! We met when I was in graduate school seven, eight years ago, when I was twenty-three or twenty-four. I saw this skinny blond-haired girl walking across the street from the campus and she was playing a flute like the Lone Pied Piper. She was all by herself. I went and flagged her down, invited her for a hot cocoa and once we started talking we have never stopped. People always comment on how different we are from each other, but we get along great and have a lot in common."

"Did Lynn tell you anything about me and how we met? You do know she's letting me stay here and sleep in my tent in your yard and keep some of my stuff upstairs?"

"Yeah, she told me about you. I figured she would already have you settled in. Lynn tells me about all kinds of people she meets and befriends. Every day is filled with new stories, new people, and the familiar ones she mentions often," says Pete. "She's talked to me about you. Are you the bohemian writer philosopher who lives out in the woods in Michigan?"

"I suppose that description could resemble me. I've actually had a former career in the automotive and banking industries as a Computer Programmer and then a Project Manager. I guess I'm sort of in denial of that right now, and I'm running in a new direction," I say.

"I'd heard that you wrote and read poetry and writings and quotes from great thinkers. That's what Lynn said anyway. She actually raves on about her times in Michigan on the recent trip with the deadheads, more so than she does about all the other places. Whatever happened had a positive impact on her memory."

"Why didn't you go with her on the trip?" I ask.

"Somebody has to stay and hold down a job and take care of this house and property," Peter says. "Like I said, I'm not a deadhead anyway. I've spent all summer thus far working on my pond project."

We're standing beside the pond looking at the water and the goldfish and the miniature waterfall.

"It's only been operational for two days now," says Peter.

He kneels down to feel the temperature in the water and to adjust some yard lights.

"The landscaping and everything looks beautiful," I say.

"Thanks! You wouldn't believe all the work and planning it took—subcontractors, a mini-bull dozer with a scoop, piles of dirt and stone, stacks of wood, power tools everywhere. It was a mess and a big headache!" Peter says.

"Everything looks great now! I wouldn't have suspected any of that if you hadn't told me. You did a great job!" I say.

"Thanks, man, I really appreciate the compliment!"

I tell Peter how I got him mixed up with Pete. How I assumed Cricket was getting married to Pete because they were always together when I met them at Lake Minnawanna. Peter gets a big kick out of this.

"Pete has been a friend of ours for many years. He can't find a woman to marry because all he loves is music. He doesn't have time for a relationship."

"Cricket, er Lynn and me, stopped by Pete's house for a visit earlier this evening," I say. "They both got a big laugh at my expense too, when I thought they were going to be the newlyweds."

We share another hearty laugh and then Peter excuses himself to go to bed. It's past midnight.

I go out to my tent and crawl into my sleeping bag. I stare out the mesh screen at the stars twinkling in the dark sky. Here I am in Rochester, New York.

ꟷꟷ

"All that mankind has done, thought, gained or been: it is lying as in magic preservation in the pages of books. They are the chosen possession of man."

—Thomas Carlyle

The next morning Cricket tells me that she will be busy and gone most of the day.

"Peter sleeps in late then gets up at mid-afternoon to get ready for work. You may see him just before he leaves," she says. "Other than that, please make yourself at home, Ted. On my chest of drawers upstairs, I put a stack of books from my personal library that I thought you might be interested in."

And then Cricket rushes out the door and is gone on her way. I go upstairs to check out the books. My day is set now. I'll just sit outside and read books and flip pages for the entire day.

When I get upstairs I see that she isn't kidding! There must be forty books stacked ten to a column in four columns.

I start looking at the titles and authors—Voltaire, Virgil, Dante, Milton, Shakespeare, Montaigne, Homer, Plato, Aristotle, books on History, Culture, Rock and Roll, The Grateful Dead, Art, Poetry, Literature, Buddha, Lao-Tzu, Baba Ram Dass, Confucius, Goethe. I spot an empty box and fill it with the books.

I need to make a couple trips. I drop off the first load of books on the patio table out back by the rock garden waterfall pond. I take the second box load of books to the deck on the front porch. I spend all morning, the entire afternoon, and well into the evening, reading alone, by myself, no conversation with anyone.

I catch sudden epiphanies by the hour it seems. Some great personage of thought and literary talent has me beaming bright as I acknowledge the swift suddenness of universal understanding.

I scatter my mind and eyes all over the pages in the books. I have a ready pen to write when the inspirations command. The recesses of my inner world expand to a boundless infinitude…

I discover I've only begun to learn. I've set myself on a path of self-learning—no educational institution or business environment can provide the direction for my self-growth. Only I can properly direct my learning. This is my obligation, my duty to myself. The power of creating demands a consistent focus. This much about myself I find to be true!

ജഗ

Chapter Eight

The Big House Party

ജഗ

"Strangers passing in the street
By chance two separate glances meet
And I am you and what I see is me."

—Pink Floyd
Echoes

The next morning I met Cricket out on the patio for coffee. She and Peter will be gone most of the day running last minute errands and preparation for the party week.

"People are going to start arriving today, tonight and tomorrow, and just keep on arriving!" Cricket says, as she settles into the porch swing with her mug in hand. "I expect us to get over a hundred people here along American Bald Eagle Street, with some of my close neighbors, and especially here at my home. Your moments of solitude are about to end, Ted!"

"So the big time parties that you've been talking about are about to begin!" I say.

"Not all at once, but when the parties get rocking I promise you the entire property—all four floors, the backyard, porch deck, garage, patio—will all be hopping with frenzied activity. It's going to start happening soon. You'll probably see a lot of people drunk and passed out all over in the next week," Cricket boasts.

"This is what I made the big cross-country trek for—Cricket's Great Adventure Party!" I put my hands to my mouth to echo my words as an announcer. "Cricket's Great Adventure Party! Come one, come all, to the week-long festival!"

She claps with much enthusiasm, enjoying my little play on her grand events! We both enjoy a few smiling cackles in anticipation of what lies ahead.

"You will need to pace yourself, Ted! There'll be lots of tents outside where you have yours set up. It will eventually look like a little campground community. There's going to be so much lively energy! You'll need to pace yourself!" she warns again.

"Now, don't start playing 'Mother Hen' on me!" I say.

"Yeah! You're right! I know!"

Cricket shakes her head and rolls her eyes in self-admonishment. Then she quickly changes the subject.

"So what did you think of all the books I loaded you down with yesterday?"

"I spent the entire day—at least a solid ten or eleven hours—reading and writing, mostly reading and skimming over things. So much knowledge and information—I plan on doing the same thing again today!"

"I won't be gone as long today as I was yesterday. Maybe we can do something interesting this evening, like talk about books, sitting around in my third floor library, passing around the purple whale. You can tell me some of the things you've read and decided to write about. Maybe I can read some more of your journal notebooks."

"Sure! I'm there! Count me in!" I say. "That would be a fine plan."

"You're going to meet a lot of interesting people in the next week. My uncle—the Professor, my brother, Don—he's an airline pilot, my Mom and Dad, Peter's parents, musicians, poets, counter-culture thinkers, hippies, deadhead historians, rainbow families, and all of my best friends."

Then Cricket twirls around in a pirouette on the patio.

"I need to get going, Ted."

She reaches over to me on the porch swing chair, leans over and hugs me and kisses my forehead.

"I'll see you later, Ted."

Cricket scurries off the porch and down the sidewalk to her car in the driveway. I wave as she pulls away and honks goodbye. I soon find myself staring into space.

> *Great Cricket! She knows. She's in touch with the hidden unseen. Inner presence! Full of life-giving energy! Spread the love. Spread the peace. Spread the wings of hope and fly through eternal infinity. We are all connected—all connected as one great big human family. A loving member, I am.*

Meanwhile, I get back to the writing and reading routine I had going the day before. I go back in the house and bring a pile of books to the front deck, and then I go back in the house and take another stack of books out back in the patio area by the rock garden, goldfish, and mini-waterfall.

I sit out here and flip through page upon page of literature. Then I switch up after a couple hours and go to the front deck and do the same thing. I pass the rest of the morning and the early afternoon hours in this manner.

ജ്ഞ

Cricket gets back around three-thirty in the afternoon with a car load of people. At the time they pull in I am sitting on the front porch deck with my stack of books. I'd been reading Goethe and Voltaire all afternoon. I spent the morning hours out back in the pages of **Sartor Resartus** by Carlyle. I still have several more books slated to crack into.

Cricket parks in the driveway and all four doors fly open at once. She has four passengers, three females and a guy. One of the women in the back seat, bolts out of the car and runs up to the porch at me—it's Mignon!

We embrace and hug. She kisses me on both cheeks. This woman defines 'beauticious' with her dark-haired, full-bodied, allure.

"It's so good to see you, Ted! I've been looking forward to visiting with you again and having fun like we did in Michigan several weeks back. Let me introduce you to some of our friends—this is Jason, Millie and Lois."

I nod my head to each person and shake hands.

Millie is the first one of the three who I speak with at length. She is short and plump with straight dishwater colored hair which she rolls in a bun and pins to her head. She is smiling and gregarious, where as, her other two friends are quiet and reserved.

"We heard a lot of good things about you, Ted! You like to write and read a lot, Cricket says. You have any published material?"

I feel a slight flush to my face over the compliment, or is it the question?

"Other than a few poetry contests and some creative writing classes in college—I don't have anything on the market that you've read!"

"Cricket calls you Bohemian Ted!" Millie says with a big admiring smile on her face.

"How do you know Cricket?" I ask.

"I'm her big witch sister! She did tell you that she is a witch? I'm a witch, Lois is a witch and Mignon is a witch in training!"

Millie giggles and looks mischievous in her playful banter. I don't know how to take her statements on witchery, so, I avoid the obvious bait into the occult by declaring: "It's always good to learn and grow and use knowledge positively."

Cricket, Lois and Jason have gone into the house together after we are initially introduced, while Mignon and Millie sit out on the front porch wraparound deck visiting with me. They ask how I traveled there and I tell them about my ride from Michigan to D.C. to New York and then the subsequent bus trip to Rochester.

"Are you ready for all the big parties and get-togethers? You've arrived at a perfect time, Ted. All this stuff has been in the planning stage for a long time," says Mignon.

"Yeah, we have more things going than is possible to do," says Millie. "I'm not going to be able to make each event, night after night, day after day—too much stuff!"

Cricket whistles and motions from the front door for us to join them inside, to come in and get some refreshments and then come back to the living room, because she has some things she wants to say to all of us together.

I follow Millie and Mignon into the house, get a glass of tea and then sit on the couch in the first floor living room next to Jason. Holding his breath, Jason hands me the lit purple whale. We pass the whale back and forth a few times.

The women are still congregated in the kitchen.

"So, you live around here Jason, or did you come from somewhere across the country like I did?"

"I'm originally from Rochester, but I hitch-hiked all the way from Duluth, Minnesota to get here for this long party week. I rode all the way here with truckers. It took me half-a-dozen rides. I wouldn't miss this for anything!" he boasts. "I've known Cricket for a long time and she's like a sister to me."

"She has a special way about herself—that's for sure!"

I say. "Did she tell you how we met at Lake Minnawanna in Michigan?"

"Sure! On the Dead tour! Isn't she a riot on a Grateful Dead Tour?"

Jason bursts out loud laughing in recall of some distant experience with Cricket. I join in with a nod of my head and a few chuckles of my own. He takes another hit from the purple whale and passes the pipe to me. Then all the women come back into the living room. I can tell something is up the way they all march into the room and take their seats and look over to Cricket.

Cricket announces to all of us that she wants to have a Symposium in her third floor library.

"I have large wine goblets, garland and ivy leaves, and all the women have agreed to change into toga sheets. We want to recreate an ancient Greek tradition—a 'Drink and Think Party!' I've nominated you to be the facilitator, Ted. You can't turn me down and you must play," she says.

"Sounds like fun," I reply.

Cricket already knows I'm deep into philosophy because we talked about Plato, Aristotle, Socrates and Pythagoras around the campfire a few weeks ago. The timeless truths of ancient wisdom have always been a great topic of interest to me.

ᘐᘏ

This is my first time checking out the third floor of Cricket's home. Ever since I came here I stay mainly outside, downstairs, or walk up the stairs to my corner on the fourth floor. This is a very big house. They have over twenty-two hundred square feet of space on each floor. When Cricket opens the door to her library I am literally flabbergasted.

The long walls that run the length of the house are filled from floor to ceiling with bookshelves full of books.

"I have over three thousand book titles! I've been building my personal library and collecting books since my early teens, close to half my life. When I'm old and grey I hope to have over ten thousand books in my collection," says Cricket.

"You'll have to make your whole house into a library then," I joke.

Cricket snickers, "Yeah, that's what Peter is worried about!"

Jason comes up the stairs with a crate of ten wine bottles from the cellar in the basement.

Cricket and the girls go to change.

Jason and I decline to wear a toga, even though the girls keep urging us on. I start scanning the bookshelves—History, Art, Literature, Ancient Civilizations, The Pyramids, Stonehenge, Atlantis, Encyclopedia collections, technical computer engineering manuals, et cetera. It just goes on and on from floor to ceiling, everything is categorized and has its own section. She even has a checkout sheet pegged to a corkboard, with book titles and signatures and the date the books were loaned out. Very efficient! The library has me in a state of shock and awe.

So this is where Cricket got the stack of books she left me a couple days ago. This helps to explain her wonder and knowledge and curiosity of people and things.

The women all come back dressed like they are ready for the movie "Animal House."

Cricket and Mignon put a garland and ivy wreath on my and Jason's heads. Cricket says to everyone in a loud voice, "We have to have ground rules in order for this to work and be fun. No one can use the words 'God' or 'Religion' and we can't speak about 'Sex.' If anyone breaks the rules they have to drink a full goblet of wine."

"What about 'sex' that we can't speak of?" questions Mignon.

"Anything about sex: having it, doing it, referring to it—gay, lesbian or straight—no talking about sex!" Cricket says. "What's so hard to understand about that?"

"Yeah, Mignon!" says Jason jokingly.

Followed by Millie and Lois, "Yeah Mignon! No Sex!"

Mignon playfully puckers her lower lip in mock exasperation.

Cricket's next rule is that whoever has the floor to speak about their chosen subject in the Symposium, has a time limit. She picks up a small hour glass filled with pink sand.

"This is a ten-minute glass. There are six of us, so in approximately one hour, all of us will have had a chance to speak."

Jason uncorks several bottles of wine and fills up the goblets. The couch is shaped into a big "U" facing the books on the opposite wall. A large table is in the middle of the couch area for everyone to put their drink, papers, pens, books, and index cards.

Cricket asks me to give a brief summation of the original Symposium with Socrates.

I tell the group about the unique drinking and thinking parties of ancient Greece.

"In the dialogue entitled, The Symposium, by the Philosopher Plato, he gives a fictional account of notable fifth century-B.C. Athenians meeting to drink and have an intellectual discussion. The central activity is the semi-ritualistic drinking of wine as the discussion flows."

"Here! Here!" everyone shouts, raising their glasses.

I continue, "In Plato's account the subject is Eros or

Love. Each person at the party gives their take on the meaning of Love. The last person to speak on the subject is Socrates. Then a drunk reveler, Alcibiades, comes in to interrupt and join the party. All he wants to talk about is Socrates," I say.

"Okay, that's enough, Ted. Does everyone get the point?" Cricket says as she hands out small two-by-four-inch index cards that are passed around to each of us.

"Your goal is to write down the subject you want to talk about. You can say anything about the topic that you want, except for the two words and one subject." Cricket adds, "If you get caught you lose your turn to continue speaking and you have to down a whole goblet full of wine. Everybody understand?"

We all nod and gesture in agreement.

We pass the purple whale around, drink from our goblets, and decide on some topics and notes to jot on our index cards.

Jason volunteers to speak first.

He announces his topic, "Killing the Earth or Saving the Planet."

Each of us writes the name of his topic on an index card.

Jason is twenty-eight years old. He wears real long dishwater blonde hair that is always in a tight ponytail that extends past the midpoint of his back. He's tall and slender at six-feet two. He plays a bass guitar and rhythm guitar at night clubs for odd jobs.

Cricket turns over the ten-minute hour glass. Jason gets out of his seat and goes over to the open area in front of the bookshelves. He paces back and forth and uses hand gestures as he speaks.

"I'm concerned that humanity is sucking all the oil out of the planet. The earth needs the oil," he says, "for lubrication from the friction of the energy produced by nature." Jason talks about Greenpeace and other planetary causes. "I'm also concerned about the ozone layer and green house gases."

He casually mentions the word "God" in his long-winded dissertation.

"You're out," I say, "and drink your full goblet of wine, Jason!"

The whole group of us laugh, as Jason downs his wine. As the facilitator I call on the next person to speak.

"It's Millie's turn. You have the option to continue speaking about Jason's subject or choose a new subject to speak on," I say.

She chooses "Witchcraft and Tarot Cards."

Each of us writes the subject down on our index card. Cricket turns down the timer device and Millie begins.

"I like the camaraderie I have with other witches. It's fun to learn about herbs and potions and star charts. I like reading tarot cards for people and helping them discover their way in life." She talks till her ten minutes run out with the last granule of pink sand.

It is now Lois' turn to speak. She chooses "Witchcraft and Crystal Balls," as her topic to speak about. Lois enjoys scaring people who are afraid of witches. She wears a dark gothic look: black hair, black pants, black blouse, black boots. Lois even wears black finger nail polish and outlines her lips with black.

"I'm not evil but if people want to think that, it's their problem!" Lois says. She talks about her black crystal ball. How sometimes she is able to see visions of things in the crystal ball. "I can be a good medium. I'm learning to channel in my trance state. I need to become mentally stronger and trust myself more often. I'm still learning to become a better witch."

Her time runs out.

Now it's Mignon's turn. She wants to talk about "Flower Children" and touring with "The Dead." This was her first tour and she loved it—changed her life, she says.

"I love the whole idea of being a flower child—perfect harmony and bliss and peace with all nature and people. It's groovy man, just spreading vibrations of love! I feel closer to earth, nature, the wilderness, other people, friends!" says Mignon with a big pearly white smile of perfectly formed teeth. "I love life and I love God."

A big shout goes up in the library as we all catch Mignon's mistake at the same time that she discovers she made the mistake and broke a rule of the game.

We all cheer her on as she drinks down her goblet of wine. The Symposium continues to move right along.

ꕥ

Taking a short break, we pass the purple whale around the U-shaped couch several times until it is now Cricket's turn. Her topic is "Rainbow Families."

She calls the rainbow families "The Purveyors of Living Light."

Cricket dashes back and forth and pirouettes around her library. Like a whirling dervish she rushes from one end to the other—a free-spirit child in her play land. Mignon turns the sand glass timer over and Cricket begins.

She positions a four-step foot ladder in the center of all of us gathered around her on the couch. She climbs to the third step and looks out upon us and speaks.

"The rainbow families pray for the planet in national forests around the country and the globe. We stand for positive causes that benefit the welfare of the environment. The rainbow families believe in intentional community building because of their passion and commitment to principles. 'Do the right thing by others, always.' This burgeoning community of like-minded brotherhood and sisterhood are the purveyors of living light!"

I look around at each of the people on the couch listening to Cricket with me: Lois, Millie, Mignon and Jason. Everyone's presence is wired into Cricket. We collectively look at this petite woman up on her ladder, with a group-minded sense of wonder.

Cricket has cast a spell on us all with her passion and compassion for others! She is an authentic soul up on her soap-box preaching.

"The vast majority of humanity is in an un-awakened state. Spiritual literature abounds that alludes to this psychic slumber. Humankind has forsaken the grains of knowledge and kernels of wisdom that nature has bestowed upon them because they choose to reside on barren soil and desert sands," Cricket says.

Cricket bemoans the fact of how hard it is to make positive change for the good in society because of all the negative forces at play.

"There is a vortex of energy in society that serves as a challenge to overcome against all odds. 'Do the right thing in the right way at the right time.' This is not easy, but we shall overcome. The rainbow families will continue to pray for the planet and the people who occupy it."

When her time runs out she says, "All hold hands in a daisy chain and say a prayer for the planet."

We do.

Then she directs us all to join in and repeat, "Please God, Help Us! Amen."

All six of us toast, repeat the words, and down our goblets of wine.

Then we pass the purple whale around.

It is now my turn to speak.

I choose the great admonition from the ancient philosophs: "Know Thyself."

I get off the corner of the couch and step into the open area to begin my ten minute oratory. Cricket suggests I can use her little step ladder as she had. I hesitate briefly to consider it before I ascend the three stairs and look out at my captive audience of five.

"One must search the Self and Soul of one's individual being to drill down to the tap-root of the sprouting seed of existence. What does 'Know Thyself' mean? I believe it means to gain an understanding from our faults, failures, ego-centric arrogance, pretensions, and negative habits. As well as the positive unique qualities of character that define us as ourselves. Do we search? Do we seek? What do we find? Do we discover that we are afraid of the truth or attracted to the truth? Only the truth can set you free!"

I am getting on a roll now like Cricket had, so I continue, "There is an infinite world—an inner cosmos contained at the heart of understanding and awareness of the statement 'Know Thyself!' A self-limiting person could eventually discover themselves to be limitless. You are what you think. Your reality is the perceptions you behold. The habit forming tendencies of thought determine the choices and opportunities a person makes out of life."

I feel my ego and my pretensions and arrogances gnaw and scratch within for expression.

I am aware of this on a different level, a deeper dimension, as I'm speaking.

It all adds up to a daily mindset of no expectations to low expectations to a substandard nullified of nothing. No being. Just existing. Struggling. Uncertainty. Unclear vision. The mental trap door closing. Seeking answers. Focusing of my will to will, to learn and grow from the trials and tribulations. Afraid to move? Afraid to act? Why is that? Fear to act is fear to grow is fear to know.

I wonder in silence about myself as I finish my oratory.

"The 'I Am that I Am' mode of thinking is an introduction to your 'Higher Self,' a knowing beyond faith. The transcendental allure of enlightenment…"

My time runs out and everyone stands and claps, cheers, whistles, hoots and hollers, as we finish the first round of our Symposium. All together we share a rousing six goblet salute. Each of us downs our wine.

Jason works on uncorking two more bottles and filling everyone back up.

Cricket is ready to go another round. This time she wants the topic to be the same for everybody. Cricket says the topic will be my topic: "Know Thyself."

So we continue our Symposium. The women look like they are ready for the Acropolis and the Parthenon, with their makeshift gimmick attire. We share laughs and stories of learning about ourselves. We discard the formality of the ten-minute time keeper. It is a lively discussion that sometimes splinters off into three different conversations. The wine is working its wonders. Hard to keep group focus.

We continue this way for a couple more hours.

All talked out after a bushel of empty wine bottles, we saunter down from the library to go out back and barbecue in the early evening. Peter is already home and outside entertaining several of his friends. They all start hollering—"Animal House! Toga! Toga! Toga!"—when the girls come outside in their Greek outfits. We tell them about our Symposium.

By nightfall the property has over fifty people present. Most of them came from the neighborhood and Peter's work. This isn't even the "Big Party," more like a pre-big-party-get-together.

By midnight it has dwindled down and I drunkenly go to my tent to hit the sack.

But I can't fall asleep right away so I write and scribble in my journal for forty-five minutes before falling asleep, attempting to recap the day's events.

ꟿ

The next morning people start arriving en masse. By the afternoon hour Cricket and Peter must have well over a hundred guests. Mostly everyone is hanging outside.

I notice a couple of horseshoe pits, so I get involved in the tournaments for the better part of the day.

I meet so many people that I lose track of names. I met several people multiple times, but it's like the first time, when it comes to remembering the names that belong to the faces.

As it gets dark the party moves into the house, mainly the first and fourth floors.

I meet Woodrow Oscar Wilferd on the fourth floor, sitting on a chair in the far corner by himself, where Cricket said I could store my stuff. He looks like a Cheech and Chong throwback hippie from the sixties. He wears an American flag bandana, long brown hair, and a large, full, furry-faced beard. A pair of wire-rimmed, John Lennon style glasses, rests on the bridge of his long roman nose.

I sit in a chair next to him with my notebook journal open on my lap, pen in one hand, beer in the other. Looking over top of his spectacles, he introduces himself and we shake hands.

"You can call me Wow—everyone does!" he says to me with a chuckle. "Wow is the name I answer to."

He repeats himself just to make sure I got it straight.

"Well, hello, Wow, I'm Ted, from Michigan. I met Cricket a few weeks back when she was on the Dead tour and she invited me out here to celebrate these happenings—and here I am!"

"Wow—I met Cricket while hiking in the state forests

of Maine. We met through the rainbow families network," he says. "We climbed Mount Kataaden together!"

"Wow, indeed! I'm impressed! I'm familiar with that mountain from reading Henry David Thoreau," I say.

"Who? Never heard of him…"

"No way, Wow! You've got to be kidding. Wow!" I say.

"Is he a writer? I don't read much. I like to draw and paint."

"Oh, I see, everyone has their own special things they're drawn to," I say. "I like books and writing for example, but I couldn't paint or draw if my life depended on it!"

"Wow! I'm just the opposite," says Wow!

We both share a quick laugh over the recognition of our polar opposite states of being. And with that I turn the pages in my notebook and click my pen to write. As I engage my mind in this activity, Wow pulls out a large drawing tablet that he has beside him leaning against his chair.

I glance up at him now and then, fumbling around himself in the various pockets of his army issue coat. He finally finds his charcoal colored drawing utensils in a secret pocket in the inside lining of his coat.

We both sit in silence in our far corner as the party rages on throughout the house—music, dancing, drinking, smoking, mixed in with a crescendo of conversing voices. Wow and I are oblivious. We continue in our silence, involved in our separate pursuits. My focus is on jotting as many bullet-point statements of things I've been experiencing so I can look back later at all my notes and write about the adventure.

I look up from my notebook jottings and say—"WOW."

Just at that moment he finishes rolling and hands a doobie to me. Then we both say "WOW" with big smiles on our faces.

"I'm going to have to start calling you Woodrow," I say, "because every other word is Wow!" I joke to him.

"Wow!" he responds. "Don't worry you'll get used to it!"

And with that we take a short time out to enhance our inebriated state. We each down our beer and Wow volunteers to go to the keg and fill up the mugs. I continue to sit in the corner of the fourth floor room and write in my notebook.

I think about this new character I've just met—Wow! Wow would fit the opposite description to Cricket's extreme, extroverted nature. On the other end of the pendulum, he seems to be Mr. Introverted. He's not the type to try to meet or introduce himself to anybody. He would rather be left alone in his "Wow" world.

Despite this, we bond and talk and have things in common. I'd like to get to know more about Mr. Woodrow Oscar Wilferd.

ꙮ

Wow comes back with a full glass of brew for each of us. We settle into the far corner of the fourth floor room, away from the hustle and bustle activity of the party taking place throughout the premises.

"So, Wow, when were you in the service and how old are you?" I ask.

"I was in Vietnam, man! It was like living through hell on earth some days. Wow!" He stares into space, perhaps rekindling memories of long ago. "I was a young kid then in 1967—right out of school, just a boy. I served till October of 1970. I'm forty-four years old now and I never thought I would live to be this old."

"I just visited the Vietnam Veterans Memorial in D.C. about a week ago. You ever been there and seen the long memorial wall?" I ask.

"No! I don't want to either. It would be like reliving every one of those days all over for me in my mind. I'd surely go nuts, if I'm not already," Wow says. "A lot of my old friend's names are on that wall. I saw so much death. It was terrible," says Wow, with anguish in his eyes from the sudden recall of memories.

Trying to steer the subject in a new direction I continue to talk about my recent visit to D.C.

"I met a former marine biker guy by the name of Baron Von Torchenstein. You remind me of him. Both of you have the same general look about yourselves," I explain. "The Baron and you have other things in common too, like painting and drawing. You do paint, don't you? Or, do you just draw?"

"I do both, but mostly draw and sketch. Painting takes a lot of discipline, which I lack at times," says Wow, laughing at himself. "I see these images in my mind and they torment me till I get them down and sketch them out."

Wow flips open his sack holder of drawing paper on his lap and pulls out numerous sketches for me to check out. He does nature scenes—flowers, winter on a farm, a serene riverside brook, mountains and canyons.

Wow also does evil clown faces and monsters from the dark depths of his imagination. His doodling is endless.

I scan through sketch after sketch as he hands them to me—look it over then hand it back with the opposite hand and receive the next sketch with the other hand. We keep up like this for several minutes, rolling through Wow's portfolio.

When I finish looking at his artwork, Wow puts all his drawings back inside the folder and he starts to talk about Vietnam again. He feels more comfortable with me now as I notice him to be in a more relaxed and loose posture.

When I first met him, Wow was stiff and rigid, keeping to himself and looking around his surroundings in a near paranoid manner. I theorize that Wow has schizophrenic tendencies or PTS-Post Traumatic Syndrome.

His demeanor is totally opposite of that now.

"There was death and carnage and horror to live through every day," he says. "Battlefield stories are nothing but living nightmares…walking through killing fields and jungles and late night ambushes and raids. I saw death everywhere, every single day during those years."

Wow stares off in a trance as he speaks until he becomes visibly upset and his hands start shaking and he begins to sweat profusely around the forehead, just staring into his deep space…

Scarred emotionally and psychically—Traumatized—we are traumatized by certain experiences. The war within and the war without. Hate and anger. Negative energy. Robotic mentality. Loss of soul. Loss of mind. Zombie-like. The trauma lives in the mind. You carry it with you. Die and die again all over. Mystic Might. Traveling from the dark to the light. Lost again. Hurt. Anger. Despair. No one can understand. Not good enough to be as good as one should be. Where was my death? Why did death forsake me? What am I supposed to be? I'm alive seeking. Still, the endless trauma is not unaware nor unseen…

"Let's talk about something else," I suggest. I cannot imagine the hell that is burnished in his memory. I have no experience with guns, weapons or the armed services. All I can do is listen to his stories with empathy and compassion.

"We're here to have a party and good times!" I say.

I drink down my cup of brew, and Wow takes the

hint and follows suit.

"Give me your cup and I'll go and get a fill up for us," I say.

Wow hands me his cup and I leave him in the dark dimly-lit corner of the upstairs room. Out in the main room of the fourth floor the party continues. I mingle with the crowd and even dance a song with a cute little female who invites me on the dance floor. Everyone is having fun.

I work my way over to the keg eventually, and fill up a couple tall cups of beer for me and Wow. I squeeze and jostle my way through the strobe lights, loud music, and smoke-filled room of party people, to the opposite corner of the floor where Wow sits in dark seclusion by himself. I hand Wow his beer.

"You're not still thinking of Vietnam are you?" I ask. "If you are, I'm going to go hang out with someone else."

"No—I'm all right! That shit gets to me sometimes. I don't need to think about it or talk about it. You brought up fricking Vietnam you know!"

Wow assumes the stern upright posture of before. I can see his edginess is still there.

"Just relax, man! No need to get riled up." I soften my voice and tone to a slight whisper. "Just relax and enjoy yourself. Peace be with you, brother." I offer my right hand to him and we shake hands.

After a few awkward moments of silence, Wow then transitions into speaking about rainbow families and deadheads and acid freaks. I listen to him go on and on with his funny anecdotes and stories.

It is well past midnight. Wow and I roam from somber introspective moods to total euphoric elation. We laugh till our bellies hurt. What is so funny? WOW! I don't know! Just saying, "WOW" is enough to make either one of us burst out laughing all over again.

ℬℴℭℛ

I have to leave the upstairs and get outside, move around, get away from Wow! He's up there farting now. I'm sure no one will bother him in his corner.

I saunter out to the front porch. Pete is playing his guitar on the deck. The drummer is banging away on a six-piece drum set with several clanging cymbals. Jason plays a bass guitar. They're doing a Cosby, Stills, Nash and Young tune—very good vocal harmonies. About fifteen people congregate out here, listening to the live band performance.

I head out back by the keg and bar. Peter is out here holding court with a dozen people. He's bartending. I haven't seen Cricket in quite a while. Neither has Peter.

Snaking back through the house from the back door entry way to the kitchen, I find Cricket in the living room with eight other partygoers, watching a Grateful Dead concert on her big screen TV. She comes over and asks me if I'm having a good time. It is real loud and hard to hear so we must cup our hands around the other person's ear to have a conversation. Cricket motions with her finger and I bend down to hear what she has to say.

"Want some acid, Ted?"

I lean into her ear as she cocks her head to hear my response.

"I never did it before and I don't think I want to," I say.

We switch positions and she responds.

"This is the time in your life to try. Your mind will just become overactive with thoughts and images and visions. It will be great for your creative writing experiences."

"You make it sound so harmless," I say.

"What are you worried about? You might be able to write better if you can control and channel the energy," Cricket says.

I yawn real big and don't hear all she says.

"Plus it will help keep you awake so you can party all night right into the next day. Try a couple hits with Wow!" she says.

We switch and Cricket gives me her ear so we can continue our talk in the noisy atmosphere of Grateful Dead music mingled with dozens and dozens of conversing voices. The room is filling up with people, as Cricket and I crowd in tight together.

"I have some in my wallet that Jeff gave me."

I pull out the cellophane wrapper and carefully hand it to Cricket. She opens it and looks inside fingering the contents.

"That's two hits. Here's two more!" she says.

And like a drugstore clerk she dispenses the medication to me and then abruptly disappears down the hall amongst the crowded rooms.

I look at the tiny little objects in the palm of my right hand and I wonder what to do.

I head back upstairs where about thirty people are dancing, drinking, talking, smoking, and having a merry good time partying on the fourth floor. They're dancing to Top Forty music.

Wow is still sitting in the far corner all by himself. He has his army fatigue jacket on like he's thinking about leaving. Wow doesn't recognize me at first, his bearded chin is resting on his chest, he fell asleep in the chair I discover. He jumps, startled.

"Wow! Yo, Wow!" I say.

He readjusts his spectacles, squints at me for a brief second or two before he realizes it's me.

"You all right? Sorry to startle you like that. What the hell are you doing falling asleep at a party?" I say.

"I was just catching a few zzzzzs," he says. "I didn't know if you were going to come back or not…"

"Yeah! Sure, I just checked out the party through the house, found Cricket, and then made my way back up here," I say. "Lot of fun stuff happening all over the premises. Here, this is from Cricket."

I hand him the hits of acid.

"What's this?" he says. "Oh…I see!"

Wow carefully lays the small LSD dots in the palm of his hand. He sticks two in his mouth, under his tongue. He hands the other two hits back to me. I hold the acid in the palm of my hand and look at Wow.

"What's the matter?" he asks.

I shrug my shoulders and don't say anything, continuing to look in my palm at the wonder drug.

Should I or shouldn't I?

"Come on, what are you waiting for?" says Wow, as he gently nudges my hand toward my face.

And just like that, I do it. The deed is done. Within a split second I have the dots stuck to my tongue.

"Yahoo! Yeah!" says Wow.

We continue with some of the conversations we were having earlier. By three in the morning we are in alternate realities. One reality is being physically present at the party. The other reality is a whole new milieu.

My thoughts are moving much too fast for my pen to keep up. It looks like scribbles and hieroglyphics on the pages. I can't write or think like I normally do. I just have to be and experience the images in my mind.

I see bright colors and distortions of fast moving scenes. Nothing is clear and everything is quick. Fleeting. Unfamiliar faces and places and things…

WOW has his big sketching pad laid out on his lap. He is drawing charcoal and pencil images—looks like he is on a mean clown trip!

My psychic slumber penetrates. Sleepwalking through life. This is a transgression against my soul. William James was right about HABITS, especially habitual ways of thinking. We think ourselves into a consistent thought groove. Selling short our tool of creation. Wandering souls. I'm a seeking soul wanting to know and understand. I will re-orient the polarity of my habitual nature. Thinking. Discerning. Learning. I will come to grips and cross the GREAT DIVIDE…

I look at myself in a mirror. This LSD thing is maybe not for me! I have tiny pinhead pupils. The whites of my eyes are bloodshot gray. I have a pit in my stomach. I drink a lot of water, never quenching my thirst—more water, more water, followed with beers. I have an ashen look, zombie-like. Then my face turns beet red. I feel spaced out, but focused.

Strange.

The music is loud, but I want it louder. CCR, "Down on the Corner." I watch all the drunk revelers dancing and the strobe lights flashing.

I feel the hair standing on my skin, the back of my neck, my arms, legs, head. I keep rubbing myself to push the hair down but it feels like my bodily hair is moving like tiny little insects in all directions throughout my whole body.

I realize I am electro-magnetized!

Creativity seeking. An epiphany—Satori. Evolutions of understanding. Searching for great thought vibes. Attuning. Seeking. Refinement. Receptors. Receiving a solid flow. Capturing and writing. Creative lightening. Proof from mind to hand to pen to paper. Solid flow. Get it out. Creative undertow swirling. Sucking. Blasting. Here it comes. Here it comes—the sudden enlightenment from within!

I proceed to the corner by my chair and grab my notebooks from my book bag and I sit next to Wow—I write and he draws—the rest of the dark early morning hours. He is concentrating on his sketches. I am in the writer zone, a receptacle to attuned thought. I receive and transcribe on the paper.

We hardly speak, both lost in the universe of our own thoughts. My writing is better now, at least I can understand and read it. Before, I was trying too hard. Now I'm letting it flow as it comes to me. I focus on the feelings and images of my heightened senses. The music blares on, song after song. We are oblivious to most everything else, stuck in our dimly lit cove in the far corner of the fourth floor of Cricket's great Victorian home.

ꕤ

Chapter Nine

Saturnalia

ꕤ

"I usually need a can of beer to prime me."
—Norman Mailer

"Whoever battles with monsters had better see that it does not turn him into a monster. And if you gaze long into an abyss, the abyss will gaze back into you."
—Friedrich Nietzsche

Unrestrained Revelry

The party lasted all night into the dawn of a new morning. Cricket comes running up the stairs full of excitement.

"Come on everybody we're going to the school yard to watch the sun come up over the hills. It will be awesome," chirps Cricket.

I am ready to go.

Wow doesn't want to move. He is wide awake and tripping pretty good. He just wants to continue doodling in his sketch pad. He is drawing motorcycles, race cars and guns from various perspectives. Wow hands me his pad and says, "Later, dude," as I flip the chart pages revealing new images and conceptions from the mind of Wow. I hand his sketch pad back after a brief perusal. Amazing skill! He continues on sketching images.

I follow Cricket downstairs. Everyone is organizing in the front yard driveway. There are twenty-two people still standing from the all-night revelry. Cricket and I make it an even two-dozen. There are a few mingled conversations, but mostly just chaotic noise and jostling around. Everyone is gathered and waiting to go.

Cricket hands me a harmonica and she carries a flute. We meet up with the rest of the crowd huddled outside. I have my notepad and pen in one hand and a tall glass of water in the other, as I scurry down the neighborhood road ahead of everyone else. I am full of boundless energy. I'm riding the wave of a great experience.

Another sunrise with Cricket and her gang after an all night party.

I'm looking forward to a transcendental moment! I was caught unawares, on previous occasions. I'm ready for the sunrise trip today. I still relish the experience of the moment of the sunrise that first day I met Cricket at Lake Minnawanna—the cheering throng followed by a silent meditation.

> *Other worldly cosmic consciousness. A life beyond death. Undulating transcendental spheres. Vibrating. Spatial Vortex pulsating. Magnetic cerebral energies. Flowing swiftly through the currents of time. Attracting to the attuned mind. Enwrapped. Absorbed. Consciousness awakening. Stream of life enrapturing. The infinite within. Seed bud, roots of soul generation. Psychical Miracle. Swift flowing transcendent measures. I am that I am that I am—a spiritual force animating a physical presence. Am I awake or self-deluded?*

I jog forward about seventy-five yards or so to stay ahead of the pack. Cricket is in front leading the group. I hear someone say, "She's just like a pied piper—she plays and we all follow."

I whip open my notebook and sit down on the curbside of the street and start writing about the unfolding scene—the great mindset and vibes of positive energy we are contributing in the group gathering—pure joy without restraint.

All feels right in my world at this moment. We are a small band of brotherhood and sisterhood of humanity.

I feel the presence of the principles of natural order. I can sense truth running a straight path through Nature and Nature's God. I receive a momentary understanding of the correlated principles in the evolutionary unfolding of individual life.

I am as one with the great Creative Intelligence—the central source of the great reservoir of knowledge and truth! I am feeling, sensing, a transformative vibe, transcending on the intuitive plane.

> *The higher order of Being has ever attracted my inward sanctum. I sense a vast power I never have reached. Am I worthy? Is my character growth heading in the right direction? Am I blind to the sense I should know? How did the historic greats tap into their inward reservoir? I want to be so self-assured to know that I know that I know—not that I continually know, that I don't know. What is this mystic treasure unrevealed within?*

> *The harmonious energy pervades all senses. Everything is AWARE and ALIVE with vibrancy, texture, energy, love. How else to explain such a phenomenon—ecstatic group energy dynamics—mastermind consciousness! I've felt this type of energy wave numerous times on this bohemian adventure, however, each culminating moment in time is extra special in its own way. The experience is the thing! Awareness! Awareness and understanding through experienced enlightenment!*

The noisy crowd of all night revelers soon approach my curbside seat. They are singing and clapping to Cricket's flute playing as they stroll down the middle of the neighborhood street. I have a harmonica in my pocket, so I give it to one of the guys passing by. He runs up front with Cricket and our small troupe follows them down the street.

I close my notebook and hurry to catch up. I hang with the pack until we come upon the elementary school playground.

The top orb of the sun's rays is starting to peak over the hill. The horizon lights up to dawn. The pillow-puff clouds reflect orange and pink.

Cheers, clapping and hooting fills the school yard.

"Here it comes—the beautiful life-giving light of nature," shouts Cricket from within the crowd.

"Feel the heat rising as a new day begins," shouts a young guy with a Harvard t-shirt. "I'm ready for it, are you?"

Our group of gatherers cheer. "Yes! Yes!" More clapping as each of us join in. We all salute the beaming bright sun, blasting it's presence over the horizon of the hilltop.

We're standing amidst swings, teeter-totters, merry-go-rounds, slides, monkey bars, and rings. I notice a huge mound of dirt off to the side of the playground area. The dirt mound is about ten feet high at the summit. Probably unloaded here from a dump truck. I climb to the top.

As the sun is growing over the horizon and everyone is spread out in the playground before me, I stare down at the scene. I hold a half-full glass of water in my left hand. In my right hand I hold my writing pen.

'Ping—Ping—Ping' I tap the pen against the top of the lightly held glass. The sound echoes off the buildings in the school yard.

Everyone is talking and enjoying the sunrise morning, but they can hear this constant echo ping.

Three pings, one—two—three, then pause for fifteen seconds then I repeat the pings like an ever-ready cuckoo clock. I am a mechanical device with my precision—creating a musical tuning-in with the universal lyre.

Eventually, with my persistence of motion, everyone stops what they are doing around the playground and look up at me on the dirt mound, creating this ping echo, in step with the sun's ever-persistent rising.

I stare down on the faces in the crowd 'Ping—Ping—Ping.' The sun rises as if being summoned for the cause. I am a transcendental bohemian at this moment in time. If only the moment could last longer than a moment lasts ...I stand on this makeshift hill pinging my glass like a robot machine for fifteen solid minutes. Everyone thought it was great for the first five minutes. I held all their attention—the ping echo calling to the rising sun. Then the group becomes restless and weary of my display and drifts apart in groups of two or three.

"Let's go!"

Enough is enough.

But I am in my own universe of understanding at this moment. Deep within. I am oblivious. My ping-ping-ping every fifteen seconds serves as a connective key to my inner self-harmony. My mind settles into a meditative alpha state.

I am mesmerized by the sun and the steady echo sound of my pings against the glass. Nothing else exists for me at the moment.

A dirt clod comes near my peripheral vision, interrupting me from my trance-like state. The gang is dispersing down the road! Two of the guys toss dirt clods near me to get my attention.

I see people talking but I can't hear. I see mouths voicing words and I see their facial expressions, but all I hear and sense is the universal lyre—ping-ping-ping.

I am temporarily tuned-in! Everything else, tuned-out.

Then I snap out of it with a quick suddenness. The transcendental connection is severed. I stand on the dirt mound, look around at the playground, then make my way down.

The human family tree is an unbroken chain of descendants and ancestors perpetuating continuity and life through place and time. Billions of lifetimes. Evolutionary growth and waste. So many lost souls struggle with living a human life. The race of humanity has generally, forever been in psychic slumber. The long unbroken chain will evolve one day to a higher order of being.

I come down off the hill and we all walk home, through the neighborhoods, back to Cricket's place. I stay in back of the pack by myself, bringing up the anchor. We walk through the side streets and down the roads. I continue to keep to myself for awhile.

I couldn't even logically explain to my own self what I had just done on the makeshift dirt mound in the school yard. I've now shown myself to be the weirdest of all the weird people, for today anyway.

I'm not a bit tired. A whole new day long party is here. I remind myself that I have to pace myself or I'll just wear right down from all this nonstop revelry atmosphere. Cricket had warned me.

I hang out by my tent in the backyard when we get back from the morning walk, in semi-solitude, and read all my notebook jottings from yesterday and last night. I discover that I shouldn't write when I drink too much. The sentences get sloppy and they don't make much sense.

Every now and then I come upon a good passage—a thought provoking quote, some intelligible conceptualization, a quick quip I think of or that someone has mentioned. But for the most part, I'm frustrated with what I produced. My quality of creative output is less than I'd imagine it to be. My standards are better than this.

I vow to myself that today I will not drink. I can party and enjoy myself amongst all these people without imbibing so much.

ഊര

Cricket comes out to my tent with Millie and Mignon trailing behind her. Mostly everyone is sleeping now. The three of them don't plan on going to bed. They want to keep on going. By mid-afternoon the house and the whole property will be full of partying people again.

We huddle together, each sitting in a lawn chair in the back yard near my tent. None of them mention what happened at the school yard this morning with me on the dirt mound. Perhaps my actions were not perceived as abnormal at all by a crew of witches.

"The earth is filled with vibratory amplification spots," says Cricket. "These lines of force, or ley lines, connect from the positions of the stars in the sky, in cooperation and harmony with the energy of the sun. There are also ancient energies that are pure and sacred, like certain Native American Indian burial grounds."

"They can be haunted if they're abused and not honored," says Millie.

"Living souls and entities—NOT resting in peace," says Mignon.

"We are more than we seem, than we give ourselves credit for being. Souls in flesh, not flesh with a soul to disregard and never mind," says Cricket.

The three women share an intense look about their eyes as all three of them laser focus on me as they talk, each jumping in to interject an added thought to the unfolding of the story.

"Ancient energies, sacred energies, are out here in my backyard," says Cricket. "Over there," she points to the far corner of the yard by rows of large sunflowers, "is our memorial to the sacredness of this land—my blessing from the spirit world to live here."

"It used to be cursed out here!" says Mignon. "This land was an old Indian burial ground."

"We invited a Shaman to come to release the curse," interjects Millie.

"I got together with all my witch friends and we had a séance," says Cricket. "Only to discover we were dealing with something more powerful and mysterious than all of our combined energies. We went to an Indian reservation to seek help. A medicine man agreed to come and look at the property. He was spooked. He said we would need a highly trained and competent Shaman. He suggested a Chief Joseph from the Black Hills of South Dakota."

"I must have missed something," I say. "What kind of problems were you having to follow through with all this stuff? Why was the medicine man spooked?"

"Oh, excuse me, Ted, I got a little ahead of myself in the story," says Cricket.

"Birds were always dying out here and the cats were scared to be out in the far corner of the yard, always hanging close to the house," says Mignon.

"Sometimes I could faintly hear muffled drums and tribal chanting. Right over there the ground would shake and vibrate," Cricket says as she points over by the rows of tall sunflowers in the far corner of her yard.

"Oh my gosh, remember that day I came over to visit you Cricket, and the ground vibrated so loud we thought we were going to have an earthquake? I was freaked," says Millie.

"The final event that caused me to realize I had to get a Shaman to visit was Peter's pond project," says Cricket. "It should have been done last year but he was repeatedly delayed by freak things—broke his thumb digging, supplies would get busted overnight, or things would be missing. The yard did not want him doing anything to it."

"Every time I would come over to visit, Cricket and Peter would have some new story about something or other happening out here. It was spooky haunted!" says Mignon.

"So we finally got Shaman Chief Joseph to visit last Fall, and he released the hold of the spirits from the property by conducting an exorcism through a Native American peyote ceremony vision quest," says Cricket.

ꟷ

"How did Chief Joseph solve the problem?" I ask.

"He went into a trance and visited dimensions of the spirit world," says Cricket. "He made a fire, took some peyote in his mouth, a chunk. He chanted until he worked himself into the proper state of mind."

"There were five of us and Chief Joseph," says Millie, "me, Mignon, Cricket, Lois and Katydid, joined in the ceremony with the Shaman Chief."

"We sat in a circle on the ground and made a makeshift fire ring," says Mignon.

"The six of us formed a circle on the ground, sitting with legs folded, around the burning sticks, kindling wood, and hot embers of the fire ring. We passed the purple whale around," says Cricket.

"When it came time for the Shaman, he declined, and instead reached into a leather sack and pulled out a long two-foot length peace pipe. He filled it up with his stuff in his magic sack. We passed it around and I choked on it," says Cricket.

"So did I!" says Millie.

"Me too!" agrees Mignon. "Katydid didn't choke though!"

"The Shaman Chief was star stuck by Katydid and he hardly paid any attention to the rest of us," says Millie. "He called her an ancient spirit!"

"Did everyone do peyote?" I ask.

"No—just the Shaman," says Cricket, as the other two nod in agreement.

Cricket continues the story and whenever she pauses for a breath, to think or recollect, then Millie or Mignon takes over in the story telling. And it goes like that until they collectively tell me the whole story.

So I'm imagining, while I'm hearing them recount the tale—five witches and a witch doctor shaman sitting around getting stoned so they can visit the spiritual dimension. It becomes too much for me when they regularly use the word "Exorcist" and "Exorcism" in the telling of the story. These women actually are scaring me a bit I must admit with their otherworldly spooky story!

Are they pulling my leg? Is this for real?

I take a break to go in the house and get a glass of water and visit the bathroom. It is all quiet in the house—people are sleeping everywhere.

When I come back outside, there are Cricket, Mignon, and Millie, my witch friends, eagerly waiting for me to come back so they can continue telling their story. The four of us get resituated in our lawn chairs in front of my tent. The women pick up right where they left off and tell me more about this "Spirit World Journey."

Cricket continues with the story. "Chief Joseph visited the ancient ancestors in the spirit world—finding unrest, disharmony and chaos. The Shaman visited a Hades-type-purgatory—a Native American Indian Nation Hell!

He spoke to the Great Spirit Chief. The peyote delivered him into a series of visions. He saw The Great Spirit Chief change forms—from an American Bald Eagle soaring in the sky, to a thousand-pound Great Grizzly, to a big bull elk, then a buffalo, and a moose. The Great Spirit Chief told the Shaman that dishonor was being heaped upon the Great Nations by the unholy manner in which the restless spirits must endure, from the treating of their sacred burial ground," says Cricket.

"He was in a trance for over three hours!" interjects Mignon. "He hardly ever blinked his eyes. He used his body as a medium."

"Like trance channeling?" I ask.

"More or less!" says Millie, with a big bright smile and arching of her brows.

"We women would hold hands, close our eyes, and meditate while the Shaman was in his universal spiritual visitation. When he came out of his vision he told us what he had seen and what we must do," says Cricket.

"Chief Joseph said we must make a simple Memorial to all the great Indian Nations!" says Mignon.

The women stand up. Millie says, "Hey, Ted, let us show you something."

We walk over to the far fence line of the property by the enormous sunflowers. On the other side of the sunflowers is a huge cairn-type rock pile. A wooden post is protruding from the middle of the large rock pile. On that wooden post is a sign—many engravings.

The three witch women continue their story.

Millie says, "We wrote down the Shaman's directions and gathered the rocks, planted the sunflower garden, built the cairn, and worked on the sign."

"We used an old fashioned wood burning kit that Peter has," says Cricket, "to burnish in the names of each tribe. I now come out each morning and light a candle and meditate out here."

"What did the Shaman want for payment of services rendered?" I ask. "Traveling so far and all."

"He didn't want any money—he wanted Katydid!" says Cricket. "Katydid was like an older big sister to all of us."

"She was a free spirit in her early forties," says Mignon.

"Chief Joseph wanted himself a squaw," says Millie with a hearty laugh.

"Katydid was unattached and childless," Cricket says. "Katydid is one of the original flower children of the sixties. She met Janis Joplin, Jimi Hendrix, Bob Dylan, Joan Baez, The Rolling Stones, Jim Morrison, Jerry Garcia."

"When can I meet Katydid?" I inquire.

"You won't—she's dead!" reply Mignon and Millie in unison.

All three women share sorrowful sad looks planted on their faces in remembrance of a still fresh grieving. Cricket hands some tissue to Millie and Mignon so they can each dab their eyes and nose.

I walk over closer to the memorial to read some of the inscriptions. The writing is small and the tribal names have been carved and wood-burned into the sign, filled with names of tribes by language family groups:

The Algonquin—Chippewa, Ojibwa, Cree, Menominee, Shawnee, Potawatomi, Miami, Ottawa, Sauk and Fox, Adirondack, Chickahominy, Delaware, Mahican, Mohegan, Penobscot, Podunk, Powhatan, Arapaho, Blackfoot, Cheyenne.

The Athapascan family of tribes—The Apache, Navajo, Kato, Hupa, Tolowa, Tlingit. The Caddoan family of tribes—The Caddo Confederacy, The Pownee Confederacy, Arikara. The Eskimouan family in Alaska—

Aleut, Inuit, Eskimo, and so on it went.

Each tribe has a place: The Aztecs, Pueblos, Shoshoni, Winnebago, Crow, Omaha, Iowa, Oglala, Dakota, Chinook, Seminole, Chocktow, Chickasaw, Creek, Cherokee, Seneca, Mohawk, The Nez Perce.

"We're sorry, Ted! We still get emotional when talking about Katydid, even though she's been gone for awhile now!" says Cricket.

I stand up from my crouching stance where I am reading the memorial sign. The women are ready to continue their story.

"So what happened?" I ask.

"Katydid went with Chief Joseph happily. She loved adventures and new experiences. They lived on a reservation in the Black Hills of South Dakota," says Cricket. "They went out west and canoed down the Colorado River and lived like Native American Indians of lore. She was so full of life and excitement."

"You guys never did tell me what this Chief Joseph looked like," I say.

"He is short and squat with long gray and black hair in a pony tail," says Mignon.

"Why would Katydid go running off with someone like that?" I ask.

"His eyes are otherworldly, like two planets," says Cricket. "Katydid was drawn to his mind and his magic and his oneness with nature and things," says Mignon.

"Then she came down with cervical cancer and died within a couple months. It was so sudden," says Cricket. "The Witch Doctor Shaman couldn't save her. We were all so devastated. It's never been the same since. Katydid was a pure soul, an old soul. She taught us all. We made a Memorial to her in our sunflower garden, also. She always maintained she was an American Indian in previous lives.

She felt she was just returning back to her roots," says Cricket, as the other two nod in agreement.

The four of us walk around the Memorial. Cricket relights a couple of candles that the wind has blown out. They point to a small inscription that has been wood-burned into the base of the post.

'Katydid, Forever The Free Spirit. 1949 – 1992.'

It is getting later in the day and people start arriving and waking up to start the party all over again. The three witches and I break off our little pow-wow and separate in different directions. Actually, I stay by my tent and the three of them scatter.

I walk back over to the sunflower garden. I stare at the pile of rocks, and the Native American Memorial, bow my head and close my eyes. I feel the spirituality, love, compassion, wildness, and nature-loving spirit of a great people—The Native American Indian Tribes!

ജ൮

I decide to walk out to the front deck and see what is happening there. Not much. Another Grateful Dead concert is on the big TV in the living room. About a dozen people are watching it.

I head upstairs and stop by the third floor to go in the library, but the door is locked. I proceed up to the fourth floor of the old Victorian home. I haven't been back up here since I left for the sunrise walk this morning, now it's nearing mid-afternoon.

As I get to the top of the stairs I see a huge mess. The floor is quiet and vacant. Empty beer cups, bottles, plastic food plates, ashtrays, and liquid spill on the floor in several spots. Each step I take my sandaled foot sticks to the floor and then peels off as I lift my leg. I make this screeching cracking sound as I walk over the area and survey the scene.

I walk over to the corner where I have my clothes in a chest of drawers. I need to shower and clean up. As I'm looking in the drawers I hear a rustling noise behind the couch and chair, up against the wall. I go over to check it out—it's Wow! He's just now waking up, and all we both can say is 'WOW!'

"It's time to get back up and start partying, Wow! The backyard, front porch deck and living room are filling up with people," I say.

He responds with, "Wow!" then rolls over on the floor, back to sleep.

Afterwards, I get cleaned up and refreshed in the fourth floor bathroom. I am ready for the new day of Saturnalia with all the people.

As I make my way back down the stairs to the activities taking place on the property, I stop by the third floor library and try the door again. It is slightly ajar. I make my way into the library to discover Lois conducting a Séance.

A big round table in the middle of the room holds a crystal ball at the center. Lois and four other people sit at the table—Jason, John, Trudy and Wilma. They ask if I would like to join them. I lock the door and take a seat at the table.

The big black crystal ball in the middle of the table is sitting on a golden chalice. Each person has a set of tarot cards face down on the table in front of them. Lois deals me two cards.

I've never been one to mess with or inquire into occult practices and black magic, so I am skeptical and apprehensive.

Perhaps I should excuse myself and leave.

"What's the matter, Ted?" asks Lois. "Are you frightened?"

"What's the goal or purpose of this séance?" I ask.

Lois thinks this is funny, then she sneers at me.

I look around at everyone else and they don't look that much more comfortable than I do. This is definitely Lois' show to run.

"John and Trudy have recently lost a close family member and they want to make contact with her in the spirit world. The group effort has been unsuccessful thus far," says Jason.

This seems too personal to me and I beg off to excuse myself and rejoin the party.

"Maybe I shouldn't be here," I say, as I rise from my chair and inch away from the table.

"Maybe we need another person in the ritual to give more mental energy for the spiritual summoning," suggests Jason to Lois.

"This is way over my head and I'm not comfortable participating," I say.

Jason and Wilma say they feel the same way, but they're willing to lend themselves to the cause to help John and Trudy get through their grief. I find out that the close family member is their oldest daughter who was recently killed in a car accident. They've already tried a Ouija board and that didn't work. Now Lois is trying her crystal ball.

I sit back down at the table and look over at Lois. She is in a quiet trance-like state and doesn't say anything.

Lois has several books stacked beside her on a stool—***Occult Practices, Spiritual Summoning, Beyond the Grave, A Witches Handbook.*** I pick up one of the books and page through it.

John and Wilma and Trudy sit quietly at the table, looking at the crystal ball and down to their laps, back and forth. Lois says nothing and Jason paces up and down the length of the bookshelves, nervous with thought.

Lois is still quiet in her trance.

I continue to page through the occult manual as I look around at everyone else. It is quiet, eerie and surreal.

"How is this process supposed to work?" I whisper to no one in particular.

No one answers. Everyone is silent, waiting on Lois.

"'Cause this isn't getting anything done!" I say.

Jason comes back to the table and sits down. Just then Lois snaps out of her trance, rife for the challenge.

"I am the medium and a spiritual entity will talk through me, or a message and vision will appear in the crystal ball, or the Ouija Board may spell out a message. It's all up to the spirit on how the communication will take place," Lois states emphatically to us all.

"What about this?" I say as I push the book over to Lois that is opened to a chapter called 'The Oracle of Napoleon.' It gives detailed instructions on how to contact the spirit of Napoleon Bonaparte. "Perhaps the spirit of Napoleon could be contacted and you could ask him questions that he could answer," I say to Lois.

I am only kidding around to break the tension in the room. She takes me serious and slides the book closer to her and begins reading the instructions.

I really don't believe in any of this and it seems to me that Lois is a charlatan. It's very unfair to lead John and Trudy on this way. They already have such broken hearts with their loss.

But what do I know?

Just then the table starts to shake and a cold breeze blows out the candles in the room. We all look at each other with frightened expressions on our faces—all except Lois.

She is smiling big now. Lois rubs her crystal ball and it fills up with a cloudy white substance. Then the planchette on the Ouija Board on the end table starts moving and jerking along the table. Lois is now in a deeper trance-like state as she wears a far off stare. She starts speaking in a voice not her own, very deep and guttural.

"Ted must leave the room now! The disbeliever must leave now!"

She repeats these two sentences over and over in a monotone, staring into the crystal ball.

What have we stirred up? After the fourth time of, "Ted must leave the room now! The disbeliever must leave now!" I get up from the round table and quickly make my way to the exit door of the library, and lock the door on my way out.

> *Fear and Caution of an Unknown Power—Polarity Blast! The great dividing line of good and bad, moral and immoral, right versus wrong, constructive and destructive—plays out each day with every individual. I sense a polarity of energy—un-human, un-earthly? Caution! Caution! Intruder Alert. My free will is not broken. I will not participate. My psychic flow is drawn only to truth and goodwill to others.*

The rest of the evening is pretty much like the night before. First the backyard and the front porch deck fill with revelers. Each place on the property reverberates a loud musical environment and cacophony of mingled voices in conversation. The ever-present Grateful Dead concert is playing on the big TV in the living room. As the night progresses, more and more people congregate and dance on the fourth floor, just like the night before.

I am the last of a dwindling crowd at two in the morning. Cricket is still going strong as the grand host and Peter is still tending bar.

I am too tired to continue with the festivities, for I

didn't sleep the night before. So I make my way to the tent for some well deserved rest.

Upon closing my eyes I see a vision of myself meditating underneath a bright luminous rainbow. The energy of the multi-colored rays penetrate my being. I proceed to levitate in the air several feet, still sitting in a lotus position, meditating under the bright rainbow.

The vision is so clear, as if a doorway into another dimension. I open my eyes and sit up in the darkness of the tent. The vision fades. As soon as I lay back down and close my eyes, the vision comes again. I slowly drift off to sleep, seeing the vision of myself in my mind's eye, levitating, while meditating under the beautiful rainbow.

ᘐᘑ

Chapter Ten

Summer Solstice

ᘐᘑ

Kairos—*A time when conditions are right for the accomplishment of a crucial action: the opportune and decisive moment.*

Garbage Day!

I wake up at noon the next day when a gentle persistent nudging on my shoulder from Cricket startles me from my REM sleep.

"Huh? What?"

In a semi-conscious fog I look up at Cricket, standing over me. I must have fallen back asleep outside my tent in a foldout lawn chair.

"Get up, Ted! It's the start of the neighborhood summer solstice party! The whole block is already revving up. Let's go walking around. Come on get up!"

She pulls on my wrist, gently yanking me fully awake. Cricket is full of vibrant energy right off the bat to start a new day.

"Can you give me a little time to wake up, use the bathroom, and shower? I can't generate so much energy within myself so quickly—what did you do, drink a pot of coffee?" I ask her.

"I start every day with Meditation and Yoga!" she responds with enthusiasm.

I stand up and stretch and twist, bending over and from side to side to loosen my joints.

"So that's one of your big secrets!"

"What big secrets?"

"The big secrets that make you so different and so special!" I say.

She smiles at me with amusement.

"I didn't mean that in a disrespectful way or as a 'come-on' to you or anything. I—I meant the uniqueness of you as a human being! I've never met anyone quite like you before, your zest for life is extraordinary."

I feel uncomfortable expressing myself to her in this way.

Long silence!

With a slight blush to her cheeks and a contented smile Cricket says, "Thank you, Ted! It's great to be acknowledged and appreciated for who I am. Hey, we're two peas in the same pod—I could tell right away that you were different too, when I met you in Michigan, Ted."

Then she starts to giggle at me as she covers her mouth trying to hold back her laughter.

"I didn't think you were 'coming-on' to me, Ted!" Then she bursts out laughing at me.

"Okay, let's change the subject!" I say. "What's that big rainbow thing you have wrapped around you?"

"This is my rainbow bag," she reponds.

She holds open a big sack that looks like a newspaper carrier bag. It is colored with rainbows, and rainbow colors of red, orange, yellow, green, blue, indigo and violet.

"Today is garbage day and the start of the summer solstice celebration."

"Wasn't summer solstice a week or two back?" I ask.

"Yes! You're right! However, the actual week of June

21st didn't work out. It was bad timing or rough scheduling for a lot of people on the block. Plus many of the residents were still on The Grateful Dead Masterpiece '93 Tour—like Pete, Mignon and me. So, a lot of us in the neighborhood agreed to have the summer solstice celebration delayed so as to lead into the 4th of July. People are going to be walking up and down the streets, house to house for the next three to four days, block after block of outdoor parties and celebrations. Let's go, Ted! Hurry up and get ready! It's garbage day!"

"What's so exciting about garbage day?"

Cricket folds up my lawn chair as soon as I get up and then leans it against my tent post. She puts her hands on her hips, as if waiting for me to get moving.

"What that means is that people in the neighborhoods are going to put out stuff that is still useful, but they have no need for anymore. Then people go garbage picking to find some treasures and useful things. This would be things you would normally see at a garage sale. There is a lot of bartering, trading and goodwill energy going on. Some people will only give up something in return for something of equal value," she says.

"So, it's not all free garbage then?" I ask.

"Right, only if it's at the curbside. People wheel and deal on their porches or in their garage. Hey, Ted, I'm going to push along a shopping cart and fill up my rainbow bag. Then we're going to re-distribute the stuff to needy families."

"So, it's not really garbage then? Why call it garbage day?"

"One person's garbage is another person's treasure! I'm sure you've heard that before," says Cricket. "Our annual garbage day is a way to make that concept into a reality."

"Well, I need to hurry up and get ready so we can go," I say.

"Yes! Hurry! Hurry! Let's go!" says Cricket.

I duck into my tent to get a change of clothes, and then rush inside to freshen up in the first floor bathroom. Within fifteen minutes I am ready to go, but that isn't fast enough for Cricket. I can hear her hollering for me from out in the yard.

"Let's go, Ted! Let's go! We have things to do! Hurry up, Ted!"

I meet Cricket out in the driveway with her shopping cart and big rainbow bag. We proceed down her block on the sidewalk. People are congregated around their homes, drinking, visiting, eating, and talking about and showing off "garbage." House after house, we see similar scenes unfold.

We are not more than a block away and I am already perspiring like a waterfall. The weather is nearing a hundred degrees already today.

Despite this, Cricket looks calm and cool in her oversized gypsy dress, wearing sandals and pushing her cart, peering through her dark sunglasses with a perpetual smile. She waves and greets people as we walk by. Every scene at each house is like a replication of the previous home and yard—joyous summer celebrations and social gatherings.

Our first stop is Pete's house. There's the giant male marijuana plant again—looking like a mystical tree, perhaps a new age bodhi. I stay outside with the empty shopping cart while Cricket runs in the house. The two of them come out to the front, Pete with his banjo in his hands, picking away, tuning it up.

Cricket motions for me to come in, she brings out her purple whale from a pocket of her gypsy dress. We visit for a half hour—drink a bottle of wine between the three of us. Pete switches from his banjo to his guitar. He works on tuning it up while we visit and share a drink together.

Pete's entire house is full of musical stuff. His piano stands in the far corner of the living room, amps, big stereo speakers, a whole wall of music CD's, a violin and three more guitars laying around on display stands.

We sit on a chair and the couch in his living room amidst all of this. I find myself sitting on score sheets tucked in between the cushions.

Pete lives alone. He is a confirmed bachelor, about thirty-years-old, I remember Cricket telling me that before.

Pete's mind works in music twenty-four hours a day, seven days a week. He's made himself into an eccentric. He's always happy and cheerful though. Pete just needs to be playing and singing and listening to music all the time. He likes all kinds of music.

"The ever-present musical beat is the pathway to the door of my soul!" says Pete. "I love to create harmonies and listen to the harmonic beat in all kinds of different music. I get myself wired into a vibration, man!"

Pete, looking down at his guitar fret bar, directs his words at Cricket and to me as we sit in a triangle facing each other, with a glass of wine and the ever-present purple whale making the round.

"You think you'll ever get married, Pete?" asks Cricket. "A woman is going to have to love you for you and pick up after you." As she surveys the dirty dishes, empty pizza boxes and fast food wrappings strewn throughout the house amongst all of Pete's musical equipment and gear.

Pete bursts out laughing at Cricket because of the squeamish look of disgust she wears planted on her face.

"Oh, Cricket, you've seen much worse than this plenty of times. I'm basically a clean guy—I just need to pick up things more often. Give me a break, girlfriend. Feel free to clean up if you want."

And with that suggestion from Pete, Cricket bolts into action while we sit back in relaxation and watch her scurry around the house picking up all of Pete's garbage and junk laying around.

"You enjoying your stay here in upstate New York?" Pete inquires.

"Yeah, man! This has been a great time and there's so much more yet to go. Cricket has plan after plan coming into focus. Always on the go, she is. Keeps me busy just trying to keep up with her," I say.

Pete continues to strum and tune his guitar as we talk.

"Where you guys off to now? Doing the garbage day deal in the neighborhoods?"

"Yep, that's what Cricket has planned for us to be doing right now," I reply.

"Okay! Time to go!" Cricket interrupts us. "Time for us to get moving, Ted. We have a lot to accomplish today! We're burning sunlight!"

Pete puts his guitar down on a guitar stand and walks down the hallway to a back room of his house and then comes back with a bag full of stuffed toys and old clothes and some canned goods.

"Here Cricket! I've been saving and collecting stuff for you." Pete hands her the bag.

We proceed outdoors to the front porch and divide the stuff between the shopping cart and her rainbow bag. Cricket and I leave Pete's house and continue our 'Summer Solstice' walk through the neighborhood blocks on garbage day.

At the next house, we meet a man who, calling out to the street for Cricket as we walk by, introduces himself as 'Phat Bob.' He is the owner of the home, a big, husky, middle-aged guy with an enormous beer potbelly. He's caught in between two young long-haired hippy types who are scuffling around on his patio deck.

"Cricket! I need your help over here! Can you come and talk some sense to these numbskulls?"

Cricket motions for me to come along. I push the shopping cart into the driveway and follow Cricket out to the front deck. The two hippie guys are arguing over a huge picture leaning up against a wall. It looks like the back of someone's hair. The picture is gigantic—it's six feet tall and four feet wide.

"This is the back of Jerry Garcia's head!" says Phat Bob. "Many a tripping party has commenced where deadheads will take LSD, put on the Grateful Dead, and space out in an all day and night trance, staring at this picture," he boasts to us.

The two young teenage boys call a private truce and sit down quietly in front of the picture.

"People have claimed to see everything under the sun in that picture: Heaven, Hell, God, Satan, angels, the antichrist, revelation, cosmic harmony, outer space, truth, light, wisdom, the past, the future—you name it!" says Phat Bob.

"Yeah, and it's all just a product of an individual's imagination!" says Cricket.

"Spaced out of their gourd imagination," I add.

"You can't deny people the experience of their own truth!" says Phat Bob. "That picture can be whatever people want it to be. That's the magic of it. Each person has their own relation and perception."

"If it's good and positive I like it. But when it can be evil and damaging then I don't," says Cricket.

I study the picture for a while with the teenagers. The three of us stand there in silence looking at a big mass of hair—gray, white, black, brown, thick and stringy hair.

"Free trips with Captain Trips!" Phat Bob raises his beer can in salute to his prized portrait, and downs the beer in one long gulp, crunch's the can into a fist, belch's real loud, and walks over to his cooler on the porch and cracks open another brew.

"One guy camped out at my house on the front lawn for two weeks because he had to see 'Garcia's Head, Man!' This guy was a total loony!" says Phat Bob. "I finally had to call the cops and have them remove the guy. He was harmless, but he wouldn't leave—spooked the shit out of my family, my wife and kids. I thought it was funny at first and advocated to let him stay. But the guy just became a spaced-out leech."

"What's the problem you're having with these two guys?" I inquire.

"The two young punks are arguing over who would get the picture if I put it out for garbage day. I tease them and suggest I may put it out for garbage day and they believe me and I almost start a damn war!" Phat Bob explains with a hearty chuckle.

"I just want to get some raw energy going and now these two want to fight about it."

"I think you all are foolish!" says Cricket. "Come on, Ted, we need to get going."

"Just a minute," says Phat Bob. "I have some stuff I've been saving for you, Cricket." She follows him into his house where he gives Cricket two big garbage bags of clothes and stuffed toys.

"I've been accumulating all this stuff just for you," Phat Bob says as they both return to the deck.

I take the bags and empty them into the cart. The cart is now full and her rainbow bag is bulging off her shoulders.

"We're going to need another shopping cart, Ted."

Cricket is only looking for a certain kind of 'garbage' to take with us, like clothes, little children's toys and canned food. Nothing else is acceptable.

"If we get too loaded down we're going to unload the stuffed animals," says Cricket. "We still have a long way to go and a lot of ground to cover. I've got a friend with a big industrial van who promised to help me out last week. I need to give him a call soon."

We walk down the sidewalk to the next block over after leaving Phat Bob's. Cricket runs across the street a couple houses down and disappears out back. I keep walking straight ahead, pushing the cart along. I pass the house where Cricket disappeared and keep on walking.

It's a party festival atmosphere everywhere. Music is emanating from almost every house and yard. Most of the time it is folk music—Bob Dylan, Joan Baez, Arlo and Woody Guthrie. It seems as if there is an amateur musician with a guitar, on every front porch or out in the yard.

Flower petals in the hair is a big thing. Everywhere we roam people seem to be into it. Cricket and I wear flower petals in our hair and ivy and garland around our ears from casual strangers coming out to greet us in merriment as we saunter by.

Cricket comes running down the sidewalk after me. She has another shopping cart she is pushing in front of her. Cricket's rainbow bag is in it and the shopping cart is overloaded and bulging just like mine.

"We need a third cart now!" I say in jest. We laugh together. "What are we going to do now?"

Cricket is huffing and puffing all out of breath. "I've got a ride for us! I made the phone call and Rex is on his way. We have to meet him at a street corner a couple blocks away. Let's go!" says Cricket.

We continue to walk at a brisk pace as I follow her,

both of us with a shopping cart, down the neighborhood streets. When we come to the designated meeting place, no one is there. Within a couple minutes Cricket spots the vehicle heading toward us as she jumps up and down waving and gesturing to the driver.

"Over here! Here we are, Rex!" she hollers down the street.

A solid white van pulls up to the curb alongside of us and I meet Rex. He runs a janitorial supply company. Rex uses his van to haul wholesale products around. He jumps out and opens a door in the back and another door on the side. Rex has an extra shopping cart in here. The whole back is cleared out so we can just load up our shopping carts right into the van. The two of us lift the full carts into the vehicle. We give Cricket back her rainbow bag, all empty, and we unload the extra shopping cart.

"I'm going to follow you guys until you get the last cart full," says Rex. "Then we're going to go into some poor neighborhoods and to an orphanage."

Cricket rushes up to a house with her cart. I hang back and talk to Rex through his open passenger window.

"Cricket is like the Robin Hood and Pied Piper of Rochester," says Rex. "She never ceases to amaze me!"

"She played the flute and led us down the road to see a sunrise the other day," I say.

"I've experienced a few sunrises around Cricket after an all night party. It's incomparable! There's nothing else like it I've ever experienced," says Rex. "She is like the goddess of the sun—sometimes seems to have the unending energy of ten people!"

"That's why it's so exciting to be around Cricket. You can't help but to pick up on her enthusiasm and excitement about life," I agree.

"I could never keep up with her on a daily basis. I love

how she is so genuine and caring for the disadvantaged and the underdogs of the world. Our son is physically disabled and my wife and I see how Cricket is so genuine in her outpouring of kindness and caring to others. She is a teacher and a healer. She heals relationships and gives people hope," says Rex.

I stand out by the driveway of a brick ranch house waiting for Cricket to emerge. My thoughts turn to the act of giving and caring for other people, strangers. I consider my life and goals.

What is my purpose? Why am I here? What am I supposed to accomplish with this life? I know what my purpose IS NOT! My purpose is not to fail, not to be negative, not to give up, not to work against myself, not to lose hope, not to be unenlightened, not to be loveless and not to be unhappy…

It feels good to be useful, to help and deliver the goods, bring peace and friendship and compassionate caring. The people of the earth are in need. Help poor souls for a day. Be cheerful. Make 'em laugh. Make 'em smile. Give 'em some food, toys, clothes. Give them heartfelt compassion. Free-flowing love…

Rex puts the van in park by the curbside and rearranges space in the back. Just then Cricket comes out from behind the house with a bulging cart much bigger and larger than the two we already have. We can't even see Cricket—just a moving cart.

Cricket endeavors to spread some good karma energy where it's most in need. "This is going to be fun, Ted," Cricket says as I hear her muffled voice from behind the cart. "Let's go do the right thing, Ted!"

Before meeting Cricket I had lost my compassion. Lost in my own delusions, my own self-overblown fantasy become nightmare, become self-pity, become the will to overcome. People become my problem, my blame, my excuses, my shame. The loveless state soon pervades. Lost. Disconnected. Numb. Disoriented. Lack of inner peace, lack of love.

Rex and I rush over to get the cart from Cricket and load it in the van. Cricket sits in the passenger seat and I squeeze into a space on the floor of the van right behind the driver's seat.

Rex drives us to an orphanage. Cricket talks with the authorities at the front desk lobby. She comes back to the van and directs Rex to take the wraparound driveway to the backdoor entrance of the group home. We unload all of our stuff from the van. Rex and I take it to a back storage room area where we separate the stuff into toys, food, clothes, and stuffed animals. We then load up the three empty carts in the van and drive back to where we left off so we can continue our 'garbage picking' day.

On our second and third trips, we visit houses and trailers in what looks like a skid row neighborhood, well below the poverty line. Cricket would always get out and talk to people and find out if they were willing to receive charity. Not surprisingly, some family homes were deeply offended, and they told us to go away. One guy even said if we didn't get away from his house he would shoot us. We left in a hurry. Rex squealed the tires of his van as we moved down the street.

We gave away six full grocery carts of stuff in the downtrodden neighborhoods. When we find a family that is happy to see us, then we spring into action unloading the charitable goods. Every once in awhile Cricket would have Rex pull over so she could grab a few canned goods—

peaches, pork and beans, soups—and run up to a porch and set it on the door step.

On our final drop off at another orphanage, we stop along the way to look under some bridges, back alleys and a couple homeless shelters. Cricket would quickly assess the situation—rummage through the carts, throw some clothes and food cans in her rainbow bag, then run out to the vagabond homeless and hand out the items.

It is such a rush watching her in action. Rex and I marvel at how quick and smooth she operates.

Here we are, the guys, and we are scared to death, paranoid half the time, while hanging out in less than stellar environments. These aren't the same neighborhoods where Cricket lives. We are looking out in all directions, craning our necks, and eyes, to be ever on the alert for danger. We are Cricket's watch dog helpers. At last, she completes all of her tasks and everything goes well.

We've used up our whole day on 'garbage day,' getting around from place to place. We've covered a lot of territory.

After the fourth run to a second orphanage, Rex says, "I've got to go. My wife and kids are expecting me for dinner."

He drops off Cricket and me at the Summer Solstice neighborhood festival. He keeps two of the empty carts in his van. We have made four rounds all told and delivered a dozen carts of stuff.

Cricket and I head down the streets, me pushing our empty cart, while she skips and hops along, her rainbow bag flopping at her side. I start thinking about the road I've traveled in life and where I've come from and where I'm going…

What am I trying to do with this life? Weakness, failure, losing, near death. Running the gauntlet of my personal truth has almost driven me to the brink. What is it I seek? Liberty and peace, inner understanding—fitting in with my fellow man—being useful to society. This gauntlet has rendered a fissure of demarcation, splitting myself in two—the false road and the royal road. One broad and wide, one narrow and deep. The unique road I must travel is opening itself to me. So easy to get lost; fear of the unknown, uncertainty. The living of a life—my life—Theodore Senario, born in Chicago, of an ancient Italian island heritage. I pledge to myself to travel my road and seek my peaceful shores.

Life is a journey, life is a lesson, life is a blessing. Rowing to my peaceful shores, floating and sailing and seeking and believing. Who am I? Where shall I go? Servicing and giving? Starting and completing? I must run this gauntlet and seek my soul.

ജ്ഞ

Cricket decides she wants to get involved with something else at somebody's home. I beg off. I just want to walk through the neighborhoods, enjoy the evening and relax. I can't continue at Cricket's pace. I feel the need to saunter along and be in solitude with my thoughts amidst the vast crowd of happenings.

I spend several hours roaming the neighborhood streets the rest of the evening. I stop at a corner hot dog stand and purchase a corn dog and a soda. I enjoy walking amongst the masses and witnessing the camaraderie and good times enjoyed by all.

The street lights are on, the front yards and porches spill over with music—guitars, tambourines, cymbals, a harmonica, a flute, drum beats, the crescendo of conversing voices at various octaves, vibrates through the night air.

I eventually find myself nearing back to Cricket and

Peter's place. There isn't much going on in the house or on the property—everyone is scattered about partying at different places in the neighborhood. I use this as a cue to hit the sack to catch up on my rest.

I walk over to my tent in the backyard but I can't sleep. My mind is busy with thoughts, images, and visions of what I've been experiencing throughout the day. I need to settle myself down. I am still too hyped up.

It is time to meditate.

I sit in my tent in a folded leg position, pyramidal, with my thumb and forefingers touching and each hand resting on a knee. I visualize the rainbow chakra energy system—the seven points of energy that Mignon and Cricket introduced to me. Each color becomes a vibrant hue: red, orange, yellow, green, blue, indigo and violet. Then all the colors of the rainbow mix into a solid burst of white light from my brain down my spine to the tailbone.

I feel a sudden rush as I become attuned within myself.

My breathing slows down and I connect with the rhythm of my breath. I meditate like this for a solid fifteen to twenty minutes. When I come out of my meditation I am more peaceful and balanced and ready for a good night's rest.

But my mind is still busy with visions and thoughts as I drift off to sleep. But everything has slowed down now. I ponder on friendship, happiness, positive goodwill toward fellow man, the Symposium, an Indian Shaman, Spirits, Witches, Hades, Purgatory, and Heaven on Earth.

I stop on the last topic and focus on that. "Heaven on Earth." I sing the phrase in my mind and smile as I recall the images of my recent experiences.

"Heaven on Earth…Heaven on Earth…Heaven on Earth…" I slowly start drifting off to unconsciousness. I'm in the hypnogogic state—between being awake and sleeping.

ꕥ

"Once it chanced that I stood in the very abutment of a rainbow's arch, which filled the lower stratum of the atmosphere, tingeing the grass and leaves around, and dazzling me as if I looked through coloured crystal. It was a lake of rainbow light, in which, for a short while, I lived like a dolphin."

—Henry David Thoreau

I feel so alive and connected to the Natural Order. The constructive correlative principles of nature are enlightening me. I can breathe in the truth of my being. The rainbow is real, I can touch it! I see the multi-colored glow in the palm of my hand, against my skin, I'm bathing in the light.

The pebbly stars in the sky are like ocean pearls, resting, making the light of their own shores. I want to pluck them and taste the morsels of their truth. Star light, shine bright—I salute the truth in Nature and Nature's God!

The Great Philosophers and Great Thinkers all had something of vital importance in common. This common thread of equilibrium, the law of balance within, universally applicable. The passion draws the inward seeker. I am of keen interest. These signs of harmony I follow. Deconstruct. Construct. A life lived and learned. The growing evolution. Connecting with people is the solution. Striving. Seeking. Experiencing. Loving. Breathing. Seeing. Feeling. I am that – I am that I am—I am. Harmonic consistency and continuity infuse my consciousness!

I fall asleep soon after, and have a wonderful refreshing night's rest.

The Summer Solstice party continues on the next day. And the day after is the 4th of July culmination celebration. I mingle with and meet hundreds of people, walking the streets and neighborhoods for hours upon hours.

I visit Pete and he plays his guitar and sings. We mastermind the lyrics to a song together. I jot it all down and then rewrite a copy for Pete and leave it with him. He says he is going to put some chords and sheet music to it.

I see Phat Bob again. Everyone is joyful and happy in summer celebration mode. I stare at the Jerry Garcia hair picture for about a half hour. Deadhead hippies keep telling me that I will see a vision and it will help me write if I stare at it and meditate in front of the picture. I give it a half hour—why not? Nothing happens for me. Moments come and moments pass. I figure the Grateful Dead must literally live on inside some of these deadhead heads.

On the Fourth of July in the evening I find myself on the river's edge watching the fireworks with a large crowd of people and I don't recognize anyone.

After the fireworks I take a long walk back to Cricket and Peter's Victorian home. The house is full and bustling once again. I can hear firecrackers going off in the distance, and I see kids with sparklers running around in their yards.

The Summer Solstice celebration has been one great big continuous event. The aura shines in multi-colored layers of enlightening light. The rainbow is real—just touch it, give it a feel!

ꕥ

Chapter Eleven

Finger Lakes—Ball & Chain Newsletter

ꕥ

"We arrive at virtue by taking its direction instead of imposing ours. It is ours when we use it, it is not ours, when we do not use it...one does not possess these powers, but is as a pipe or channel by which these powers of nature flow."

—Ralph Waldo Emerson

Waterfall Ceremony Plans

After the 'Summer Solstice Independence' parties, we have a four day period before we leave for the Finger Lakes region for the next series of celebrations, culminating with Cricket and Peter's wedding. I sleep quite a bit, and keep to myself for the first day, resting and reading in my tent.

The next day Cricket wakes me early, just after sunrise. "Ted, time to rise," she whispers through the window flap of the tent. "Ted, it's time to get up. We've got a lot of things to do. I've brought you a hot herbal tea."

I roll around and stretch in my sleeping bag, semi-conscious, listening to this whispering voice in my head.

It's Cricket chirping at sunrise with the songbirds.

I sit up and yawn, unzip my tent, get out and greet Cricket with a little hug. She hands me the cup of tea and then we walk down to the pond. We sit on a bench without talking and watch the goldfish swim while we sip our hot tea. No one else is up.

"We have about twenty-five people staying in the house or camping in the yard," she says. "Peter still has his Best Man, and his parents, to come in from Michigan tomorrow or the next day."

"Is Peter from Michigan?" I ask.

"Peter graduated from the University of Michigan. His buddy Dave has an Engineering degree from U of M also. Dave now works in Ann Arbor. Peter's parents live in Grand Rapids," says Cricket.

She hands me a sheet of paper—it's titled, 'The Ball and Chain Newsletter—Vol. 2.' In the right-hand corner of the paper is a silhouette of a man and woman sitting close together on a park bench under a streetlamp. The document is directions to the 'BIG SHOW'—a series of parties and celebrations out in nature.

"From Rochester take I-390 south to Exit number 408," she says with exuberance. "Take a right on Route 36 and it leads to the Park entrance. Follow the Park road about fifteen to twenty miles and follow the signs for Middle Falls and the Glen Iris Inn."

"How am I going to get there?" I ask.

"Keep these directions so you'll be sure to know how to get there," Cricket says. "I'll find someone for you to hitch a ride with. It will be very hectic with people everywhere rushing about, so don't lose this," she says, pointing at the ball and chain newsletter directions.

"I think I'm going to set you up with a ride from my brother, Don. He's a Southwest Airlines pilot, and he's coming by himself in a brand new red convertible. I think it's a Ferrari!" she says, amping up with excitement. "You two will enjoy each other's company. Don likes to read a lot too. He's on a tight schedule so I'm still waiting for a confirmation phone call from him," Cricket says.

"How many brothers and sisters do you have?" I ask.

"Just Don and me, but we're over a dozen years apart.

He was gone to college and moved on by the time I started school," Cricket says. "All of my rainbow family clan and friends are like my brothers and sisters."

She downs her cup of tea in a big gulp, and jumps up pulling on my hand, ready to get moving.

"I want to spend some quality time with you today and tomorrow because after that I will be unavailable," she explains, "getting involved with all the last minute preparations and organizing people and things. So, let's get going this morning and get out of here before anybody wakes up."

Cricket takes our empty cups and hurries up to the backdoor of her home and then comes out a few seconds later with a thick stack of newsletters she cradles in her arms.

"What are you going to do with those?" I whisper.

"Come on, let's go," she whispers back to me and motions to follow. "I've got to get these spread out today!"

We get in her car like a couple of escapees and head into town—the 'Greenwich Village' area of Rochester. It is still too early in sleepy dawn and most of the businesses aren't open yet, except for a small coffee shop that looks deserted just opening up. She runs in with a stack of papers while I wait in the car. She comes rushing back a few moments later with a cup of coffee for each of us.

"Let's go do something fun! We can drop off newsletters a little later. I've got a surprise, an epiphany to share with you," Cricket says with a beaming smile.

Then she hands me my cup of coffee and hops in the car and drives us to the place for the unveiling of her new brainchild.

ꕥ

"We will drive to the shores of Lake Ontario and then go to Greece," Cricket says.

I give her a double-look of bewilderment when she says, 'Greece.' Cricket ignores my questioning glance as she smiles with a mischievous look in her eye that serves to only pique my curiosity.

"I have an idea I've been intending to share with you for some time, and now is finally the time. I want to tell you about it when we are in Greece," Cricket says.

I look out at the roadway as she enters the highway entrance ramp.

"So, you can't tell me about your idea till we get there?"

"Not till we're in Greece, Ted. It's a symbolic thing. Be Here Now! The Higher the Fewer!" Cricket exclaims. "You may not like my idea at all, we'll see! There is a city named 'Greece,' northwest of Rochester, before the lake, actually a little village town. We will stop there after visiting Lake Ontario. There is a tree in a park in Greece that I like to go meditate under—my own personal Bodhi, not a real one, mind you—but the symbolic intent is there."

Twenty minutes down the road, Cricket pulls over to a roadside entrance to the lakeshore. She parks near a path that leads down to the lake. We walk along the shores of Lake Ontario as Cricket tells me all about the details and plans for her waterfall marriage ceremony with Peter.

"The most beautiful nature setting you can imagine, a huge waterfall backdrop and flowers and music and food and games and liquid refreshments. This is going to be a one-hundred-hour party, Ted! People and friends and family are coming from all over the country. I have so many things to do. That's why I want to get away with you today before everything starts getting unmanageable and out of control. I have a lot of coordination to oversee. We have to get all our gear, everyone's gear and equipment, transported to the scene. Can't forget anything," she says.

"Is there anything I can do?" I ask.

"Yes! Yes! Enjoy yourself!" she says. "Write! Think! Socialize! Have fun! It was meant for you to be here and it was meant for us to meet. You are the 'Bohemian Writer' I was destined to meet on my grand grateful gathering tour. I've known—I've always known!"

"What have you always known?" I ask.

"That this time would be special and a mysterious confluence of forces and energies would align," she responds. "Come, let's sit on the beach over here, Ted, in the sand and stare at the horizon."

We take a seat next to each other and without speaking look out on nature—water, sky, sun. We are in complete solitude on the sandy shore.

Stillness. A calm breeze.

A meditative quiet contentment takes hold from within.

Breathe in. Breathe out …

Have I been running from people, running from relationships, running from life? Why am I so torn asunder? It feels good reconnecting with people and society. The vast relationships feed my creative energy. I sense an obligation and responsibility to my fellow man. Why have I never felt this way before? Because I was trapped in my own ego of self-deluded habits. I will recapture my mental liberation. With Thankfulness and in Gratitude, I am at peace.

Cricket nudges me, which startles me out of my reverie.

"Let's walk back to the car, Ted. Time for me to take you to my favorite spot in Greece. Satori! Kairos! Epiphany! I'm a catalyst converter!" she jumps up and exclaims as she runs away from me towards the car.

"Come on, Ted," she hollers back to me, "let's go!"

I hurry along after her and meet up at the car. Cricket then drives us to Greece.

"Are you still curious?" she asks. "Curious about my proposal plan?"

"So, now it's a proposal plan," I say.

"Well, you have to agree to let me do it," she responds. "I can't proceed without your cooperation and trust in me."

"Yes, you have my curiosity piqued. When can we end the suspense, already?" I ask in feigned exasperation.

Then we drive by a sign that reads—'Greece Canal County Park.'

"A small tributary river from Lake Ontario runs through the park," Cricket says. "It's very peaceful here."

Cricket enters the quaint town's park and drives us to a small secluded alcove overlooking the river.

"That tree over there is my special tree. We understand each other. She is my Bodhi. I pray and meditate under her," says Cricket as she points out the car window at her favorite tree.

After she parks the car we walk over to the huge wide-girth mangrove-like tree and sit down on the rippled and gnarled roots that protrude from the ground at the base. We clutch our hands together from our outstretched arms, facing each other, and meditate in silence with closed eyes for several minutes. Then Cricket suddenly bursts up from the tree, unclasping my fingers and scurries down to the river's edge, then runs back up to me sitting under the tree.

"The Higher the Fewer! Be Here Now!" she exclaims. "Come on, let's take a stroll, Ted!"

Cricket is obviously too excited and full of bundled up energy to sit under a tree—even if it is her favorite tree—she must move as she expresses herself. She's ready to spill the beans on her new idea-proposal plan.

"Okay! Okay! I'm with you!" I say. "I can't wait to hear what all this excitement is about."

We walk through the park in Greece, sauntering along the riverside while skipping small stones across the water. Cricket whistles to herself and moves like a cheetah through the park as I hurry to keep up with her. We pass by a few people out walking their dogs.

"All right, I've had enough," I say. "I'm not going to chase after you all through the park. Let's hear what you have to say."

She stops about ten yards in front of me, where we meet up and then walk back together to her special tree.

"Ted, would you trust me with your writing notebooks?" she asks.

"Why would I need to do that?"

"I want to keep them for a couple of days and work on a project with Mignon. I have a desktop publishing software package and I want to use it to structure and format my idea for some of your writings and poetry," Cricket says. "This is the only time I will have available to do this—just today and tomorrow. Mignon has agreed to help me."

"What do you want to do?" I ask.

"Remember when we first met and I read some of your writings and you read some to me, and I said your stuff must be seen, read and heard?"

I nod in acknowledgement.

"I want to put some of your more meaningful writings into a simple one page pamphlet booklet," she explains.

"I don't see where you're going with this," I reply.

"If you would indulge me a little longer," Cricket says, "I will fully explain myself. I've known for some time now. I've always known I would eventually meet up with someone. Not just anyone, but someone special with a unique message that would serve and uplift humanity. I've been all over the United States and Canada in the last few years, meeting all kinds of wonderful people and joining up with beneficial causes and leading the way as an exemplar. I've discovered the higher the fewer, Ted. I've learned to be here now! There is a great struggle taking place amongst the masses everyday across this country, the globe," she explains. "People need and hunger for self-illumination, self-liberty, happiness and contentment, but they don't know how to go about it. I believe you have a unique way with thoughts and words that fills a need, Ted Senario—Mr. Bohemian!"

"Thank you for the high praise, which I doubt I deserve," I respond. "I don't know if I have the courage and belief in my own self, as much as you have in me. You see a greater me than I can aspire to, it seems. I need to write to survive, to suffer and struggle and overcome, to understand."

"But you suffer, Ted, because you are in search of truth. Some of your pages of writings are just glowing with overflowing wisdom. I feel the power surge right through me," she says. "This is a rare gift! I can't do it. I have passionate artist friends in writing, painting, music—and the commonality they all have is a deep suffering from their inner core to self-express the art encapsulated within. You get where I'm coming from, Ted? You are a natural! You give voice and soul to the vibe that permeates at the gatherings—positively feeding off the energy with written words of deep meanings, Ted."

With a serious look our eyes and senses lock as I stare back at my muse.

"So, what is your plan with my notebooks?" I inquire.

"To create a bohemian buzz, Ted!"

Cricket walks to her car and then comes back with a sheet of paper, a copy of the Ball & Chain newsletter directions.

"Just a minute, watch this—I'll show you," she says. Cricket folds the sheet in half and then folds it again. Then she takes a pen from her gypsy dress pocket and numbers the four sides—one, two, three, four. "Side number one is the cover title—sides number two and three open up together—we can fill this up with prose and poetry you've already written. Then on the back page, side number four—you can conclude with a poem or final word from the author—You—The Bohemian."

She jumps in the air like a cheerleader, with a big beaming smile of self-assurance. Then Cricket leans into a semi-huddle with me to continue with her plan, "We won't use your name, just the moniker—by 'The Bohemian.' We can hand them out at small colleges, University campuses, coffee houses, libraries, concerts, bookstores, events, parks—everywhere!"

"I'm not so sure of this idea of yours," I respond. "What do you need me to do? Some of my private journal passages are meant to stay that way."

"You told me once that you almost died several times in your life, right?" inquires Cricket.

"Yes."

"Don't you think that your repeated near miss of death has left a burden on you?"

"Yes."

"This burden is your soul asking you to 'Heal Thyself!'—to coordinate your habit energies into a constructive flow that pays back and serves nature," Cricket says. "This is why you pour yourself into your writings and express such startling creativity, Ted."

"So, you want to exploit my stuff then, like an agent or a marketer?"

"Yes and No," she replies.

"First, we have to have a product that caters to your streams of thought. That's where my idea comes in—how to package some of your creative work for edible consumption, without blowing people away or talking way over their heads. So, 'yes,' it is a marketing thing and 'no,' I'm not proposing to be an agent for your genius. However, I'd like to think of myself as the 'Catalyst Converter' of this process. Like I said before, I've known and been aware and on the look-out for quite some time—my intuition tells me this is the right thing to do. Do you trust me, Ted?"

"Yes—yes! I do," I respond.

"Then, I'll ask you again—can I have your notebooks when we get back to the house? I'll need them for the rest of the day and tomorrow. I already talked this over with Mignon and told her I was going to spring this on you and if you go for it then she and I are going to work together to build the pamphlets," Cricket says.

"Sure," I say. "I'm interested to see what you come up with."

Cricket hops and jumps around her favorite tree in Greece.

"You will see for yourself tomorrow night," she says. "I'm the Catalyst Converter!"

Soon after, we get in her car and drive back to the 'Greenwich Village' area of her town.

"I'm going to head out of Greece and get back to Rochester. I never took you on a proper tour of our town," she says. "We have a lot of interesting places and sites in Rochester."

She drives thru the small town of Greece and enters

the highway to take us back south. Several miles later she takes the Rochester exit. Cricket parks the car and I follow along as she stops in the coffee shops, book stores, cafés, bar lounges and record stores to leave copies of her Ball & Chain Newsletter. She encourages the owners of the small businesses to make more copies if they need to, and spread the word.

We get rid of her stack of newsletters in short order, and then head back to the parking lot just before the noon hour. I rush to keep up as she skips and jumps along the sidewalk and across the streets.

ꕥ

Cricket backs up her car and drives out of the parking lot, as I sit in the seat beside her, anticipating the next things she will be taking us to experience.

"How come you're being so quiet, Ted?"

"Just enjoying the time and listening to you. I'm thinking of the actual Greece—Athens, Sparta, Socrates, Plato, Pericles, Herodotus, Aristotle, Homer, Euripides, Alexander the Great!" I say. "Just thinking about those famous lifetimes and the traces they've left on human history."

"That's why I knew you would appreciate it, symbolically, of course," she says, "if we spent some time here. I love my little meditation tree. Don't you, too?"

"Yes—yes! I have special places and trees I feel that way about, back home in Michigan," I respond.

Cricket beams a big smiley face at me, "You just wait till I show you the materialization of my idea! By tomorrow night Mignon and I will have something to show you."

"I'm excited to see what you have up your sleeve," I say.

"This first place I'm going to stop at is Cobb's Hill Park," Cricket says. "Peter and I go bike riding and roller blading through here. They have bands and poetry readings out here sometimes at the outdoor auditorium."

Cricket then pulls the car into the entrance of Cobbs Hill Park. After she finds a parking space, we get out and head to the hilltop. I look up at Cricket as she runs up the hill.

"Come on, Ted! From the top you can see the city of Rochester!" Cricket says with excitement as she continues to usher ahead of me, finally reaching the top of the hill. I make it up the hill right after her. Both of us take a minute to catch our breath. We stand there for a few minutes overlooking the city—skyline, industry, homes and roads.

"Isn't this wonderful, Ted? We need to get going to the next place!" she says. "I have a beautiful waterfall to show you!"

And with a burst of exuberance she races back down the hill and I chase after her.

Cricket drives us to the next nature park on her grand tour about town. We enter the Upper Falls Park by the Genessee River.

"I've always loved waterfalls," she says. "I think a waterfall is mesmerizing. Waterfalls and rainbows are two of my most favorite things in nature. Water bringing life and a rainbow, light."

We take a seat in the grass and view the hundred-foot Upper Falls.

"This waterfall use to power the city's flour mills at the turn of the century," Cricket says. "So Rochester was called the 'Flour City' because of its milling industries. Now it's known as the 'Flower City' because of our abundant parks, nurseries and garden areas," she says.

We sit in silence for about fifteen minutes staring at the vast waterfall—white water crashing, perpetual waves reverberating echoes…

Then Cricket drives us to one more park in the city of Rochester.

"You'll love this view too, Ted! Manhattan Square Park has a huge observation tower," she says, "over a hundred feet in the air."

She parks the car and we jump out like jackrabbits.

"Come on, Ted, I'll race you to the top!" she boasts as I rush to trail along. "Another nice view, Ted!" Cricket outstretches her arms to the sky. "Perspective! Natural Nature!" She takes in a deep breath through her nostrils and blows the air out of her mouth. "Exhale! Inhale!" A big beaming smile spreads across her petite face.

"I'm with you, Cricket!" I say. "I love the raw elements! Nature is harmony!" I look down upon rows and rows of flowers and flowering shrubbery and green-leafed trees blowing in the breeze. "The beautiful color scheme of breathing life."

"We need to get going again, Ted. This is fun but I have more places to take you and show you," she says. As she scurries down the stairs, she stops and looks back up at me, trailing behind by a half-dozen steps or so. "Let's go to the cemetery next!" Cricket says. "We have some historic people who were great leaders of civil rights, who lived and died here."

Then she motors on down the rest of the stairwell and I rush along after her. Cricket drives us to Mount Hope Cemetery.

As we enter the gates and she parks the car, Cricket whispers, "This is where Susan B. Anthony and Frederick Douglas are buried. Come on, I'll take you to their burial sites."

Cricket gets out of the car and opens her trunk to retrieve a couple stems of plastic red roses she has stored there. After she shuts the trunk and locks the car, I follow along.

"Do you come here often?" I ask.

"Often enough," she says, "when I need to! Why?"

"Just because you have plastic flowers ready for just such a thing," I say.

"I always have plastic flowers and candles in my trunk. You've seen what a collector I am. I collect and redistribute," she says.

We walk by huge granite stones dotted along the grass line throughout the cemetery. Cricket then veers off the edge of the roadway and walks across a field of grave markers. As she gets closer to her destination, she bursts into a slight gallop and I must jog to keep up. When I catch up to her, she is standing at the gravestone of Frederick Douglas. In silent reverence we stand with bowed heads and stare at the name 'Frederick Douglas' etched in the stone, for a solid ten minutes. I think about the great struggles for civil rights and equality for African-Americans.

"He was their Moses, even more so than Martin Luther King Jr.," Cricket says. "He was a slave who trained himself to be a writer and a speaker, and he became the greatest exemplar for his struggling race in his time."

"I remember reading about him in school," I say. "He met with Abe Lincoln several times. Sure would have liked to be in that room to hear their conversations."

"Come on, let's go! I have another historic gravesite for you to see—Susan B. Anthony." Cricket gestures with a wave for me to follow her to the next site.

As we walk along the edge of a well traveled dirt pathway in the cemetery, my mind drifts:

Civil rights and equality, the end of slavery, the thought of being alive during slavery, Women's suffrage and the well fought fight for the right to vote for half the human race in America. The tide turned—endless lives finally given a new meaning of perspective for ensuing generations. A strong melancholy feeling takes hold of me, such as when I was visiting the Memorials in DC, or the Native American Shrine in Cricket's backyard—a strong reverence for life and energy and historic directions through time. Civilization evolves and plods along. I'm reminded of my recent trip to the Statue of Liberty. Freedom is not free. It never has been. So many have suffered in the struggles to unbind mankind. This persistent fact seems to gloss over the present thinking of the vast multitudes. We sell ourselves short as individuals, again and again. Do we truly appreciate our lives?

"Susan B. Anthony was arrested for voting in 1872," says Cricket. We stand in silence before the granite rock monument. Cricket bows her head and I can tell she is thinking of thankfulness and gratitude, with her eyes closed and her voiceless lips moving, she concludes her prayer and then kneels to place the red rose on the ground near the grave marker.

After a long ten-minutes of silence Cricket breaks the quietude with, "Let's go visit Susan B. Anthony's home. Her red brick Victorian home is right here in the town. Just take a few minutes."

And with that I am back on her trail, following Cricket to the car to head to the next destination. As she drives up to the house we discover the museum home will be closed today—doesn't matter because Cricket is like my own personal tour guide. We park and get out of the car and walk around the perimeter of the home.

"This is where she lived during the most politically active period of her life," Cricket says. "This is where she was living when she was arrested for voting in 1872. This place should be like a shrine to all women. It is for me. I've been through the home dozens of times and I know the tour guides. I've been through her writing room and her bedroom and her reading room," says Cricket as fast as she can, as I look out on the red-bricked façade. I imagine the life presence of the great female pioneer who inhabited this domain with her undying energy for the reform she must personally bring about.

Living history. Hallowed ground.

"Come on, Ted, I have a couple more things to show you before we must head to the house."

Back on the road looking out the passenger window, my mind drifts to the great lives, the great characters of history:

> *Thoreau and Emerson and Whitman and Plato and Aristotle—Transcendent thought unleashed! Socrates, Pythagoras, Jesus, Confucius, Buddha—connecting with the great mind and spirits of all time—Soul Sensations! Copernicus, Galileo, Kepler and Newton—universal pedigrees—Understanding Nature's vast mechanical system! Einstein, Leonardo da Vinci, Michelangelo, Shakespeare and Edison—invoking the fires of creation!*

Cricket drives by a big mansion estate. "This is the George Eastman House. You know—the Eastman Kodak Company. He was the co-founder. Became the richest man in Rochester in his day," Cricket says. "It has over fifty rooms!"

"It sure would be something to have more money than you know what to do with, wouldn't it?" I say, looking out at the rich aristocratic structure. "I'm sure you must have toured through there, too, huh?"

"I did when I first moved out here to settle down with Peter, but I'm not too impressed with opulent displays of wealth," Cricket says. "Money should be used to serve and enhance, not bind and imprison."

"Aren't you being a bit overly critical of the guy, what's his name—George?" I say. "He worked with inventors and had a business relationship with Thomas Edison. He was a pioneer for revolutionary changes."

"True! True! I'm speaking of the misuse of wealth in general by the wealthy. I didn't mean to denigrate George Eastman," Cricket says. "Things could work better in society for the unfortunate—that's all I meant."

And with that last uttered word we sit staring out the window of the car as she drives.

Silence. Lost in our own thoughts.

We then proceed through a neighborhood and over to Cricket's final stop of her whirlwind morning tour.

"We're going to finish our little trip by going through a walk in one of our nation's largest municipal rose gardens. Roses of all kinds and colors!" she exclaims.

Cricket twirls, skips and jumps all the way through the multi-colored displays of endless rose petals. After following along for awhile through the rose garden, I find a park bench and stare at Cricket in her energizer-bunny-mode pirouetting through the rows and columns of park flower bushes.

Afterwards, we head back to Cricket's home.

"Wow, Ted! We used up the whole morning and now we're burning afternoon light," Cricket says. "We have to get back. Everyone should be up and about by now. I'm excited to get my hands on your notebooks and get busy with Mignon on my idea and plan!"

ᢒᢓ

When we get back, Cricket says she is going to find Mignon and that I should meet her in the third floor library in forty-five minutes with all my notebooks. I tell her that I only brought four journals with me, but I will give them all to her.

I walk over to my tent in the backyard to get the rest of my notebooks. People are milling about on the property and in the house, gearing up for another day of group energy vibes.

I sit back on the grass in my private secluded spot under the tree beside my tent, flipping through the pages of my notebook journal entries—drifting off into the quiet summer afternoon breeze:

The arc of time—this small span of time encases my short lifetime. I cannot waste it! I will not be empty and hollow. This arc of space and time is all I will ever have to work with. I must refine myself, redefine myself—grab a hold of my wayward character. Redirect myself—reconnect myself. When I come to the end of the line of this short lifetime, I don't want to discover that I had really never 'lived' at all. I am in jeopardy of this soul transgression. Life is a lesson.

Then I hear Cricket and Mignon's voices jointly calling for me from within the house—the upstairs window overlooking the backyard from the fourth floor.

"Ted, Ted Senario! Ted, come on upstairs!"

Then I hear whistles and catcalls, coming from the house interior on multiple floors. An echo phone—blow horn!

"Ted! Ted Senario! Ted, come on upstairs to the library!"

I gather my notebook journals and hurry into the house and up the stairs to the third floor library. I brush past numerous men and women filtering about in the house, being told repeatedly by others that someone is looking for me. The two women are waiting for me at the library door.

"Come on in," says Cricket.

She locks the library door after I enter the room. I hand Cricket my four notebook journals.

"Thank you, Ted," she says.

She hands two of the journals to Mignon, and keeps the other two notebooks for herself. Mignon walks over to a corner office within the library. She sits on a chair beside the door and buries her eyes and mind within the pages of the notebooks.

Mignon looks up briefly and forces a rushed smile. "Thanks, Ted! Cricket and I have a game plan. I'm like her assistant, but she's the one with the idea," says Mignon.

"That's not totally true," replies Cricket. "It was your class in school Mignon, that English composition or creative writing class, when you used that new publishing software. Remember?"

Mignon nods and shrugs her shoulders.

"Well, anyway, I have a PC in this office and I want to pour through your stuff and find little tidbits, sound bites, wisdom sentences, truthful poetry, stuff like that," says Cricket. "But, what I need from you, Ted, is some general direction. Could you choose a dozen themes and come up with a corresponding quote that exemplifies each one? If you can do that for us, then that's all I would need you to do, for what Mignon and I are going to create. Can you do that, Ted?"

"You need this right now? How much time do I have?" I ask.

"We're going to go in my corner office and get setup and read and take notes and jot down ideas and thoughts, get the software going and such," Cricket says. "You just sit here in the library and take as long as you need. I'll have Mignon come out and check up on you now and then. No pressure, Ted! Just relax and enjoy the process as the three of us work out this project. It will be fun I promise you!" she says, with a big, beaming, toothy smile.

"Okay! I'm good to go! I'm with you on this!" I respond.

Cricket and Mignon go off into the corner office and

close the door. I walk up and down the rows of books in the library, grab a sheet of paper and start jotting down words, a column of words, then another column of words. I look over my list for several minutes and then check mark a dozen themes. Cricket has a large chalkboard in the far corner of the library, so, I go over and write out the dozen titled themes for Cricket's research. I stare at my list and wonder, reconsider—erase a couple lines by rubbing the heel of my hand on the chalkboard.

Must keep the thought on a positive philosophical vein, metaphysical spirituality, duality/polarity, creative learning, igniting the spark of the divine within.

Then I write down some famous quotes that I readily remember. I find several quotation books on the library shelves to aid in my research. Mignon comes to check on me and I ask for another thirty minutes to finish the job. When she returns I have the following title and quote affiliations written on the chalkboard:

I **Transcendence**

"A Good Writer speaks to the intellect and heart of mankind, to all in any age who can understand him."

—Thoreau

II **Realities**

"It is not only for an exterior show or ostentation that our soul must play her part, but inwardly within ourselves, where no eyes shine but ours."

—Montaigne

III **Magnetized**

"Of all knowledge, the wise and good seek most to know themselves."

—Shakespeare

IV **The Human Planet**

"Come forth into the light of things,
Let Nature be your teacher."

—Wordsworth

V **Actualization**

"The soul is the perceiver and revealer of truth. We know truth when we see it, let skeptic and scoffer say what they choose."

—Emerson

VI **Uniqueness**

"The great law of culture is: Let each become all that he was created capable of being."

—Carlyle

VII **Infiniteness**

"Man is the sun; his senses the planets."

—Novalis

VIII **Thought Creation**

"Serious things cannot be understood without laughable things, nor opposites at all without opposites."

—Plato

IX **Discovering**

"Not everything that counts can be counted, and not everything that can be counted counts."

—Einstein

X **Seeker Within**

"Nay, be a Columbus to whole new continents and worlds within you, opening new channels, not of trade, but of thought."

—Thoreau

XI **Modernity**

"Money makes money and the money that money makes, makes more money."

—Benjamin Franklin

XII **Momentary**

"Each moment is an age between me, and the consummation of my existence."

—Margaret Fuller

Cricket and Mignon come out of the tiny corner office into the library. They both look over my list on the chalkboard. Then Cricket walks over to the table where I sit and reads out loud each of the dozen themed statements.

Afterwards, she says, "This is exactly what I'm looking for, Ted!"

Mignon stands tall and lanky with her silky thick brunette tresses curled to one side of her slender neck. Her head in motion in a perpetual nod, as if to say, "I understand now!" Mignon looks over Cricket's shoulders to follow along and reread to herself what Cricket has just read.

"I'm so excited! This idea is going to be great," Mignon says.

"Let's get to work," says Cricket.

Then off the two of them go, to the tiny office, behind a closed door.

I sit back lounging on the couch in the library reading some Goethe and Milton and Dante from Cricket's book shelves, keeping me company deep into the evening.

ഌര

Mignon and Cricket cloister themselves behind the office door, and I never see the two of them again for the rest of the day and night.

I leave the serenity and quiet of the library study on the third floor in the late evening and saunter out to the backyard.

There are pockets of people mingling about on the deck, in the backyard, the first floor TV room, and the kitchen. Peter is tending bar and the BBQ pits at his regular hosting post, near the garage area.

"Where are Cricket and Mignon?" Peter asks.

"They're still up in the library in that small office room with the door shut. Mad Scientists!" I joke.

"They always have some type of project they're working on. Now they've got you baited and hooked into one of their schemes," Peter laughs.

"I'm anxious to see what she's going to come up with," I respond.

"What did she do, take your notebooks?"

"Yeah! She's going to 'build something from them' for me Cricket said. So I gave her my journals and she and Mignon have been working together ever since. It's so quiet and serene up there. You become totally oblivious to anything happening elsewhere around the house. I've been up there reading by myself for hours," I say.

"Lynn loves her library and books and little private office," says Peter. "It's a great environment for learning and reading and creativity and writing, drawing, painting, computer projects, whatever."

"I'm very impressed with it," I concur.

"Thanks! It was all Cricket's idea and plan. She talked about it and talked about it over the years and then we bought this house and she finally had all the room she needs, so she designed the library and we put it together. It was a lot of work lugging up all her boxes and crates of books," Peter says. "Cripes, she had a storage shed full of books and encyclopedias and stuff!"

"You two are perfect for each other," I say. "I'm looking forward to this big wedding nature celebration."

"We've been planning it for a long time and it's finally here. I can't believe it," Peter says with a disbelieving grin of denial as he shakes his head.

"You nervous? Having second thoughts?" I ask.

"No! No! Never!" he says heartily. "I'll be glad to get through all this and have it behind me. Meanwhile, there's a lot of fun to be had!"

Peter gulps down his ale and cracks open another brew and motions to offer me one. I decline his offer and move off to the thoroughfare in the backyard when several people come up to Peter's makeshift bar for refills.

I decide to make my way to my tent and call it an evening.

The next morning I walk upstairs to the library and discover Cricket and Mignon are still locked up in the office room.

ᘓᘐ

I need to put the books back on the shelves Cricket had given me to read earlier in the week. I have them stacked in columns in my tent so I make several trips up the stairs to the library and then back to the yard.

I find a book on the bookshelf Cricket has always praised, "Be Here Now" by Baba Ram Dass. I decide to spend the rest of the morning hours outdoors by the sun garden reading this book of 'Presence.'

"Be Here Now. Now Be Here. Be Here Now."

I repeat the phrases of the main theme of the book to myself as I skim through the pages. Cricket's character and manners with people reflect of this material. I can sense a deeper understanding of what makes her tick. She is a living proponent of the 'Be Here Now' philosophy.

My association with Cricket over the last few weeks has driven my inward seeking for greater understanding to uncharted depths:

Teamwork success is a natural aphrodisiac. I feel great! I feel wonderful! Succeeding on projects is much of what the economy of life is about. The work-a-day world stirs the pot of finances, budgets, and paychecks-—The materialistic engine. Harmonic teamwork is usually not so easy. The living example sells greater than all the self-help books ever could.

Cricket is Kant's 'Categorical Imperative' personified. She practices, participates and applies the principles. I'm often at the opposite pole—stuck on theory, learning, knowledge accumulation and integration. And I feel lost so often on my journey. Cricket is naturally adept. Her energetic gears of action lead the way.

I'm thinking of these things, lounging back on a lawn chair, reflecting, contemplating, reading…when I hear loud noises and hollering erupting from within the house. Cricket and Mignon come running out back to my tent area where I'm relaxing. They are filled with overzealous enthusiasm and cheerfulness.

Their project is finished and they've come to show me the results.

Cricket hands me back my notebooks. Then Mignon hands me a couple pamphlets—one reads 'Seed & Roots' by The Bohemian, on the front cover—the other reads 'Self & Soul' by The Bohemian.

I open the pamphlets and read excerpts of my prose and poetry. The women are excited in anticipation of my reaction. I take several minutes to read the passages they've pulled from the notebooks. The two smiling women are quiet with built-up energy like a steamed-pressure cooker about to release.

When I start to speak they each grab one of my arms to brace themselves as they jump up and down like little children.

"This is very unique! I like the concept!" I say.

"We have created original pieces of creative-art word-works," says Mignon.

"Yeah!" replies Cricket, pumping her fist in the air, "We had a wonderful time doing this and creating these little intellectual pieces of property. This is how you start, Ted, as The Bohemian, at the grass roots!"

"The grass-roots man, groovy!" says Mignon, as she embraces me in a hug. Then slowly Mignon backs away from me and says, "Thank you, Ted. Thanks so much for trusting us. This was very fun and these pamphlets can be inspirational to others."

"Okay, it's my turn," says Cricket.

I give Mignon one last quick hug and then we brush lips in a rushed kiss.

"My turn! My turn," says Cricket.

Then I bend down to hug my sweet little petite Muse.

"This is a start of a new life for a new you, Ted," she whispers in my left ear. "You need to write a book and then a whole bunch of books. These pamphlets are a baby step in the right direction. People will read them and want to know more from the Bohemian," Cricket says.

"I appreciate what both of you have done," I reply. "These pamphlets, if anything, will be solid mementos of this time period in life. Creativity, Art, Literature and Teamwork all coming together—what is that phrase you call yourself?"

"The Catalyst Converter!" says Cricket.

"Yeah—the Catalyst Converter! You have done just that," I say. "This is a good creative idea—a short concise way to express deep meanings and profound thought!"

"The hardest part was custom-fitting each mini-page to contain different formats without overlapping or having to edit out stuff," says Mignon.

"Then we had to make sure we matched the content

with our theme for each pamphlet," says Cricket. "We spent a lot of time mixing and matching statements, paragraphs and sentences, until we got it just right. You're going to want to sit down quietly somewhere and go through each one of these to make sure you agree with everything and the editing we did."

"I don't know what else to say except—Thank you! Both of you! Thank you for deeming my stuff worthy and spending your time on this to create these."

I hold up my stack of a dozen pamphlets, shuffling through them like a deck of cards.

Then the three of us share a group hug. I thank them again for their efforts. Cricket wants to go all over and hand them out with some more of her Ball & Chain newsletters.

"It takes less than five minutes to read a pamphlet and if you do the whole dozen, you can be done in just about an hour. Mignon and I timed it for both of us," says Cricket.

They give me an additional two full sets of the dozen pamphlets, with one set tied in a red ribbon. I sit outside the rest of the afternoon looking over the work they've done with the writing compositions in my journals. It is a great mastermind effort.

ꙮ

The following day is all about the waterfall ceremony plans and the big nature party. Many of the relatives and friends begin arriving and stopping by. Last minute preparations are in full swing.

Then around noon Cricket receives a terrible phone call. The florist in town was burglarized over night and all the wedding flowers are ruined. The owner of the floral shop is sobbing as she describes the scene to Cricket over the phone. The florist had a heated argument with her husband the day before and he stormed off drinking and no one has seen him since. She suspects he may have done the damage. The police have the husband on their main suspect list.

The bottom line—no flowers for Cricket's wedding!

After Cricket gets off the phone with the distraught florist she makes several phone calls to local florists, but with no luck on such short notice. And then word gets around from her inner circle of girlfriends spreading the news, "No flowers! No flowers for the wedding!"

The sobering news filters through the house and then picks up steam to become an immediate panic of concern for everyone throughout the house and property. Several of the women are sobbing over this. Cricket is angry, upset, confused—has compassion for the circumstances of the florist—but she needs to spring into action with a plan to solve this problem. There are over sixty people on the property and in the house at this point and everyone is concerned about this emergency.

"What am I going to do, Ted?" asks Cricket. "I can't find an answer to this problem and it's critical that we have flowers. The flowers are supposed to play a major role in this event. I'm bringing together flower children from all across the country to my wedding and I won't have flowers. This can't be happening," she mutters.

"How ironic—a great gathering of flower children without flowers." I say.

"Peter's parents are supposed to arrive from Michigan tomorrow—and they have already paid the florist for the flowers. She said she will refund the money. But what do I do? It's over two grand of flowers," says Cricket.

"Wait a minute…did you say Peter's parents are still in Michigan? Where at?" I ask.

"Yes—Grand Rapids area—why?" asks Cricket.

Suddenly it occurs to me that I may have the possible solution to the unfolding dilemma.

"I have a friend in southeast Michigan who owns a flower shop. Peter's parents are in Grand Rapids and they will be heading east on their trip out here," I say.

"Yes!"

"I can call my florist friend, Loreen, and if she agrees to do it, then maybe we can have Peter's parents stop by and pick up the flowers and drive them through Canada. It will take five to six hours if they shortcut through at the Blue Water Bridge in Port Huron," I say.

Cricket hands me the phone receiver.

"Please make the call right now, Ted! I've run out of options."

"Okay! I have her business card in my wallet. Let me dig it out and then I'll call her and see what she has to say."

Cricket and I walk into a bedroom and close the door on the second floor. It's a nice guest bedroom for young children, twin bunk beds and a play area. Once I get my florist friend, Loreen, on the line I tell her the circumstances of the dilemma we find ourselves in. Cricket huddles in close by the phone with her left ear to hear.

"So, how have you been Ted, and why are you way out in New York? I haven't heard from you in a couple years," says Loreen.

"It's a long story. I'll have to fill you in some other time. You ever heard of the deadheads and the Grateful Dead?" I ask.

"I've heard of the names but I don't know anything about it or about them," says Loreen.

"Well, anyway, do you think you could talk with my friend Cricket and advise her or come up with something? Her in-laws are coming through and it will only be six hours of driving or so if they cross the Blue Water Bridge," I say.

"Put her on the phone and let me talk to her."

I pull the phone away from my ear and hand it to Cricket. The two women talk for about forty-five minutes. Cricket tells my florist friend all the details of everything she will need—stargazer lilies, lotus blossoms, roses, baby's breath, miniature white gardenias, spring rye ferns and climbing vine of English ivy. All of this will need to be made into a dozen bouquets and boutonnieres, flower head wreaths, a bridal bouquet and a special bridal headpiece.

When they finish talking Cricket motions for me to get the phone—Cricket has transformed as she wears a big excitable grin of accomplishment spread across her face.

"Wow! You just made someone real happy and eternally grateful! What did you two agree on?" I ask Loreen.

"Well first, I'm waiting for a return confirmation phone call from you guys that her parents will hold off for a day before coming out there," says Loreen. "So you need to arrange that right away. Then I'll need to get my wholesalers on the line and get a bunch of stuff delivered. I've never done an out-of-state wedding before!"

"Don't worry! I'm sure you will do great. You just saved the day and the wedding and the nature party on this end. Thank you so much. You are a sweetheart! You've made me a hero out here now!"

She laughs on the other end of the phone line.

"Glad I can help! Thanks for the business and thanks for thinking of me," Loreen says. "I miss our talks. It was fun being your friend. Let me know when you are back in the area."

"Sure thing! Thanks again, Loreen! I'm going to get off the line now and let Cricket make the other arrangements and get back with you. Hope to talk to you again soon. Bye!"

"Bye Ted! Thanks!"

Cricket then calls Peter's mom. Luckily they hadn't left yet. Cricket explains all the details. Peter's parents, June and Butch, agree to wait an extra day and then pick up the flowers in Richmond, Michigan at Flower Carousel.

The flowers are here to smile and bring warmth, beauty and good cheer to the occasion. Crisis averted. The lovely flower lady came through. What a sweet compassionate acquaintance.

So, we call back my florist friend, Loreen, and tell her the good news. Cricket gives the florist the number of her soon to be in-laws. The deal is sealed.

After Cricket hangs up and passes on the good news there is a big raucous cheer that wells up throughout the house and the property. Everyone is clapping and hollering and congratulating Cricket, Peter and me. We have saved the day and rescued the Big Show!

ꙮ

Five of us hop in Cricket's car. We have a quick mission to accomplish. Cricket needs to spread the word about her Big Show. She's recruited several of us to come along with her. Cricket drives us up town and parks the car on a side street. She opens her trunk and pulls out her rainbow bag. She must have been busy doing some printing because she has new stacks of flyers and pamphlets in the rainbow bag. Cricket hands a stack of papers to each of us.

Mignon, Molly, Jason, Cricket and I fan out in teams of two and three. We saunter into the core pathways of unconventional bohemian living in the 'Village.' We visit the coffee shops, art houses, cafe's, record stores, book stores, poet corners, night club bars, nature parks, college campuses—all over the Rochester area.

The Bohemian Adventure

Together we scatter 'Self & Soul' and 'Seed & Roots' with the Finger Lakes Ball & Chain Newsletter.

Spreading good cheer and inspiration. Socially connecting. Creating positive karma. What you give, you get. You sow what you reap. Life is a mirror echo when perspective is fine-tuned. For you see the authentic inner self reflected in your everyday character.

Can words and thoughts and stories make a difference? Mass market appeal is frightening and alluring. Can one voice reach from the highest mountain peaks to the lowest valley floors?

ജ്യ

Chapter Twelve

The Wedding

ജ്യ

"Let us go singing as far as we go:
the road will be less tedious."

—Virgil

Traveling and Setting up Camp

We leave the next day for the park in the Finger Lakes Region. I carry my copy of directions from the Ball & Chain newsletter in my back pocket. I still don't have a ride though. I'm patiently waiting on the front porch. Cricket's brother, with his shiny red Ferrari, hasn't shown up yet. Cricket made arrangements for me to ride with him.

I have my tent, sleeping bag and book bag bundled together on the front deck, name tags on each parcel. Everything is in a corner on the deck porch, as I watch the pace of activity from the various people going in and out of the house with more stuff to go on the trip.

I decide to send my stuff ahead with a small caravan of four trucks, each with trailers packed full. I walk over to a huge GMC truck with my possessions. It's packed with equipment, gear, bags, suitcases and personal effects. I take each of my things—tent, sleeping bag, backpack, book bag—and fit them into a slot of space in the u-haul trailer hitched to the back of the truck.

Everyone has their own personal agenda of planning activity going on—clothes for each day, food, beer and liquor, outdoor games, musical equipment and sound systems, camping gear, etc. The great Victorian house and property will soon be shut down and quiet for the next several days.

I'm still waiting for my ride. I may need to hitch a ride with someone else. I've noticed the chances for a ride are dwindling as each vehicle gets loaded with people and camp gear. I'm watching all this activity from the porch when a beautiful red Ferrari pulls up to the curb across the street.

I'm the first to introduce myself to Cricket's brother. Walking down the porch and across the street, I meet him as he gets out of his car.

"Hello! I'm Ted! I believe Cricket arranged for me to ride with you!"

We shake hands.

"Nice car you have here," I say.

"Thanks! Nice to meet you—I'm Don," he says. "So you're the special writer guy my sister has me setup with to ride out to her big shindig?" says Don, with a wide grin.

He is medium-built, athletically fit and slender, wearing a polo shirt and khaki shorts and sandals, clean-shaven, with a deep right-cheek dimple that he persistently displays when he smiles. With dark brown eyes and close cropped rusty red hair, I notice that he hardly resembles Cricket at all.

"Is my sister around?"

"I'm sure she's somewhere around here," I say.

At that moment, as if on cue, Cricket comes rushing out of the house and they share a big hug embrace near Don's car.

"How you doing, Sis!" Don says. "Getting cold feet?"

"Not at all. I'm ready!" she responds.

A few more hugs and kisses later Cricket is quickly pushing Don back to his car so he can take her for a ride around the block.

"Let's go! I want a ride right now!" she says.

Then Cricket looks over to me standing on the sidewalk, "If Peter, Mignon or anybody wants to know where I'm at, let them know I'm on a short ride with my brother, Don, in his new car and I'll be right back—okay?"

I nod in agreement.

"No problem! Enjoy your ride!"

Don and Cricket speed off down the neighborhood road in the splash red Ferrari. I pace up and down the sidewalk in front of the house as people rush about inside and outside the house, continuing with the never ending packing chores.

Twenty minutes later Cricket and Don are back. Cricket is standing up in the convertible on the passenger side, her hair and braids blowing in the wind, as Don honks the horn on their approach. She is mouthing something in a yell but it is inaudible to me. Finally, Don lets up on the horn as he pulls up beside the curb and parks. Cricket jumps out of the car and comes running over to me.

"Ted, I want to introduce you to my brother," she says. "Come on over here with me."

She grabs my right hand and pulls me toward her. We walk over to Don who is still sitting in his car, wearing a big smile on his face.

"I know you two already met initially, but I didn't properly introduce you," Cricket explains.

I reach over and shake Don's hand again.

"Don, this is a special friend of mine I met on the road recently, his name is Ted. Ted, this is my big brother, Don," says Cricket.

"So, you're riding with me?" asks Don.

"It sure looks that way or else I'm going to get left behind," I say.

"Are you ready? If so—hop in!"

"Sure! I have my stuff loaded up on the trucks that already left," I say.

Then I rush around to the other side of the car and get in the passenger seat and fasten the seat belt. We both wave goodbye to Cricket.

"See you there later on," I say.

"You know how to get there, right?" asks Cricket.

I pull out my folded up copy of the Ball & Chain newsletter flyer and wave it over my head.

"Good! I'll see you there later after everyone is all setup. Bye!"

She blows us a kiss and then heads back inside her Victorian home.

Don shifts the car into gear and takes off down the road and through the neighborhoods to the highway. We take I-390 south.

"What do you do to afford a slick ride like this?" I ask.

We must lean over to each other when we speak because the road noise and wind in the face makes it difficult to hear.

"I've been a pilot for over fifteen years. Work for Delta Airlines. Used to work for United and then Northwest," says Don. "Saved up for quite a few years to buy this here vehicle—my own little big boy toy for myself," he says.

The ride in the Ferrari is breathtaking. You know you are in something special just because of the persistent stares and long gawking effect the car draws on people's eyes.

Don opens it up past one-hundred miles-per-hour in split seconds it seems. Then he eases up and slows it down so he won't get caught speeding. I hold on tight to my seat cushion, squeezing the leather fabric, and staring intently at the roadway, the wind in my face full throttle, hair blowing, gulping for fresh breath as we slither out of the fast lane.

"Aren't you afraid of getting caught?" I ask.

"I have this here radar," he says, pointing to a small electronic contraption with digital readout on his dashboard. "I'm just showing off a little bit! Can't help it in a vehicle like this! I've only received one ticket so far, and that was for a rolling stop," Don says.

"So, where do you fly to?"

"All over—it depends," he says. "I've been around the world—Europe, Down Under, The Orient, South America, and all over the States. I work out of Logan International Airport in Boston now, and most of my flights are quick trips all along the eastern seaboard—D.C., Baltimore, New York, Philly, Portland."

"What did it take to learn how to fly and get certified as a pilot?" I ask.

"I went into the Air Force out of high school. I learned everything there. Then when I finished my enlistment and became a civilian I got my commercial pilot's license and it's what I've been doing ever since," Don says.

"So how often do you see Cricket?" I ask.

"Hardly ever," he responds. "She was just a baby kid when I left home, just starting school. I got married young and had a couple kids right away. So we didn't see much of each other."

"Where's your family?" I ask.

"The wife and I are separated right now and she has custody of the kids. We decided it would be better if I just went to the wedding by myself," Don says.

"Sorry to hear that. I've just went through a divorce and the recovery process can be rough going at times," I say.

"You have any kids?" he asks.

"No—we never started a family," I say.

"Well, let's not get each other all gloomy here," Don says with a sly grin. "So, why are you out here and how did you get to know my sister?"

"I met her at a park in Michigan when she came through with the traveling community of deadheads. We were intellectually attracted to each other during the course of her stay at the campgrounds. I've been mesmerized by her energy and her persona ever since," I say. "She is really something else. Just before they left Michigan she invited me to the wedding. One of the deadheads came back ten days later and picked me up and brought me out here. We went to the last show in D.C. then they dropped me off in New York and I got a bus ride up here."

"No shit!" he says. "You a deadhead, too?"

"No—not really—not like these people. Some of them are really hard-core into it. I'm in to the great gatherings and the camaraderie and the energetic vibes, though," I say. "I'm more of a Pink Floyd and Led Zeppelin fan than I am of the Dead. I really don't know much about them other than what everyone has been telling me and teaching me since I met all these people."

"What do you do for a living?" Don asks.

"I'm on a self-chosen sabbatical right now. I'm taking a long time-out from the normal grind of daily life. I used to work in high tech in the automotive industry—computers, programming and systems analysis. I burned out from the malaise of the routine. Something was missing! The marriage didn't work out and I had an investment failure—so, I just had to get away and rediscover myself and my direction in life. So, that's why I guess I'm available to do something on a whim across the country like this. Strange how things happen and come about."

"My sister says you write. Ever publish anything?"

Don inquires.

I stare out the window at the roadway as we pass vehicles in the slow lane. I remain silent.

"I said, did you ever publish anything?"

"No! Not yet, nothing substantial," I answer.

"Well, good luck to you anyway!" he says. "I admire people who step out from the crowd and have something meaningful to say and share with others. You interested in politics?" Don asks.

"Not at all! Period! I have no interest to go down that line of discussion," I respond.

Don chuckles over my reply, "Yeah, we start out as friends and then we'll be arguing and disagreeing on viewpoints. Kick back and let me see if I can find some Floyd for you on the radio."

He presses a few buttons until he finds "Comfortably Numb" on a station. Then he cranks the volume up full blast. I sit back in my seat and let my mind drift.

The day I proposed we were so happy. The day we got married I felt so sure and secure. The day we got divorced I realized I'd taken my false self-delusion for truth. But the love was real while it lasted. I had never let myself care for another so deep. Then I took that love for granted and let it slip away. I got what I deserved. Precious is the love between a couple. It must be nurtured and catered to, consistently, for that love to preserve and grow. True love is deserving of a lifetime of celebration. Next time I will be a better man and uphold my end of the relationship. Love can be fleeting, but love is eternal. I'm thankful for the love I've shared, the deep traces on my soul. I've been blessed!

We arrive at the Park after listening to an album's

worth of assorted rock music. The ride in the Ferrari has been great!

Don is staying at the Glen Iris Inn with the rest of the wedding party, so he drops me off in the organization campground area. There are big signs that read—"Peter & Cricket's Big Show Campers." They also have a section of the park set aside for motor homes and RV's. I walk over to a pavilion with picnic tables loaded with camping equipment and gear. I easily locate my stuff. I load up my gear and start walking out to the woods.

I'm looking to find a nice secluded spot deep within the wooded forest. There are dozens of tents all setup side by side in the open areas and then more tents are being pitched, slowly dotting the periphery of the forest and filling in the gaps.

This doesn't work for me. I desire deep woods seclusion. I make my way into the hickory, oak and pine to find myself a spot nestled under a wide-girth tree. Right here it is. I brush aside the pine needles and leaves to create a flat even surface for my new tent home.

Every now and then I spot somebody walking deeper into the dense woods, backpack and gear on their backs, looking for a nice patch of ground like I just found to pitch their tent and setup camp.

After setting up my tent I unroll my sleeping bag inside and put a flashlight in the corner. I have Thoreau's ***Walden*** and Emerson's ***Nature***—old hardcover books published in the late 1800's. These are the two books, along with my four writing notebooks, that I've carried with me on this 'Bohemian Odyssey.'

Here they are, my faithful companions. I put ***Walden*** next to my flashlight by the sleeping bag. I gather a notebook, a couple pens and Emerson's ***Nature***—a little skinny book of the essay. I love to walk in solitude and read this book out in nature. Inspires me every time!

Awesome Emerson! This will balance my mind and set me in the right frame as I partake on this hundred hour 'Big Show' party scene.

ഇന്ദ

As I walk along a trail on the forest floor, I look up everywhere at a big green canopy—the blue sky and shafts of light peeking and peering in with shiny bursts of rays—and blue-eyed nature mixed with white-cloud azure, smoky pillow puffs. The wind blows ever so slightly—rearranging the bursts and shadows from the movements in the high branches of the canopy to the seeing eyes on the forest floor.

I wander for an hour, until I come upon a vast waterfall. I descend to the river bed several feet below and walk along the shore till I find a huge boulder to sit on as I look out at the falls. I sit in a lotus position to balance my energy in meditation with the environment.

Breathe out—cleansing. Breathe in—purity! The serenity is mystical! Breathe out...Breathe in! Omm! Om!

I soon place myself in a relaxed mode. Open Mind. Clear Mind. Steady Consciousness. I experience several moments of bliss—becoming attuned with raw nature. Breathe out...Breathe in! Omm! Om!

I slide down from the boulder onto the ground of the riverside shore. I lean my back against the great rock and sit here to read Nature. From page to Falls to page, my roving eyes and thoughts meld.

I look out on the vast spillage of water continuously falling, falling, falling down the mountain side. The crushing sound of the crashing waves on the water and rocks below, leaves a blistering echo that persists and vibrates down the canal of the forested riverbed. I am mesmerized by the sheer beauty and power.

Nature is a natural wonder!

Emerson writes and speaks of a spiritual optimism, inner self-discoveries, the unobtained obtainable, intuitive reception instinctively, inherent truths in physical nature exposed, the principles and laws of nature, the nature within and the nature without, unprecedented probabilities and possibilities for us as individuals to realize our greatness.

I find Mr. Ralph Waldo Emerson to be very inspirational.

The raw elements of natural nature have a magnetic, draw-like pull on my inward senses. Nature energizes and refreshes me. I'm aiming to find the connection with my soul through nature. The creative spark is divine. When I find myself and truly know my self—then I can forge and mold that self to the new me I'm supposed to be. My self needs to know my soul, and my soul needs to know my self. Why have I built and erected such walls and detours and trap doors? The nature of my character has suffered and struggled. I will endure and overcome and grow and develop. The attraction of nature is combining with my inward being to arrive at the alignment and balance I must secure within my character to reveal my unknown hidden purpose. Here I am—searching and seeking!

The constant echoes of the waterfall serenity lapse me out of my inspirational stream. Natural Nature is so awe-inspiring! It is easy to get lost, literally engulfed in the beauty— flowing through my daydreams.

Hey—I've got a big celebration to get back to!

Refreshed and exhilarated, I make my way back through the woods to the main campground organization areas, working my way up the park mountainside and through the trails in the woods. I saunter along the path in reverie with my surroundings. I see chipmunks chasing each other, a doe and her fawn, a raccoon scurrying up a tree, blue jays, cardinals, orange breasted robins, a hawk devouring a rabbit kill. The wildness of the wilderness is part of the natural order of things. Nature is raw and pure and beautiful and worthy of our attention and affection.

ജ്ങ

I come up to a huge field, a vast grassy open area. People are gathering in groups all around. The space is three to four soccer fields in length and width. This will be our vast nature party environment. A small stage and musical equipment are being erected at both the north and south ends of the field. Picnic tables cluster under a covered roof structure near each end of the field, a pavilion, but on the opposite side of the band setup. The catered food and bartending will fill up a dozen tables or so.

A thousand people can eat, drink and be merry under the pavilion. Cricket has mentioned to me several times before that she hoped to get over fifteen hundred people to show up for her 'Big Show.'

"Ted, I expect a little over a third of that amount, say five-hundred people to be from my Deadhead and Rainbow Family networks. That could be a very conservative estimate though. I think it could even exceed a thousand people if everyone I've talked to and invited end up coming. Even more than that—I'm figuring a solid third to come from the neighborhoods and Rochester area."

"Sound check. Sound check…"

Cricket is on stage at the far end of the field, talking into the live mic—"sound check…one, two, three… Testing!"

I walk over to an empty fold out chair leaning on a post in the pavilion. I sit and listen as I look back across the field at Cricket on the stage. She has her hands in the air gesturing like she is about to make an announcement—"Hello everyone!" she bellows. A slight applause and some shrill whistles emanate from the various pockets of people scattered on the vast field.

"Hello all my good friends and revelers!" Cricket shouts into the mic.

The audience responds several decibels louder than the first time. I leave my seat to walk in closer to the stage, likewise as does many others across the field, getting closer to the upcoming entertainment. Everyone seems to have a beverage, some double-fisted. The grateful gathering is shifting into a new gear.

"I have a couple of announcements I want to make before we cut loose with all the activities. First and foremost—have fun and be safe!" Cricket hollers into the mic. She pauses as the audience cheers heartily to her suggestion. She's organizing a big raffle drawing so she can get an accurate headcount by tomorrow.

"Don't forget your two dollar raffle ticket. Everyone has to get one and register. I have a sealed and locked box underneath both pavilions where you can drop off your ticket. Only one ticket per person," she says.

The people keep arriving throughout the Park. Cricket had mentioned that Peter and she have a list of over three-hundred people between both their families and relatives and friends from college days.

A guy nudges in alongside of me, wearing a big red and white Dr. Seuss hat and holding a sixty-four-ounce mug of brew. The hat increases his height by two feet.

"How ya doin'?" he says. "Isn't she the one that's gonna get married tomorrow?"

He leans into me to catch his balance as he stumbles while pointing at the stage. I grab hold of the young fellow to steady him from falling.

"Yes! That's Cricket," I say.

The young guy readjusts himself, checks to make

sure he didn't spill a drop of his beer, then looks up at me and back out to the stage. His eyes are bloodshot and grey and glassy. He seems to have trouble focusing. He sways back and forth as he stands.

"You want to take a seat right here on the ground, man? Do you good to rest a bit," I say.

We sit down on the grass together and listen to the rest of what Cricket is saying.

"Furthermore, we have three different bands and many solo musicians. So there will always be music playing at one stage or the other throughout this big event," Cricket says. "We have volleyball and horseshoes and kickball and bocce ball—plenty of things for everyone to have fun doing—plus we're talking about organizing a softball game. You can locate the beer kegs by following lines of thirsty folks. Everyone knows where to go for food—am I right?" she shouts into the mic and thrusts her hand upward toward the sky.

A big raucous cheer wells up throughout the huge field. I look over to the guy sitting next to me and he is laying flat on the grass passed out with his big hat covering his snoring face. A drummer and a guitarist start playing their instruments as they look forward to Cricket finishing her spiel so they can bust loose with music and dance and celebration.

Cricket bellows into the microphone. "Remember people! Take it lightly tonight—this is not the big party evening yet. We have a big wedding to get through tomorrow!"

People jump up and down cheering on the field.

"One more thing—I love you all! Thanks for sharing this moment with us!"

Then Cricket blows a big kiss to the crowd as the cheering reaches a new crescendo, gradually drowned out by the music from the band taking over on stage. This huge wedding party is more like a rock festival concert.

The cost of this type of gathering has to be enormous! Evidently there is some big money footing the core of this bill. The floral order alone came to over twenty-five-hundred dollars. I'm thinking that ten times that amount would have to cover the costs of all the catered foods, beverages and rental equipment setup.

But then everyone pitches in and contributes, and I'm experiencing the unfolding of it all right before my eyes. I look out to the opposite far end of the field and I can hear the other band doing sound check. The big huge party field is constantly moving with people walking in groups, splaying out in all directions. The gathering places are wherever the kegs are. Several spots on the field are queued up in lines and mini-circles as soon as a new keg is setup and flowing. I've counted eight different spots on the field so far. Then we have the bar areas under each pavilion.

People keep coming and coming and coming from all directions. I see a lot of hugging and embraces from friends who are happy to see each other.

I watch the reunions take place throughout the day—so much happiness and joy from friendships that endure the passages of times past, from far and wide.

ഌ൮

We spent the first night doing all the last minute preparations and enjoying the nature celebration atmosphere. Cricket comes up to me in the evening around the campfire and says she received a call from Peter's parents.

"They already picked up the flowers and are in route," she says. "The florist packed them in Styrofoam containers with ice packs. All the flowers are traveling with them in their Winnebago motor home. They should be here in the early morning. Butch and June decided to take the longer stateside route through Pennsylvania to upstate New York. They figure it would be too much of a hassle to go through customs in Canada with all the flowers."

Cricket updates me with this news and then she is gone in a heartbeat.

I stare into the giant bonfire and let my mind wonder…

The essence of beauty is the nature of Being. Lotus of the true law beaming brightness and energy of rightfulness, emitting the fragrance of truth, pureness, infinity. Life giving forces of compassion and trusting happiness. Nature smiles and laughs with her flowers. The lotus of the true law is a sacred symbol for the joining of this love. In the love of truth is the power to nourish love—flowing gently to the shores of our Being.

The next morning is the long awaited wedding day. I meet Butch and June around eight-thirty when I spot a Winnebago in the parking lot. A couple in their sixties is working together at the back of their camper to unhitch the trailer that holds the small compact car they've been pulling.

"Hello, are you Butch and June—Peter's parents?" I ask. "Do you need any help?"

The two look up at me from their bent over postures at the trailer hitch.

"I'm sorry, didn't mean to sneak up on you like that," I reassure them.

"Yes, we're Peter's parents and you must be Ted!" says the woman.

"Yes, I am! When did you get here?" I offer a handshake of greetings to both of them.

"Late at night in the wee hours of the morning, around

two," says Butch. "The park was pretty quiet and dark so we just found a spot and parked and got some sleep."

"Loreen was wonderful! Such a nice lady," says June. "Oh, she gave me something for you, a letter. It's in the front of the camper. I'll go get it."

June walks over to the front-end of the vehicle while I stay back and help Butch finish his project. We unhitch the trailer and block the wheels. Then June comes back and hands me the envelope from Loreen.

"I'm so excited, you must see the professional job your florist friend did," says June.

"Thanks for picking up the flowers and delivering the letter," I say as I put the letter in my back pocket to open later.

June opens their motor home door and invites me in to see the flowers. I look over to Butch, who is still preoccupied with his trailer.

"Just a minute," I say to June. "So, you going to be all right back here? Need help with anything else?" I ask Butch.

"No, I'm finished now. Let's go into the camper so you can see the flowers," says Butch with a big grin. "That flower lady friend of yours in Michigan saved this wedding."

I follow him over to the side door of the Winnebago where June is waiting for us on the top step.

"She really did a good job!" he says.

"Hurry up! I can't leave the door open, I've got the air-conditioning on to keep the flowers cool," says June, waving to rush us in.

Butch motions for me to go in first and I hurry up the three stairs and into the camper. Butch then follows and closes the door. The inside is filled with a nice cool crisp chill in the air. They have over a dozen Styrofoam coolers stacked three high in several spots. June pulls one down and takes off the lid. Inside are Lotus blossoms and lily pads floating in water. Then she pulls down another cooler and it is full of red roses. The cooler is packed with ice and they've made two shelf layers.

"We had to buy these coolers at a meat-packing place," says Butch. "That was the big worry—could we get everything transported out here without it all wilting and dying on us," he says. "How they looking honey?" Butch says to June.

"Everything is looking just fine and dandy," responds June.

Then she pulls the top off another Styrofoam cooler and I look inside.

"Flower head wreaths and some bouquets," she says. "We have ice packs in each of the coolers and they're holding out strong and keeping everything fresh."

"Seems like you guys did a great job and have everything under control," I say. "It took a lot of teamwork and coordination to pull this off. Cricket and Peter are really going to be happy."

"Do you know where they are? Have you seen them?" asks June, frowning with worry. "I haven't and I need to know where to send the flowers!"

"The wedding party is staying at the Glen Iris Inn up the road a ways. I haven't been there, but I know that's where you should be able to find them," I say. "I'm sure everyone in the wedding party is starting to get ready for the noon wedding."

"They reserved a room for us honey," says June. "We should go up there with the bus then, right now."

"We should just leave everything in here on high AC right until they need it," says Butch.

"Yes—let me get out of here and you two get going! It

was nice meeting the both of you. I'm glad the flowers look great. See you later," I say.

I shake both their hands again and then exit the Winnebago. Butch and June then drive the bus up to the Inn.

Cricket will be so happy to see the flowers.

After they leave I go walking on a short trail in the woods until I find a comfortable shade tree to sit under. Then I pull out the envelope from my back pocket and open it. It's a letter from my florist friend, Loreen.

Hello Ted,

I had to work a twenty-hour shift and have a couple of my floral designers work overtime to meet the short deadline and get everything done.

I'm worried about the flowers staying cool. I've never sent an order so far before.

Thank you for thinking of me and passing along the business opportunity. Call me when you get a chance. I'm anxious to hear how the flowers are and how the wedding went. Stay in touch!

Your Friend,
Loreen

On page two of the letter, Loreen has taped a hundred-dollar bill to the page in gratitude. I'll put the money in a card for the newlyweds.

ഗ്ര

The wedding ceremony is scheduled for noon sharp at the waterfall. It's another scorching summer day coming—ninety-five degrees. I make my way across the field to the scenic overhang backdrop. I stand here looking out at the waterfall. Pretty soon the ceremony will take place right here where I am standing. I've already agreed to take pictures for several people in the wedding party. I'm going to have my book bag filled with cameras.

I peer out from the shade of the overhang at the waterfall as my mind drifts into a relaxed-mode trance. I'm thinking about my own marriage several years ago. I had the right person at the wrong time. When is it ever the right time? My struggle is self-induced. I tell myself these things to rationalize myself to myself.

I'm staring into the center of the waterfall, into the rushing white waves of perpetual motion. My mind is transfixed on the mental imagery of a wedding, beautiful flowers, a blushing bride, the groomsmen and maids of honor. I look deep into the Falls and see images of the faceless people in the ceremony. They could be any people, anywhere throughout the United States or other countries and cultures, the sea of humanity. It has been a tradition from time immemorial to celebrate the great coming together of two separate souls in a partnership union of love, companionship and faithfulness.

I lost my love and I lost my way. I must find myself before I can ever love again. Authentic love will come again because I am going to be a beacon—a beacon of love. If I forgive myself then I am forgiven. I Forgive. I am Ted Senario—alive and driven. My former love has gone so that a new love may be reborn. A love built on a foundation of truth. I am the generator of this love. The caretaker, decision-maker. I am an open channel to the natural flows in my sacred quest to find true meaning.

Some of the people from the wedding party come over to the overhang lookout where I'm standing in a trance-like state, overlooking the waterfall. Their sudden presence breaks me out of the train of mental reverie I am in.

The women are dressed in pink chiffon with flower

wreaths of roses and baby's breath on their heads. They are carrying stargazer lilies with lots of pink roses strewn about. The fragrance of the flowers fills the summer air. The men are dressed in dark tuxedos with tiny pink roses on their lapels. Soon people are congregating and gathering from all wayward directions to this spot where the wedding will take place.

Soon after arrives the bride and groom in a white horse-drawn carriage. Peter wears a big Abe Lincoln top hat and long tails for a tux, with a big red cummerbund around his midsection.

Cricket is dressed in an all-white lace wedding gown—looking beautiful! Her hair is sprinkled with roses, baby's breath, fern, and small fragrant white gardenias.

The big story going around amongst the crowd is how Cricket finally shaved her legs and underarms. Also, that Peter and Cricket made the decision to give something up physical about themselves to dedicate and symbolize their past. Cricket chose a long piece of her braided hair. Peter chose his mustache and the hair on his legs too! He shaved his mustache the night before, and then put the stache back together on the sticky side of clear tape and then taped over the other side. The two of them will conduct this small ceremony before their wedding vows.

When they exit the horse-drawn carriage and Peter assists Cricket down the steps, I notice that Cricket carries a shoebox in her hands. Everyone crowds around to hear what she will say. Cricket opens the shoebox and pulls out a piece of her braided hair, then she puts it back in the box. Someone hands a wireless mic to Cricket so she can be heard as she completes her dedication.

I look around and spot a big boulder to jump onto to get a better view.

Peter, in his top hat, assists Cricket back up the two

stairs to the opening of the carriage door. Cricket speaks into the mic, "First of all I'd like to thank everyone for being a part of our lives and sharing this great moment with us."

The swarming group of guests hoot, holler, cheer, and clap voraciously. Cricket pauses for a moment before she speaks again.

I have my book bag strapped to my back, full of cameras, so I start taking pictures with one camera after the next, shooting photographs with one camera roll after another while the rest of the proceeding unfolds. A young guy with a camera is eyeing my spot on the big boulder, so, I invite him up to take pictures, too.

"I would like to bless the life I've lived thus far," Cricket says. "Life is a blessing everyday! I'm full of gratitude and thankfulness. I have been a free earth child for over twenty-eight years now! I hope to receive many many more years than this when it's all said and done. But I don't want to address the future at this moment," she says.

Someone hands over the shoebox to Cricket and she pulls out an object and lifts it in the air.

"This braided piece of hair was cut from my head at midnight last night. This symbolizes all I have been in my life, all I have grown, all I have failed, all I have succeeded, all I have learned, all I have cried, all I have loved."

Then she bows her head in silence, still standing at the carriage step. The crowd grows quiet. Waiting. Silence. Waiting…

Then Cricket lifts up her head and puts her hand out to Peter. He ascends the carriage stairs and stands on the top step with her.

"Dear Great Creative Intelligence, I dedicate this piece of myself as a remembrance of times past," she says into the mic. Then she puts the six-inch piece of braided hair back in the shoebox. "My past was a gift. Life is a holy treasure. The jewels of my days have sparkled and shined. I give up this piece of me in remembrance of the sacredness of this life journey. This represents all I have matured and grown and evolved to at this point in time. Amen!" Then she hands the mic to Peter.

Peter then pulls out his baggy of leg hair and his taped up mustache from the same shoe box where Cricket put her braided piece of hair. A big roar of laughter and giggles erupts from the crowd, as he lifts his dedication to the air.

"I had to come up with something and here it is!" Peter waves his lunch bag of leg hair round and round his head. "Since Cricket finally shaved her legs for this occasion, I thought I would, too."

Everyone in the crowd seems to get a big kick out of his act. Cricket was taking her dedication very seriously, but now she's joining in the laughs with everyone else. A chant rises up from the crowd, "No more hairy legs! No more hairy legs!" Cricket pulls up her gown with the help of her bridesmaid and Peter pulls up the pant legs on his tux. Cricket stands next to Peter smiling and shaking her head in feigned disgust and exasperation. Then she reaches into the shoebox, which is sitting on the carriage seat behind them, and pulls out her own big lunch bag of leg hair. The hysterical laughing bellows out from the crowded wedding guest revelers.

It is hot and muggy as everyone is beading up with sweat. They laugh and carry on for several minutes. Peter finally takes back hold of the mic to get some order.

"Hey, we still got a wedding to do here, people!"

After a few minutes the noise quiets down with spirited giggles still kicking up amongst the people.

With a big grin on his face, Peter continues, "No—in all seriousness, when Cricket first told me it was her wish to dedicate a part of our old selves, I didn't know what I was going to do. I don't have all the sentimental things to say like she does, but I understand where she's coming from."

Then Cricket motions for the mic from Peter. He puts up his finger to ward her off because he has more he wants to say.

"We have been blessed! We'd like to thank all of you for sharing this moment with us."

Then Peter hands the mic back to Cricket. Cricket hollers into the mic. "I'm melting here people! Let's get this show going!"

ꕥ

Peter and Cricket walk down the carriage stairwell to the pavement. The crowd parts to create an aisle that leads all the way from the carriage to the scenic overlook where the ceremony will take place. Peter and Cricket hold hands and walk down the makeshift aisle to their places on the mini-stage platform.

I am still standing on the huge boulder taking picture after picture. Now it's time for the Waterfall Wedding Ceremony.

The bridesmaids line up on one side and the groomsmen take their positions on the other side. Peter is standing with the pastor up front on the platform. He still wears his big top hat. Cricket is led down a shorter makeshift aisle with her proud father by her side. The aisle opens as they pass by—then closes up and fills in with bobbing, craning heads.

I wonder about her parents because I have not met them and Cricket hasn't said much to me about them.

Cricket takes her place next to Peter on the platform. I'm snapping pictures all the way. The ceremony is short and brief. The picture taking and posing afterwards is long and arduous. There's always one more pose and one more picture to take. I have all the cameras laid out on a folding chair. I keep taking pictures, winding the film, and switching to the next camera.

Finally, the wedding party jumps in the decorated cars and drives through the park honking their horns. It is a noisy, loud, cheerful, happy experience.

Now it's time to have a never-ending Nature Party!

ꙮ

Chapter Thirteen

A Nature Party

ꙮ

"Now is the time for drinking,
now is the time to beat the earth
with unfettered foot."

—Horace

The Rainbow Warriors

After the wedding ceremony, the reception out in nature kicks into high gear. Activity ramps up all over, up and down the vast field—volleyball, horseshoes, bocce ball, badminton, soccer, hack-e-sack. Small groups and huddles of people dot the landscape. The bands setup musical equipment at each end of the field. Tables of catered food fill the pavilions. Soon, a vast sea of people inhabits the open spaces of the park, flowing from activity to activity.

I head for some food and refreshments as the long lines are forming. I'm sure I will meet a lot of interesting characters in the next few days. While waiting in line I notice that each table has a folded newsletter by each plate setting. It is Cricket and Peter's Ball & Chain Newsletter—Volume #3. I open up a folded newsletter and discover tucked inside one of the pamphlets Cricket and Mignon made of my writings. I peruse the newsletter of well-wishes and good tidings from the newlyweds—a listing of all the activities taking place in the next three days—"*Socialize, celebrate, eat, drink, play games, dance and share in the fun!*"

I check a few more plate settings. Every table setting has a different copy of 'Self & Soul' or 'Seed & Roots,' tucked inside a folded newsletter. I'm flattered and my surprise is genuine. The Catalyst Converter strikes again! I figure Cricket and Mignon and their circle of close friends must have really been busy to plan and prepare all this.

After I finish a delicious plate of burgers and fries, I decide to walk around and mingle about—listen to both Folk/Rock bands and a deejay playing Oldies but Goodies dance music. They alternate throughout the afternoon and into the early evening. Several groups of people are dancing around on the turf. I make the rounds from beer keg to beer keg for refills and top-offs, sharing small talk with various individuals hanging around the bartending area.

Eventually, I gravitate towards a group of people at a table under the pavilion, where I notice the enthusiastic response they are receiving from two other tables of listeners. Their name tags denote that Bobby and Joan work for Greenpeace. They are talking about their recent adventures and mission. I notice that mostly everyone wears tie-dyed shirts that read, 'Rainbow Warriors' on the front and back of the shirt.

As I huddle in and move closer to hear, more and more people congregate—our little semi-circle grows from a couple tables of listeners to over fifty people at a half-dozen crowded tables.

"This is about saving the oceans, eliminating toxic chemicals, stopping climate change, stopping the nuclear threat, protecting the ancient forests, and stopping the innocent slaughtering in whaling," says the young woman standing on a chair addressing the growing crowd. "Greenpeace is for the health of our planet and the welfare of current and future generations of inhabitants."

The crowd breaks out into an extended applause. Then a young man pulls a chair alongside Joan, and he stands on it. His name is Bobby.

"Greenpeace focuses on the most crucial worldwide threats to our planet's biodiversity and environment," he says. "The fragile earth deserves a voice."

Joan and Bobby clasp hands in a high-five to each other. They hand out Greenpeace buttons and some literature on their mission. I browse through a flyer and continue to look up and listen to the two speakers.

"You can make a difference," Bobby says. "Everyone makes choices everyday that impacts the health and welfare of the planet. We are Rainbow Warriors!" He holds his right hand high in the air, holding out two fingers for the universal peace sign. "The fragile earth deserves a voice. We are that voice—you and me, all of us! Peace and brotherhood."

Then Bobby steps down from the chair and Joan takes over.

"Be sure to get your Greenpeace button," she says. "We also have a few more t-shirts available to sell. The 'Rainbow Warrior' comes from a North American Cree Indian legend. It describes a time when humanity's greed has made the earth sick. At that time, a tribe of people known as the 'Warriors of the Rainbow,' would rise up to defend Mother Earth." Joan shouts out to the crowd, "We are the Rainbow Warriors!"

The audience responds with shouts of, "We are the Rainbow Warriors! We are the Rainbow Warriors! We are the Rainbow Warriors!"

Joan steps down from the chair as the gathering of people clusters around the tables in this far corner of the pavilion, amidst clapping and cheering. It is a nice makeshift pep rally for old Mother Earth.

Then another woman ascends onto the speaker's chair, motioning with her hands to quiet down so she can speak. I sit back down at my crowded table to hear what she has to say. She is a cute little smiling dark-haired beauty and her name tag says, 'Crystal.'

"I'd like to speak for just a couple minutes about a group that I belong to that you may or may not be aware of," she says. "We identify ourselves as Lohasian. LOHAS are people interested in a lifestyle of health and sustainability. We are dedicated to personal and planetary health. Lohasians identify themselves as spiritual, but not religious. In a nutshell, we buy recycled paper and goods, purchase natural or organic personal care products, we pay more to get foods without pesticides, and we want our vehicles to be fuel efficient."

A young woman raises her hand at a table for a question.

"Yes?" says Crystal, pointing at the young girl.

"So, what does L-O-H-A-S stand for again?"

"Lifestyle of Health and Sustainability!" answers Crystal. "We have some flyers here to handout to those who are interested and we have some buttons too!"

Then she steps down from the speaker's chair and the gathering crowd claps and then slowly disperses.

I decide to go for a contemplative walk along a short path in the nearby woods. It's all starting to make sense to me now. This fits right in with Cricket's topic of 'Rainbow Families' from that day when we had the symposium in her library. My mind drifts—

All is One and One is all. Planet earth is vibrating with energy that charges every human soul and living thing. The great miracle is always present in everyday creation. We are infinitely blessed and hardly ever acknowledge the blessings. The mystical rainbow beholds the energetic colors of manifestation. This great earth will always need her Rainbow Warriors, generation after generation. All is One and One is All.

The day progresses into the early evening hours. By nightfall, I find myself to be seriously inebriated. I notice several huge community bonfires torch up. The crowds of people cluster around the fires—singing, laughing, dancing, drinking and storytelling fill up the party atmosphere. I haven't seen the bride and groom since they shoved cake in each other's face earlier in the day.

It is late, and I realize I went past my limit long ago. I decide to call it an evening. I leave the warmth of the bonfires and head to my tent in the chilly woods. I soon realize I have a young woman tailing me on my trek through the woods. I see her silhouette in the moon light from a distance. I carry a makeshift walking stick and a small flashlight to lead my way through the dark path. Noticing her off in the distance I wave my flashlight and wait till she comes closer.

I shout out to her shadow in the dark—"Are you lost? Can I help you?"

Once she comes within thirty yards she hollers back in the cool night air, "Are you the bohemian writer? Ted? If so, I want your autograph!"

I wait as she draws closer.

"Are you the guy that wrote these cute little booklets? Several people pointed you out to me and said you are the author."

She holds out a few pamphlets in front of her, as she draws within a few feet of me. She is wearing a tie-dyed Rainbow Warrior shirt with white khaki shorts. Her silky, thick-black, tresses, curl down each shoulder and part down her back. She looks familiar, from earlier in the day. She wears daffodils and roses and daisies and vines spread throughout her hair. She smiles with the face of an angel, pearly white beautiful teeth.

"Hello, my name is Serenity Crystal," she says.

Then she curtsies and holds out her left hand for me to kiss. I am mesmerized! Plus I am inebriated, riding on an extreme exquisite high. I reach out to her hand and gently raise it to my lips as I bend down and kiss her soft hand in greetings. We both strain to see each other up close in the dark woods, as I dropped the flashlight.

"Weren't you speaking on a chair at the pavilion earlier in the day?" I ask.

"Yes, that was me! You were there!"

I snap my finger in recall, "You are the LOHAS Rainbow Warrior?"

"Yes, that's me! I thought I recognized you from somewhere," she says.

With sweaty palms I nervously drop my flashlight again and the light goes out. Then I start sweating everywhere all at once. I am overheated by the presence of Serenity Crystal.

We stand next to each other in the dark, peeking through the forest canopy, looking up at the moon and the endless stars.

"What time do you think it is—getting close to midnight?" I ask. "I've lost all track of time as the day progressed. No watch. You don't have one either I see. I'm having a great time! You?"

"It's been a wonderful day!" she responds. "I think it's about a half-hour before midnight. I asked someone just before I started following you out here. I thought I was going to lose you in the dark."

I feel her hand reach out to my arm and down to my right hand as we grip each other, standing side by side continuing to look up at the sky as we talk. The soft wind blows and cools me down.

"I thought maybe someone was stalking me at first," I joke. "Couldn't tell if you were safe or not," as both of us giggle and laugh. "You drink much tonight? I think I had more than I needed. I was on my way to pass out in my tent for the night."

"I'm okay. I've had just enough to feel good and enjoy myself. You alone?" she asks.

"Yes, I hitched a ride out here from Michigan. I met Cricket a few weeks back and she invited me to her wedding. The whole experience has been a wonderful adventure," I say. "Are you related to the bride or groom?"

"No! I really don't know them. I came with a bunch of friends," Crystal says.

I slip my arm around her shoulder and hold her tight as we stare up at the moon.

"Sorry if I stumble now and then, with the drinking and the dark woods and this little flashlight, I can hardly stand straight," I laugh at myself. "What was that you said about an autograph?"

"Oh," she giggles, "I read a few of your little mini-booklets and I thought it would be wonderful to meet you and talk with you and maybe get your autograph on one of them," she says.

Crystal reaches into the back pocket of her shorts and pulls out several of the pamphlets.

"Here's one," she says, handing it to me, "could you sign it, please? I have to leave early in the morning."

"Let's go to my tent where I have a pen. How come you have to leave so soon?"

"The people I came with are leaving in the morning. They are my ride home. I live in Maine not far from Portland," she says.

We walk through the woods, holding hands, watching our steps from the lighted pathway from my dim flashlight.

"You have a boyfriend?"

"I've had an 'on-again, off-again' relationship with a guy named Eddie, but nothing real serious right now!"

"There's my tent up ahead."

We walk over to the tent and I unzip the screen flap and invite her in. I locate a pen and sign a pamphlet under the flashlight glare, 'Dear Crystal Serenity, Great to meet you! Your Friend, Bohemian Ted.' I hand the paper back to her.

We proceed to kiss and make out and feel each other up as we roll around on the sleeping bag inside the dark tent. I haven't been this close to a woman in a couple years, since my wife, and it feels good to hold this beautiful stranger in my arms.

We hardly speak again, just moans and grunts and smacking lips as I wrap myself into the sweet voluptuousness of her body—sacred feminine energy sparking flames of pure joy.

ꟷ

When I wake up in the morning, Crystal Serenity is gone.

Was she ever there or was I only dreaming?

My head is pounding from the hangover so I just stay in my tent and sleep into the early afternoon hours. Then upon reawakening and emerging from my hideout in the woods, I discover that I have become a controversial figure over night.

Several people, in passing, have asked me if I am—"The bohemian, the guy who wrote the pamphlets?" This doesn't sound good, just from the tone of the question. Perhaps I am on the defensive. With reluctance I groggily admit I am the guy. Several people tell me that a grey-haired man is looking for me—since last night and earlier this morning.

I have been hiding out in the deep forest, sleeping off my drunkenness from the day and night before.

And, whatever happened to Crystal?

And, who is 'the guy' looking for me?

I walk a path in the woods that leads to the big show at the party field. It looks as if everything is starting to gear up for another whole day of celebrations out in nature. People are continuing to congregate and join in fun and games like the days before. I make a conscious decision to lay off imbibing alcoholic liquid refreshments today. I want to write and try to capture the essence of the moment today. I can't do that when I'm drinking too much. I head over to the Park showers and restrooms, then to the pavilion to get something to eat.

What a sweet little woman that was I met last night! Will I ever see her again?

I'm sitting at a table by myself, eating lunch and flipping through a couple of my notebooks when a man in his mid-fifties, baldheaded and bespectacled, introduces himself as Professor Henry Farthington. I stand up and we shake hands in greeting.

"I was wondering if you are the bohemian author? Several people directed me to you. You are Ted, right?" he inquires.

"Yes, I am! I'm Ted Senario. Nice to meet you, Professor Farthington."

"So, you're the guy who wrote this bunk? You're the bohemian fellow?"

I sit back down in my chair as the professor stands over the table peering down at me from over the top of his glasses. He wears a strict, edgy look about himself. Stern. Authoritative. Overbearing. I hesitate, and then take a bite of food and slowly chew, staring back at him. Our eyes are locked on each other. The silence between us is loud. When I swallow my bite of food, I clear my throat and answer him.

"Are you talking about the little pamphlets that Cricket and Mignon made of my notebook writings?"

He pulls out several copies from inside his folded newspaper and lays them on the table.

"I mean these," he says, with a mean steady glare in his eyes aimed at me like laser beams.

"Yes, those are my writings," I admit. "They weren't meant to be offensive or taken negatively by anyone. Everything written is about being positive, optimistic, knowing oneself, seeking truth, spirit, soul, compassion. What gives? I didn't print anything to get upset about."

"Now hold on here, young fellow," says the Professor. "Let's just sit here and I got a thing or two to tell you, if you don't mind and have the time."

"Sure," I say.

He pulls out a chair and sits at the table across from me.

"So, you are the writer of these words then?"

He holds up a couple of pamphlets and sets them on the table. I acknowledge once again, with a slight nod of my head.

"I teach Psychology and Sociology at Columbia University in New York City. I enjoyed most of your literature—you like some amateur philosopher or something?"

"I write, read and think about deep mindful things," I say, "or at least I try to anyway. But I'm no Buddha or Socrates, far from it. I don't have all the answers. Just trying to grow and learn."

"I have to take exception with some of your word

usage, and question the semantics of what you really mean," he says. "For instance, the use of the word 'Adamites' in reference to humanity in some of your prose—I didn't like that!"

Then he opens the pamphlet that offends him and points out the passage on the page. He thumps the pamphlet repeatedly with his index finger as he expresses his misgivings to me.

"You shouldn't use a religious point of view in your philosophical literature if you want to be taken seriously. As soon as you do that, it erases all the good you wrote up to that point."

Then he stares at me across the table, waiting for my response. His two eyes glare back like a pair of black oil sockets, steely, hard and dark.

"I borrowed that word from a poem I read by Walt Whitman or Robert Frost, I forget which. I think it is a clever way to refer to mankind. As for religion, it's closer to mythology, if you think about it. Adam and Eve, who really knows, come on man!" I say, with a bewildering look of exasperation from this topic of disagreement.

The professor then blows his stack in response. He jumps back from the table and then pounds the ball of his fist like a hammer into the pamphlets lying on the table. My plate and silverware and cup of tea jump on the table top. The professor starts raising his voice and shouting at me, making a big scene.

"Who the hell do you think you are anyway? What if I'm an agnostic? What if I'm an atheist?" he shouts. "Then you're preaching to the choir, boy! You understand where I'm coming from, son?"

"No, I don't!" I respond as I stand up from the chair and table. "Is this your teaching method—hollering and yelling and being belligerent when you don't agree with someone? And if the only people I have to worry about upsetting is atheists and agnostics—well I'm fine with that!" I say.

"Now hold on there," says the professor. "I don't claim a perfect sympathy with either of those words, or class groups in society. I was just saying—what if I was? I wanted to see what kind of reaction I would get out of you! See if you would defend your work. See if I could jerk your chain."

I can't believe this: I'm sitting at a vacant table in the far corner of the pavilion, eating my food, bothering no one. This man has literally ambushed me as he continues heaping louder abuse and anger toward me. He is very demonstrative with his non-verbal—arms and hands in constant movement as he slaps and fingers and crumbles and slaps the small set of pamphlets in his hand. At that moment he reminds me of an outraged football coach who just witnessed his team make a massive game-changing failure, say a Woody Hayes or Bo Schembechler or Mike Ditka type.

"Can you please lower your voice and stop shouting and talking so loud," I request. "I'll have a courteous conversation with you only if you will calm down."

"I'm not an atheist and I'm not an agnostic," he claims. "I'm an In-betweener! The Bible is a bunch of crap and lies!" he shouts again. "Biblical references are bullshit! Especially in literature meant to be considered seriously."

"Now just relax and sit down and lower your voice and we can talk about this," I say. "So, you are not an agnostic and you are not an atheist and you don't believe in the Bible. Now that we've established all that, what's an 'in-betweener?'" He's the first person I've ever met who labeled himself in this manner.

All this huff-n-puff because I used the word 'Adamites'—I don't get it.

Professor Farthington pulls up a seat and sits back down, looking at me with a calm expression. I'm startled by his sudden change of behavior. It must all be an act, or else this guy is completely loony and I'd better watch out and move on.

"Ultimate knowledge can't be known and God can't be proven to exist," he says. "End of story! You die, you get buried or you get cremated, whatever!"

"So, you don't believe you have a soul then?" I ask.

"What's a soul? Prove to me what a soul is! Show me I have a soul!" he says. "If you can do that, then you just went from amateur philosopher to philosopher of the ages! Can you do that?"

I stare at him and don't move a muscle or respond in any way. He peers back at me for a few seconds of silence, looking over the top of his glasses.

"Didn't think so! See! So, essentially all this is nothing but hogwash," he says as he slaps the pamphlets in his hands again.

I'm totally stunned and taken unawares by his persistent over-reactions. I need to diffuse the situation and move on. The professor will have none of that—he wants to argue and debate. I get up to gather my stuff and throw my uneaten food away. He then starts following me around.

"Why do you write and publish this stuff if you don't want to talk about it and explain yourself?"

"I really don't know what to say to you," I respond. "It seems like you want to argue for the sake of being argumentative and disagreeable. That's not how I operate—sorry! I'm going for a walk in the woods. You're welcome to come along if you want and we can talk about this further."

Finally, a big smile spreads across Professor

Farthington's face as we proceed to take a quiet stroll out to a path in the woods.

Much in life is based on speculation, dogmas, and borrowed beliefs. We assume to know what we don't know and can't prove. Consciousness is reined in and shackled to a small corner of density. The immense reality of truth is hidden within. A closed mind is not open to know. Skepticism and pessimism is a poison to growth. The negative allure has resounding effects. Uplifting optimism and idealism always have a strong opposing force. But Truth is stronger than all forms of resistance. The wayward light shines through the engulfing darkness. The tides of humanity gravitate to all the dark directions. The Earth will always need Rainbow Warriors…

ꕥ

We walk along a path I have taken several times before. It curls back around to just less than a mile in circumference. We saunter along, keeping quiet to ourselves and enjoying the views of nature. The sky is a clear ocean blue without a cloud in sight. Another beautiful summer day!

I look over at Professor Farthington and can tell his mind is churning on something to debate about or discuss.

"So, what's on your mind?" I ask. "Can we give that 'Adamites' thing a rest though?"

After a long pause of silence the volatile professor speaks to me in a calm measured tone.

"Do you have guilts that arise when your personal needs and desires—your burning passions—come into conflict with the demands of society?" he inquires of me. "Are the urgencies of your instincts in an endless struggle with the restrictions of civilization?"

"I'm not sure where you're coming from or what you mean," I say.

"I'm quoting from Freud's ***Civilization and Its Discontents,*"** he says. "Have you ever read the book?"

"No, I haven't!" I say.

"Well, I think you fit the mold. You are a bohemian, at least you call yourself that," he says. "Your writing is based on counterculture themes, idealism, antirealism, against the mainstream."

"What the hell is antirealism?" I interject. "Just because you don't believe in a soul doesn't mean I'm antirealism. But you're entitled to your opinion and you can believe or say whatever you want."

He thinks I fit the mold. I don't get it. He comes up with this assumption about me from reading my pamphlets? Perhaps I can learn something from his line of questioning.

"Yes, I am discontent, disenchanted, socially disaffected. How very astute of you. Do you always question your students and associates from this angle?"

"Sometimes, but not usually. I find most people to be so caught up in the dramas of their lives that they wouldn't even understand what I mean. But I could tell you are different, from the style and tone of your writings," replies Professor Farthington. "You seem to have some unknown artistic purpose you are striving for."

As we walk through the paths into the deep woods I open up and spill forth my views.

"I painted myself into a corner, slotted my spot on the Grand Machine. I adapted and became part of an ineffectual bureaucracy. The demands of a professional services culture, operating within a self-defeating system, was too much for me after five years, and within seven years into my career I struck out on my own. Every day was a day of troubleshooting emergencies. I was burning out and losing myself in the process. I had to escape. In my escape I failed miserably," I say.

"So, you admit you are in a struggle with the restrictions of civilization and have strong conflicts with the demands of society?" Professor Farthington inquires once again. "You admit that your passions are against what the mainstream says you should do?"

"Exactly! That's how and why I connected with Cricket and all these alienated deadhead rainbow family people," I say. "Writing has been my angle for exploring my struggle."

"So, tell me about the nature of your discontent," he says.

"I am discontent with my life. Of this I have no doubt. It all started around 1988. I had a great situation but I felt I should be living a different life—more exciting and adventurous—with me in control of my financial independence and how I use my time. I realized I was selling myself short, falling into the slotted hole. It is so inviting to adapt and sell oneself short. You only get one chance at this life. I attempted repeatedly to affect situations in my work life, my professional career, to promote myself on a faster path. It just wouldn't happen—couldn't happen to my satisfaction. The system is all wrong. I couldn't beat it. The mega-corporate mainstream had all my best hours delivered to them each day," I admit with dejection.

"Where did you work and what did you do?" he asks.

"I worked in the banking industry and the automotive industry, worked with high-tech systems and programmers," I reply. "Anyway, I became so disillusioned. The rose-colored tints soon turned to a pale grey. I needed freedom. I was stifled, choked, lifeless, a living zombie. I'd show up each week and put in my time to collect a paycheck. Where's my soul-growth? How can

I evolve and unfold to my utmost? I can't. I won't. I'm not going to live this life as if I'm digging my grave each day. There is an inward universe to conquer and behold, an infinite power to activate from within, outward. I owe this to myself, my soul, the seed and roots of my being!"

"So, that's why you became a writer, almost as a vehicle of self-preservation?" the professor inquires.

"Yes, yes! My whole work ethic and mental frame of mind has been through a complete flip from when I graduated from college and anxiously entered the corporate work force environment of Midwest Americana. I had unbridled enthusiasm, idealistic goals and mega ambitions. In the first couple of years I'm advancing well on my career path. I've completed several technical certifications and have been promoted to the title of Systems Engineer."

"Well, that all sounds good and fine, so what happened?" he says.

"In the next few years in my career I slowly start to become disillusioned. I felt trapped by the corporate rat race—mortgage, cars, credit cards, bills, bills, bills. I discover that I've made my life about living to pay my bills. How depressing is that realization? That's what you do as an adult—make bills, take on increasing debt responsibility and tie yourself down. This is the adult way of doing things. I think I can live with this program for awhile. I talk myself into it—so this is why I work now? Then my investments went bad and my marriage soon followed," I say.

"So, how did you get to this point in your life—right now, right here?" the professor questions me further. "Sounds like you've had a 'Meaning Crisis' or something to that effect."

"Exactly! I started asking myself everyday—'What is

the purpose of my life?' I discovered I'm not living for a true purpose. I'd sided with the false self, the false me, the untrue existence of my reality. Before the end of the 1980's I knew I must make a drastic upheaval move. I couldn't live on false pretense anymore. I refuse to grow old with secret despair, unspoken dread, and suppressed darkness. I could not live on this false foundation anymore. I decided these chains of self-imposed and self-limiting tyranny must be broken and unshackled. But, then I made all the wrong moves for all the right reasons," I say.

"What happened?" he asks.

"Bottom-line, I repelled and chased away the love of my life. My inner turmoils need only my company. She was so patient with me. She understood that I had these intense fires burning within me, strong ambitions and aspirations, an undefined purpose I am seeking. I was impatient. I blew our investment money on some deals that went sour and that was the beginning of the end for us," I say.

"Here's what I think," responds the Professor.

We stop walking the path in the woods as we stand facing each other. I listen with focused attention to what he has to say.

"The instincts of your natural nature are sublimated, submerged, hidden. You increased your efforts to change and self-growth only to discover that man has not an unlimited amount of mental energy, not individually. You witnessed the drowning of the evolution of your character into the sea of conformity. Am I close? Am I right?"

"Very much so," I agree with his assessment. "I could sense this repetitive scenario to be against the art of life, opposed to the natural order of myself and soul, at the seed and roots core. I had to escape, only to place myself in a new self-imposed prison. I'm now seeking to know the laws and principles of my inner nature. There is an in-depth relation to perpetual forces of creation. There is a guiding force to knowing thyself. The seeker continuously peals away the false coverings hiding the kernels of truth. The mission must go on."

"You sure seem to have a handle on things now. I wish you well in your endeavors," says Professor Henry Farthington.

"Thank you! I appreciate your frank and candid nature."

We walk together in silence along the forest path for several minutes, but my mind is still busy processing:

> *My character is my temple, my moral directive. I neglected to acknowledge this critical truth at previous stations in my life, and this denial resulted in my unraveling. My foundation was built on falsehoods and materialism. The temple came crashing down. I'm rebuilding the inner me. I know what tools to use and what tools to avoid. Destructive chaos is everywhere inviting. The sacred temple within has no room for negative functioning. A sound temple is a ringing bell of Truth for the owner individual.*

I am long-winded in my talk as we walk through the trails. The professor listens intently, all the while. It is as if he assumes the role of psychologist, priest, father confessor.

"You sound like a philosopher experimenting with his own life to gain the personal experiences of wisdom one needs to grow forth," he says.

"That is a lofty goal, but in no way do I think of myself as worthy of the title—'Philosopher.' I do aspire to become a published author one day, though. I feel I have many books inside of me, waiting to be coaxed out," I say.

We are fast approaching the end of our trail in the woods, back to where we started. Professor Farthington laughs out loud about the pressure he created in getting me to cough up my background story.

"I do that with my students all the time. I like to test people on what they think about things, about others and about themselves," he says.

The professor laughs some more and squeezes me around both shoulders with his hands and tells me to, "Keep on writing what you honestly feel and believe, and especially what you know of truth from your own personal experience of truth. However, I must warn you about being pretentious or speaking of things as an expert or master when you really don't know. And try to avoid biblical references or religious semantics when you express yourself. The English language is rich and powerful. You don't need to resort to gimmicks to get your point across. Good luck to you, Ted."

I thank him for his advice. We shake hands again. The end of our trail looped back around to the big party field near a pavilion. We split apart, heading in different directions.

ജ്ജ

Who is Crystal Serenity? Where is she now? The cute little Lohasian Rainbow Warrior from Portland, Maine.

Was that a real experience or a dream?

I continue walking and embark on a steeper footpath that connects to a new trail. The air is fresh and cooler as I near a gurgling brook. I kneel down and feel the cold soft water rush past my finger tips. Another beautiful day in nature!

My thoughts revert to an incident I had yesterday, way before the liquid refreshments took the toll on me.

I met Gary Morris. I saw this man by himself,

struggling with a cane and a food tray to get to a table to eat. The guy was very unsteady on his feet. I rushed over to help him get settled. We sat at a table, just the two of us, and talked for several minutes, with all this endless hullabaloo of activity about us. We connected on a deep level of understanding. Gary shared his life history and awakening with me.

Gary is sixty-five years old. He wears graying action in his receding hairline, but he has a paradoxical youthful exuberance to his character, his self-understanding. Gary lives alone. He's an uncle to one of the bridesmaids. It is very inspirational just being around Gary and listening to him speak.

"I was involved in a serious one car accident twenty years ago," he said. "I lost control with my red corvette on a dark night on a lonely winding road along the Pacific Ocean in California. My wife and I had recently divorced and I was mean and belligerent with her and my new girlfriend. They both told me to go to hell. I was drinking and carousing every night, hardly sleeping," Gary said.

He paused and took a deep breath and looked at me laser-like, square in the eyes. I could sense his giving of trust in me to talk so deeply of his tender sensibilities and vulnerability.

He began again, "I was full of self-pity. It was everybody else's fault—never mine! I was self-centered, egotistical, controlling, arrogant, irresponsible and I cheated whenever I got the chance at whatever competitive games I played," he said. "I sound like a son-of-a-bitch, when I think about it, even now. Put it this way—I was not a nice person or balanced in mind, and I only cared about myself first, and everyone else second."

"What caused you to gain the awareness to turn it all around?" I asked.

"Then the doctors told me I would never walk again. My spirit just collapsed," with a deep sigh, Gary continued, "just bedridden and useless for the rest of my life! Imagine that! One day I am fully healthy as I lived a tumultuous life—then BANG! It all ends, and I will never have what I always took for granted. Just like that!"

Gary made a motion to snap his fingers, but the snap was only symbolic to emphasize his point, because his hands and limbs were contorted, irregular.

"What happened to you in the accident?" I asked.

"I was in the hospital for damn near a year. I should have died," he said. "The car rolled several times and I was trapped inside, unconscious. It was a few weeks before I woke up again. The doctors induced the coma so I would just rest and heal and not think. I was paralyzed," Gary Morris said. "Messed up pretty bad—I have a spinal cord injury. It will never totally heal. But I can get around and I'm generally independent now. I go to physical therapy two-three times every week. I can drive."

"So you spent almost a year in the hospital?" I asked.

"The doctors told me I would never function normally, walk, or leave the bed. I fooled them," he said. "I willed myself to get better. It was a long grueling recovery process. I lost my ego. I surrendered to the universal forces—begged forgiveness! I found purpose and I found my inner power," Gary said.

"What was your secret?" I asked him. "How did you grow for the good with so much negativity surrounding you and within you? Most people would just give up."

"I learned to know myself," Gary enthusiastically proclaimed, "to know my inner faults, weaknesses and demons. I had to go through all my unhappiness and emptiness to discover the other self within me. It was very difficult, heart-rending, hopeless at times. But what the hell, I had time." Gary laughed, "I'm in bed forever it seems. So all I can do is lay there and think! During this time, say six to nine months later, I've reconstructed my character, personality, who I am—everything! All this reinvention has happened in my mind."

"Did you read a lot of self-help books, philosophy, meditation? Pray to God?" I asked. "What caused you or helped you turn the corner?"

"All of that and more!" he said. "I came to the realization that I was still in control of how I think. I changed how I think and how I feel, essentially changed my entire habit nature. And with that I came in touch with my spirit more than ever before in my entire life," he boasted. "A whole new perception and clarity and decisiveness prevailed!"

Gary stared off into the woods beyond, looking past me. He had talked himself into an exquisite trance, recalling his enlightenment process.

"What happened next?" I asked.

Gary shook his head from side to side to snap out of his momentary meditative state.

"I said, what happened next? You transformed yourself from the inside and then began walking again?"

"Then one day, miraculously, I feel tingling in my extremities. I didn't say anything for at least a week or two. I started practicing moving my toes and fingers late at night. I would do this and not tell anybody, and I just felt so thankful, so gifted, so honored, so loved by God. I just knew I was going to walk and get up from that bed and I eventually did!" Gary's glassy eyes emit a few tears descending down his cheeks as he recalls his story.

"Wow! That's amazing!" I said.

"Of course it took many, many months of hard physical therapy almost every day. It was tough, but I did it!" he said. "Now I have an energy healer lady who visits me twice a week and she gives me these deep massages and readjusts my bodily energy flow. Plus I still do physical therapy every other day. I'm independent and getting along just fine now!" Gary said.

We later shook hands and wished each other well after our little chat. What a unique man, a free soul who shed all his personal demons and destructive tendencies to grow into the individual liberty that is always there.

He willed his own miracle unto himself!

How has my spirit grown through my years of troubling turmoil? Is my distant soul closer to the inward self I acknowledge as me? I feel a closer kinship to my soul presence. But, still, I sense a wide gulf from my inward faith to my experience of knowingness. The intangible unseen is so real, but yet I cannot prove a thing. The soul is shrouded in mystery. My spiritual evolution is what remains.

ꕥ

I continue with my nature walk and head in a direction that leads to the grateful gathering of revelers. As I draw nearer I can hear the cacophony of noises and playful yells, yelps and hollering, rising out of the belly of the forested woods in the park. The party with a thousand-plus is evidently ramping up to energetic levels once again. I scurry along to join in on another day of festivities.

I participate in several games of horseshoes and then jump in as a substitute in a volleyball game. The bands are warming up for the night shows. The countdown to the end of this big celebration is coming soon.

Later in the afternoon I decide to take a long walk down by the riverside overlooking the waterfall like I did the day before. It is my intent to sit out in the solitude of nature and write in my journal notebook.

I notice a couple walking hand-in-hand along the

river's edge as I descend the hilly mountain side until I am at the foot of the falls. By the time I get to the bottom the couple has disappeared into the woods along the riverbed. I walk over to the big boulder I sat on previously, take my book bag off my back, and commence to write in my notebook.

I write about my understanding and lack of understanding of the word 'Transcendental.' I focus on a literal dictionary definition of the word: *Being beyond ordinary or common experience, thought or belief.* As I stare at the waterfall and the surrounding scenes of nature, I ponder this definition, this word—*transcendental; transcendent.*

I begin writing in my journal:

> This whole trip has been a transcendental experience for me~starting from that first night when I awoke at Lake Minnawanna to a mixture of music, noise and chaos from the deadhead village forming at the campgrounds. From that moment I've been on an odyssey. Moreover, I was already in the midst of my own self-chosen odyssey, before the deadheads appeared in my life. I've just been riding this long, continuous wave ever since I met the Heads. What have I discovered about myself during this process? What kind of truths have I discovered and/or validated? I feel that my consciousness elevated to a deeper level of awakening. But what do I really mean by that? Have I found insight into my life's purpose? What have I learned from my failures, painful experiences and fears? Do I misrepresent the truth to myself? What attitudes do I have that disempower me? My broken heart is mending. My soul needed the tonic of this bohemian adventure. I've grown into a new awareness of insights. I will love

once again. I feel a group love for all the people in the grateful gatherings. Compassion and kindness and cheerfulness are a connective binding force with others. The energetic vibe resonates. Meeting Cricket and the Grateful Gatherers showed me how to break free. Now I'm opening myself up to a new life, a future of love~a new way to be. This 'beyond the ordinary experience' qualifies as 'transcendental' for me! I feel a universal connection to the spark of the divine! It's up to me to maintain and enhance this connection throughout my days. Natural nature awaits!

I write all this in my journal for my quest of self-knowledge and understanding. I realize that many of my thoughts are open-ended questions, not readily answerable. But I trust in the evolving state of my mind. My habit energies are growing and developing constructively. Self-liberty will one day be at hand.

I put my writing materials in my book bag, fold my legs in a sitting position and meditate on the rock by the river side, looking out at the beautiful falls.

Omm. Ommm.

&

After meditating for about half an hour, I make my way up the mountainside to the party scene. The myriad activities of partying and drinking and dancing and cavorting about are going on strong in all directions. Today I vow to be a non-drinker, so things that seemed perfectly normal yesterday, appear strange and funny today. Like the guy walking around with the empty twelve-pack box on his head as if it's a football helmet, or the young woman lying on a blanket in the field by herself, laughing hysterically, or the heave-ho tree where several revelers lean against as they vomit.

I spot the groom in the midst of the crowd. I haven't seen Peter since he got married. I walk over to him to congratulate him on his nuptials. Peter is surrounded by his college fraternity house brothers. Everyone is loud, boisterous and pretty well inebriated.

One of his college buddies asks me where I went to school.

"Michigan State University—I graduated from MSU in 1982," I respond.

An immediate roar of boos and hisses rains down on me. All of these guys are from the University of Michigan in Ann Arbor. Both schools have a major rivalry in sporting events, especially football and basketball. The fraternity brothers from U of M throw paper cups and plastic bottles and pieces of Doritos and pretzels at me. It is all done in good-natured fun. I'm a good sport about it and absorb the razzing.

Every one of Peter's buddies has an engineering degree and they work in the automobile industry. What a coincidence of commonality. I explain to them that I worked in the automotive industry too, in the eighties at General Motors.

"I actually started my first job in the Engineering Change Control Department at GM. I worked for Electronic Data Systems—EDS. This was the time when Roger B. Smith bought EDS from H. Ross Perot," I say.

"The guy that just ran for President last year?" asks Peter.

"Yeah! Same guy!" I say. "I was one of the original hires, right when the deal happened and Perot sold EDS to GM for something like three billion dollars. I was just a raw greenhorn out of college learning the ropes and barely six months into my job and then we got word that

GM bought us."

"Were you happy about that?" asks one of Peter's buddies.

"Sure, at first!" I say. "It was a great opportunity. I'd been living and training down in Dallas and it meant I could move back home to Michigan and continue my career living in my preferred state. I was all for it. Plus I got an immediate boost in salary. But the job and the company owned me night and day. Then when I started working at the GM Tech Center in Warren, I discovered a stressful unwelcome working environment. Nobody at GM wanted us around! Upper management on both sides were always arguing and at odds with each other. Plus EDS had to absorb GM's technical services division, and these lifelong GMers did not want to change allegiance and become EDS."

"Why not?" asks Peter. "They still work for GM because GM bought EDS."

"It didn't work that way though," I reply. "The people who had to transfer to EDS lost half their fringe benefits. So GM people didn't like us and former GM people who were now EDS people, didn't like us. Every day was filled with animosity and tensions. After awhile it wears on you," I say.

"How long did you work there?" asks Peter.

"Almost eight years. The local papers said it was like the minnow was trying to swallow the whale. It did get better after awhile though, and I worked with a lot of General Motors people on successful projects. There's just so much bureaucracy and red tape and unions and bullshit going on in a big corporate environment."

"How come your boy quit?" inquires one of Peter's frat brothers.

"I don't know what you're talking about?" I say.

"H. Ross Perot! How come he quit on the people?" he says. "My whole family and all my relatives were going to vote for him."

"I don't know what happened for sure. He didn't really want to win, I guess. He just wanted to make sure the Republicans didn't get re-elected," I say. "He took almost twenty percent of the popular vote as an Independent. Theodore Roosevelt was the last Independent to do so well, something like 1912 or so. That's why Clinton won with the lowest percentage in history at thirty-nine percent, because Perot split the Republican vote."

"That's probably what he had in mind to do all along," says Peter.

"I think so, too," I say. "My major regret is that Perot didn't create a viable third party that could challenge the two-party system legitimately in each election. Something like the 'American Party' as an alternative for voters who don't like the Republican and Democratic nominees."

"I think he's an asshole!" says one of Peter's buddies.

Then the frat brothers start pushing and shoving against each other, playfully jostling around.

No more talk about MSU, GM, EDS or Perot! Some of these guys are on the borderline of getting out of hand.

I discover all these guys work as engineers at Chrysler, Ford and Toyota. Soon the discussion turns to their shop talk. I listen in on the conversation and stand around with them joining in on the small talk about work-related issues in corporate America. Peter eventually roams off amongst the throng. So, I find myself standing here with these five guys, when all of a sudden two of the guys, Brett and Dave, start threatening me.

"Why are you living in Peter's backyard?" says Dave in an aggressive tone.

"Yeah! You're just a freeloader and a bull-shitter!"

says Brett. "Just an asshole from MSU!"

The two guys crowd in closer towards me. They snap from fun and games and laughter to pure anger and it's all directed at me.

"Why don't you have a job?" asks Brett.

"I was invited by Cricket to come out here," I respond. "I haven't been freeloading and bullshitting about anything. What's you guys' problem anyway?"

"You don't belong around here or at Cricket and Peter's house," shouts Dave. "Get lost, loser!"

He pushes me in the chest with his outstretched hand and I stagger back a few feet. I find myself separated from the main crowd with these two guys on each side of me shooting menacing looks at me like bullets. The other fraternity brothers had drifted off in the crowd. I see some people at a distance take notice of my predicament. My first thought is that I have to be ready to defend myself in case they jump me. The second thought is just to get away and move on.

Just then Peter appears out of the crowd, hollering at his two friends. He comes up and grabs both of them by the shirt collar in back and violently pulls his two drunk buddies away from me. Full beer cups spill in the air with a whooshing splash. The three of them fall to the ground on top of each other, soaked in beer. They're rolling around laughing.

Peter hollers up to me, "I'm sorry for my friend's attitudes. They don't mix well with people from MSU or Ohio State, especially when they're drinking. Go on and have a good time, Ted."

Peter and his frat brothers continue wrestling around with each other—throwing half-empty cups of beer into each other's faces, pushing and pulling and tackling one another. I move along before it turns into a full-blown fraternity brouhaha.

Back in the solitude of the woods I walk a short trail, thinking of conflict, rivalry and not getting along:

No person, group, organization or institution can keep me down. Only I have this power. I will not submit and give away this power to anyone. My choice is life, growth, development and self-evolution. I am a mere microcosm of what I aim to be. Rivals and naysayers and strong competition will always be present. The choice is to fear or be fearless. The choice is mine alone.

I spend the rest of the day having fun, watching the bands, dancing to the music, conversing with people, and socially drinking a few non-alcoholic beverages. The party forms into big round moving circles around the bonfires at night. I hang out around the kegs off and on throughout the evening, sitting off to the side in a folding chair and writing in my notebook.

I enjoy watching and hearing all the happy boisterous faces coming for refills. Every now and then someone approaches me and asks, "What are you writing?" or inquires if I'm the bohemian writer who wrote the pamphlet booklets?

These questions spawn various conversations about the act of writing and thinking and creativity. Most everyone I talk to is very positive and encouraging. The deadhead types in the crowd stop by and read something back to me from 'Self & Soul' or 'Seed & Roots.' I enjoy the camaraderie and repartée. Cricket's idea for my writings has sparked interest and numerous conversations.

ꕤ

I wake up in my tent on Day Number Four at the park and I can sense that today will be different. I need to say goodbye to the newlyweds and figure out my journey back home. Many people are busy breaking down camp and packing up. Some people are staying an extra day, but most of the people are vacating. I notice the stage on the north end of the field was dismantled last night.

I get out of the tent, back out on my knees, stand up, turn around—I'm startled.

"Oh shit! You freaked me out dude!" I exclaim.

A short, rotund, unshaven guy is standing in front of me staring at me. He wears a serious-minded look on his face and he doesn't react to my surprised jerky jump and jolt reaction to his sudden presence. He stares at me in silence for a long moment.

"I'm Allen and I've been hired to watch Cricket and Peter's Victorian home for the next three months. Do you have anything of yours in the house?" he asks.

"Yes, I do!" I say. "On the fourth floor in the far corner of the room in the front of the house. Why?"

"You have to leave!" says Allen. "All your stuff has to be off the property right now!"

"What do you mean—right now? I need to make arrangements, get a greyhound bus ticket home or something," I complain.

"You need to take care of that right now!" he says.

"Hold on a minute here guy. I'm sure Peter and Cricket would let me stay a day or two until I make the arrangements."

"That's them—not me!" he responds. "I'm not going to be held responsible for their home and have anyone staying on the property. These were my conditions when I agreed to do this for them."

He pulls out a signed sheet of paper from the back pocket of his jeans and tells me he has an agreement, as he jabs his index finger into the paperwork.

"So, you're kicking me out into the streets, just like

that?" I ask.

"Cricket and Peter are leaving today for a three-month-long, West Coast, car trip. They plan on catching up with the Grateful Dead in late August in Oregon and northern California," he says. "I think they just left in fact! I'm in charge of their home now!"

I never talked about any of this with Cricket. I should have made plans for my departure before I came to Finger Lakes. Whenever I was with Cricket it was always about the now moment and the next party, the next activity, the next celebration. We never discussed the aftermath and I haven't considered as much as a thought about my planned departure.

Now I'm in a bind. I have dwindling funds and I don't know how I'm going to get back. Cricket is my patron—*was my patron*. I've just been living it up from day-to-day for weeks now. I've been to a party here, a party there, always meeting and seeing new people, having interesting conversations, and enjoying the events.

Now Bohemia has come to an end. Dissolved. The queen of all bohemians left the environment. The energy vacuum is pronounced. Only the unique Cricket can claim command of the mysterious force that surrounds her wherever she goes. I've partied along, written along, read along, ridden along, walked along, talked alongside Cricket, the mystical muse. Athena could not have served me better. My muse is no longer here. It's time for me to depart.

Unwanted and unwelcome! Time to move on and be on my way. This moment will not mar the great times, the companionships with new friends, the sense of purpose I've regained. But I'm sad and depressed right now and I can't get these feelings out of my head. My exciting adventure is coming to an end.

PART III

End of The Road Show Rainbow

"Not till we are lost, in other words, not till we have lost the world, do we begin to find ourselves, and realize where we are and the infinite extent of our relations."

—Henry David Thoreau, ***Walden***

"Lately it occurs to me,
what a long strange trip it's been."

—Grateful Dead *Truckin'*
(The Band's unofficial Motto)

Catharsis:
1) A purging
2) an emotional purification or relief, usually by sharing in the experience of another

Satori:
sudden enlightenment and a state of consciousness attained by intuitive illumination; representing the spiritual goal of Zen Buddhism.

"We shall not cease from exploring
And the end of our exploring
Will be to arrive where we started
And know the place for the first time."

—T.S. Eliot

ꕥ

Chapter Fourteen

The Honeymoon is Over

ꕥ

"The Queen of Light took her bow, then she turned to go."

—Led Zeppelin
'The Battle of Evermore'

Lost My Patron

I spend most of the day after talking to Allen, walking trails in the woods. I saunter over to the Inn, by the off chance, to say goodbye to the newlyweds. Alas, they've already left, no such luck. I will not be able to see Cricket again.

I arrange to hitch a ride back into Rochester with a group of people who are leaving early tomorrow morning. I tried to find a ride with various people leaving today but no one heading to Rochester has room for me.

By the time I get back from my all day walk in the woods, I discover a note paper clipped to my tent. It's from Allen. He says he will have all my belongings on the front porch deck, and that the entire property is locked up.

A vast majority of the party crowd is now gone from the park. There is a small group of people, perhaps a dozen or so, on the southeast end of the big field near the pavilion. I take a walk down there, grab a bite to eat from the leftover food available—a hamburger, hot dog, chips and soda.

I hear from others about the grand send off of Cricket and Peter earlier in the day. The newlyweds plan on spending ten to twelve hours a day driving until they get to the west coast, where they have a honeymoon suite waiting for them in San Francisco, overlooking the Pacific Ocean. I have no doubt Cricket will be walking North Beach and checking out the Haight Ashbury district on her visit.

Without the Queen of Bohemia, I'm a lost bohemian, once again, here anyway—social misfit, non-conformist, drifter that I am. This little idyll of time with Cricket, in my life's passageway, has left a deep impression on my mind, my heart, my soul. I'm especially aware, but without the full understanding, of the profundity, the ethos, the anomalous nature of the recent experiences:

She is an original, a unique—a bundle of positive energy! I missed saying goodbye! I've got to be moving on and get myself a means to get back home. Damn, the funds are low, always low. Cricket will be missed. This adventure on a bohemian odyssey has all been her doing. Moving along, I need to be moving along.

She's gone, she's gone. Will I ever see her again? Goodbye Bohemian Queen. Thank You, thank you. The whirling dervish has left the premises. She's off to the west coast. Cricket the Queen of Bohemia, my Mystic Muse. I will miss our times together, the great causes, the great vibes, the learning and power of words.

Great book reader—classical literature, history, poetry, philosophy. People in need. Ahhh Cricket, you are special indeed—I'll miss you girl.She is the magnet that brought me here. Intense fire burning within. Electro-magnetic force. Bursting flames of energy. Boundless. Cheerful. Exasperating. Tireless. What an overwhelming force of Nature little Cricket is.

As I look around and survey the nature party platform, I see that everyone here, including myself, shares a common trait of appearance—looking extremely tired, lethargic, and worn down from the persistent days of celebration.

My mind must switch into a new gear. I have my self-preservation instincts on high alert. I need to find a way to get back home. My bohemian adventure of fun activity is now over. It's time for me to come to grips with the new reality.

I stop by the camping area of the couple who promised to give me a ride back to town tomorrow. Just double-checking to make sure. Betsy and Ron tell me to be ready first thing in the morning. They have a big "old yeller" dog that I'll be sharing the backseat with. I find out that Ron is a distant cousin of the groom, and they live in Portland, Maine.

I wonder if they know Crystal Serenity?

There is a small fire ring with a few dozen people hanging around at night. Every now and then there is a burst of laughter and excitement in a passing conversation, but mostly it's a small community of silence, all eyes staring into the crackling embers of the campfire. The high octane energy of the past few days has morphed into a lethargic zombie-like state with the remaining stragglers.

I decide to head for my tent and a restless night of sleep. I don't know where I'm staying tomorrow night, and I don't know how I'm going to get back home.

ꕥ

In the morning Ron and his dog wake me up just after sunrise. He says his wife is riding to Rochester with some other friends and that it will just be him, me and the dog, Jake. I quickly clear out my tent and break it down and fold it into a tight roll. Then I roll up my sleeping bag and stuff all my gear in my backpack. I walk through the woods and over to Ron's campsite and put my backpack in the back of his oversized GM pickup truck. He's having a coffee and throwing a stick for his dog to chase down and retrieve.

"Good Morning!" he says. "Sorry about waking you so early! My wife already caught a ride with someone else and they left when it was still dark."

"So, you're ready to go right now then, I bet, huh?" I say. "The sooner the better is fine with me."

"Yesiree, I am, too!" Ron says, as he tosses the stick far off into the edge of the woods for his dog Jake to fetch.

"I've got some coffee brewing on the campfire. Want a cup? We have some time for a coffee or two and a chat."

"Don't mind if I do," I say.

Ron and I talk about the big party celebrations and the wedding and the fun times we had. I explain to him how I met Cricket last month and how I had made the trip out here. He says he doesn't know Cricket that well (he always refers to her as Lynn), but that she seems to him like quite a character. He chuckles as he says it. I tell him about a couple of sunrises I experienced with Cricket and what we did on 'Garbage Day.' He enjoys hearing me rehash the stories.

"So, you mentioned yesterday that you are from Maine?" I inquire.

"Yes, but we have some friends near Rochester who we've been visiting on this trip, too. But, yeah, we have to get back to Maine," he says. "Near Portland! And you're from where?"

"Michigan!" I say. "I'm wondering if you know a brunette girl named Crystal who was here at the gathering a couple days ago. She wore a Rainbow Warriors shirt and she said she was from Portland, Maine?"

"My wife Betsy and I are the only ones from Maine that I know of on this trip! Not to say that there weren't others. There were so many people that I barely saw a tenth of them that I actually met and talked with. Wish I would've met her," he says. "We didn't really get too rowdy here. There was so much stuff going on and so much to eat and drink and things to do and people to watch enjoying themselves. Shit, I was tired and ready for bed by nightfall every night!" Ron says.

I finish my cup of coffee and Ron tosses the stick for Jake one last time.

"Well, I'm ready to go if you are," I say. "We can finish this pot of coffee and put out the coals and get going."

"Sounds good to me!" Ron says.

We gather up our final things and Ron lets the dog in the backseat of his truck. I take one last look at the surrounding environment of raw natural nature—the trees and woods and birds and footpaths, the sound of the waterfall, and the flowing streams and the mountains backdrop. I take it all in one last moment and then hop into the passenger seat.

Ron starts up his truck and we set off on the road to exit this huge park. I silently look out my window at the passing nature scenes—wildflowers, oak, pine, hickory, sumac, maple, and birch trees, squirrels and chipmunks, a hawk circling, rabbits scattering, an owl in a tree, a little red fox crossing the street, a herd of deer racing through the woods, robins, blue jays, cardinals…

"My vacation is almost over in a few more days," he says. "We have to get back to the daily grind. You know how that goes."

"Yes, I do!" I reply. "What kind of job do you have, Ron?"

"I work as a district salesman of fifty-gallon hydraulic

drums," he says. "Spend a lot of time on the roads visiting clients at various small to mid-size machine shops. The whole deal can get monotonous at times though."

I look over to the console dash and notice some cassettes of Zig Ziglar and Og Mandino.

"You read self-help books and listen to tapes?" I ask.

"I listen to positive motivational tapes all the time," Ron says. "I try to keep up with the latest self-improvement stuff. You need to do that in my line of business. Being a salesman can be tough sometimes. There's always pressure for new sales," he complains. "I want more out of life but I feel trapped with the mortgage, car payments and debt. Go to bed with that responsibility every night—so, then I wake up and do my routine."

I laugh out loud—can't help it! The familiar refrain! I'm not laughing at him or with him, but in spite of his similar story of fate.

The disillusioned! Quiet desperation! We are everywhere!

"What's so funny?" he says.

"Just listening to you go on about the everyday pressures of life makes me laugh at myself," I say. "That's why I'm in the woods writing, being a hermit and trying to figure it all out. I burned out from the grind, man! I'm trying to rekindle that flame and come back at it with a different approach," I say.

"Life can be tough! A never-ending struggle at times it seems. I just want to be able to have peace of mind one day," Ron says. "You know what I mean? No worries or doubts or fears—just bliss and happiness and contentment!" Ron laughs to himself, "I'm talking shit now, aren't I?"

"Not at all!" I respond. "All of us human beings are each in our own personal struggle for self-liberty and self-freedom. It's just that so many people, the walking multitudes, are unaware! That's the heart of the issue."

"I read some of those folded booklets from a sheet of paper that you wrote. That was a cool idea, man! I think I have some copies in my luggage," he says.

"That was Cricket's idea," I say. "My words and her idea. She took my notebooks and got with one of her friends and they created the little pamphlets. Neat idea. I was pretty surprised."

"I've had various times in my life where I was seeking answers for myself to the great questions and mysteries of life," Ron says. "I never find legitimate answers to what I'm seeking because the reality of life gets in the way."

"That's why I write and read so much. There are a lot of trap doors and detours in life that can take you down roads that will never lead to true understanding. Then ten years go by, a couple decades, whole lifetimes of psychic slumber," I say. "You ever heard of Mindfulness?"

"I've heard of the term," he says.

"Thoreau's social experiment at Walden Pond for two years and two months and two days was most of all an experiment in Mindfulness," I say.

"Doesn't that word 'Mindfulness' originate with the Orientals and Buddhists?"

"Exactly! Buddha, himself!" I say.

"You see, Ted, my problem is that I see stuff, hear stuff, learn things, but nothing really sticks. It's like it's good for that moment as it passes through my mind, but two weeks later I won't remember any of it, and I sure won't be applying it to my life, unless it's what I've got to do to earn my paycheck. And companies don't care about their employees getting self-illumination—it's all bottom-line," Ron says. He rubs his thumb against his two fingers back and forth to signify the power of money over us as a human race.

"Well, mindfulness is about being in the present moment with all your senses as you experience the unfoldment of each moment. You can get there through meditation and awareness," I say.

"Stuff like that sounds simple but it can be very distracting and hard to concentrate or find the time regularly to do it." Ron says.

"That's precisely why we are supposed to do it, so we can relax and de-stress and disconnect from our busy lives," I say.

"I just fall asleep whenever I try to meditate," Ron says.

"I've had that problem, too. Or the opposite effect when you can't slow your mind down from thinking of a multitude of things all at once, can't concentrate or focus. Those two mindsets can make meditation impossible. I'm not real good at it yet, but Cricket sure is," I say. "I think that's one of her big secrets!"

"So, what did you do before you started writing and ended up out here?" Ron inquires.

"I was part of corporate America, just like you. Worked as a computer programmer and a project manager. Ended up getting a divorce, losing the house, made some bad investments, yadda, yadda, yadda," I say. "I guess you could say that I'm on my own personal mindfulness journey right now!"

"The big difference between you and me, Ted—I would never be willing to take a big risk like that! I live in economic fear all the time. Worries about my job, my clients, meeting my quotas, paying the bills and keeping the relationship solid with Betty and the kids. These things consume my mind and my waking hours every day." Ron complains, "I have no time to get in touch with my spirituality."

"Myself, I had to take the time and make the time or I was just going to burnout—Period! Each of us is different," I say.

We both stare out at the roadway, silently contemplating, as the passing traffic road sounds meld into the background of our private thoughts. Having a deep spiritual discussion about self-knowledge, individual evolution, and finding one's purpose in life, is a great way to get to know someone. We went far enough.

We continue to sit in silence for the next twenty minutes until I spot a Rochester city limits sign. When we arrive within the town I ask Ron if he could take me to the Greyhound Bus Depot. He takes me there, and I get a ticket from Rochester to Buffalo. The clerk at the ticket counter says I can choose from several destinations heading west from Buffalo. I decide to just buy the one-way ticket to Buffalo and then make my decision when I get to the bus depot from there. My bus leaves at noon tomorrow.

Ron then takes me to Cricket and Peter's Victorian home. No one is here and my stuff is not on the deck porch. Everything is locked up. I get my gear out of the back of the truck. Ron says he's going to meet up with his wife at a friend's house on the other side of town. We thank each other for the lively conversation and wish each other well. We shake hands and then I watch Ron and Jake head down the neighborhood road.

I sit down on the front porch and wait for somebody to come by, hopefully. The time drags on the rest of the morning, and no one comes by. I thumb through one of my journals and jot a few things down now and then. I'm nearly broke now. I have less than fifty bucks for another bus ticket and food till I get home. I already know this won't be enough.

Finally, in the early afternoon, Allen comes by to check on the house. I've been sitting on the porch waiting and worrying for several hours. As soon as he pulls into the driveway and parks his car, he opens up the door and hollers at me, "You can't be here!"

"I'm just here to pick up my stuff. I have a bus ticket that leaves tomorrow at noon for Buffalo," I say. "Can I pitch my tent in the backyard just for tonight?"

"No way!" he shouts as he approaches me on the front deck. "You have to be out of here right now!"

Allen leaves no room for negotiation or discussion of the issue. I re-explain to him that I have nowhere to go.

He says, "That's your problem, not mine! Maybe you can stay in a homeless shelter downtown or something."

"I'd rather not do that," I complain.

He quips back to me, as he jams the key in the front door to unlock it, "Doesn't seem like you have any options then!"

With a stern look on his face, he invites me in to go upstairs and collect my stuff. He follows me up the stairs and watches over me as I pack my clothes and things. He then leads me quickly down the stairs and out the front door as he locks up the house again.

"You can't hang around the property and wait till your bus leaves tomorrow either. I want you to load up and start walking down the street right now," he says.

I feel like he is punishing me and I don't get it. Everyone has been so friendly, caring, kind, and compassionate throughout this trip and now the whole thing ends in a big thud like this. On the verge of boiling over with his red hot face and clenched fists, Allen watches me move along on the deck porch in slow motion, fiddling with my gear. I'm trying to stretch out the time to see if there is a way to talk any reasoning sense to him but he is totally shut off to any of my pleas. Finally, I load my repacked backpack on my shoulders, and I head down the street.

I'm now homeless and unwanted in a strange town, in a strange state, a strange wasteland. My bohemian odyssey is turning into a personal nightmare. I don't say anything to Allen as I walk away. I just leave.

I remember walking these same neighborhood streets just last week with Cricket. Everything was abnormal everywhere then. Now the neighborhood blocks are back to the normalcy of everyday living. Just a few scattered individuals are outside—checking mail, tending to a garden, trimming bushes, mowing lawns, kids playing.

I walk by banjo playing Pete's house. He isn't home. I walk a few blocks and come up to Phat Bob's house, the guy with the huge portrait of the back of Jerry Garcia's head. He isn't home either. I walk from block to block the rest of the day, the heavy backpack wearing me down as I sweat like a waterfall.

It will be nightfall soon, and I'm in a serious quandary. I walk to a telephone booth at a gas station and look through the yellow pages. I don't have enough money to stay in a hotel tonight and then buy another bus ticket in Buffalo. I have to rough it. And now the sky is getting dark and cloudier. Looks like a serious storm coming.

> *Here you are again, Ted—lost again! Rejection is a part of me, for the habit seems ingrained. Here I am again! I can't dwell on these things and I can't ignore my persistent feeling either. The human condition! What lesson am I supposed to be learning from all this? Just be a free and easy bohemian, moving on.*

ഋ

I hang out at the phone booth, sifting through the yellow pages until I find a Christian Missionary homeless shelter.

I call the number and a woman answers.

"Hello, can I help you?"

"Yes! I'm stranded with nowhere to go. It's storming out here, and I'm at Fifth and Main."

The woman on the phone says, "You can stay here for the night. It's less than a mile from where you're currently at."

"Thank you! I'll be there shortly." *Click.*

I head to the homeless shelter as the sky busts loose again, drenching me from head to toe. I arrive at the homeless shelter like a beaten down man in a miserable state. The trials of the day, the endless walking, the heavy backpack, and the drenching rain have taken a toll on me. In addition, I've acquired huge, bleeding raw blisters on my feet.

The receptionist directs me to fill out some forms. Then she gives me a small mat to lay on the floor for sleeping. I walk into a large room that is filled with homeless hobos, drunks, junkies, and in general, the mentally unfit. Now I feel like I've hit rock bottom. I don't like where I'm at. *Why?* I feel like a loser in a room full of lost souls.

I try to locate a secluded empty spot on the floor in a far corner. The caretaker of the place rushes over to me from his desk on the far side of the room, stepping over sleeping people to get to me quickly.

He's clearly agitated as he says, "You have to sleep in the next open spot on the floor or you can leave if you don't like it!"

I huddle up against a wall and stand there by myself, trying not to make eye contact or talk with anyone. I am thankful to be out of the drenching storm. My mind drifts as I ponder my role in life:

I've got to realign myself. If I don't readily define myself, the net of society will. Am I a writer? or am I deluding myself to aim so high? Why not just be satisfied with joining an organization and working, having a regular job? I feel trapped when I settle in. Lost. Seeking. The art of an artist is something he or she must strive for, and weather the trials and tribulations of living a life—and still get the passionate nature of the work of the art, out!

I enter the restroom with my backpack so I can change into some dry clothes and cleanup. A couple of old bums—dirty, greasy, smelly—with claw-like hands snatch at my backpack. I holler at them and slap their hands away.

"Do you have anything to drink, Mister?"

"I don't have what you want."

They ignore me, and keep grabbing at my stuff. No sooner do I knock one guy's hands away than the other guy is grabbing at my possessions.

I take my backpack and walk out to the main floor of the homeless shelter. An attendant is making the rounds handing out blankets. I take one. I am too nerved up to be able to sleep tonight. I change into dry clothes out in the open, then I put everything back in my backpack and secure it. I unroll my sleeping bag onto the floor mat. I leave my gear by my head, as I lie down, and keep a hand on my stuff in case anybody tries to steal something.

There must be over two hundred floor mats filled with homeless individuals. I lay awake staring at the ceiling, watching the fans rotate. I'm now surrounded by floor mats of people. The place is filled to capacity because of the storm.

It stinks so bad—rank odors everywhere!

I have one hand over my nose the whole night, the other hand holding on to my backpack gear. The guard and attendants breakup several altercations happening on the floor. A couple guys get into a fight. The guards separate them and then kick them out.

There is a disgusting, gosh-awful-stink coming from the man laying on the mat right next to me. He pulls his pants down and starts fondling himself out in the open. I jump up and holler for the guard and attendants. By the time they get to him, he has his pants up and he denies he did anything. So they let him stay.

As soon as they have their backs turned and get involved in something else, the dirty old man does it again. I holler for the guard, jump up. Grab my stuff and move over to the wall. It feels like I'm in an insane asylum more than a homeless shelter. The guard and attendants come rushing over. The guy just keeps on playing with himself. People are hollering and egging him on. The guard starts hitting the guy about the head with a rolled up newspaper. The old man won't stop flogging himself. Finally, the two attendants and the guard grab the guy and hold him to the floor. They throw a blanket over him then grab each of his feet and an arm as they drag him all the way across the floor to the exit door.

The homeless are jeering at the attendants and rooting for the dirty old man. The poor guy isn't laughing and smiling now as I hear his muffled screams and hollers. The other homeless people jerk their mats up off the floor to make way for the exit of this dirty old stinking man. Back to the streets and the mud holes!

The room calms down after this episode runs its course. I lay back down and stare at the whirring fan overhead. It's late and dark and the thundering is still rolling like cannon fire every now and then. I attempt to close my eyes and meditate on my breath. My mind is so busy, I can't hold my attention. Noises and smells about the big room, whispers and shuffling, as I wonder and worry about things:

Life is so short. Have I been selling myself short—selling out? Settling for a slot—nowhere near a worthy capacity of my potential. Have I been working against myself?

Am I my own worst enemy? I'm in my own way! I caused the detours, mental blocks, ill-advised moves. I'm the cause and I'm the effect. Mis-wired! Off-Balance! Get out of your own way, Ted! O' sweet life! Much too short to continue on this way.

ꕥ

I lay back down on my mat in my sleeping bag, still holding my nose and checking to make sure my backpack is safe. It's around two in the morning when I look at my watch. The place is quiet, but the stench increases a few more levels. I plug both nostrils with balled up tissue, and decide to breath only with my mouth. When it becomes very quiet and still I close my eyes for the last time and drift off.

Startled, I wake up at six in the morning. *Something is wrong*. The big lights are on and guards urge people to get up and get moving. *My backpack is missing*! My heart jolts in my chest and I feel a surge of adrenaline turn into panic. *I've been robbed!*

I jump up from the mat and scurry around, looking everywhere, scanning everything. Then I spot my stuff in a corner, up against a wall, clothes strewn around. I'm really pissed off as I run to the opposite corner of the huge shelter room.

The attendants are folding up blankets and gathering mats and setting up tables and chairs for coffee, tea, and juice at breakfast.

I dart in and out amongst the stragglers, dodging someone still on the floor, and finally get to the corner where my possessions lay strewn around. I gather my stuff to find out what is missing. My wallet is here but my cash is gone, all of it. They didn't take my bus ticket, because I slept with it in my front pants pocket. I pull out the ticket stub to make sure I still have it and look through my empty wallet again.

The only other thing missing, that I notice right away, is a valuable notebook journal. I feel so violated. The guard and attendants say they didn't see anything. I fold up my sleeping bag and gather my stuff in my backpack, and stomp out of the homeless shelter.

Have I made myself a victim in my own mind? Why? What causes me to be drawn to these wayward stations in life? I'm here to learn. I am learning. I am a learner. Will I ever be competent enough to teach what I have learned? I'll just keep learning. Am I a victim? Do I have a victimized mindset? No, maybe not…yes, maybe true. Could be rationalized and defended from both angles equally I suppose. I just need to dust myself off, pick up and get on my way. I have a lot of traveling to go. I am not going to reassume the role of a victim all the way through. This was just a blip on my screen of life. No, I'm not a victim!

ꙮ

Chapter Fifteen

End of The Rainbow

ꙮ

"Up with the sun, gone with the wind,
some people think I'm crazy…"

—Bob Seger
'Trav'lin Man'

Greyhound Bus to Buffalo

I walk a couple miles to the bus depot and wait for my ride. Now I'm broke, and I have no way of getting back home to Michigan. I'm quite depressed about my situation at this point when my nemesis, Allen, shows up. He stops by to see how I'm doing. I tell him about my terrible night. I don't know if he feels guilty or what, as he offers me a twenty dollar bill to at least be able to get some food as I set out on this long journey home. I thank him for his generosity and then he departs. I offer to shake his hand but he abruptly turns his back and walks away. The small gift is highly appreciated. I walk to a vending machine and buy four dollars worth of chips, coke and candy bars. I suddenly realize I haven't eaten since yesterday afternoon.

I board the bus at noon for the trip to Buffalo. I'm still quite worried, stressed-out a bit, but I'm settling in for the next stages of my journey. *What am I going to do? How am I going to get home?* I've got a headache and nausea! Just nerves and stress hastening the consequences on my mind. I close my eyes and try to slow down the thoughts. Detach from all thought and just be—silent meditation. The bus rolls on down the highway. When I get to Buffalo I will need to do something. Slowing down and drifting—

Traveling on the road as a loner is a time to think about the progress of this life I lead. Where am I going? Where have I been? What have I learned? What character defects are keeping me down? What does the future hold as my destiny and fate? There is no gold at the end of this rainbow. The multi-colored light has gone dark, a great void—light missing. I'm in the dark, traveling—a traveler in the dark!

When we arrive in Buffalo it's getting late in the afternoon approaching dinner time. I'm determined not to stay in another homeless shelter, so I head to the nearest truck stop from the bus depot, to try to hitch a ride with truckers. This seems to be my one and only option. After a couple hours of walking through downtown Buffalo I come upon a truck stop restaurant. I'm a little apprehensive because I've never hitchhiked in my life.

I go into the restaurant and enjoy a bowl of soup and a glass of water. I tell my waitress about my problem of being stranded. I ask her if she knows any truckers that are heading west via Pittsburgh or Cleveland or driving through Canada to the Blue Water Bridge in Port Huron, Michigan? She puts out the word but has no luck. All I can do is wait.

It gets dark and then into the late evening, as several hours pass by. I have the entire waitress staff looking out for me now. They keep filling up my coffee cup and giving me updates whenever a new trucker comes in. Finally, nearing midnight, trucker James Thompkins comes over to my table and introduces himself and says he's heading to Pittsburgh. He offers me a ride and I gladly jump at the opportunity. I gather my stuff and go over to his booth in the restaurant and sit with him while he finishes his meal.

James is a big, husky, beer-bellied giant of a man—over six-feet-four and all of three-hundred pounds or more. He bellows a hearty laugh and a gregarious good-natured manner. James constantly flirts with the waitresses. The women adopted me and my plight as their 'cause' for the night. They're exuberant, cheerful, and high-fiving when they land James T. as my ride. He offers to buy me a dinner, so we sit there together and enjoy a good meal. When we get ready to leave I thank all the waitresses and share several hugs with the crew.

Then I load my backpack on my back and we walk out to his big Mack Truck. He's hauling a trailer full of livestock. A whiff of the smell jolts my senses. Whew! It's full of hogs I discover, and they are squealing and snorting. I climb up to the passenger seat and make myself comfortable. I put my gear in the back behind my seat. We're on the road less than a half-hour when I fall asleep. I sleep through the rest of the night.

ჲ

I wake up in the morning and James T. informs me that we drove clear through most of northern Pennsylvania during the night.

"We'll be in Pittsburgh soon," he says. "You want to be dropped off at a bus station or a truck stop?"

I stretch and yawn as I look out at the open road. I have a crimp in my shoulder and neck from how I slept up against the door.

"I'd like to try to hitch another ride at a truck stop," I yawn. "Hopefully, I won't have to wait as long as yesterday."

"Then how about we stop here at the next truck stop

and I'll buy you a breakfast?" he says. "At least you'll have a full belly while you're waiting!" James T. chuckles.

"Sounds good to me," I respond. "I really appreciate your generosity."

He parks his rig in the far corner of a vast overcrowded trucker rest stop. We share a quick breakfast together because he's in a hurry. The big man clears his plate and downs his coffee before I've had three bites from my still full plate.

"Time is money! I've got to get on down the road to my destination," he says.

"Thank you for the ride and the meals!"

We shake hands.

"You have any money for food and whatnot?" he inquires.

I pull out a bill from my pocket. "I'm down to my last ten dollars, but I'll be all right," I say.

James T. unhitches a bill fold hooked to a chain connected to his belt loop and hands me a twenty dollar bill. I refuse at first, but he insists. I ask for his address so I can pay him back. He says not to worry about it. I thank him once again. We shake hands and then trucker James Thompkins departs.

I sit in the restaurant the rest of the morning and into the afternoon. I buy a lunch and ask the waitress staff to keep an eye out for me. They don't seem to want to be as helpful, so I must look around for a ride by myself. By the noon hour I figure I'd better get off my duff and start talking to truckers or I might end up spending all day and night here in Pittsburgh. I stare out the window and around the restaurant:

Self-pity will not be my friend—I refuse the companionship. But still it clings and sings to the destitute, the hopeless, the pity seeker. Like an evil parasitic leech it sucks and drains and lingers. Yes, I'm in a pinch—but self-pity will not conquer me. I will find a way. I will make something happen. How did I get this way? Just a couple of days ago I was celebrating with over a thousand people. Break free from this mental hold, Ted! Time to get up and go!

I find a new ride shortly thereafter, from trucker Chet Bazynski. I meet him at the checkout line where he is waiting behind several others to pay for his meal. He says he is heading to Cleveland and then Toledo. That would get me real close to my home in Michigan. Chet is hauling new cars to a dealership. Mr. Chet B. is not your normal looking truck driver. He has a regal look about himself. He's in his late fifties, sports a well-groomed full white beard. He's very fit and trim. Chet says he runs 10K with his wife at the break of dawn when he's at home. Says she is way better than him and he struggles to finish sometimes, but his wife runs in marathons. The guy really likes to talk. I gather my stuff and follow him out to his rig.

"I love being out in the wilderness of nature," he says. "My job allows me to take a few weeks or a month whenever I need it, to explore the National Parks of the United States. I love camping all over Canada, too!"

"I'm a nature lover myself," I respond. "It's nice to meet someone who has such passion about the great outdoors!"

This guy relishes his life. He owns his rig and subcontracts to get hauling jobs. After I'm settled into his cab, he starts up the truck and heads for the highway, with a big beaming smile planted on his face.

"I love the freedom of the open roads!" he says. "Yessirree, I love the freedom of the open roads!"

As he enters the ramp for the highway I look out on the roads and towards the horizon and up to the sky, as I thank my lucky stars!

"I have a goal to backpack and hike at every U.S. National Park," trucker Chet proclaims. "There's fifty-seven and I've done fifty-one! My next big adventure is going to be Isle Royale National Park in Upper Michigan. You ever been there?"

"No, I haven't," I say, "but I'd like to one day. I love it in the Upper Peninsula in Michigan—very scenic and undeveloped and natural."

Chet raves on and on about the history of the island and the raw wild elements of untapped wilderness. His eyes sparkle and gleam as he stares at the road, rehashing his research for his next big adventure. I enjoy listening to Chet tell his stories with boyish enthusiasm for enjoying great experiences.

I'm newly inspired, refreshed, re-energized from this chance meeting. The commonality and passion for nature is a bulls-eye with me.

"Yessirree, I love the freedom of the open roads!"

I close my eyes and let my mind drift. I drift into my resistance:

> *I'm going against my stream, upriver, against the heavy current. I'm always resisting. Stop resisting, Ted. Go with the flow of nature. Go Ted, go! But here I drift in the wrong direction. I've made my natural life flow one of resistance. Nature is calling. I must heed. Foolish to fight the powers of universal nature, mechanical laws operating, regardless of me. Get with the flow. Ted, get with the flow.*

ᢒᢔ

Chet segues into a new set of stories. We drive from Pittsburgh to Cleveland and the time just flies. He keeps talking with the same consistent enthusiasm and determination to make sure he tells his stories in the right context, with all the details laid bare. Chet's story is about building a boat from scratch in the Upper Peninsula of Michigan when he was a younger man, over thirty years back, he says.

"I built this boat at a cabin in the early spring of 1962. I had to get moving if I was going to be ready to set sail with my twenty-eight-foot craft by mid-spring," he says. "I dropped her in the shores of Lake Superior for the first time, up there at Whitefish Point."

"Did you christen the boat and give it a name?"

"Sure did! Bought a nice bottle of champagne for the occasion," Chet says. "I cracked the bottle over the front bow and christened the boat 'Destiny.' A couple of my old buddies were with me at the time, and my wife, but she was my girlfriend then. We dropped the boat in the water and I said goodbye to Kathy and then the three of us set sail—headed for the Soo locks."

"How did you learn to build a boat? You ever done that before?"

"No, I hadn't, but I had blueprints, tools, supplies and the place to build it. You know how it is when you're young—you can do anything!" Chet chuckles to himself reminiscing. "When I was a young man I wanted adventure, then Vietnam came along, but that's another story. Anyway, we left the locks at Sault St. Marie and followed the waterways in Georgian Bay in Lake Huron. We followed this to the mouth of the St. Clair river in Port Huron, down the channel through the Detroit river and into Lake Erie, then onto Lake Ontario. We went the rest of the way through the Great Lakes system to the Hudson River. The Hudson led us out to the ocean."

"How long did it take to do all that?" I ask.

"About a week! We weren't in a hurry or anything. We went up to Nantucket to get resupplied for the trip across 'the big pond'—The Atlantic Ocean!"

"No way! You're bullshitting, right?"

"Yes, we did!" Chet insists. "It took me and my two pals thirty-three days to get across. That was ten days longer than we had anticipated. We finally spotted land—Portugal! We were happy as hell, let me tell you. Everyone was so worn out and tired from the trip. Couldn't wait to get out of that damn boat and step on dry land. We floated into the harbor in Lisbon and then I sold my boat. The three of us then flew back to the States."

"What did you guys eat? Did you have any harrowing experiences during the trip, bad weather, sea sickness, stuff like that?" I inquire.

"We had plenty of food, dried goods and stuff, although it was getting down pretty low at the end there." Chet lets out a big belly laugh recalling some of the details of his adventure story. "One of my buddies, John, was seasick the whole time. The poor guy couldn't keep anything down and he lost close to thirty pounds on the trip. He was just fine and dandy when we did all the lakes and inland routes. He loved sailing and fishing. But when we hit that ocean he was done for, almost immediately! We kept thinking he would get better and get use to it, but he never did. The poor guy suffered everyday all the way across. He was useless, so the other two guys had to do the work of a three-man crew. We managed though."

"What about storms and high waves?"

"There was a weeklong period where we didn't know if we were going to live through it. The worst of it was three days straight. It was treacherous, menacing, severely critical situations. We were thrown way off course. Everyone was drenched in saltwater and the boat was rocking so hard. Big ten-to-fifteen-foot waves would slam up against and over the boat, crashing and crackling.

Sea storms can really be a bitch."

"I would like to do something like that one day, but I probably never will, just for that reason. I'd need to be on one of those big cruise liner ships," I say.

"My poor buddy, John, was down below the whole time holding on tight, in near hysterics, crying and bellowing and thinking we were all going to die. Me and Joe spent a lot of time laughing at him and bitching at him. I wasn't going to let him being miserable make me miserable and ruin my adventure trip. We kept threatening to throw him overboard some nights, then he'd shut up."

Chet laughs and pounds his open right hand onto his pant leg, remembering the scenario. "We had him under control near the end, we'd just holler 'Sharks!' and he'd stop bitching and just moan to himself."

Chet continues laughing, as we approach our destination—"Here we are coming into Cleveland!" I say.

ꙮ

Trucker Chet drops off his trailer load and hooks up to another trailer load of new cars. We're now off to Toledo. Chet wants to hear some things about me, he says he's done telling stories for awhile. I fill him in on my bohemian odyssey. He gets a kick out of Cricket, Baron Von Torchenstein and Wow, as I recall various anecdotes from my adventure. Chet pounds his open hand on the steering wheel when he thinks something is funny. I'm thoroughly enjoying the road conversations with this enthusiastic fellow. His laughing is contagious. I become aware that I have a permanent smile planted on my face as we converse. It feels good to smile and laugh and feel free.

It seems like we just left Cleveland and here we are approaching Toledo. Chet doesn't have another hauling contract to fulfill, so he is in limbo. He spends some time at the car lot in a corner office making phone calls. I sit in the truck cab and wait. Then he comes back to the truck with a big smile on his face. He contracted a load to pick up in Flat Rock, Michigan, then he has to drive up to the Bay Area in Saginaw Valley. He says he can drop me off in Pontiac along I-75. Excellent!

We head back out on the road. We're not hauling anything so the vehicle runs differently, much easier, quicker. Chet opens it up on the highway, slamming into the next higher gear with the clutch. He's hooting and hollering as we pass other truckers in the slower lanes. Soon we cross the Michigan state boundary line. When we get to our next stop in Flat Rock, Chet wants to talk about nature again.

"I like a philosophy that creates freedom for the individual mind. My nature trips do this for me. Nature is my philosophy," he says. "All my children are grown-up and married, but I still arrange one-on-one nature outings with my two daughters and son. We'll go on long hikes or a bike ride or a canoe trip. Helps me keep a pulse on their lives and stay connected to them in a way, and offer fatherly advice if need be."

"Have you ever read Thoreau, Emerson and Whitman—*Walden Pond, Nature, Leaves of Grass*?" I inquire.

"I've read them all and know them quite well," he responds.

"Somehow, that doesn't surprise me one bit," I reply.

"My favorite is Robert Frost. My wife and I read Frost to each other all the time. *'Two roads diverged in a wood, and I took the one less traveled by, and that has made all the difference.'* All of those true nature writers know what they're talking and writing about. Those writers experience their work first-hand."

"They write about intuition, being in touch with your senses, a wakeful consciousness, intuitive instincts,"

I interject. "And everyone and everything interconnects through nature. Enlightenment comes from gaining this awareness and understanding—bringing the energy of your being, your body, your aura, into equilibrium with the forces of nature!"

"You really get into that stuff, ehh?" Chet says. "I'm more on the surface and not as deep as you, but I understand where you're coming from."

Chet then bursts out with a big hearty belly laugh. I'm not sure what for this time. After he gets himself under control, he says, "That Walt Whitman guy sure was a dirty old man! I can't believe some of the sexual innuendo he wrote in his blank verse, especially for that period of time in the 1800's. He was an original, that's for sure!"

"*Song of Myself, I Sing the Body Electric, O Captain! My Captain!* Walt Whitman had a universal vision of man and woman and society around the globe," I say.

"And he was a dirty old man, too!" says Chet. We laugh and carry on in our conversations, truckin' on down the road. I'm sure I could drive all through the United States and Canada and never run out of things to talk about with this guy. I look out on the roads and passing scenery as I ponder my continuing adventure in the living of a life:

> *Go on. Go on. Go on. I must go on. I am the wayward traveler. This individual life is my vehicle. I adventure to learn. Experience is my mission. Understanding my goal. Why am I here? Where am I heading next? Go on, Ted—go on, Ted, go on…Life is but a dream. Life is but a dream—towns and roads and skylines changing with the people.*

ꙮ

Chet switches gears into a new set of subjects. "Awhile ago I took a trip into the Yukon Territory in Alaska over to British Columbia. Saw polar bears, grizzlies, bald eagles, bison, moose, elk, coyotes, wolf. Encountered huge whales, orcas, sharks. I climbed to the summit of Mt. McKinley—did it when I turned forty," Chet proclaims as he pounds his chest proudly.

We both agree that life is so short and there is much to learn and do and discover.

Now here we are approaching the Pontiac city limits, along I-75. "If you can drop me off at a restaurant that would work out real well for me," I say. "I have a buddy from college days who lives near Lapeer. I can call him to come and pick me up."

"What are you going to do then?"

"Split my time between camping in the deep woods on some acres of my buddy's property and camping at the state park nearby."

"No job?"

"That is my job for now. I'm in the process of writing and reading and studying out in nature every day. I'll come out of the woods on Thanksgiving and decide which way I want to go with a job and making money and all that comes with that. But for now, I'll just continue on with my nature journey. I've got a lot to write in my journal everyday—keeps me busy and focused."

"You ever publish anything?" Chet inquires.

"Not really! I've never been interested or focused on writing to be published. My career was in business and high-tech. My writing is my unpaid, unknown art," I reply.

"Let me rephrase my question then—do you plan on publishing your work one day—say as a book, a novel, a screenplay?" Chet questions me.

"Yes, I do, some day!"

"Well, it may be sooner than you think. Keep at it. I'll

be scanning the new book lists one day, and hopefully I'll find you. Good luck to you my friend."

"That's a good place to stop at the next exit." I point to a billboard. "This is my drop-off point."

Trucker Chet exits the highway and pulls his rig into a Denny's truck stop restaurant. He wants to keep moving, so he waits for me to get my stuff out of his cab. I feel through my backpack to my book bag and locate a copy of the twelve pamphlets all together in a red bow tie. I pull the package out and then walk over to the driver's side of the cab. Chet opens the door and hands me a business card with his home address and phone number.

"You take this card and get a hold of me someday. Maybe we can pal around and do something adventurous out in nature," he says. "It's been a pleasure to make your acquaintance and I wish you well, Ted."

I take the card from him then climb onto the top step of his rig, holding on to the sidebar handle as we shake hands.

"I have something for you too," I say. I pull the pamphlets out of my back pocket and hand them to Chet. "Remember the stories I told you about Cricket, back around the Pittsburgh to Cleveland part of our trip. Anyway, she had this idea for some of my journal writings and this is the outcome of what she produced."

"Thank you very much, Ted! I'll enjoy reading some of your work. You be sure to keep in touch." We shake hands one last time and then I leap off the rig and he shuts the door and slowly pulls away. I'm going to miss trucker Chet. What an interesting, fun guy!

After Chet leaves I stare at the traffic on the highway interchange. The busy traffic patterns—everybody going somewhere, living a life. I have come nearly full circle, to the end of the rainbow of my Bohemian Odyssey.

Mental states of consciousness decide so many fates. We are what we think. Self-destructive thinking takes place everywhere. We do not see. We do not hear. We do not smell. We do not taste. We do not truly touch and feel. We choose our individual self-imposed thinking curse. We choose not to live to the fullest, not to enjoy the gift of our birth. To struggle, to struggle in vain.The changing mind, the equalized mind. Balanced polarity. Positivity inclined to a constructive flow of thoughts. Feeling fine and cheerful and optimistic in continuity over time. I'm arriving at a proper state of mind. Harmonic convergence dividing line. Fun loving people, friendly, caring, helpful. Sweet Mother Earth, blessed universe. Thank you for our creation!

I shoulder my backpack and walk to the nearby restaurant, where I call an old college dorm room buddy to come pick me up. All the anxiety, worry and stress I experienced that last day in Rochester on into Buffalo, is now completely gone. There's something to be said about a comfort zone and home turf. I was drowning in self-doubt there for awhile. I think it was the suddenness of it all. I have only myself to blame for not planning my departure beforehand. I was so caught up in the moments of each day that it completely slipped my mind.

ЖЖ

Chapter Sixteen

Lake Minnawanna

ЖЖ

"Divine imaginings, like gods, come down to the groves of our Thessalies, and there, in the embrace of wild, dryad reminiscences, beget the beings that astonish the world."

—Herman Melville

The Bohemian Odyssey

My lovely familiar home in nature, my refuge from the chaos of society—nature sweet, strong and wild!

Where does life go from here?

Right now it's time to finish my 'rebirthing process' in the womb of mother nature. Rebirth myself into the self and soul of truth I must own up to. It's time for me to get to work and write and walk and read and saunter through the byways of raw elemental nature!

Thoreau and Emerson and Whitman set a great example to me for appreciating the wonderful diversity in nature and human life—the awesome mystery of transcendent existence! The magic earth is mystical—Myth Earth!

Has it all been a dream?

I'm back where I started thirty-three days ago. Here I am like Dorothy back from her Oz journey.

Reality used to be a friend of mine, now how does life seem?

The Bohemian Adventure

I still have four months of self-imposed exile, to live out in nature with the sky as my roof. I have a full cooler of food on ice. I'm ready to settle down into the contemplative mode, the zone, out in nature, where I was before Cricket and the Deadheads appeared.

I am a bohemian—a real artist or pretend artist? I shall see where my will and passion will take me. I have the freedom to be free. I've been in denial of myself for far too long. To scale the peak with a mere brushstroke is to land on never before charted terrain. Am I worthy? Ted, yes you are!

I'm staring into the surface edge of Lake Minnawanna which reflects my face shrouded with branches of leaves from the over-hanging tree. I'm sitting on the base of a tree in a secluded area that curves and skirts the water line before shooting upwards toward the sky. The horizontal tree trunk holds my body aloft over the water, as I dangle my feet in the cool liquid. Little schools of minnows swim around, darting to the movement of my toes.

I look into the pebbly sand of this mere six inches of water, imagining the sand to be the grains of truth to my being—unleashing my imagination to behold a symbolic meaning, fine-tuning a message from pure universal spirit to lead my way. I pick some sand out of the water and hold it aloft, as I rub the sand through my fingers, searching for my inner meaning:

What is the truth of my Being? How do I learn to align to my Purpose? Know thyself through individual development, individual discovery, individual self-analysis, individual growth through learning by rightly using knowledge applied. The personal experience of individual enlightenment can only be earned in this manner! Earn it through self-reliance, Ted!

Every soul is on their own individual life journey. Every life has a story. I rub the sand through my fingers. I sense a tremendous growth in character, waiting for my aims. I have far to go, but I'm closer than I've ever been. For wherever I go, there I am, changing with the flow of the universe. I know that I know that I know, and I also know—I know nothing at all!

As I look back in reflection on my life, I realize I have always sensed an attraction to an unknown cause. By the age of thirty I knew I had to design a new pattern of life and thought. I need something higher and noble and truly worth my while.

I attained the nobility of failure, by society's rules. But I know better than this. I know my self-worth. I just need time for diversion to gain the proper perspective. Time to grow into my new awareness! Time to adjust. Time to be my best. But time waits for no one. Now is always now!

Our culture of mediocrity and materialism rules the day. Negativity and belligerence is the greatest sales job played out on the public mind. This all-pervading energy infiltrates our schools, classrooms, homes, daily thought process. We breed and feed on the anachronism.

Lake Minnawanna exudes a cool breeze. The shoreline ripples move in for that final slap on the shore, followed a few seconds later by the next small wave—simple, loving, passionate nature. Just being!

Fully relaxed, I'm wrapped in a solitude of mental reverie.

I glare out from the shoreline to the mid-depths of the small body of lake water. The trance-like lapping of the shore stills my mind. I lay back along the tree with my feet dangling, ankle deep, as I close my eyes, nestled comfortably in the tree.

What is Freedom of Consciousness? How have I constrained myself, chained myself, limited my existence in past endeavors? The dormant consciousness drivels and drones and groans in chains. Stuck on oneself, within oneself. There is no liberty when you choose to be a prisoner within. Scale the heights of character to build yourself an exemplary life of adventures, learning, and wonders. I've learned the dormant mind has no connection to certain realities of life.

How have I constrained myself, detoured and detained myself—and limited the existence of my past endeavors? Getting in my own way—keeping myself down! The interpenetration of prolonged psychic slumber has left a misalignment of mental energies. I now have the freedom to learn and gain the message to grow rightly from the added knowledge. I'm transforming into my rightful consciousness—being present in the now!

Sudden images from my adventure filter through my mind. In a visual stream-of-consciousness state, I watch the rapid fire unfolding of all I have recently seen, done, and experienced. The events, people and places are random, not in the proper chronological order of happening:

I'm in Rochester, NY, then Washington D.C., New York City, The Vietnam Memorial, Frederick, Maryland rest stop, Cleveland, Cricket, Mignon, Wow, Baron Von Torchenstein, Buffalo, Pittsburgh, The Nature Party, Deadheads, The Symposium, Garbage Day, Trucker Chet, Rainbow Warriors, Greenpeace, Self & Soul, Seed & Roots. I see visions of Indians, tribes, clans, counterculturalists—tie-dyed, dreadlocks, headbands, miracles, tattoos, village shows, campfire rings, balloons, a waterfall, a sunrise, a peace sign, doobie circles, a stoned face, love, permeating love, music, constant music, harmony, mind of peace, and a mysterious mystical energy of mental, spiritual wonder and brotherhood.

ജ്ഞ

I fall deep asleep lying on the tree watching my visions in a constant flow of images as I drift off.

I dream of an American Bald Eagle circling in the sky above me. I'm in a meadow lying in the tall grass, staring at the sky. I watch the bird of prey descend lower and lower. I can see his sharp talons as he moves them back and forth as if flexing to make a grip.

We make direct eye-to-eye contact as I look over that great big yellow killer peak beak. He fully extends his wings as he glides through the sky. The bald eagle is only fifty feet above me now. I stand up in the meadow and wrap a towel and shirt around my arm, as I look up and hold out my arm as a perch.

With a short quick whistle I holler "Ace," in my dream, and he descends down to my arm and lands gracefully, pulling in his folded wings. I feel the hard firm grip of his talons.

It's surprising how much we work against ourselves and get in the way of ourselves. Character growth principles are a major struggle. To capitalize one must grow and learn and develop and master the principles of positive constructive nature—to be kind and friendly and of beneficial service to others. Mastering specific particulars, developing an accumulation of enacted principles, learning to acquire knowledge needed. I'm growing into the spirit of my True Nature.

Ace and I stand out in the middle of the meadow and stare at each other for several long minutes. Somehow we are communing on a spiritual plane. Words cannot describe it nor feelings either—we are two beings connected ethereally.

For a brief millisecond I feel, I know, I have direct insight into the very nature of things. I see and understand the correlation of universal forces in Nature—the fundamental principles of life—the superstructure of moral certainty. I yearn for the millisecond to last a millennium, for eternity, never ending.

But in a snap of a finger the direct insight is gone, vanished. The ethereal cosmic connection is no more.

Ace launches into the air from my outstretched arm. He flies several hundred feet above me. His pattern is a figure-eight diagram. I watch him fly the entire pattern seven, eight times. On completion of the eighth mobius strip trip, I awake from my daydream.

Where am I, and what have I seen? What is the meaning?

I stretch out and look up into the sky, out to space, into the cosmos of my dreams.

ꙮ

Lake Minnawanna is my Walden Pond.

Nature is, Nature was, Nature will be!

I decide to leave my comfortable little perch along the shoreline to go out walking in the woods, along the trails. Henry David Thoreau had it right in his perspective of cleansing, balancing nature. Ahhh…the sweet odor of the natural woods—sumac, berries, hickory, pine, maple—the magnetic allure infiltrates the vital senses.

Transcendental intuitions aroused…

> *My mental state is settling into a harmonic convergence within. I can feel and sense the balanced equilibrium. A cerebral magnetic harmony pervades. I am an open channel to Nature's natural flows. I'm flowing to the alignment of my life's proper direction. I am free to be who and what I want to be. I have the freedom to be free!*

I locate a favorite little spot by a babbling brook. I'm inspired to write in my journal.

> This Lake Minnawanna park is like an old trusted honest friend, the very best a friend can be. I love her well and treat her kindly as I explore her inner depths. She is my natural muse~sacred feminine mother nature. Our natural affection is mutual.
>
> I come and go as I please, all along her body I explore. She unfolds her welcoming arms and greets me warmly every time.
>
> I'm back, O' Lake Minnawanna Park~I'm back!

I get up and walk further along the creek trail for awhile, then sit down by the babbling brook at the creek side and open up my journal notebook, and began to write, once again.

> I'm thinking about Cricket. She really is the self-proclaimed 'Catalyst Converter.' I realize that everything that transpired in the last month, every experience I've had, would not have happened if I hadn't met and befriended Cricket. She named me 'The Bohemian,' but I declare that she is truly bohemia, 'The Queen of Bohemia.' I would never expect to meet such an individual as Cricket, ever again.

I stop writing and stare off into the distance of the rolling, flowing, babbling brook. Smooth waters gently caress the pebbles and stones and sharp rocks, glistening wet bark, and over and around a fallen tree. The sweet water bottlenecks and flows, only temporarily impeded, moving, rolling, flowing…

The exemplar worthies are those who live for the passion of their dreams. Constructing a character seed with foundational roots firm and deep. Unleashing the self-evident limits of being and growing, to be limitless. Ted—you are in control of your choices! Ted—you are in control of your will! Ted—you have it all, don't you see? Life is worthy of truly living!

Thoreau and Emerson and Whitman have been a beacon to me because of their inspirational words and deeds. Each man connected and aligned his character to nature. From this viewpoint, a natural emanation of transcendental harmony pervades. A lifetime student of Nature, becomes a teacher and a learner ever onward. The small pond lakeshore has a reflective depth of infinite range.

Reaching into the inner sanctum sanctorum—extending outward to right action, right thought, right being.

To achieve the insight to reconcile an understanding of connected oneness to all world cultures in human history—the golden tree, the Golden Mean—east to west, north to south, generation upon generation, age to age. The Great Earth, peopled with souls, struggling in the search for self-emancipation.

Right here, right now—Lake Minnawanna serves as my Walden Pond!

ꕥ

I flip through my pages and rummage through the other notebooks in my book bag. I had written phone numbers, addresses, names of over three hundred people during my bohemian odyssey. I've discovered that the missing notebook from that night in the homeless shelter, is the notebook I'm looking for.

I've lost everyone!

It's as if those people came into my life, appearing from nowhere, and now they've disappeared back to nowhere. I'm depressed, dejected, melancholy.

> *Lost in a life of self-induced delusions is an improper illusion of fantasy, not reality. Following this route is a recipe for individual catastrophe. The unending cycle turns and turns. Life is akin to a game of action and reaction, cause and effect, as above so below, flowing out and in—rhythm. I'm working on becoming finely-tuned. I will live for a purpose. I am thankful with never-ending gratitude!*

I wonder about Baron Von Torchenstein. Perhaps we could meet up at Torch Lake. Or he could come riding through here on his chopper one day. His wooden wizard sculpture is the other thing missing from that harrowing night at the homeless shelter in Rochester, New York. I didn't know it was missing at the time. I forgot about Baron giving it to me. I just knew right away that my money and a notebook were gone. Now I've lost the wooden sculpture from Baron Von Torchenstein, too.

Did my Bohemian Odyssey really happen or is this story an illusion in my head?

Of course it happened, I tell myself. But I wonder what is real and what is unreal.

I want the raw pure truth, even if I discover this truth to be opposite to all I have known. I want to live in truth and bear witness to falsehoods, especially in myself. I want to know. I've got to know. 'Know thyself,' the ancient philosopher proclaimed.

I'm a seeker…

I flip to an open blank page in my notebook. I write some names across the top line:

"Cricket, Baron Von Torchenstein, Pete, Wow, Trucker Chet, Jeff...These people were at the heart of my Bohemian Odyssey. My whole adventure could be summed up by what I did, talked about and experienced with these individuals. I'm trying to locate a larger meaning, a deeper impress on my mind. Why do things happen? What shapes circumstance and consequence? Synchronicity. Serendipity. Luck. Is life a continuous cycle of evolutionary learning and discovering moments? The answer to the 'Why?' of my questions is the secret to the 'Who?' and 'How?' of my recent experiences. The utter mystical mystery remains. I'm thinking about energy, matter, light, space, time, gravitation, electro-magnetic energy, polarity, synergy, circumstance, event, choice, chance, action at a distance and the constants of relativity... Each of us are like an island universe unto ourselves. I have the inner and outer me.You have the inner and outer you. No one knows the inner being of another. Everyone is under the scope of evolutionary character development by the mere process of living a life. There is an alignment pattern to attain with possession of the key to self-knowledge, mastery of the inner being. The power of your island universe progressively unfolds."

I flip through some pages in another notebook and locate the paradoxical quotes I am looking for to sum up my train of thought:

"Wherever You Go, There You Are."

—Jon Kabitt-Zinn

The Bohemian Adventure

"If the Universe is hidden in the Universe itself,
then there can be no escape from it.
This is the great truth of things in general."
—Chuang-Tzu

I close my notebook and put my writing materials in my book bag. I need to stretch and walk and move to get some exercise. I feel like I'm going to get lost in mind-numbing abstractionism and ambiguity if I don't get moving.

I hike the outer perimeter of the six-hundred acre park. I use a big wooden walking stick to assist me on the unlevel terrain. I proceed through a six-mile network of trails, wandering from marshy swamp to woods to open fields and then back again to towering pines and hardwoods to lightly forested oaks and maples. My walking stick is an invaluable ally in my hiking efforts. Then down to the shore of the lake I saunter—beautiful little Lake Minnawanna.

This seemingly natural lake is really man-made, a sixty-acre impoundment of the south branch of a creek. Her life giving waters are teeming with bass, bluegill, perch, and an occasional northern pike. I bend down and brush my fingers softly in the liquid, enjoying a brief meditation at the shore.

Long silent stretches of natural bliss awaken my inner senses. The long dormant, latent, sleeping me briefly jostles from my life-long slumber.

The unborn self, the unlived me, my future being—I'm evolving to the unmanifested me. Translating potential into being from a work-in-progress generates its own energy field. I'm awake to a previously hidden source of inner power. The constructive will in action suffused with vision, attention, passion, intention, and hope is a will of positive force.

In a sudden jolt to full consciousness my brief meditation ends. Thereafter, I head back out on the trails to circle around the lake by walking the outer perimeter. I eventually come to a wider main trail that leads to a cove on the shores of Lake Minnawanna.

I follow the path. When I arrive at a small secluded spot I discover I'm not alone. Two young teenage lovers are holding hands sitting on a rise by the shore with their feet soaking in the water. The young couple abruptly leaves when I take off my shoes and walk in the water. I take my book pack off my shoulders, unzip and locate what I'm looking for, and drink some bottled water. I have a parched throat. I'm now seated comfortably in the sand by the shore as I proceed to write in my notebook:

> "How does one become a positive influence, make a beneficial impact to the world and mankind? I'm thinking of the Rainbow Warriors of Greenpeace, LOHAS, Rainbow Families, Cricket~ahh Cricket... My muse is gone but her influence remains. I've discovered a newer wakeful way to perceive existence. This bohemian odyssey was like a beacon to awaken all my senses. There is more to life, so much more. I know that I don't know, and I want to know through my personal experience. I will continue to seek. To be a positive influence to anyone at anytime, one must constantly be tilling the gardens and planting and harvesting an ever growing germination of overflowing fruits. The evolutionary unfoldment is driven from within."

ജ്ജ

I saunter out to some more trails around the park. I ponder Thoreau and his daily walks around Walden Pond—walking out in nature in solitude, secluded from society, carrying along his writing utensils—inspired to pen his greatest thoughts while engulfed in raw nature.

As a nature walker something happens to my mind, my body, my being. I'm tuning-in to the Universal Lyre, the natural order of things. Henry David Thoreau created this phenomenon for himself. He tuned in his spiritual being with nature. So did Ralph Waldo Emerson and Walt Whitman.

I'm attempting to emulate this facet of these great thinkers—the American Transcendentalists. It's now evolving to the nature of my character.

I'm aiming for a balance, an alignment, equilibrium of harmonic forces converging within. I'm arriving, traveling the full course. Life is a miracle from beginning to end. I am in charge of my direction, my choices, my mistakes, my development, my growth. Inner harmony is attainable and sustainable. I will that I will make it so!

I continue sauntering along through the trails, feeling the utter ecstasy of being in the now with nature. I soon find myself pondering the intellectual meetings Emerson would lead in his library study in Concord. Ralph Waldo would invite several to a dozen visitors—Bronson Alcott, Thoreau, Margaret Fuller, Elizabeth Peabody, Theodore Parker, Jones Very. These people would write and speak of transcendental things, great thinkers and writers and exploring nature.

I can visualize a young Thoreau quietly participating, soaking up the atmosphere. Then I see Henry running off to Walden, to pen inspiring words in his journals.

The ancient adepts, the worthies of remotest antiquity, must have felt this affinity with nature. The great thinkers and writers and artists of history, share a keen sense of the infinitude. The connection is there to be made.

Internal Light! Electro-magnetic gravitational frequencies! Sparking divine thoughts and actions. Blazing like thunderbolts through my being. I am that I am! Pulsating dimensions of hope and truth and eternal life…

I've about come full circle from my all day walk through the park. It's time to head to my campsite and bring an end to this day and this story.

ഇരു

From my experiences I've discovered I'm in a struggle for my individual liberty, my self-liberation.

I must move forward, gaining strength from the pathways of life I've traveled. Moving forward day by day. I'm living in the present, in touch with the now, aspiring to noble claims, moving on to the great beyond. The journey is so much greater when one has a genuine and sincere appreciation of gratitude and thankfulness for the individual human life lived. Living a life is a gift not ever to be taken for granted. This I know and believe.

To recognize the negativities and to consciously relinquish the terminal hold is enlightenment in action—a principle withdrawn and cashed in, to profit by. Onward through the inward journey into the uplifting outer experiences of life. The struggle for individual liberty has afflicted humanity from the dawn of creation. We struggle and grope and sell ourselves short again and again, lifetime after lifetime.

I will not be partial to this death march. My drum beats a different rhythm. I will not live in constant desperation.

FREEDOM—I'm seeking you!

I continue walking through the woods, following the trails, until I come upon my campsite. I gather some kindling to build a small campfire. The sunset over the horizon is coming soon. I see a faint moonlight, dimly lit, through the clouds.

All is well.

The bohemian road show adventure is tucked securely in my memory, and now relegated to an experience of my past.

I still have my own nine-month rebirthing social/cultural experiment to complete. At Thanksgiving when I come out of the woods for good, I plan on getting re-acclimated to work-a-day society. I will set a new course and live out my dreams.

Moreover, I will forever be a bohemian!

Nature's laws, principles and processes are my seeking wonderment. I must bring my personal character, my nature—into compliance, alignment, natural order. The constructive evolutionary unfoldment of my being is no longer hindered. I'm getting out of my own way. Simple. The constructive laws of nature in individual life, can be aligned, lived through, and experienced. The goal is set, the ship is launched!

In the final analysis of things, it seems as if we all have an individual path to lead, and purpose to discover.

There is music in us—a universal symphony!

There is light in us—bright galaxies!

Never stop searching for the music and that light because it's always within, awaiting your beckoning calls!

—The Bohemian
LAKE MINNAWANNA
Summer of 1993

ᘓᘐ

Epilogue

ᘓᘐ

I'm walking on a trail in the back woods from Lake Minnawanna. A lone hiker, a man in his mid-fifties, approaches from the opposite direction. We nod 'hello' to each other as we pass by along the trail. I soon find a side path off the main trail. This path leads to a babbling brook. Further down the path, I notice a huge tree that spans across the creek, serving as a bridge. I walk to the fallen tree and cross to the other side of the stream. This is a wonderful place to write in my journal and doodle some nature sketches.

The autumn afternoon is crisp, clear and mildly warm for the season. Soon, though, late fall is coming then winter and colder weather with the changing seasons. Several hours pass as I'm lost in my imaginative mental reveries out in nature. I pen page after page in my notebook journal. I'm on a creative roll, producing new material, enjoying the work of a free artist.

"Excuse me! Mind if I join you?"

I look across the stream by the fallen tree bridge and there is the man I passed earlier along the hiking trail.

"How are you? I'm Ed, we passed each other on the path…"

Ed walks across the tree to my side of the stream as he's talking. I watch him without saying anything.

The man snaps his fingers and whistles, "You, who—anybody home?"

I spring alert. "Just lost in the beauty of nature," I say as I get up from my sitting position on the log. I put my notebook and pen down on the log and walk over from the creek shore to where Ed stands at the end of the tree bridge. We shake hands.

"I'm Ted. Nice to meet you."

Ed is a tall lanky man—lean and fit.

"You seem to really enjoy it out here in the elements of the raw outdoors," he says.

"Absolutely I do. Great for the soul—cleansing, refreshing, revitalizing," I respond.

"What are you doing out here, writing, drawing, planning?" Ed inquires.

"Yes to all three. How do you know? Why do you ask?"

"I'm always interested in the creative types wherever I go in the world. Seeing you on the trail carrying a notebook and pen is intriguing to me. Then spotting you again way out here alongside this creek—I just had to introduce myself. I'm not from these parts. We're visiting some of my wife's distant relatives because of a recent death in the family."

"Where are you from?" I ask.

"Originally from Vancouver, Canada, but I live down under now in Australia and New Zealand," he says.

"What kind of work you do?" I ask.

"I own an IT company, a publishing company, and a few other things. I have my own venture capital company to fund my interests."

"What about you?" he inquires.

"I'm an IT project leader. Or I use to be. Right now I'm unemployed. Just enjoying myself out in nature. Been doing it for seven months straight now. When I come out of the woods in a couple months I'll need a job. Maybe I should give you a call," I joke.

"Maybe you should," says Ed. He proceeds to hand me a business card. "I'll look forward to hearing from you."

I take the card from him. "Thank you!" We shake hands.

Edward Kingsley, CEO
GIVE—Global Initiative Venture Enterprises

Ed then walks back across the fallen tree to the hiking trail and disappears into the woods.

ABOUT THE AUTHOR

Author, F.T. Burke is a lifelong resident of the State of Michigan where he now lives with his wife. He enjoyed a prior career in the high-tech sector serving as a systems engineer and project manager.

Mr. Burke's debut novel, 'The Bohemian Adventure,' kicks off a series of books centered around the adventures of the main character, Ted Senario.

For more information about the author, visit the website: AuthorFTBurke. com

CPSIA information can be obtained
at www.ICGtesting.com
Printed in the USA
FFOW03n0721080417
34274FF